ALSO BY GREG EGAN FROM GOLLANCZ

LUMINOUS
GREG EGAN

Copyright © Greg Egan 1998

First published in Great Britain in 1999 by Millennium

This edition published in Great Britain in 2008 by Gollancz
an imprint of the Orion Publishing Group
Orion House, 5 Upper St Martin's Lane, London WC2H 9EA
An Hachette Livre UK Company

10 9 8 7 6 5 4 3 2 1

A CIP catalogue record for this book is
available from the British Library

ISBN 978 0 57508 2 083

Typeset at The Spartan Press Ltd,
Lymington, Hants

Printed and bound at Mackays of Chatham plc,
Chatham, Kent

The Orion Publishing Group's policy is to use papers that
are natural, renewable and recyclable products and made
from wood grown in sustainable forests. The logging and
manufacturing processes are expected to conform to the
environmental regulations of the country of origin.

www.orionbooks.co.uk

CONTENTS

CHAFF

El Nido de Ladrones – the Nest of Thieves – occupies a roughly elliptical region, fifty thousand square kilometres in the western Amazon Lowlands, straddling the border between Colombia and Peru. It's difficult to say exactly where the natural rain forest ends and the engineered species of El Nido take over, but the total biomass of the system must be close to a trillion tonnes. A trillion tonnes of structural material, osmotic pumps, solar energy collectors, cellular chemical factories, and biological computing and communications resources. All under the control of its designers.

The old maps and databases are obsolete; by manipulating the hydrology and soil chemistry, and influencing patterns of rainfall and erosion, the vegetation has reshaped the terrain completely: shifting the course of the Putumayo River, drowning old roads in swampland, raising secret causeways through the jungle. This biogenic geography remains in a state of flux, so that even the eyewitness accounts of the rare defectors from El Nido soon lose their currency. Satellite images are meaningless; at every frequency, the forest canopy conceals, or deliberately falsifies, the spectral signature of whatever lies beneath.

Chemical toxins and defoliants are useless; the plants and their symbiotic bacteria can analyse most poisons, and reprogram their metabolisms to render them harmless – or transform them into food – faster than our agricultural warfare expert systems can invent new molecules. Biological weapons are seduced, subverted, domesticated; most of the genes from the last lethal plant virus we introduced were found three months later, incorporated into a benign vector for El Nido's elaborate communications network. The assassin had turned into a messenger boy. Any attempt to burn the vegetation is rapidly smothered by carbon dioxide – or more sophisticated fire retardants, if a self-oxidising fuel is employed. Once we even pumped in a few tonnes of nutrient laced with powerful radio-isotopes – locked up in compounds chemically indistinguishable from their natural counterparts. We tracked the results with gamma-ray imaging: El Nido separated out the isotope-laden molecules – probably on the basis of their diffusion rates across organic membranes – sequestered and diluted them, and then pumped them right back out again.

So when I heard that a Peruvian-born biochemist named Guillermo Largo had departed from Bethesda, Maryland, with some highly classified genetic tools – the fruits of his own research, but very much the property of his employers – and vanished into El Nido, I thought: At last, an excuse for the Big One. The Company had been advocating thermonuclear rehabilitation of El Nido for almost a decade. The Security Council would have rubber-stamped it. The governments with nominal authority over the region would have been delighted. Hundreds of El Nido's inhabitants were suspected of violating US law – and President Golino was aching for a chance to prove that she could play hard ball south of the border, what-ever language she spoke in the privacy of her own home. She could have gone on prime time afterwards and told the nation that they should be proud of Operation Back to Nature, and that the thirty thousand displaced farmers who'd taken refuge in El Nido from Colombia's undeclared civil war – and who had now been liberated for ever from the oppression of Marxist terrorists and drug barons – would have saluted her courage and resolve.

I never discovered why that wasn't to be. Technical prob-lems in ensuring that no embarrassing side-effects would show up down-river in the sacred Amazon itself, wiping out some telegenic endangered species before the end of the present administration? Concern that some Middle Eastern warlord might somehow construe the act as licence to use his own feeble, long-hoarded fission weapons on a troublesome minority, destabilising the region in an undesirable manner? Fear of Japanese trade sanctions, now that the rabidly anti-nuclear Eco-Marketeers were back in power?

I wasn't shown the verdicts of the geopolitical computer models; I simply received my orders – coded into the flicker of my local K-Mart's fluorescent tubes, slipped in between the updates to the shelf price tags. Deciphered by an extra neural layer in my left retina, the words appeared blood red against the bland cheery colours of the supermarket aisle.

I was to enter El Nido and retrieve Guillermo Largo.

Alive.

* * *

Dressed like a local real-estate agent – right down to the gold-plated bracelet-phone, and the worst of all possible three-hundred-dollar haircuts – I visited Largo's abandoned home in Bethesda: a northern suburb of Washington, just over the border into Maryland. The apartment was modern and spacious, neatly furnished but not opulent – about what any good marketing software might have tried to sell him, on the basis of salary less alimony.

Largo had always been classified as *brilliant but unsound* – a potential security risk, but far too talented and productive to be wasted. He'd been under routine surveillance ever since the gloriously euphemistic Department of Energy had employed him, straight out of Harvard, back in 2005 – clearly, too routine by far . . . but then, I could understand how thirty years with an unblemished record must have given rise to a degree of complacency. Largo had never attempted to disguise his politics – apart from exercising the kind of discretion that was more a matter of etiquette than subterfuge; no Che Guevara T-shirts when visiting Los Alamos – but he'd never really acted on his beliefs, either.

A mural had been jet-sprayed onto his living-room wall in shades of near infra-red (visible to most hip fourteen-year-old Washingtonians, if not to their parents). It was a copy of the infamous Lee Hing-cheung's *A Tiling of the Plane with Heroes of the New World Order*, a digital image that had spread across computer networks at the turn of the century. Early nineties political leaders, naked and interlocked – Escher meets the Kamasutra – deposited steaming turds into each other's open and otherwise empty braincases, an effect borrowed from the works of the German satirist George Grosz. The Iraqi dictator was shown admiring his reflection in a hand mirror – the image an exact reproduction of a contemporary magazine cover in which the moustache had been retouched to render it suitably Hitleresque. The US President carried – horizontally, but poised ready to be tilted – an egg-timer full of the gaunt hostages whose release he'd delayed to clinch his predecessor's election victory. Everyone was shoe-horned in, somewhere – right down to the Australian Prime Minister, portrayed as a pubic louse, struggling (and failing) to fit its tiny jaws around the mighty presidential cock. I could imagine a few of the neo-McCarthyist troglodytes in the Senate going apoplectic if anything so tedious as an inquiry into Largo's defection ever took place, but what should we have done? Refused to hire him if he owned so much as a *Guernica* tea-towel?

Largo had blanked every computer in the apartment before leaving, including the entertainment system, but I already knew his taste in music, having listened to a few hours of audio surveillance samples full of bad Korean Ska. No laudable revolutionary ethno-solidarity, no haunting Andean pipe music; a shame – I would have much preferred that. His bookshelves held several battered college-level biochemistry texts, presumably retained for sentimental reasons, and a few dozen musty literary classics and volumes of poetry, in English, Spanish, and German. Hesse, Rilke, Vallejo, Conrad, Nietzsche. Nothing modern – and nothing printed after 2010. With a few words to the household manager, Largo had erased every digital work he'd ever owned, sweeping away the last quarter of a century of his personal archaeology.

I flipped through the surviving books, for what it was worth. There was a pencilled-in correction to the structure of guanine in one of the texts . . . and a section had been underlined in 'Heart of Darkness'. The narrator, Marlow, was pondering the mysterious fact that the servants on the steamboat – members of a cannibal tribe, whose provisions of rotting hippo meat had been tossed overboard – hadn't yet rebelled and eaten him. After all:

> No fear can stand up to hunger, no patience can wear it out, disgust simply does not exist where hunger is; and as to superstition, beliefs, and what you may call principles, they are less than chaff in a breeze.

I couldn't argue with that – but I wondered why Largo had found the passage noteworthy. Perhaps it had struck a chord, back in the days when he'd been trying to rationalise taking his first research grants from the Pentagon? The ink was faded – and the volume itself had been printed in 2003. I would rather have had copies of his diary entries for the fortnight leading up to his disappearance, but his household computers hadn't been systematically tapped for almost twenty years.

I sat at the desk in his study, and stared at the blank screen of his work station. Largo had been born into a middle-class, nominally Catholic, very mildly leftist family in Lima, in 1980. His father, a journalist with *El Comercio*, had died from a cerebral blood clot in 2029. His seventy-eight-year-old mother still worked as an attorney for an international mining company – going through the motions of *habeas corpus* for the families of disappeared radicals in her spare time, a hobby her employers tolerated for the sake of cheap PR Brownie points in the shareholder democracies. Guillermo had one elder brother, a retired surgeon, and one younger sister, a primary-school teacher, neither of them politically active.

Most of his education had taken place in Switzerland and the States; after his PhD, he'd held a succession of research posts in government institutes, the biotechnology industry, and academia – all with more or less the same real sponsors. Fifty-five, now, thrice divorced but still childless, he'd only ever returned to Lima for brief family visits.

After *three decades* working on the military applications of molecular genetics – unwittingly at first, but not for long – what could have triggered his sudden defection to El Nido? If he'd managed the cynical doublethink of reconciling defence research and pious liberal sentiments for so long, he must have got it down to a fine art. His latest psychological profile suggested as much: fierce pride in his scientific achievements balanced the self-loathing he felt when contemplating their ultimate purpose – with the conflict showing signs of decaying into comfortable indifference. A well-documented dynamic in the industry.

And he seemed to have acknowledged – deep in his heart, thirty years ago – that his 'principles' were *less than chaff in a breeze*.

Perhaps he'd decided, belatedly, that if he was going to be a whore he might as well do it properly, and sell his skills to the highest bidder – even if that meant smuggling genetic weapons to a drugs cartel. I'd read his financial records, though: no tax fraud, no gambling debts, no evidence that he'd ever lived beyond his means. Betraying his employers, just as he'd betrayed his own youthful ideals to join them, might have seemed like an appropriately nihilistic gesture, but, on a more pragmatic level, it was hard to imagine him finding the money, and the consequences, all that tempting. What could El Nido have offered him? A numbered satellite account, and a new identity in Paraguay? All the squalid pleasures of life on the fringes of the Third World plutocracy? He would have had everything to gain by living out his retirement in his adopted country, salving his conscience with one or two vitriolic essays on foreign policy in some unread left-wing netzine – and then finally convincing himself that any nation that granted him such unencumbered rights of free speech probably deserved everything he'd done to defend it.

Exactly what he *had* done to defend it, though – what tools he'd perfected, and stolen – I was not permitted to know.

* * *

As dusk fell, I locked the apartment and headed south down Wisconsin Avenue. Washington was coming alive, the streets already teeming with people looking for distraction from the heat. Nights in the cities were becoming hallucinatory. Teenagers sported bioluminescent symbionts, the veins in their temples, necks, and pumped-up forearm muscles glowing electric blue, walking circulation diagrams who cultivated hypertension to improve the effect. Others used retinal symbionts to translate IR into visible light, their eyes flashing vampire red in the shadows.

And others, less visibly, had a skull full of White Knights.

Stem cells in the bone marrow infected with Mother – an engineered retrovirus – gave rise to something halfway between an embryonic neuron and a white blood cell. White Knights secreted the cytokines necessary to unlock the blood-brain barrier – and, once through, cellular adhesion molecules guided them to their targets, where they could flood the site with a chosen neurotransmitter – or even form temporary quasi-synapses with genuine neurons. Users often had half a dozen or more sub-types in their bloodstream simultaneously, each one activated by a specific dietary additive: some cheap, harmless, and perfectly legitimate chemical not naturally present in the body. By ingesting the right mixture of innocuous artificial colourings, flavours and preservatives, they could modulate their neurochemistry in almost any fashion – until the White Knights died, as they were programmed to do, and a new dose of Mother was required.

Mother could be snorted, or taken intravenously, but the most efficient way to use it was to puncture a bone and inject it straight into the marrow – an excruciating, messy, dangerous business, even if the virus itself was uncontaminated and authentic. The good stuff came from El Nido. The bad stuff came from basement labs in California and Texas, where gene hackers tried to force cell cultures infected with Mother to reproduce a virus expressly designed to resist their efforts – and churned out batches of mutant strains ideal for inducing leukaemia, astrocytomas, Parkinson's disease, and assorted novel psychoses.

Crossing the sweltering dark city, watching the heedlessly joyful crowds, I felt a penetrating, dream-like clarity come over me. Part of me was numb, leaden, blank – but part of me was electrified, all-seeing. I seemed to be able to stare into the hidden landscapes of the people around me, to see deeper than the luminous rivers of blood; to pierce them with my vision right to the bone.

Right to the marrow.

I drove to the edge of a park I'd visited once before, and waited. I was already dressed for the part. Young people strode by, grinning, some glancing at the silver 2025 Ford Narcissus and whistling appreciatively. A teenaged boy danced on the grass, alone, tirelessly – blissed out on Coca-Cola, and not even getting paid to fake it.

Before long, a girl approached the car, blue veins flashing on her bare arms. She leant down to the window and looked in, inquiringly.

'What you got?' She was sixteen or seventeen, slender, dark-eyed, coffee-coloured, with a faint Latino accent. She could have been my sister.

'Southern Rainbow.' All twelve major genotypes of Mother, straight from El Nido, cut with nothing but glucose. Southern Rainbow – and a little fast food – could take you anywhere.

The girl eyed me sceptically, and stretched out her right hand, palm down. She wore a ring with a large multifaceted jewel, with a pit in the centre. I took a sachet from the glove compartment, shook it, tore it open, and tipped a few specks of powder into the pit. Then I leant over and moistened the sample with saliva, holding her cool fingers to steady her hand. Twelve faces of the 'stone' began to glow immediately, each one in a different colour. The immunoelectric sensors in the pit, tiny capacitors coated with antibodies, were designed to recognise several sites on the protein coats of the different strains of Mother – particularly the ones the bootleggers had the most trouble getting right.

With good enough technology, though, those proteins didn't have to bear the slightest relationship to the RNA inside.

The girl seemed to be impressed; her face lit up with anticipation. We negotiated a price. Too low by far; she should have been suspicious.

I looked her in the eye before handing over the sachet.

I said, 'What do you need this shit for? The world is the world. You have to take it as it is. Accept it as it is: savage and terrible. Be strong. Never lie to yourself. That's the only way to survive.'

She smirked at my apparent hypocrisy, but she was too pleased with her luck to turn nasty. 'I hear what you're saying. It's a bad planet out there.' She forced the money into my hand, adding, with wide-eyed mock sincerity, 'And this is the last time I do Mother, I promise.'

I gave her the lethal virus, and watched her walk away across the grass and vanish into the shadows.

*   *   *

The Colombian air-force pilot who flew me down from Bogotá

didn't seem thrilled to be risking his life for a DEA bureaucrat. It was seven hundred kilometres to the border, and five different guerilla organisations held territory along the way: not a lot of towns, but several hundred possible sites for rocket launchers.

'My great-grandfather,' he said sourly, 'died in fucking Korea fighting for General Douglas fucking MacArthur.' I wasn't sure if that was meant to be a declaration of pride or an intimation of an outstanding debt. Both, probably.

The helicopter was eerily silent, fitted out with phased sound absorbers, which looked like giant loudspeakers but swallowed most of the noise of the blades. The carbon-fibre fuselage was coated with an expensive network of chameleon polymers – although it might have been just as effective to paint the whole thing sky blue. An endothermic chemical mixture accumulated waste heat from the motor, and then discharged it through a parabolic radiator as a tightly focused skywards burst, every hour or so. The guerillas had no access to satellite images, and no radar they dared use; I decided that we had less chance of dying than the average Bogotá commuter. Back in the capital, buses had been exploding without warning, two or three times a week.

Colombia was tearing itself apart; *La Violencia* of the 1950s, all over again. Although all of the spectacular terrorist sabotage was being carried out by organised guerilla groups, most of the deaths so far had been caused by factions within the two mainstream political parties butchering each other's supporters, avenging a litany of past atrocities which stretched back for generations. The group who'd actually started the current wave of bloodshed had negligible support; *Ejército de Simon Bolívar* were lunatic right-wing extremists who wanted to 'reunite' with Panama, Venezuela, and Ecuador – after two centuries of separation – and drag in Peru and Bolivia, to realise Bolívar's dream of *Gran Colombia*. By assassinating President Marín, though, they'd triggered a cascade of events that had nothing to do with their ludicrous cause. Strikes and protests, street battles, curfews, martial law. The repatriation of foreign capital by nervous investors, followed by hyperinflation, and the collapse of the local financial system. Then a spiral of opportunistic violence. Everyone, from the paramilitary death squads to the Maoist splinter groups, seemed to believe that their hour had finally come.

I hadn't seen so much as a bullet fired, but from the moment I'd entered the country there'd been acid churning in my guts, and a heady, ceaseless adrenaline rush coursing through my veins. I felt wired, feverish . . . alive. Hypersensitive as a pregnant woman: I could smell blood, everywhere. When the hidden struggle for power which rules all human affairs finally breaks through to the surface, finally ruptures the skin, it's like witnessing some giant primordial creature rise up out of the ocean. Mesmerising, and appalling. Nauseating – and exhilarating.

Coming face to face with the truth is always exhilarating.

*　　*　　*

From the air, there was no obvious sign that we'd arrived; for the last two hundred kilometres, we'd been passing over rain forest – cleared in patches for plantations and mines, ranches and timber mills, shot through with rivers like metallic threads, but most of it resembling nothing so much as an endless expanse of broccoli. El Nido permitted natural vegetation to flourish all around it – and then imitated it . . . which made sampling at the edges an inefficient way to gather the true genetic stock for analysis. Deep penetration was difficult, though, even with purpose-built robots – dozens of which had been lost – so edge samples had to suffice, at least until a few more members of Congress could be photographed committing statutory rape and persuaded to vote for better funding. Most of the engineered plant tissues self-destructed in the absence of regular chemical and viral messages drifting out from the core, reassuring them that they were still *in situ* – so the main DEA

11

research facility was on the outskirts of El Nido itself, a collection of pressurised buildings and experimental plots in a clearing blasted out of the jungle on the Colombian side of the border. The electrified fences weren't topped with razor wire; they turned ninety degrees into an electrified roof, completing a chain-link cage. The heliport was in the centre of the compound, where a cage within the cage could, temporarily, open itself to the sky.

Madeleine Smith, the research director, showed me around. In the open, we both wore hermetic biohazard suits – although if the modifications I'd received in Washington were working as promised, mine was redundant. El Nido's short-lived defensive viruses occasionally percolated out this far; they were never fatal, but they could be severely disabling to anyone who hadn't been inoculated. The forest's designers had walked a fine line between biological 'self-defence' and unambiguously military applications. Guerillas had always hidden in the engineered jungle – and raised funds by collaborating in the export of Mother – but El Nido's technology had never been explicitly directed towards the creation of lethal pathogens.

So far.

'Here, we're raising seedlings of what we hope will be a stable El Nido phenotype, something we call beta seventeen.' They were unremarkable bushes with deep-green foliage and dark-red berries; Smith pointed to an array of camera-like instruments beside them. 'Real-time infra-red microspectroscopy. It can resolve a medium-sized RNA transcript, if there's a sharp surge in production in a sufficient number of cells, simultaneously. We match up the data from these with our gas chromatography records, which show the range of molecules drifting out from the core. If we can catch these plants in the act of sensing a cue from El Nido – and if their response involves switching on a gene and synthesising a protein – we may be able to elucidate the mechanism, and eventually short-circuit it.'

'You can't just . . . sequence all the DNA, and work it out from first principles?' I was meant to be passing as a newly appointed administrator, dropping in at short notice to check for gold-plated paper clips, but it was hard to decide exactly how naïve to sound.

Smith smiled politely. 'El Nido DNA is guarded by enzymes which tear it apart at the slightest hint of cellular disruption. Right now, we'd have about as much of a chance of *sequencing it* as I'd have of . . . reading your mind by autopsy. And we still don't know how those enzymes work; we have a lot of catching up to do. When the drug cartels started investing in biotechnology, forty years ago, *copy protection* was their first priority. And they lured the best people away from legitimate labs around the world – not just by paying more, but by offering more creative freedom, and more challenging goals. El Nido probably contains as many patentable inventions as the entire agrotechnology industry produced in the same period. And all of them a lot more exciting.'

Was that what had brought Largo here? *More challenging goals?* But El Nido was complete, the challenge was over; any further work was mere refinement. And at fifty-five, surely he knew that his most creative years were long gone.

I said, 'I imagine the cartels got more than they bargained for; the technology transformed their business beyond recognition. All the old addictive substances became too easy to synthesise biologically – too cheap, too pure, and too readily available to be profitable. And addiction itself became bad business. The only thing that really sells now is novelty.'

Smith motioned with bulky arms towards the towering forest outside the cage – turning to face south-east, although it all looked the same. '*El Nido* was more than they bargained for. All they really wanted was coca plants that did better at lower altitudes, and some gene-tailored vegetation to make it easier to camouflage their labs and plantations. They ended up with a small *de facto* nation full of gene hackers, anarchists, and refugees. The cartels are only in control of certain regions; half the original geneticists have split off and founded their own little jungle utopias. There are at least a dozen people who know how to program the plants – how to switch on new patterns of gene expression, how to tap into the communications networks – and with that, you can stake out your own territory.'

'Like having some secret, shamanistic power to command the spirits of the forest?'

'Exactly. Except for the fact that it actually works.'

I laughed. 'Do you know what cheers me up the most? Whatever else happens, the *real* Amazon, the *real* jungle, will swallow them all in the end. It's lasted – what? Two million years? *Their own little utopias!* In fifty years' time, or a hundred, it will be as if El Nido had never existed.'

Less than chaff in a breeze.

Smith didn't reply. In the silence, I could hear the monotonous click of beetles, from all directions. Bogotá, high on a plateau, had been almost chilly. Here, it was as sweltering as Washington itself.

I glanced at Smith. She said, 'You're right, of course.' But she didn't sound convinced at all.

* * *

In the morning, over breakfast, I reassured Smith that I'd found everything to be in order. She smiled warily. I think she suspected that I wasn't what I claimed to be, but that didn't really matter. I'd listened carefully to the gossip of the scientists, technicians and soldiers; the name *Guillermo Largo* hadn't been mentioned once. If they didn't even know about Largo, they could hardly have guessed my real purpose.

It was just after nine when I departed. On the ground, sheets of light, delicate as auroral displays, sliced through the trees around the compound. When we emerged above the canopy, it was like stepping from a mist-shrouded dawn into the brilliance of noon.

The pilot, begrudgingly, took a detour over the centre of El Nido. 'We're in Peruvian air space, now,' he boasted. 'You want to spark a diplomatic incident?' He seeemed to find the possibility attractive.

'No. But fly lower.'

'There's nothing to see. You can't even see the river.'

'Lower.' The broccoli grew larger, then suddenly snapped into focus; all that undifferentiated *green* turned into individual branches, solid and specific. It was curiously shocking, like looking at some dull familiar object through a microscope and seeing its strange particularity revealed.

I reached over and broke the pilot's neck. He hissed through his teeth, surprised. A shudder passed through me, a mixture of fear and a twinge of remorse. The autopilot kicked in and kept us hovering; it took me two minutes to unstrap the man's body, drag him into the cargo hold, and take his seat.

I unscrewed the instrument panel and patched in a new chip. The digital log being beamed via satellite to an air-force base to the north would show that we'd descended rapidly, out of control.

The truth wasn't much different. At a hundred metres, I hit a branch and snapped a blade on the front rotor; the computers compensated valiantly, modelling and remodelling the situation, trimming the active surfaces of the surviving blades – and no doubt doing fine for each five-second interval between bone-shaking impacts and further damage. The sound absorbers went berserk, slipping in and out of phase with the motors, blasting the jungle with pulses of intensified noise.

Fifty metres up, I went into a slow spin, weirdly smooth, showing me the thickening canopy as if in a leisurely cinematic pan. At twenty metres, free fall. Air bags inflated around me, blocking off the view. I closed my eyes, redundantly, and gritted my teeth. Fragments of prayers spun in my head – the detritus

15

of childhood, afterimages burned into my brain, meaningless but unerasable. I thought: *If I die, the jungle will claim me. I am flesh, I am chaff. Nothing will remain to be judged.* By the time I recalled that this wasn't true jungle at all, I was no longer falling.

The air bags promptly deflated. I opened my eyes. There was water all around, flooded forest. A panel of the roof between the rotors blew off gently with a hiss like the dying pilot's last breath, and then drifted down like a slowly crashing kite, turning muddy silver, green, and brown as it snatched at the colours around it.

The life raft had oars, provisions, flares – and a radio beacon. I cut the beacon loose and left it in the wreckage. I moved the pilot back into his seat, just as the water started flooding in to bury him.

Then I set off down the river.

* * *

El Nido had divided a once-navigable stretch of the Rio Putumayo into a bewildering maze. Sluggish channels of brown water snaked between freshly raised islands of soil, covered in palms and rubber plants, and the inundated banks where the oldest trees – chocolate-coloured hardwood species (predating the geneticists, but not necessarily unmodified) – soared above the undergrowth and out of sight.

The lymph nodes in my neck and groin pulsed with heat, savage but reassuring; my modified immune system was dealing with El Nido's viral onslaught by generating thousands of new killer T-cell clones *en masse*, rather than waiting for a cautious antigen-mediated response. A few weeks in this state, and the chances were that a self-directed clone would slip through the elimination process and burn me up with a novel autoimmune disease – but I didn't plan on staying that long.

Fish disturbed the murky water, rising up to snatch surface-dwelling insects or floating seed pods. In the distance, the thick coils of an anaconda slid from an overhanging branch and slipped languidly into the water. Between the rubber plants, hummingbirds hovered in the maws of violet orchids. So far as I knew, none of these creatures had been tampered with; they had gone on inhabiting the prosthetic forest as if nothing had changed.

I took a stick of chewing gum from my pocket, rich in cyclamates, and slowly roused one of my own sets of White Knights. The stink of heat and decaying vegetation seemed to fade, as certain olfactory pathways in my brain were numbed, and others sensitised – a kind of inner filter coming into play, enabling any signal from the newly acquired receptors in my nasal membranes to rise above all the other, distracting odours of the jungle.

Suddenly, I could smell the dead pilot on my hands and clothes – the lingering taint of his sweat and faeces – and the pheromones of spider monkeys in the branches around me, pungent and distinctive as urine. As a rehearsal, I followed the trail for fifteen minutes, paddling the raft in the direction of the freshest scent, until I was finally rewarded with chirps of alarm and a glimpse of two skinny grey-brown shapes vanishing into the foliage ahead.

My own scent was camouflaged; symbionts in my sweat glands were digesting all the characteristic molecules. There were long-term side-effects from the bacteria, though, and the most recent intelligence suggested that El Nido's inhabitants didn't bother with them. There was a chance, of course, that Largo had been paranoid enough to bring his own.

I stared after the retreating monkeys, and wondered when I'd catch my first whiff of another living human. Even an illiterate peasant who'd fled the violence to the north would have valuable knowledge of the state of play between the factions in here, and some kind of crude mental map of the landscape.

The raft began to whistle gently, air escaping from one

sealed compartment. I rolled into the water and submerged completely. A metre down, I couldn't see my own hands. I waited and listened, but all I could hear was the soft *plop* of fish breaking the surface. No rock could have holed the plastic of the raft; it had to have been a bullet.

I floated in the cool milky silence. The water would conceal my body heat, and I'd have no need to exhale for ten minutes. The question was whether to risk raising a wake by swimming away from the raft, or to wait it out.

Something brushed my cheek, sharp and thin. I ignored it. It happened again. It didn't feel like a fish, or anything living. A third time, and I seized the object as it fluttered past. It was a piece of plastic a few centimetres wide. I felt around the rim; the edge was sharp in places, soft and yielding in others. Then the fragment broke in two in my hand.

I swam a few metres away, then surfaced cautiously. The life raft was decaying, the plastic peeling away into the water like skin in acid. The polymer was meant to be cross-linked beyond any chance of biodegradation, but obviously some strain of El Nido bacteria had found a way.

I floated on my back, breathing deeply to purge myself of carbon dioxide, contemplating the prospect of completing the mission on foot. The canopy above seemed to waver, as if in a heat haze, which made no sense. My limbs grew curiously warm and heavy. It occurred to me to wonder exactly what I might be smelling if I hadn't shut down ninety per cent of my olfactory range. I thought: *If I'd bred bacteria able to digest a substance foreign to El Nido, what else would I want them to do when they chanced upon such a meal? Incapacitate whoever had brought it in? Broadcast news of the event with a biochemical signal?*

I could smell the sharp odours of half a dozen sweat-drenched people when they arrived, but all I could do was lie in the water and let them fish me out.

*   *   *

After we left the river, I was carried on a stretcher, blindfolded and bound. No one talked within earshot. I might have judged the pace we set by the rhythm of my bearers' footsteps, or guessed the direction in which we travelled by hints of sunlight on the side of my face . . . but in the waking dream induced by the bacterial toxins, the harder I struggled to interpret those cues, the more lost and confused I became.

At one point, when the party rested, someone squatted beside me – and waved a scanning device over my body? That guess was confirmed by the pinpricks of heat where the polymer transponders had been implanted. Passive devices – but their resonant echo in a satellite microwave burst would have been distinctive. The scanner found, and fried, them all.

Late in the afternoon, they removed the blindfold. Certain that I was totally disoriented? Certain that I'd never escape? Or maybe just to flaunt El Nido's triumphant architecture.

The approach was a hidden path through swampland; I kept looking down to see my captors' boots not quite vanishing into the mud, while a dry, apparently secure stretch of high ground nearby was avoided.

Closer in, the dense thorned bushes blocking the way seemed to yield for us; the chewing gum had worn off enough for me to tell that we moved in a cloud of a sweet, ester-like compound. I couldn't see whether it was being sprayed into the air from a cylinder, or emitted bodily by a member of the party with symbionts in his skin, or lungs, or intestines.

The village emerged almost imperceptibly out of the impostor jungle. The ground – I could feel it – became, step by step, unnaturally firm and level. The arrangement of trees grew subtly ordered – defining no linear avenues, but increasingly *wrong* none the less. Then I started glimpsing, to the left and right, 'fortuitous' clearings containing 'natural' wooden buildings, or shiny biopolymer sheds.

I was lowered to the ground outside one of the sheds. A man I hadn't seen before leaned over me, wiry and unshaven, holding up a gleaming hunting knife. He looked to me like the archetype of human as animal, human as predator, human as unselfconscious killer.

He said, 'Friend, this is where we drain out all of your blood.' He grinned and squatted down. I almost passed out from the stench of my own fear, as the glut overwhelmed the symbionts. He cut my hands free, adding, 'And then put it all back in again.' He slid one arm under me, around my ribs, raised me up from the stretcher, and carried me into the building.

* * *

Guillermo Largo said, 'Forgive me if I don't shake your hand. I think we've almost cleaned you out, but I don't want to risk physical contact in case there's enough of a residue of the virus to make your own hyped-up immune system turn on you.'

He was an unprepossessing, sad-eyed man; thin, short, slightly balding. I stepped up to the wooden bars between us and stretched my hand out towards him. 'Make contact any time you like. I never carried a virus. Do you think I believe your *propaganda*?'

He shrugged, unconcerned. 'It would have killed you, not me – although I'm sure it was meant for both of us. It may have been keyed to my genotype, but you carried far too much of it not to have been caught up in the response to my presence. That's history, though; not worth arguing about.'

I didn't actually believe that he was lying; a virus to dispose of both of us made perfect sense. I even felt a begrudging respect for the Company, for the way I'd been used – there was a savage, unsentimental honesty to it – but it didn't seem politic to reveal that to Largo.

I said, 'If you believe that I pose no risk to you now, though, why don't you come back with me? You're still considered valuable. One moment of weakness, one bad decision, doesn't have to mean the end of your career. Your employers are very pragmatic people; they won't want to punish you. They'll just need to watch you a little more closely in future. Their problem, not yours; you won't even notice the difference.'

Largo didn't seem to be listening, but then he looked straight at me and smiled. 'Do you know what Victor Hugo said about Colombia's first constitution? He said it was written for a country of angels. It only lasted twenty-three years – and on the next attempt, the politicians lowered their sights. Considerably.' He turned away, and started pacing back and forth in front of the bars. Two Mestizo peasants with automatic weapons stood by the door, looking on impassively. Both incessantly chewed what looked to me like ordinary coca leaves; there was something almost reassuring about their loyalty to tradition.

My cell was clean and well furnished, right down to the kind of bioreactor toilet that was all the rage in Beverly Hills. My captors had treated me impeccably, so far, but I had a feeling that Largo was planning something unpleasant. Handing me over to the Mother barons? I still didn't know what deal he'd done, what he'd sold them in exchange for a piece of El Nido and a few dozen bodyguards. Let alone why he thought this was better than an apartment in Bethesda and a hundred grand a year.

I said, 'What do you think you're going to do if you stay here? Build your own *country for angels*? Grow your own bioengineered utopia?'

'Utopia?' Largo stopped pacing, and flashed his crooked smile again. 'No. How can there ever be a *utopia*? There is no *right way to live* which we've simply failed to stumble upon. There is no set of rules, there is no system, there is no formula. Why should there be? Short of the existence of a creator – and a perverse one, at that – why should there be some blueprint for perfection, just waiting to be discovered?'

I said, 'You're right. In the end, all we can do is be true to our nature. See through the veneer of civilisation and hypocritical morality, and accept the real forces that shape us.'

Largo burst out laughing. I actually felt my face burn at his response – if only because I'd misread him, and failed to get him on side; not because he was laughing at the one thing I believed in.

He said, 'Do you know what I was working on, back in the States?'

'No. Does it matter?' The less I knew, the better my chances of living.

Largo told me anyway. 'I was looking for a way to render mature neurons *embryonic*. To switch them back into a less differentiated state, enabling them to behave the way they do in the foetal brain: migrating from site to site, forming new connections. Supposedly as a treatment for dementia and stroke . . . although the work was being funded by people who saw it as the first step towards viral weapons able to rewire parts of the brain. I doubt that the results could ever have been very sophisticated – no viruses for imposing political ideologies – but all kinds of disabling or docile behaviour might have been coded into a relatively small package.'

'And you sold that to the cartels? So they can hold whole cities to ransom with it next time one of their leaders is arrested? To save them the trouble of assassinating judges and politicians?'

Largo said mildly, 'I sold it to the cartels, but not as a weapon. No infectious military version exists. Even the prototypes – which merely regress selected neurons, but make no programmed changes – are far too cumbersome and fragile to survive at large. And there are other technical problems. There's not much reproductive advantage for a virus in carrying out elaborate, highly specific modifications to its host's brain; unleashed on a real human population, mutants that simply ditched all of that irrelevant shit would soon predominate.'

'Then . . . ?'

'I sold it to the cartels as *a product*. Or, rather, I combined it with their own biggest seller, and handed over the finished hybrid. A new kind of Mother.'

'Which does what?' He had me hooked, even if I was digging my own grave.

'Which turns a subset of the neurons in the brain into something like White Knights. Just as mobile, just as flexible. Far better at establishing tight new synapses, though, rather than just flooding the interneural space with a chosen substance. And not controlled by dietary additives; controlled by molecules they secrete themselves. Controlled by each other.'

That made no sense to me. '*Existing neurons* become mobile? Existing brain structures . . . melt? You've made a version of Mother that turns people's brains to mush – and you expect them to pay for that?'

'Not mush. Everything's part of a tight feedback loop: the firing of these altered neurons influences the range of molecules they secrete – which, in turn, controls the rewiring of nearby synapses. Vital regulatory centres and motor neurons are left untouched, of course. And it takes a strong signal to shift the Grey Knights; they don't respond to every random whim. You need at least an hour or two without distractions before you can have a significant effect on any brain structure.

'It's not altogether different from the way ordinary neurons end up encoding learned behaviour and memories – only faster, more flexible . . . and much more widespread. There are parts of the brain that haven't changed in a hundred thousand years, which can be remodelled completely in half a day.'

He paused, and regarded me amiably.

The sweat on the back of my neck went cold. 'You've used the virus—?'

'Of course. That's why I created it. For myself. That's why I came here in the first place.'

'For do-it-yourself neurosurgery? Why not just slip a

screwdriver under one eyeball and poke it around until the urge went away?' I felt physically sick. 'At least . . . cocaine and heroin, and even White Knights, exploited *natural* receptors, *natural* pathways. You've taken a structure that evolution has honed over millions of years, and—'

Largo was greatly amused, but this time he refrained from laughing in my face. He said gently, 'For most people, navigating their own psyche is like wandering in circles through a maze. That's what *evolution* has bequeathed us: a miserable, confusing prison. And the only thing crude drugs like cocaine or heroin or alcohol ever did was build short cuts to a few dead ends – or, like LSD, coat the walls of the maze with mirrors. And all that White Knights ever did was package the same effects differently.

'*Grey Knights* allow you to reshape the entire maze, at will. They don't confine you to some shrunken emotional repertoire; they empower you completely. They let you control *exactly who you are.*'

I had to struggle to put aside the overwhelming sense of revulsion I felt. Largo had decided to fuck himself in the head; that was his problem. A few users of Mother would do the same, but one more batch of poisonous shit to compete with all the garbage from the basement labs wasn't exactly a national tragedy.

Largo said affably, 'I spent thirty years as someone I despised. I was too weak to change, but I never quite lost sight of what I wanted to become. I used to wonder if it would have been less contemptible, less hypocritical, to resign myself to the fact of my weakness, the fact of my corruption. But I never did.'

'And you think you've erased your old personality, as easily as you erased your computer files? What are you now, then? A saint? An *angel*?'

'No. But I'm exactly what I want to be. With Grey Knights, you can't really be anything else.'

I felt giddy for a moment, light-headed with rage; I steadied myself against the bars of my cage.

I said, 'So you've scrambled your brain, and you feel better. And you're going to live in this fake jungle for the rest of your life, collaborating with drug pushers, kidding yourself that you've achieved redemption?'

'The rest of my life? Perhaps. But I'll be watching the world. And hoping.'

I almost choked. 'Hoping for *what*? You think your habit will ever spread beyond a few brain-damaged junkies? You think Grey Knights are going to sweep across the planet and transform it beyond recognition? Or were you lying – is the virus really infectious, after all?'

'No. But it gives people what they want. They'll seek it out, once they understand that.'

I gazed at him, pityingly. 'What people *want* is food, sex, and power. That will never change. Remember the passage you marked in "Heart of Darkness"? What do you think that *meant*? Deep down, we're just animals with a few simple drives. Everything else is *less than chaff in a breeze.*'

Largo frowned, as if trying to recall the quote, then nodded slowly. He said, 'Do you know how many different ways an ordinary human brain can be wired? Not an arbitrary neural network of the same size, but an actual, working *Homo sapiens* brain, shaped by real embryology and real experience? There are about ten-to-the-power-of-ten-million possibilities. A huge number: a lot of room for variation in personality and talents, a lot of space to encode the traces of different lives.

'But do you know what Grey Knights do to that number? They multiply it by the same again. They grant the part of us that was fixed, that was tied to "human nature", the chance to be as different from person to person as a lifetime's worth of memories.

'Of course Conrad was right. Every word of that passage was true – when it was written. But now it doesn't go far enough. Because now, all of human nature is *less than chaff in a breeze*. "The horror", the heart of darkness, is *less than chaff in a breeze*. All the "eternal verities" – all the sad and beautiful insights of all the great writers from Sophocles to Shakespeare – are *less than chaff in a breeze*.'

* * *

I lay awake on my bunk, listening to the cicadas and frogs, wondering what Largo would do with me. If he didn't see himself as capable of murder, he wouldn't kill me – if only to reinforce his delusions of self-mastery. Perhaps he'd just dump me outside the research station – where I could explain to Madeleine Smith how the Colombian air-force pilot had come down with an El Nido virus in midair, and I'd valiantly tried to take control.

I thought back over the incident, trying to get my story straight. The pilot's body would never be recovered; the forensic details didn't have to add up.

I closed my eyes and saw myself breaking his neck. The same twinge of remorse passed over me. I brushed it aside irritably. So I'd killed him – and the girl, a few days earlier – and a dozen others before that. The Company had very nearly disposed of me. Because it was expedient – and because it was possible. That was the way of the world: power would always be used, nation would subjugate nation, the weak would always be slaughtered. Everything else was pious self-delusion. A hundred kilometres away, Colombia's warring factions were proving the truth of that, one more time.

But if Largo had infected me with his own special brand of Mother? And if everything he'd told me about it was true?

Grey Knights only moved if you willed them to move. All I had to do in order to remain unscathed was to choose that fate. To wish only to be exactly who I was: a killer who'd always understood that he was facing the deepest of truths. Embracing savagery and corruption because, in the end, there was no other way.

I kept seeing them before me: the pilot, the girl.

I had to feel nothing – and wish to feel nothing – and keep on making that choice, again and again.

Or everything I was would disintegrate like a house of sand, and blow away.

One of the guards belched in the darkness, then spat.

The night stretched out ahead of me, like a river that had lost its way.

MITOCHONDRIAL EVE

With hindsight, I can date the beginning of my involvement in the Ancestor Wars precisely: *Saturday, 2 June 2007*. That was the night Lena dragged me along to the Children of Eve to be mitotyped. We'd been out to dinner, it was almost midnight, but the sequencing bureau was open twenty-four hours.

'Don't you want to discover your place in the human family?' she asked, fixing her green eyes on me, smiling but earnest. 'Don't you want to find out exactly where you belong on the Great Tree?'

The honest answer would have been: *What sane person could possibly care?* We'd only known each other for five or six weeks, though; I wasn't yet comfortable enough with our relationship to be so blunt.

'It's very late,' I said cautiously. 'And you know I have to work tomorrow.' I was still fighting my way up through post-doctoral qualifications in physics, supporting myself by tutoring undergraduates and doing all the tedious menial tasks which tenured academics demanded of their slaves. Lena was a communications engineer – and at twenty-five, the same age as I was, she'd had real paid jobs for almost four years.

'You always have to work. Come on, Paul! It'll take fifteen minutes.'

Arguing the point would have taken twice as long. So I told myself that it could do no harm, and I followed her north through the gleaming city streets.

It was a mild winter night; the rain had stopped, the air was still. The Children owned a sleek, imposing building in the heart of Sydney, prime real estate, an ostentatious display of the movement's wealth. ONE WORLD, ONE FAMILY proclaimed the luminous sign above the entrance. There were bureaux in over a hundred cities (although Eve took on various 'culturally appropriate' names in different places, from Sakti in parts of India, to Ele'ele in Samoa) and I'd heard that the Children were working on street-corner vending-machine sequencers, to recruit members even more widely.

In the foyer, a holographic bust of Mitochondrial Eve herself, mounted on a marble pedestal, gazed proudly over our heads. The artist had rendered our hypothetical ten-thousand-times-great grandmother as a strikingly beautiful woman. A subjective judgement, certainly, but her lean, symmetrical features, her radiant health, her purposeful stare, didn't really strike me as amenable to subtleties of interpretation. The aesthetic buttons being pushed were labelled, unmistakably: *warrior, queen, goddess.* And I had to admit that I felt a certain bizarre, involuntary swelling of pride at the sight of her . . . as if her regal bearing and fierce eyes somehow 'ennobled' me and all her descendants . . . as if the 'character' of the entire species, our potential for virtue, somehow depended on having at least one ancestor who could have starred in a Leni Riefenstahl documentary.

This Eve was black, of course, having lived in sub-Saharan Africa some 200,000 years ago, but almost everything else about her was guesswork. I'd heard palaeontologists quibble about the too-modern features, not really compatible with any of the sparse fossil evidence for her contemporaries' appearance. Still, if the Children had chosen as their symbol of universal humanity a few fissured brown skull fragments from the Omo River in Ethiopia, the movement would surely have vanished without a trace. And perhaps it was simply mean-spirited of me to think of their Eve's beauty as a sign of fascism. The Children had already persuaded over two million people to acknowledge, explicitly, a common ancestry which transcended their own superficial differences in appearance; this all-inclusive ethos seemed to undercut any argument linking their obsession with *pedigree* to anything unsavoury.

I turned to Lena. 'You know the Mormons baptised her posthumously, last year?'

She shrugged the appropriation off lightly. 'Who cares? This Eve belongs to everyone, equally. Every culture, every religion, every philosophy. Anyone can claim her as their own; it doesn't diminish her at all.' She regarded the bust admiringly, almost reverently.

I thought: *She sat through four hours of Marx Brothers films with me last week – bored witless, but uncomplaining. So I can do this for her, can't I?* It seemed like a simple matter of give-and-take – and it wasn't as if I was being pressured into an embarrassing haircut, or a tattoo.

We walked through into the sequencing lounge.

We were alone, but a disembodied voice broke through the ambience of endangered amphibians and asked us to wait. The room was plushly carpeted, with a circular sofa in the middle. Artwork from around the world decorated the walls, from an uncredited Arnhem Land dot painting to a Francis Bacon print. The explanatory text below was a worry: dire Jungian psycho-babble about 'universal primal imagery' and 'the collective unconscious'. I groaned aloud, but when Lena asked what was wrong I just shook my head innocently.

A man in white trousers and a short white tunic emerged from a camouflaged door, wheeling a trolley packed with impressively minimalist equipment, reminiscent of expensive Scandinavian audio gear. He greeted us both as 'cousin', and I struggled to keep a straight face. The badge on his tunic bore his name, Cousin André, a small reflection hologram of Eve, and a sequence of letters and numbers which identified his mitotype. Lena took charge, explaining that she was a member, and she'd brought me along to be sequenced.

After paying the fee – a hundred dollars, blowing my recreation budget for the next three months – I let Cousin André prick my thumb and squeeze a drop of blood onto a white absorbent pad, which he fed into one of the machines on the trolley. A sequence of delicate whirring sounds ensued, conveying a reassuring sense of precision engineering at work. Which was odd, because I'd seen ads for similar devices in *Nature* which boasted of no moving parts at all.

While we waited for the results, the room dimmed and a large hologram appeared, projected from the wall in front of us: a micrograph of a single living cell. *From my own blood?* More likely, not from anyone's – just a convincing photorealist animation.

'Every cell in your body,' Cousin André explained, 'contains hundreds or thousands of mitochondria: tiny power plants which extract energy from carbohydrates.' The image zoomed in on a translucent organelle, rod-shaped with rounded ends, rather like a drug capsule. 'The majority of the DNA in any cell is in the nucleus, and comes from both parents, but there's also DNA in the mitochondria, inherited from the mother alone. So it's easier to use mitochondrial DNA to trace your ancestry.'

He didn't elaborate, but I'd heard the theory in full several times, starting with high-school biology. Thanks to recombination – the random interchange of stretches of DNA between paired chromosomes, in the lead-up to the creation of sperm or ova – every chromosome carried genes from tens of thousands of different ancestors, stitched together seamlessly. From a palaeogenetic perspective, analysing nuclear DNA was like trying to make sense of 'fossils' which had been forged by cementing together assorted bone fragments from ten thousand different individuals.

Mitochondrial DNA came, not in paired chromosomes, but in tiny loops called plasmids. There were hundreds of plasmids in every cell, but they were all identical, and they all derived from the ovum alone. Mutations aside – one every 4,000 years or so – your mitochondrial DNA was exactly the same as that of your mother, your maternal grandmother, great-grand-mother, and so on. It was also exactly the same as that of your siblings, your maternal first cousins, second cousins, third cousins . . . until different mutations striking the plasmid on its way down through something like 200 generations finally imposed some variation. But with 16,000 DNA base pairs in the plasmid, even the fifty or so point mutations since Eve herself didn't amount to much.

The hologram dissolved from the micrograph into a multicoloured diagram of branching lines, a giant family tree starting from a single apex labelled with the ubiquitous image of Eve. Each fork in the tree marked a mutation, splitting Eve's inheritance into two slightly different versions. At the bottom, the tips of the hundreds of branches showed a variety of faces, some men, some women – individuals or composites, I couldn't say, but each one presumably represented a different group of (roughly) 200th maternal cousins, all sharing a mitotype: their own modest variation on the common 200,000-year-old theme.

'And here you are,' said Cousin André. A stylised magnifying glass materialised in the foreground of the hologram, enlarging one of the tiny faces at the bottom of the tree. The uncanny resemblance to my own features was almost certainly due to a snapshot taken by a hidden camera; mitochondrial DNA had no effect whatsoever on appearance.

Lena reached into the hologram and began to trace my descent with one fingertip. 'You're a Child of Eve, Paul. You know who you are, now. And no one can ever take that away from you.' I stared at the luminous tree, and felt a chill at the base of my spine, though it had more to do with the Children's proprietary claim over the entire species than any kind of awe in the presence of my ancestors.

Eve had been nothing special, no watershed in evolution; she was simply defined as the most recent common ancestor, by an unbroken female line, of every single living human. And no doubt she'd had thousands of female contemporaries, but time and chance – the random death of daughterless women, catastrophes of disease and climate – had eliminated every mitochondrial trace of them. There was no need to assume that her mitotype had conferred any special advantages (most variation was in junk DNA, anyway); statistical fluctuations alone meant that one maternal lineage would replace all the others, eventually.

Eve's existence was a logical necessity: some human (or hominid) of one era or another had to fit the bill. It was only the timing which was contentious.

The timing, and its implications.

A world globe some two metres wide appeared beside the Great Tree; it had a distinctive Earth-from-space look, with heavy white cumulus swirling over the oceans, but the sky above the continents was uniformly cloudless. The Tree quivered and began to rearrange itself, converting its original rectilinear form into something much more misshapen and organic, but flexing its geometry without altering any of the relationships it embodied. Then it draped itself over the surface of the globe. Lines of descent became migratory routes. Between eastern Africa and the Levant, the tracks were tightly bunched and parallel, like the lanes of some palaeolithic freeway; elsewhere, less constrained by the geography, they radiated out in all directions.

A recent Eve favoured the 'Out of Africa' hypothesis: modern *Homo sapiens* had evolved from the earlier *Homo erectus* in one place only, and had then migrated throughout the world, out-competing and replacing the local *Homo erectus* everywhere they went – and developing localised racial characteristics only within the last 200,000 years. The single birthplace of the species was most likely Africa, because Africans showed the greatest (and hence oldest) mitochondrial variation; all other groups seemed to have diversified more recently from relatively small 'founder' populations.

There were rival theories, of course. More than a million years before *Homo sapiens* even existed, *Homo erectus* itself had spread as far as Java, acquiring its own regional differences in appearance – and *Homo erectus* fossils in Asia and Europe seemed to share at least some of the distinguishing characteristics of living Asians and Europeans. But 'Out of Africa' put that down to convergent evolution, not ancestry. If *Homo erectus* had turned into *Homo sapiens* independently in several places, then the mitochondrial difference between, say, modern Ethiopians and Javanese should have been five or ten times as great, marking their long separation since a much earlier Eve. And even if the scattered *Homo erectus* communities had not been totally isolated, but had interbred with successive waves of migrants over the past one or two million years – hybridising with them to create modern humans, and yet somehow retaining their distinctive differences – then distinct mitochondrial lineages much older than 200,000 years probably should have survived too.

One route on the globe flashed brighter than the rest. Cousin André explained, 'This is the path your own ancestors took. They left Ethiopia – or maybe Kenya or Tanzania – heading north, about 150,000 years ago. They spread slowly up through Sudan, Egypt, Israel, Palestine, Syria and Turkey while the interglacial stretched on. By the start of the last Ice Age, the eastern shore of the Black Sea was their home . . .' As he spoke, tiny pairs of footprints materialised along the route.

He traced the hypothetical migration through the Caucasus Mountains, and all the way to northern Europe – where the limits of the technique finally cut the story dead: some four millennia ago (give or take three), when my Germanic two-hundredish-great grandmother had given birth to a daughter with a single change in her mitochondrial junk DNA: the last recorded tick of the molecular clock.

Cousin André wasn't finished with me, though. 'As your ancestors moved into Europe, their relative genetic isolation, and the demands of the local climate, gradually led them to acquire the characteristics which are known as Caucasian. But the same route was travelled many times, by wave after wave of migrants, sometimes separated by thousands of years. And though, at every step along the way, the new travellers interbred with those who'd gone before, and came to resemble them . . . dozens of separate maternal lines can still be traced back along the route – and then down through history again, along different paths.'

My very closest maternal cousins, he explained – those with exactly the same mitotype – were, not surprisingly, mostly Caucasians. And expanding the circle to include up to thirty base pair differences brought in about 5 per cent of all Caucasians – the 5 per cent with whom I shared a common maternal ancestor who'd lived some 120,000 years ago, probably in the Levant.

But a number of that woman's own cousins had apparently headed east, not north. Eventually, their descendants had made it all the way across Asia, down through Indochina, and then south through the archipelagos, travelling across land bridges exposed by the low ocean levels of the Ice Age, or making short sea voyages from island to island. They'd stopped just short of Australia.

So I was more closely related, maternally, to a small group of New Guinean highlanders than I was to 95 per cent of Caucasians. The magnifying glass reappeared beside the globe, and showed me the face of one of my living 6000th cousins. The two of us were about as dissimilar to the naked eye as any two people on Earth; of the handful of nuclear genes which coded for attributes like pigmentation and facial bone structure, one set had been favoured in frozen northern Europe, and another in this equatorial jungle. But enough mitochondrial evidence had survived in both places to reveal that the local homogenisation of appearance was just a veneer, a recent gloss over an ancient network of invisible family connections.

Lena turned to me triumphantly. 'You see? All the old myths about race, culture, and kinship – instantly refuted! These people's immediate ancestors lived in isolation for thousands of years, and didn't set eyes on a single white face until the twentieth century. Yet they're nearer to you than I am!'

I nodded, smiling, trying to share her enthusiasm. It *was* fascinating to see the whole naïve concept of 'race' turned inside out like this – and I had to admire the Children's sheer audacity at claiming to be able to map hundred-thousand-year-old relationships with such precision. But I couldn't honestly say that my life had been transformed by the revelation that certain white total strangers were more distant cousins to me than certain black ones. Maybe there were die-hard racists who would have been shaken to the core by news like this . . . but it was hard to imagine them rushing along to the Children of Eve to be mitotyped.

The far end of the trolley beeped, and ejected a badge just like Cousin André's. He offered it to me; when I hesitated, Lena took it and pinned it proudly to my shirt.

Out on the street, Lena announced soberly, 'Eve is going to change the world. We're lucky; we'll live to see it happen. We've had a century of people being slaughtered for belonging to the wrong kinship groups – but soon *everyone* will understand that there are older, deeper blood ties which confound all their shallow historical prejudices.'

You mean . . . like the biblical Eve confounded all the prejudices of fundamentalist Christians? Or like the image of the Earth from space put an end to war and pollution? I tried diplomatic silence; Lena regarded me with consternation, as if she couldn't quite believe that I could harbour any doubts after my own unexpected *blood ties* had been revealed.

I said, 'Do you remember the Rwandan massacres?'

'Of course.'

'Weren't they more to do with a class system – which the Belgian colonists exacerbated for the sake of administrative convenience – than anything you could describe as enmity between *kinship groups*? And in the Balkans—'

Lena cut me off. 'Look, sure, any incident you can point to will have a convoluted history. I'm not denying that. But it doesn't mean that the solution has to be impossibly complicated, too. And if everyone involved had known what we know, had *felt* what we've felt—' she closed her eyes and smiled radiantly, an expression of pure contentment and tranquillity '—that deep sense of belonging, through Eve, to a single family which encompasses all of humanity . . . do you honestly imagine that they could have turned on each other like that?'

I should have protested, in tones of bewilderment: *What 'deep sense of belonging'? I felt nothing. And the only thing the Children of Eve are doing is preaching to the converted.*

What was the worst that could have happened? If we'd broken up, right there and then, over *the political significance of palaeogenetics*, then the relationship was obviously doomed from the start. And however much I hated confrontation, it was a fine line between tact and dishonesty, between accommodating our differences and concealing them.

And yet. The issue seemed far too arcane to be worth fighting over – and though Lena clearly held some passionate views on it, I couldn't really see the topic arising again if I kept my big mouth shut, just this once.

I said, 'Maybe you're right.' I slipped an arm around her, and she turned and kissed me. It began to rain again, heavily, the downpour strangely calm in the still air. We ended up back at Lena's flat, saying very little for the rest of the night.

I was a coward and a fool, of course – but I had no way of knowing, then, just how much it would cost me.

*   *   *

A few weeks later, I found myself showing Lena around the basement of the UNSW physics department, where my own research equipment was crammed into one corner. It was late at night (again), and we were alone in the building; variously coloured fluorescent display screens hovered in the darkness, like distant icons for the other post-doctoral projects in some chilly academic cyberspace.

I couldn't find the chair I'd bought for myself (despite security measures escalating from a simple name tag to increasingly sophisticated computerised alarms, it was always being borrowed), so we stood on the cold bare concrete beside the apparatus, lit by a single fading ceiling panel, and I conjured up sequences of zeros and ones which echoed the strangeness of the quantum world.

The infamous Einstein–Podolosky–Rosen correlation – the entanglement of two microscopic particles into a single quantum system – had been investigated experimentally for over twenty years, but it had only recently become possible to explore the effect with anything more complicated than pairs of photons or electrons. I was working with hydrogen atoms, produced when a single hydrogen molecule was dissociated with a pulse from an ultraviolet laser. Certain measurements carried out on the separated atoms showed statistical correlations which only made sense if a single wave function encompassing the two responded to the measurement process instantaneously – regardless of how far apart the individual atoms had travelled since their tangible molecular bonds were broken: metres, kilometres, light-years.

The phenomenon seemed to mock the whole concept of distance, but my own work had recently helped to dispel any notion that EPR might lead to a faster-than-light signalling device. The theory had always been clear on that point, though some people had hoped that a flaw in the equations would provide a loophole.

I explained to Lena, 'Take two machines stocked with EPR-correlated atoms, one on Earth and one on Mars, both capable of, say, measuring orbital angular momentum either vertically or horizontally. The results of the measurements would always be random . . . but the machine on Mars could be made to emit data which either did, or didn't, mimic precisely the random data coming out of the machine on Earth at the very same time. And that mimicry could be switched on and off – instantaneously – by altering the type of measurements being made on Earth.'

'Like having two coins which are guaranteed to fall the same way as each other,' she suggested, 'so long as they're both being thrown right-handed. But if you start throwing the coin on Earth with your left hand, the correlation vanishes.'

'Yeah – that's a perfect analogy.' I realised belatedly that she'd probably heard this all before – quantum mechanics and information theory were the foundations of her own field, after all – but she was listening politely, so I continued. 'But even when the coins are magically agreeing on every single toss, they're both still giving equal numbers of heads and tails, at random. So there's no way of encoding any message into the data. You can't even tell, from Mars, when the correlation starts and stops – not unless the data from Earth gets sent along for comparison, by some conventional means like a radio transmission – defeating the whole point of the exercise. EPR itself communicates nothing.'

Lena contemplated this thoughtfully, though she was clearly unsurprised by the verdict.

She said, 'It communicates nothing between separated atoms, but if you bring them together, instead, it can still tell you what they've done in the past. You do a control experiment, don't you? You make the same measurements on atoms which were never paired?'

'Yeah, of course.' I pointed to the third and fourth columns of data on the screen; the process itself was going on silently as we spoke, inside an evacuated chamber in a small grey box concealed behind all the electronics. 'The results are completely uncorrelated.'

'So, basically, this machine can tell you whether or not two atoms have been bonded together?'

'Not individually; any individual match could just be chance. But given enough atoms with a common history – yes.'

Lena was smiling conspiratorially.

I said, 'What?'

'Just . . . humour me for a moment. What's the next stage? Heavier atoms?'

'Yes, but there's more. I'll split a hydrogen molecule, let the two separate hydrogen atoms combine with two fluorine atoms – any old ones, not correlated – then split both hydrogen fluoride molecules and make measurements on *the fluorine atoms* to see if I can pick up an indirect correlation between them: a second-order effect inherited from the original hydrogen molecule.'

The truth was, I had little hope of getting funded to take the work that far. The basic experimental facts of EPR had been settled now, so there wasn't much of a case for pushing the measurement technology any further.

'In theory,' Lena asked innocently, 'could you do the same with something much larger? Like . . . DNA?'

I laughed. 'No.'

'I don't mean: could you do it, here, a week from tomorrow? But if two strands of DNA had been bonded together, would there be any correlation at all?'

I baulked at the idea, but confessed, 'There might be. I can't give you the answer off the top of my head; I'd have to borrow some software from the biochemists, and model the interaction precisely.'

Lena nodded, satisfied. 'I think you should do that.'

'*Why?* I'll never be able to try it, for real.'

'Not with this junkyard-grade equipment.'

I snorted. 'So tell me who's going to pay for something better?'

Lena glanced around the grim basement, as if she wanted to

record a mental snapshot of the low point of my career – before everything changed completely. 'Who'd finance research into a means of detecting the quantum fingerprint of DNA bonding? Who'd pay for a chance of computing – not to the nearest few millennia, but to the nearest *cell division* – how long ago two mitochondrial plasmids were in contact?'

I was scandalised. *This* was the idealist who believed that the Children of Eve were the last great hope for world peace?

I said, 'They'd never fall for it.'

Lena stared at me blankly for a second, then shook her head, amused. 'I'm not talking about pulling a confidence trick – begging for a research grant on false pretences.'

'Well, good. But—?'

'I'm talking about taking the money – and doing a job that has to be done. Sequencing technology has been pushed as far as it can go, but our opponents still keep finding things to quibble about: the mitochondrial mutation rate, the method of choosing branch points for the most probable tree, the details of lineage loss and survival. Even the palaeogeneticists who are on our side keep changing their minds about everything. Eve's age goes up and down like the Hubble constant.'

'It can't be that bad, surely.'

Lena seized my arm. Her excitement was electric; I felt it flow into me. Or maybe she'd just pinched a nerve. '*This* could transform the whole field. No more guesswork, no more conjecture, no more assumptions – just a single, indisputable family tree, stretching back 200,000 years.'

'It may not even be possible—'

'But you'll find out? You'll look into it?'

I hesitated, but I couldn't think of a single good reason to refuse. 'Yes.'

Lena smiled. 'With *quantum palaeogenetics* . . . you'll have the power to bring Eve to life for the world in a way that no one has ever done before.'

*   *   *

Six months later, the funds ran out for my work at the university: the research, the tutoring, everything. Lena offered to support me for three months while I put together a proposal to submit to the Children. We were already living together, already sharing expenses; somehow, that made it much easier to rationalise. And it was a bad time of year to be looking for work, I was going to be unemployed anyway . . .

As it turned out, computer modelling suggested that a measurable correlation between segments of DNA could be picked out against the statistical noise – given enough plasmids to work with: more like a few litres of blood per person than a single drop. But I could already see that the technical problems would take years of work to assess properly, let alone overcome. Writing it all up was good practice for future corporate-grant applications, but I never seriously expected anything to come of it.

Lena came with me to the meeting with William Sachs, the Children's West Pacific Research Director. He was in his late fifties, and *very* conservatively dressed, from the classic Benetton AIDS ISN'T NICE T-shirt to the Mambo World Peace surfing dove motif board shorts. A slightly younger version smiled down from a framed cover of *Wired*; he'd been guru of the month in April 2005.

'The University physics department will be contracted to provide overall supervision,' I explained nervously. 'There'll be independent audits of the scientific quality of the work every six months, so there's no possibility of the research running off the rails.'

'The EPR correlation,' mused Sachs, 'proves that all life is bound together holistically into a grand unified meta-organism, doesn't it?'

'No.' Lena kicked me hard under the desk.

But Sachs didn't seem to have heard me. 'You'll be listening in to Gaia's own theta rhythm. The secret harmony which underlies everything: synchronicity, morphic resonance, transmigration . . .' He sighed dreamily. 'I *adore* quantum mechanics. You know my Tai Chi master wrote a book about it? *Schrödinger's Lotus* – you must have read it. What a mind-fuck! And he's working on a sequel, *Heisenberg's Mandala*—'

Lena intervened before I could open my mouth again. 'Maybe . . . later generations will be able to trace the correlation as far as other species. But in the foreseeable future, even reaching as far as Eve will be a major technical challenge.'

Cousin William seemed to come back down to Earth. He picked up the printed copy of the application and turned to the budget details at the end, which were mostly Lena's work.

'Five million dollars is a lot of money.'

'Over ten years,' Lena said smoothly. 'And don't forget that there's a 125 per cent tax deduction on R&D expenditure this financial year. By the time you factor in the notional patent rights—'

'You really believe the spin-offs will be valued this highly?'

'Just look at Teflon.'

'I'll have to take this to the board.'

*　　*　　*

When the good news came through by e-mail, a fortnight later, I was almost physically sick.

I turned to Lena. 'What have I done? What if I spend ten years on this, and it all comes to nothing?'

She frowned, puzzled. 'There are no guarantees of success, but you've made that clear, you haven't been dishonest. Every great endeavour is plagued with uncertainties, but the Children have decided to accept the risks.'

In fact, I hadn't been agonising over the morality of relieving rich idiots with a global motherhood fixation of large sums of money – and quite possibly having nothing to give them in return. I was more worried about what it would mean for my career if the research turned out to be a cul-de-sac, and produced no results worth publishing.

Lena said, 'It's all going to work out perfectly. I have faith in you, Paul.'

And that was the worst of it. She did.

We loved each other – and we were, both, using each other. But I was the one who kept on lying about what was soon to become the most important thing in our lives.

*　　*　　*

In the winter of 2010, Lena took three months off work to travel to Nigeria in the name of technology transfer. Her official role was to advise the new government on the modernisation of the communications infrastructure, but she was also training a few hundred local operators for the Children's latest low-cost sequencer. My EPR technique was still in its infancy – barely able to distinguish identical twins from total strangers – but the original mitochondrial DNA analysers had become extremely small, rugged and cheap.

Africa had proved highly resistant to the Children in the past, but it seemed that the movement had finally gained a foothold. Every time Lena called me from Lagos – her eyes shining with missionary zeal – I went and checked the Great Tree, trying to decide whether its scrambling of traditional notions of familial proximity would render the ex-combatants in the recent civil war more, or less, fraternal towards each other if the sequencing fad really took off. The factions were already so ethnically mixed, though, that it was impossible to come to a definite verdict; so far as I could tell, the war had been fought between alliances shaped as much by certain twenty-first-century acts of political patronage as by any invocation of ancient tribal loyalties.

Near the end of her stay, Lena called me in the early hours of the morning (my time), so angry she was almost in tears. 'I'm flying straight to London, Paul. I'll be there in three hours.'

I squinted at the bright screen, dazed by the tropical sunshine behind her. 'Why? What's happened?' I had visions of the Children undermining the fragile cease-fire, igniting some unspeakable ethnic holocaust – then flying out to have their wounds tended by the best microsurgeons in the world, while the country descended into chaos behind them.

Lena reached off-camera and hit a button, pasting a section of a news report into a corner of the transmission. The headline read: Y-CHROMOSOME ADAM STRIKES BACK! The picture below showed a near-naked, muscular, blond white man (curiously devoid of body hair – rather like Michelangelo's *David* in a bison-skin loincloth) aiming a spear at the reader with suitably balletic grace.

I groaned softly. It had only been a matter of time. In the cell divisions leading up to sperm production, most of the DNA of the Y chromosome underwent recombination with the X chromosome, but part of it remained aloof, unscrambled, passed down the purely paternal line with the same fidelity as mitochondrial DNA passed from mother to daughter. In fact, with more fidelity: mutations in nuclear DNA were much less frequent, which made it a much less useful molecular clock.

'They claim they've found a single male ancestor for all northern Europeans – just 20,000 years ago! And they're presenting this *bullshit* at a palaeogenetics conference in Cambridge tomorrow!'

I scanned the article as Lena wailed. The news report was all tabloid hype; it was difficult to tell what the researchers were actually asserting. But a number of right-wing groups who'd long been opposed to the Children of Eve had embraced the results with obvious glee.

I said, 'So why do you have to be there?'

'To defend Eve, of course! We can't let them get away with this!'

My head was throbbing. 'If it's bad science, let the experts refute it. It's not your problem.'

Lena was silent for a while, then protested bitterly, 'You *know* male lineages are lost faster than female ones. Thanks to polygyny, a single paternal line can dominate a population in far fewer generations than a maternal line.'

'So the claim might be right? There might have been a single, recent "northern European Adam"?'

'Maybe,' Lena admitted begrudgingly. 'But . . . *so what*? What's that supposed to prove? They haven't even *tried* to look for an Adam who's a father to the whole species!'

I wanted to reply: Of course it proves nothing, changes nothing. *No sane person could possibly care.* But . . . who made *kinship* such a big issue in the first place? Who did their best to propagate the notion that everything that matters depends on *family ties*?

It was far too late, though. Turning against the Children would have been sheer hypocrisy; I'd taken their money, I'd played along.

And I couldn't abandon Lena. If my love for her went no further than the things we agreed on, then that wasn't love at all.

I said numbly, 'I should make the three o'clock flight to London. I'll meet you at the conference.'

*   *   *

The tenth annual World Palaeogenetics Forum was being held in a pyramid-shaped building in an astroturfed science park, far from the University campus. The placard-waving crowd made it easy to spot. HANDS OFF EVE! DIE, NAZI SCUM! NEANDERTHALS OUT! (*What?*) As the taxi drove away, my jet-lag caught up with me and my knees almost buckled. My aim was to find Lena as rapidly as possible and get us both out of harm's way. Eve could look after herself.

She was there, of course, gazing with serene dignity from a dozen T-shirts and banners. But the Children – and their marketing consultants – had recently been 'fine-tuning' her

46

image, and this was the first chance I'd had to see the results of all their focus groups and consumer-feedback workshops. The new Eve was slightly paler, her nose a little thinner, her eyes narrower. The changes were subtle, but they were clearly aimed at making her look more 'pan-racial' – more like some far-future common descendant, bearing traces of every modern human population, than a common ancestor who'd lived in one specific place: Africa.

And in spite of all my cynicism, this redesign made me queasier than any of the other cheap stunts the Children had pulled. It was as if they'd decided, after all, that they couldn't really imagine a world where everyone would accept an African Eve, but they were so committed to the idea that they were willing to keep bending the truth, for the sake of broadening her appeal, until . . . *what*? They gave her, not just a different name, but a different face in every country?

I made it into the lobby, merely spat on by two or three picketers. Inside, things were much quieter, but the academic palaeogeneticists were darting about furtively, avoiding eye contact. One poor woman had been cornered by a news crew; as I passed, the interviewer was insisting heatedly, 'But you must admit that violating the origin myths of indigenous Amazonians is a crime against humanity.' The outer wall of the pyramid was tinted blue, but more or less transparent, and I could see another crowd of demonstrators pressed against one of the panels, peering in. Plain-clothes security guards whispered into their wrist-phones, clearly afraid for their Masarini suits.

I'd tried to call Lena a dozen times since leaving the airport, but some bottleneck in the Cambridge footprint had kept me on hold. She'd pulled strings and got us both listed on the attendance database – the only reason I'd been allowed through the front door – but that only proved that being inside the building was no guarantee of non-partisanship.

Suddenly, I heard shouting and grunting from near by, then

a chorus of cheers and the sound of heavy sheet plastic popping out of its frame. News reports had mentioned both pro-Eve demonstrators and pro-Adam – the latter allegedly much more violent. I panicked and bolted down the nearest corridor, almost colliding with a wiry young man heading in the opposite direction. He was tall, white, blond, blue-eyed, radiating Teutonic menace . . . and part of me wanted to scream in outrage: I'd been reduced, against my will, to pure imbecilic racism.

Still, he was carrying a pool cue.

But as I backed away warily, his sleeveless T-shirt began flashing up the words: THE GODDESS IS AFOOT!

'So what are you?' he sneered. 'A Son of Adam?'

I shook my head slowly. *What am I?* I'm a *Homo sapiens*, you moron. Can't you recognise your own species?

I said, 'I'm a researcher with the Children of Eve.' At faculty cocktail parties, I was always 'an independent palaeogenetics research physicist', but this didn't seem the time to split hairs.

'Yeah?' He grimaced with what I took at first to be disbelief, and advanced threateningly. 'So *you're* one of the fucking patriarchal, materialistic bastards who's trying to reify the Archetype of the Earth Mother and rein in her boundless spiritual powers?'

That left me too stupefied to see what was coming. He jabbed me hard in the solar plexus with the pool cue; I fell to my knees, gasping with pain. I could hear the sound of boots in the lobby, and hoarsely chanted slogans.

The Goddess-worshipper grabbed me by one shoulder and wrenched me to my feet, grinning. 'No hard feelings, though. We're still on the same side, here – aren't we? So let's go beat up some Nazis!'

I tried to pull free, but it was already too late; the Sons of Adam had found us.

*   *   *

Lena came to visit me in hospital. 'I knew you should have stayed in Sydney.'

My jaw was wired; I couldn't answer back.

'You have to look after yourself; your work's more important than ever, now. Other groups will find their own Adams – and the whole unifying message of Eve will be swamped by the tribalism inherent in the idea of recent male ancestors. We can't let a few promiscuous Cro-Magnon men ruin everything.'

'Gmm mmm mmmn.'

'We have mitochondrial sequencing . . . they have Y-chromosome sequencing. Sure, our molecular clock is already more accurate . . . but we need a spectacular advantage, something anyone can grasp. Mutation rates, mitotypes: it's all too abstract for the person in the street. If we can construct exact family trees with EPR – starting with people's known relatives, but extending that same sense of precise kinship across 10,000 generations, all the way back to Eve – then *that* will give us an immediacy, a credibility, that will leave the Sons of Adam for dead.' She stroked my brow tenderly. 'You can win the Ancestor Wars for us, Paul. I know you can.'

'Mmm nnn,' I conceded.

I'd been ready to denounce both sides, resign from the EPR project – and even walk away from Lena, if it came to that.

Maybe it was more pride than love, more weakness than commitment, more inertia than loyalty. Whatever the reason, though, I couldn't do it. I couldn't leave her.

The only way forward was to try to finish what I'd started. To give the Children their watertight, absolute proof.

*　　*　　*

While the rival ancestor cults picketed and fire-bombed each other, rivers of blood flowed through my apparatus. The Children had supplied me with two-litre samples from no fewer than 50,000 members, worldwide; my lab would have put the most garish Hammer Horror film set to shame.

Trillions of plasmids were analysed. Electrons in a certain low-energy hybrid orbital – a quantum mixture of two different-shaped charge distributions, potentially stable for thousands of years – were induced by finely tuned laser pulses to collapse into one particular state. And though every collapse was random, the orbital I'd chosen was – very slightly – correlated across paired strands of DNA. Quadrillions of measurements were accumulated, and compared. With enough plasmids measured for each individual, the faint signature of any shared ancestry could rise up through the statistical noise.

The mutations behind the Children's Great Tree no longer mattered; in fact, I was looking at stretches of the plasmid most likely to have stayed unblemished all the way back to Eve, since it was the intimate chemical contact of flawless DNA replication which gave the only real chance of a correlation. And as the glitches in the process were ironed out, and the data mounted up, results finally began to emerge.

The blood donors included many close family groups; I analysed the data blind, then passed the results to one of my research assistants, to be checked against the known relationships. Early in June 2013, I scored 100 per cent on sibling detection in a thousand samples; a few weeks later, I was doing the same on first and second cousins.

Soon, we hit the limits of the recorded genealogy; to provide another means of cross-checking, I started analysing nuclear genes as well. Even distant cousins were likely to have at least some genes from a common ancestor – and EPR could date that ancestor precisely.

News of the project spread, and I was deluged with crank mail and death threats. The lab was fortified; the Children hired bodyguards for everyone involved in the work, and their families.

The quantity of information just kept growing, but the Children, horrified by the thought that the Adams might outdo them with rival technology, kept voting me more and more money. I upgraded our supercomputers, twice. And though mitochondria alone could lead me to Eve, for bookkeeping purposes I found myself tracing the nuclear genes of hundreds of thousands of ancestors, male and female.

In the spring of 2016, the database reached a kind of critical mass. We hadn't sampled more than the tiniest fraction of the world's population, but once it was possible to reach back just a few dozen generations all the apparently separate lineages began to join up. Autosomal nuclear genes zigzagged heedlessly between the purely maternal tree of the Eves and the purely paternal tree of the Adams, filling in the gaps . . . until I found myself with genetic profiles of virtually everyone who'd been alive on the planet in the early ninth century (and left descendants down to the present). I had no names for any of these people, or even definite geographical locations, but I knew, precisely, the place of every one of them on my own Great Tree.

I had a snapshot of the genetic diversity of the entire human species. From that point on there was no stopping the cascade, and I pursued the correlations back through the millennia.

*　　*　　*

By 2017, Lena's worst predictions had all come true. Dozens of different Adams had been proclaimed around the world, and the trend was to look for the common paternal lineage of smaller and smaller populations, converging on ever more recent ancestors. Many were now supposedly historical figures; rival Greek and Macedonian groups were fighting it out over who had the right to call themselves the Sons of Alexander the Great. Y-chromosomal ethnic classification had become government policy in three eastern European republics and, allegedly, corporate policy in certain multinationals.

The smaller the populations analysed, of course – unless they were massively inbred – the less likely it was that everyone targeted really would share a single Adam. So the first male ancestor to be identified became 'the father of his people' . . .

and anyone else became a kind of gene-polluting barbarian rapist, whose hideous taint could still be detected. And weeded out.

Every night I lay awake into the early hours, trying to understand how I could have ended up at the centre of so much conflict over something so idiotic. I still couldn't bring myself to confess my true feelings to Lena, so I'd pace the house with the lights out, or lock myself in my study with the bullet-proof shutters closed and sort through the latest batch of hate mail – paper and electronic – hunting for evidence that anything I might discover about Eve would have the slightest positive effect on anyone who wasn't already a fanatical supporter of the Children. Hunting for some sign that there was hope of ever doing more than preaching to the converted.

I never did find the encouragement I was looking for, but there was one postcard which cheered me up, slightly. It was from the High Priest of the Church of the Sacred UFO, in Kansas City.

> Dear Earth-dweller:
> Please use your BRAIN! As anyone KNOWS in this SCIENTIFIC age, the origin of the races is now WELL UNDERSTOOD! Africans travelled here after the DELUGE from Mercury, Asians from Venus, Caucasians from Mars, and the people of the Pacific islands from assorted asteroids. If you don't have the NECESSARY OCCULT SKILLS to project rays from the continents to the ASTRAL PLANE to verify this, a simple analysis of TEMPERAMENT and APPEARANCE should make this obvious even to YOU!
> But please don't put WORDS into MY mouth! Just because we're all from different PLANETS doesn't mean we can't still be FRIENDS.

* * *

Lena was deeply troubled. 'But how can you hold a media conference tomorrow, when Cousin William hasn't even seen the final results?' It was Sunday, 28 January 2018. We'd said goodnight to the bodyguards and gone to bed in the reinforced concrete bunker the Children had installed for us after a nasty incident in one of the Baltic States.

I said, 'I'm an independent researcher. I'm free to publish data at any time. That's what it says in the contract. Any advances in the measurement technology have to go through the Children's lawyers, but not the palaeogenetic results.'

Lena tried another tack. 'But if this work hasn't been peer-reviewed—'

'It has. The paper's already been accepted by *Nature*; it will be published the day after the conference. In fact,' I smiled innocently, 'I'm really only doing it as a favour to the editor. She's hoping it will boost sales for the issue.'

Lena fell silent. I'd told her less and less about the work over the preceding six months; I'd let her assume that technical problems were holding up progress.

Finally she said, 'Won't you at least say if it's good news – or bad?'

I couldn't look her in the eye, but I shook my head. 'Nothing that happened 200,000 years ago is any kind of news at all.'

*   *   *

I'd hired a public auditorium for the media conference – far from the Children's office tower – paying for it myself, and arranging for independent security. Sachs and his fellow directors were not impressed, but short of kidnapping me there was little they could do to shut me up. There'd never been any suggestion of fabricating the results they wanted – but there'd always been an unspoken assumption that only *the right data* would ever be released with this much fanfare – and the Children would have ample opportunity to put their own spin on it, first.

Behind the podium, my hands were shaking. Over two

thousand journalists from across the planet had turned up, and many of them were wearing symbols of allegiance to one ancestor or another.

I cleared my throat and began. The EPR technique had become common knowledge; there was no need to explain it again. I said, simply, 'I'd like to show you what I've discovered about the origins of *Homo sapiens*.'

The lights went down and a giant hologram, some thirty metres high, appeared behind me. It was, I announced, a family tree – not a rough history of genes or mutations, but an exact generation-by-generation diagram of both female and male parentage for the entire human population – from the ninth century, back. A dense thicket in the shape of an inverted funnel. The audience remained silent, but there was an air of impatience; this tangle of a billion tiny lines was indecipherable – it told them absolutely nothing. But I waited, letting the impenetrable diagram rotate once, slowly.

'The Y-chromosome mutational clock,' I said, 'is wrong. I've traced the paternal ancestries of groups with similar Y-types back hundreds of thousands of years – and they never converge on any one man.' A murmur of discontent began; I boosted the amplifier volume and drowned it out. '*Why not?* How can there be so little mutational diversity if the DNA doesn't all spring from a single, recent source?' A second hologram appeared, a double-helix, a schematic of the Y-typing region. 'Because mutations happen, again and again, at *exactly the same sites*. Make two, or three – or fifty – copying errors in the same location, and it still only looks like it's one step away from the original.' The double helix hologram was divided and copied, divided and copied; the accumulated differences in each generation were highlighted. 'The proof-reading enzymes in our cells must have specific blind spots, specific weaknesses – like words that are easy to misspell. And there's still a chance of purely random errors, at any site at all, but only on a time scale of millions of years.

'All the Y-chromosome Adams,' I said, 'are fantasy. There are no individual fathers to any race, or tribe, or nation. Living northern Europeans, for a start, have over a thousand distinct paternal lineages dating to the late Ice Age – and those thousand ancestors, in turn, are the descendants of over two hundred different male African migrants.' Colours flashed up in the grey maze of the Tree, briefly highlighting the lineages.

A dozen journalists sprang to their feet and started shouting abuse. I waited for the security guards to escort them from the building.

I looked out across the crowd, searching for Lena, but I couldn't find her. I said, 'The same is true of mitochondrial DNA. The mutations overwrite themselves; the molecular clock is wrong. There was no Eve 200,000 years ago.' An uproar began, but I kept talking. '*Homo erectus* spread out of Africa – dozens of times, over two million years, the new migrants always interbreeding with the old ones, never replacing them.' A globe appeared, the entire Old World so heavily decorated with criss-crossing paths that it was impossible to glimpse a single square kilometre of ground. '*Homo sapiens* arose everywhere, at once – maintained as one species, worldwide, partly because of migrant gene flow and partly thanks to the parallel mutations which invalidate all the clocks: mutations taking place in a random order, but biased towards the same sites.' A hologram showed four stretches of DNA, accumulating mutations; at first, the four strands grew increasingly dissimilar, as the sparse random scatter struck them differently, but as more and more of the same vulnerable sites were hit they all came to bear virtually the same scars.

'So modern racial differences are up to two million years old – inherited from the first *Homo erectus* migrants – but all of the subsequent evolution has marched in parallel, everywhere . . . because *Homo erectus* never really had much choice. In a mere two million years, different climates could favour different genes for some superficial local adaptations, but everything leading to *Homo sapiens* was already latent in every migrant's DNA before they left Africa.'

There was a momentary hush from the Eve supporters – maybe because no one could decide any more whether the picture I was painting was *unifying* or *divisive*. The truth was just too gloriously messy and complicated to serve any political purpose at all.

I continued. 'But if there was ever an Adam or an Eve, they were long before *Homo sapiens*, long before *Homo erectus*. Maybe they were . . . *Australopithecus*?' I displayed two stooped, hairy, ape-like figures. People started throwing their video cameras. I hit a button under the podium, raising a giant Perspex shield in front of the stage.

'Burn all your *symbols*!' I shouted. 'Male and female, tribal and global. Give up your Fatherlands and your Earth Mothers – it's Childhood's End! Desecrate your ancestors, screw your cousins – just do what you think is right *because it's right*.'

The shield cracked. I ran for the stage exit.

The security guards had all vanished, but Lena was sitting in our armour-plated Volvo in the basement car park, with the engine running. She wound down the mirrored side window.

'I watched your little performance on the net.' She gazed at me calmly, but there was rage and pain in her eyes.

I had no adrenaline left, no strength, no pride; I fell to my knees beside the car. 'I love you. Forgive me.'

'Get in,' she said. 'You've got a lot of explaining to do.'

LUMINOUS

I woke, disorientated, unsure why. I knew I was lying on the narrow, lumpy single bed in Room 22 of the Hotel Fleapit; after almost a month in Shanghai, the topography of the mattress was depressingly familiar. But there was something wrong with the way I was lying; every muscle in my neck and shoulders was protesting that nobody could end up in this position from natural causes, however badly he'd slept.

And I could smell blood.

I opened my eyes. A woman I'd never seen before was kneeling over me, slicing into my left tricep with a disposable scalpel. I was lying on my side, facing the wall, one hand and one ankle cuffed to the head and foot of the bed.

Something cut short the surge of visceral panic before I could start stupidly thrashing about, instinctively trying to break free. Maybe an even more ancient response – catatonia in the face of danger – took on the adrenaline and won. Or maybe I just decided that I had no right to panic when I'd been expecting something like this for weeks.

I spoke softly, in English. 'What you're in the process of hacking out of me is a necrotrap. One heartbeat without oxygenated blood, and the cargo gets fried.'

My amateur surgeon was compact, muscular, with short black hair. Not Chinese; Indonesian, maybe. If she was surprised that I'd woken prematurely, she didn't show it. The gene-tailored hepatocytes I'd acquired in Hanoi could degrade almost anything from morphine to curare; it was a good thing the local anaesthetic was beyond their reach.

Without taking her eyes off her work, she said, 'Look on the table next to the bed.'

I twisted my head around. She'd set up a loop of plastic tubing full of blood – mine, presumably – circulated and aerated by a small pump. The stem of a large funnel fed into the loop, the intersection controlled by a valve of some kind. Wires trailed from the pump to a sensor taped to the inside of my elbow, synchronising the artificial pulse with the real. I had no doubt that she could tear the trap from my vein and insert it into this substitute without missing a beat.

I cleared my throat and swallowed. 'Not good enough. The trap knows my blood-pressure profile exactly. A generic heart-beat won't fool it.'

'You're bluffing.' But she hesitated, scalpel raised. The hand-held MRI scanner she'd used to find the trap would have revealed its basic configuration, but few fine details of the engineering – and nothing at all about the software.

'I'm telling you the truth.' I looked her squarely in the eye, which wasn't easy given our awkward geometry. 'It's new, it's Swedish. You anchor it in a vein forty-eight hours in advance, put yourself through a range of typical activities so it can memorise the rhythms . . . then you inject the cargo into the trap. Simple, fool-proof, effective.' Blood trickled down across my chest onto the sheet. I was suddenly very glad that I hadn't buried the thing deeper, after all.

'So how do you retrieve the cargo, yourself?'

'That would be telling.'

'Then tell me now, and save yourself some trouble.' She rotated the scalpel between thumb and forefinger impatiently. My skin did a cold burn all over, nerve ends jangling, capillaries closing down as blood dived for cover.

I said, '*Trouble* gives me hypertension.'

She smiled down at me thinly, conceding the stalemate, then peeled off one stained surgical glove, took out her notepad, and made a call to a medical-equipment supplier. She listed some devices which would get around the problem – a blood-pressure probe, a more sophisticated pump, a suitable computerised interface – arguing heatedly in fluent Mandarin to extract a promise of a speedy delivery.

Then she put down the notepad and placed her ungloved hand on my shoulder. 'You can relax now. We won't have long to wait.'

I squirmed, as if angrily shrugging off her hand, and succeeded in getting some blood on her skin. She didn't say a word, but she must have realised at once how careless she'd been; she climbed off the bed and headed for the washbasin, and I heard the water running.

Then she started retching.

I called out cheerfully, 'Let me know when you're ready for the antidote.'

I heard her approach, and I turned to face her. She was ashen, her face contorted with nausea, eyes and nose streaming mucus and tears.

'Tell me where it is!'

'Uncuff me, and I'll get it for you.'

'No! No deals!'

'Fine. Then you'd better start looking, yourself.'

She picked up the scalpel and brandished it in my face. 'Screw the cargo. *I'll do it!*' She was shivering like a feverish child, uselessly trying to stem the flood from her nostrils with the back of her hand.

I said coldly, 'If you cut me again, you'll lose more than the cargo.'

She turned away and vomited; it was thin and grey, blood-streaked. The toxin was persuading cells in her stomach lining to commit suicide *en masse*.

'Uncuff me. It'll kill you. It doesn't take long.'

She wiped her mouth, steeled herself, made as if to speak, then started puking again. I knew, first-hand, exactly how bad she was feeling. Keeping it down was like trying to swallow a mixture of shit and sulphuric acid. Bringing it up was like evisceration.

I said, 'In thirty seconds, you'll be too weak to help yourself, even if I told you where to look. So if I'm not free . . .'

She produced a gun and a set of keys, uncuffed me, then stood by the foot of the bed, shaking badly but keeping me targeted. I dressed quickly, ignoring her threats, bandaging my arm with a miraculously spare clean sock before putting on a T-shirt and a jacket. She sagged to her knees, still aiming the gun more or less in my direction, but her eyes were swollen half-shut, and brimming with yellow fluid. I thought about trying to disarm her, but it didn't seem worth the risk.

I packed my remaining clothes, then glanced around the room as if I might have left something behind. But everything that really mattered was in my veins; Alison had taught me that that was the only way to travel.

I turned to the burglar. 'There is no antidote. But the toxin won't kill you. You'll just wish it would, for the next twelve hours. Goodbye.'

As I headed for the door, hairs rose suddenly on the back of my neck. It occurred to me that she might not take me at my word – and might fire a parting shot, believing she had nothing to lose.

Turning the handle, without looking back, I said, 'But if you come after me – next time, I'll kill you.'

That was a lie, but it seemed to do the trick. As I pulled the door shut behind me, I heard her drop the gun and start vomiting again.

Halfway down the stairs, the euphoria of escape began to give way to a bleaker perspective. If one careless bounty hunter could find me, her more methodical colleagues couldn't be far behind. Industrial Algebra were closing in on us. If Alison didn't gain access to Luminous soon, we'd have no choice but to destroy the map. And even that would only be buying time.

I paid the desk clerk for the room until the next morning,

stressing that my companion should not be disturbed, and added a suitable tip to compensate for the mess the cleaners would find. The toxin denatured in air; the bloodstains would be harmless in a matter of hours. The clerk eyed me suspiciously, but said nothing.

Outside, it was a mild, cloudless summer morning. It was barely six o'clock, but Kongjiang Lu was already crowded with pedestrians, cyclists, buses, and a few ostentatious chauffeured limousines ploughing through the traffic at about ten k.p.h. It looked like the night shift had just emerged from the Intel factory down the road; most of the passing cyclists were wearing the orange, logo-emblazoned overalls.

Two blocks from the hotel I stopped dead, my legs almost giving way beneath me. It wasn't just shock – a delayed reaction, a belated acceptance of how close I'd come to being slaughtered. The burglar's clinical violence was chilling enough, but what it implied was infinitely more disturbing.

Industrial Algebra were paying big money, violating international law, taking serious risks with their corporate and personal futures. The arcane abstraction of the defect was being dragged into the world of blood and dust, boardrooms and assassins, power and pragmatism.

And the closest thing to certainty humanity had ever known was in danger of dissolving into quicksand.

*   *   *

It had all started out as a joke. Argument for argument's sake. Alison and her infuriating heresies.

'A mathematical theorem,' she'd proclaimed, 'only becomes true when a physical system tests it out: when the system's behaviour depends in some way on the theorem being *true* or *false*.'

It was June 1994. We were sitting in a small paved courtyard, having just emerged, yawning and blinking, into the winter sunlight from the final lecture in a one-semester course on the philosophy of mathematics – a bit of light relief from the hard grind of the real stuff. We had fifteen minutes to kill before meeting some friends for lunch. It was a social conversation – verging on mild flirtation – nothing more. Maybe there were demented academics, lurking in dark crypts somewhere, who held views on the nature of mathematical truth which they were willing to die for. But we were twenty years old, and we *knew* it was all angels on the head of a pin.

I said, 'Physical systems don't create mathematics. Nothing *creates* mathematics – it's timeless. All of number theory would still be exactly the same, even if the universe contained nothing but a single electron.'

Alison snorted. 'Yes, because even *one electron*, plus a space-time to put it in, needs all of quantum mechanics and all of general relativity – and all the mathematical infrastructure they entail. One particle floating in a quantum vacuum needs half the major results of group theory, functional analysis, differential geometry—'

'OK, OK! I get the point. But if that's the case . . . the events in the first picosecond after the Big Bang would have "constructed" every last mathematical truth required by *any* physical system, all the way to the Big Crunch. Once you've got the mathematics which underpins the Theory of Everything . . . that's it, that's all you ever need. End of story.'

'But it's not. To *apply* the Theory of Everything to a particular system, you still need all the mathematics for dealing with *that system* – which could include results far beyond the mathematics which the TOE itself requires. I mean, fifteen billion years after the Big Bang, someone can still come along and prove, say . . . Fermat's Last Theorem.' Andrew Wiles at Princeton had recently announced a proof of the famous conjecture, although his work was still being scrutinised by his colleagues, and the final verdict wasn't yet in. 'Physics never needed *that* before.'

I protested, 'What do you mean, "before"? Fermat's Last

Theorem never has – and never will – have anything to do with any branch of physics.'

Alison smiled sneakily. 'No *branch*, no. But only because the class of physical systems whose behaviour depends on it is so ludicrously specific: the brains of mathematicians who are trying to validate the Wiles proof.

'Think about it. Once you start trying to prove a theorem, then even if the mathematics is so "pure" that it has no relevance to any other object in the universe . . . you've just made it relevant to *yourself*. You have to choose *some* physical process to test the theorem – whether you use a computer, or a pen and paper . . . or just close your eyes and shuffle *neuro-transmitters*. There's no such thing as a proof which doesn't rely on physical events, and whether they're inside or outside your skull doesn't make them any less real.'

'Fair enough,' I conceded warily. 'But that doesn't mean—'

'And maybe Andrew Wiles's brain – and body, and note-paper – comprised the first physical system whose behaviour depended on the theorem being true or false. But I don't think human actions have any special role . . . and if some swarm of quarks had done the same thing blindly, fifteen billion years before – executed some purely random interaction which just happened to test the conjecture in some way – then *those quarks* would have constructed FLT long before Wiles. We'll never know.'

I opened my mouth to complain that no swarm of quarks could have tested the infinite number of cases encompassed by the theorem, but I caught myself just in time. That was true, but it hadn't stopped Wiles. A finite sequence of logical steps linked the axioms of number theory – which included some simple generalities about *all* numbers – to Fermat's own sweeping assertion. And if a mathematician could test those logical steps by manipulating a finite number of physical objects for a finite amount of time – whether they were pencil marks on paper, or neurotransmitters in his or her brain – then all kinds of physical systems could, in theory, mimic the structure of the proof . . . with or without any awareness of what it was they were 'proving'.

I leant back on the bench and mimed tearing out hair. 'If I wasn't a die-hard Platonist before, you're forcing me into it! Fermat's Last Theorem didn't *need* to be proved by anyone, or stumbled on by any random swarm of quarks. If it's true, it was always true. Everything implied by a given set of axioms is logically connected to them, timelessly, eternally . . . even if the links couldn't be traced by people – or quarks – in the lifetime of the universe.'

Alison was having none of this; every mention of *timeless and eternal truths* brought a faint smile to the corners of her mouth, as if I was affirming my belief in Santa Claus. She said, 'So who, or what, pushed the consequences of "There exists an entity called zero" and "Every X has a successor", et cetera, all the way to FLT and beyond, before the universe had a chance to test out any of it?'

I stood my ground. 'What's joined by logic is just . . . *joined*. Nothing has to happen: consequences don't have to be "pushed" into existence by anyone, or anything. Or do you imagine that the first events after the Big Bang, the first wild jitters of the quark-gluon plasma, stopped to fill in all the logical gaps? You think the quarks reasoned: Well, so far we've done A and B and C, but now we mustn't do D, because D would be logically inconsistent with the other mathematics we've "invented" so far . . . even if it would take a five-hundred-thousand-page proof to spell out the inconsistency?'

Alison thought it over. 'No. But what if event D took place, regardless? What if the mathematics it implied *was* logically inconsistent with the rest, but it went ahead and happened anyway . . . because the universe was too young to have computed the fact that there was any discrepancy?'

I must have sat and stared at her, open-mouthed, for about ten seconds. Given the orthodoxies we'd spent the last two-and-

a-half years absorbing, this was a seriously outrageous statement.

'You're claiming that . . . *mathematics* might be strewn
with primordial defects in consistency? Like space might be
strewn with cosmic strings?'

'Exactly.' She stared back at me, feigning nonchalance. 'If
space-time doesn't join up with itself smoothly, everywhere,
why should mathematical logic?'

I almost choked. 'Where do I begin? What happens – now –
when some physical system tries to link theorems across the
defect? If theorem D has been rendered "true" by some over-
eager quarks, what happens when we program a computer to
disprove it? When the software goes through all the logical steps
which link A, B and C – which the quarks have also made true –
to the contradiction, the dreaded not-D, does it succeed or
doesn't it?'

Alison side-stepped the question. 'Suppose they're both true:
D and not-D. Sounds like the end of mathematics, doesn't it?
The whole system falls apart, instantly. From D and not-D
together you can prove anything you like: one equals zero, day
equals night. But that's just the boring-old-fart Platonist view,
where logic travels faster than light, and computation takes no
time at all. People live with omega-inconsistent theories, don't
they?'

Omega-inconsistent number theories were non-standard
versions of arithmetic, based on axioms which 'almost' contradicted each other – their saving grace being that the
contradictions could only show up in 'infinitely long proofs'
(which were formally disallowed, quite apart from being physically impossible). That was perfectly respectable modern
mathematics, but Alison seemed prepared to replace 'infinitely
long' with just plain 'long', as if the difference hardly mattered,
in practice.

I said, 'Let me get this straight. What you're talking about is
taking ordinary arithmetic – no weird counter-intuitive axioms,

just the stuff every ten-year-old *knows* is true – and proving that it's inconsistent, in a finite number of steps?'

She nodded blithely. 'Finite, but large. So the contradiction would rarely have any physical manifestation – it would be "computationally distant" from everyday calculations, and everyday physical events. I mean . . . one cosmic string, somewhere out there, doesn't destroy the universe, does it? It does no harm to anyone.'

I laughed drily. 'So long as you don't get too close. So long as you don't tow it back to the solar system and let it twitch around slicing up planets.'

'Exactly.'

I glanced at my watch. 'Time to come down to Earth, I think. You know we're meeting Julia and Ramesh—?'

Alison sighed theatrically. 'I know, I know. And this would bore them witless, poor things – so the subject's closed, I promise.' She added wickedly, 'Humanities students are so *myopic*.'

We set off across the tranquil leafy campus. Alison kept her word, and we walked in silence; carrying on the argument up to the last minute would have made it even harder to avoid the topic once we were in polite company.

Halfway to the cafeteria, though, I couldn't help myself.

'If someone ever *did* program a computer to follow a chain of inferences across the defect, what do you claim would actually happen? When the end result of all those simple, trustworthy logical steps finally popped up on the screen, which group of primordial quarks would win the battle? And please don't tell me that the whole computer just conveniently vanishes.'

Alison smiled, tongue-in-cheek at last. 'Get real, Bruno. How can you expect me to answer that, when the mathematics needed to predict the result doesn't even *exist* yet? Nothing I could say would be true or false – until someone's gone ahead and done the experiment.'

I spent most of the day trying to convince myself that I wasn't being followed by some accomplice (or rival) of the surgeon, who might have been lurking outside the hotel. There was something disturbingly Kafkaesque about trying to lose a tail who might or might not have been real: no particular face I could search for in the crowd, just the abstract idea of a pursuer. It was too late to think about plastic surgery to make me look Han Chinese – Alison had raised this as a serious suggestion, back in Vietnam – but Shanghai had over a million foreign residents, so with care even an Anglophone of Italian descent should have been able to vanish.

Whether or not I was up to the task was another matter.

I tried joining the ant-trails of the tourists, following the path of least resistance from the insane crush of the Yuyuan Bazaar (where racks bursting with ten-cent watch-PCs, mood-sensitive contact lenses, and the latest karaoke vocal implants, sat beside bamboo cages of live ducks and pigeons) to the one-time residence of Sun Yatsen (whose personality cult was currently undergoing a mini-series-led revival on Phoenix TV, advertised on ten thousand buses and ten times as many T-shirts). From the tomb of the writer Lu Xun ('Always think and study . . . visit the generals, then visit the victims; see the realities of your time with open eyes' – no prime time for *him*) to the Hongkou McDonalds (where they were giving away small plastic Andy Warhol figurines, for reasons I couldn't fathom).

I mimed leisurely window-shopping between the shrines, but kept my body language sufficiently unfriendly to deter even the loneliest Westerner from attempting to strike up a conversation. If foreigners were unremarkable in most of the city, they were positively eye-glazing here – even to each other – and I did my best to offer no one the slightest reason to remember me.

Along the way I checked for messages from Alison, but there

were none. I left five of my own, tiny abstract chalk marks on bus shelters and park benches – all slightly different, but all saying the same thing: CLOSE BRUSH, BUT SAFE NOW. MOVING ON.

By early evening, I'd done all I could to throw off my hypothetical shadow, so I headed for the next hotel on our agreed but unwritten list. The last time we'd met face-to-face, in Hanoi, I'd mocked all of Alison's elaborate preparations. Now I was beginning to wish that I'd begged her to extend our secret language to cover more extreme contingencies. FATALLY WOUNDED. BETRAYED YOU UNDER TORTURE. REALITY DECAYING. OTHERWISE FINE.

The hotel on Huaihai Zhonglu was a step up from the last one, but not quite classy enough to refuse payment in cash. The desk clerk made polite small-talk, and I lied as smoothly as I could about my plans to spend a week sightseeing before heading for Beijing. The bellperson smirked when I tipped him too much – and I sat on my bed for five minutes afterwards, wondering what significance to read into *that*.

I struggled to regain a sense of proportion.

Industrial Algebra *could* have bribed every single hotel employee in Shanghai to be on the lookout for us, but that was a bit like saying that, in theory, they could have duplicated our entire twelve-year search for defects, and not bothered to pursue us at all. There was no question that they wanted what we had, badly, but what could they actually do about it? Go to a merchant bank (or the Mafia, or a Triad) for finance? That might have worked if the cargo had been a stray kilogram of plutonium, or a valuable gene sequence, but only a few hundred thousand people on the planet would be capable of understanding what the defect *was*, even in theory. Only a fraction of that number would believe that such a thing could really exist, and even fewer would be both wealthy and immoral enough to invest in the business of exploiting it.

The stakes appeared to be infinitely high, but that didn't make the players omnipotent.

Not yet.

I changed the dressing on my arm, from sock to handkerchief, but the incision was deeper than I'd realised, and it was still bleeding thinly. I left the hotel – and found exactly what I needed in a twenty-four-hour emporium just ten minutes away. Surgical-grade tissue-repair cream: a mixture of collagen-based adhesive, antiseptic, and growth factors. The emporium wasn't even a pharmaceuticals outlet: it just had aisle after aisle packed with all kinds of unrelated odds and ends, laid out beneath the unblinking blue-white ceiling panels. Canned food, PVC plumbing fixtures, traditional medicines, rat contraceptives, video ROMS. It was a random cornucopia, an almost organic diversity – as if the products had all just grown on the shelves from whatever spores the wind had happened to blow in.

I headed back to the hotel, pushing my way through the relentless crowds, half seduced and half sickened by the odours of cooking, dazed by the endless vista of holograms and neon in a language I barely understood. Fifteen minutes later, reeling from the noise and humidity, I realised that I was lost.

I stopped on a street corner and tried to get my bearings. Shanghai stretched out around me, dense and lavish, sensual and ruthless – a Darwinian economic simulation self-organised to the brink of catastrophe. The Amazon of commerce: this city of sixteen million had more industry of every kind, more exporters and importers, more wholesalers and retailers, traders and re-sellers and recyclers and scavengers, more billionaires and more beggars, than most nations on the planet.

Not to mention more computing power.

China itself was reaching the cusp of its decades-long transition from brutal totalitarian communism to brutal totalitarian capitalism: a slow seamlesss morph from Mao to Pinochet set to the enthusiastic applause of its trading partners and the international financial agencies. There'd been no need for a counter-revolution – just layer after layer of carefully reasoned Newspeak to pave the way from previous doctrine to the stunningly obvious conclusion that private property, a thriving middle class, and a few trillion dollars' worth of foreign investment were exactly what the Party had been aiming for all along.

The apparatus of the police state remained as essential as ever. Trade unionists with decadent bourgeois ideas about uncompetitive wages, journalists with counter-revolutionary notions of exposing corruption and nepotism, and any number of subversive political activists spreading destabilising propaganda about the fantasy of free elections, all needed to be kept in check.

In a way, Luminous was a product of this strange transition from communism to not-communism in a thousand tiny steps. No one else, not even the US defence research establishment, possessed a single machine with so much power. The rest of the world had succumbed long ago to networking, giving up their imposing supercomputers with their difficult architecture and customised chips for a few hundred of the latest mass-produced work stations. In fact, the biggest computing feats of the twenty-first century had all been farmed out over the Internet to thousands of volunteers, to run on their machines whenever the processors would otherwise be idle. That was how Alison and I had mapped the defect in the first place: seven thousand amateur mathematicians had shared the joke, for twelve years.

But now the net was the very opposite of what we needed, and only Luminous could take its place. And though only the People's Republic could have paid for it, and only the People's Institute for Advanced Optical Engineering could have built it . . . only Shanghai's QIPS Corporation could have sold time on it to the world – while it was still being used to model hydrogen-bomb shock waves, pilotless fighter jets, and exotic anti-satellite weapons.

I finally decoded the street signs, and realised what I'd done:

I'd turned the wrong way coming out of the emporium, it was as simple as that.

I retraced my steps, and I was soon back on familiar territory.

* * *

When I opened the door of my room, Alison was sitting on the bed.

I said, 'What is it with locks in this city?'

We embraced, briefly. We'd been lovers, once, but that was long over. And we'd been friends for years afterwards, but I wasn't sure if that was still the right word. Our whole relationship now was too functional, too spartan. Everything revolved around the defect, now.

She said, 'I got your message. What happened?'

I described the morning's events.

'You know what you should have done?'

That stung. 'I'm still here, aren't I? The cargo's still safe.'

'You should have killed her, Bruno.'

I laughed. Alison gazed back at me placidly, and I looked away. I didn't know if she was serious – and I didn't much want to find out.

She helped me apply the repair cream. My toxin was no threat to her: we'd both installed exactly the same symbionts, the same genotype from the same unique batch in Hanoi. But it was strange to feel her bare fingers on my broken skin, knowing that no one else on the planet could touch me like this, with impunity.

Ditto for sex, but I didn't want to dwell on that.

As I slipped on my jacket, she said, 'So guess what we're doing at five a.m. tomorrow.'

'Don't tell me: I fly to Helsinki, and you fly to Cape Town? Just to throw them off the scent.'

That got a faint smile. 'Wrong. We're meeting Yuen at the Institute – and spending half an hour on Luminous.'

'*You* are brilliant.' I bent over and kissed her on the forehead. 'But I always knew you'd pull it off.'

And I should have been delirious, but the truth was my guts were churning; I felt almost as trapped as I had upon waking cuffed to the bed. If Luminous had remained beyond our reach (as it should have, since we couldn't afford to hire it for a microsecond at the going rate) we would have had no choice but to destroy all the data, and hope for the best. Industrial Algebra had no doubt dredged up a few thousand fragments of the original Internet calculations, but it was clear that, although they knew exactly what we'd found, they still had no idea where we'd found it. If they'd been forced to start their own random search – constrained by the need for secrecy to their own private hardware – it might have taken them centuries.

There was no question now, though, of backing away and leaving everything to chance. We were going to have to confront the defect in person.

'How much did you have to tell him?'

'Everything.' She walked over to the washbasin, removed her shirt, and began wiping the sweat from her neck and torso with a flannel. 'Short of handing over the map. I showed him the search algorithms and their results, and all the programs we'll need to run on Luminous – all stripped of specific parameter values, but enough for him to validate the techniques. He wanted to see direct evidence of the defect, of course, but I held out on that.'

'And how much did he believe?'

'He's reserved judgement. The deal is, we get half an hour's unimpeded access, but he gets to observe everything we do.'

I nodded, as if my opinion made any difference, as if we had any choice. Yuen Ting-fu had been Alison's supervisor for her PhD on advanced applications of ring theory, when she'd studied at Fu-tan University in the late nineties. Now he was one of the world's leading cryptographers, working as a consultant to the military, the security services, and a dozen international corporations. Alison had once told me that she'd heard he'd found a polynomial-time algorithm for factoring the product of two primes; that had never been officially confirmed, but such was the power of his reputation that almost everyone on the planet had stopped using the old RSA encryption method as the rumour had spread. No doubt time on Luminous was his for the asking, but that didn't mean he couldn't still be imprisoned for twenty years for giving it away to the wrong people, for the wrong reasons.

I said, 'And you trust him? He may not believe in the defect now, but once he's convinced—'

'He'll want exactly what *we* want. I'm sure of that.'

'OK. But are you sure IA won't be watching, too? If they've worked out why we're here, and they've bribed someone—'

Alison cut me off impatiently. 'There are still a few things you can't buy in this city. Spying on a military machine like Luminous would be suicidal. No one would risk it.'

'What about spying on unauthorised projects being run on a military machine? Maybe the crimes cancel out, and you end up a hero.'

She approached me, half naked, drying her face on my towel. 'We'd better hope not.'

I laughed suddenly. 'You know what I like most about Luminous? They're not really letting Exxon and McDonnell-Douglas use the same machine as the People's Liberation Army. Because the whole computer vanishes every time they pull the plug. There's no paradox at all, if you look at it that way.'

* * *

Alison insisted that we stand guard in shifts. Twenty-four hours earlier, I might have made a joke of it; now I reluctantly accepted the revolver she offered me, and sat watching the door in the neon-tinged darkness while she went out like a light.

The hotel had been quiet for most of the evening, but now it came to life. There were footsteps in the corridor every five minutes – and rats in the walls, foraging and screwing and probably giving birth. Police sirens wailed in the distance; a couple screamed at each other in the street below. I'd read somewhere that Shanghai was now the murder capital of the world – but was that *per capita*, or in absolute numbers?

After an hour, I was so jumpy that it was a miracle I hadn't blown my foot off. I unloaded the gun, then sat playing Russian roulette with the empty barrel. In spite of everything, I still wasn't ready to put a bullet in anyone's brain for the sake of defending the axioms of number theory.

*   *   *

Industrial Algebra had approached us in a perfectly civilised fashion. They were a small but aggressive UK-based company, designing specialised high-performance computing hardware for industrial and military applications. That they'd heard about the search was no great surprise – it had been openly discussed on the Internet for years, and even joked about in serious mathematical journals – but it seemed an odd coincidence when they made contact with us just days after Alison had sent me a private message from Zürich mentioning the latest 'promising' result. After half a dozen false alarms – all due to bugs and glitches – we'd stopped broadcasting the news of every unconfirmed find to the people who were donating runtime to the project, let alone any wider circle. We were afraid that if we cried wolf one more time, half our collaborators would get so annoyed that they'd withdraw their support.

IA had offered us a generous slab of computing power on the company's private network – several orders of magnitude more than we received from any other donor. *Why?* The answer kept changing. Their deep respect for pure mathematics . . . their wide-eyed fun-loving attitude to life . . . their desire to be seen to be sponsoring a project so wild and hip and unlikely to succeed that it made SETI look like a staid blue-chip investment. It was, they'd finally 'conceded', a desperate bid to soften their corporate image after years of bad press for what certain unsavoury governments did with their really rather nice smart bombs.

We'd politely declined. They'd offered us highly paid consulting jobs. Bemused, we'd suspended all net-based calculations – and started encrypting our mail with a simple but highly effective algorithm Alison had picked up from Yuen.

Alison had been collating the results of the search on her own work station at her current home in Zürich, while I'd helped co-ordinate things from Sydney. No doubt IA had been eavesdropping on the incoming data, but they'd clearly started too late to gather the information needed to create their own map; each fragment of the calculations meant little in isolation. But when the work station was stolen (all the files were encrypted, it would have told them nothing) we'd finally been forced to ask ourselves: *If the defect turns out to be genuine, if the joke is no joke . . . then exactly what's at stake? How much money? How much power?*

On 7 June 2006, we met in a sweltering, crowded square in Hanoi. Alison wasted no time. She was carrying a backup of the data from the stolen work station in her notepad and she solemnly proclaimed that, this time, the defect was real.

The notepad's tiny processor would have taken centuries to repeat the long random trawling of the space of arithmetic statements which had been carried out on the net, but, led straight to the relevant computations, it could confirm the existence of the defect in a matter of minutes.

The process began with Statement S. Statement S was an assertion about some ludicrously huge numbers, but it wasn't mathematically sophisticated or contentious in any way. There were no claims here about infinite sets, no propositions concerning 'every integer'. It merely stated that a certain (elaborate) calculation performed on certain (very large) whole numbers led to a certain result – in essence, it was no different from something like '5+3 = 4x2'. It might have taken me ten years to check it with a pen and paper, but I could have carried out the task with nothing but primary-school mathematics and a great deal of patience. A statement like this could not be undecidable; it had to be either true or false.

The notepad decided it was true.

Then the notepad took statement S . . . and, in 423 simple, impeccably logical steps, used it to prove not-S.

I repeated the calculations on my own notepad, using a different software package. The result was exactly the same. I gazed at the screen, trying to concoct a plausible reason why two different machines running two different programs could have failed in identical ways. There'd certainly been cases in the past of a single misprinted algorithm in a computing textbook spawning a thousand dud programs. But the operations here were too simple, too basic.

Which left only two possibilities. Either conventional arithmetic was intrinsically flawed, and the whole Platonic ideal of the natural numbers was ultimately self-contradictory; or Alison was right, and an alternative arithmetic had come to hold sway in a 'computationally remote' region, billions of years ago.

I was badly shaken, but my first reaction was to try to play down the significance of the result. 'The numbers being manipulated here are greater than the volume of the observable universe, measured in cubic Planck lengths. If IA were hoping to use this on their foreign-exchange transactions, I think they've made a slight error of scale.' Even as I spoke, though, I knew it wasn't that simple. The raw numbers might have been trans-astronomical, but it was the mere 1,024 bits of the notepad's binary representations which had actually, physically misbehaved. Every truth in mathematics was encoded, reflected, in countless other forms. If a paradox like this – which at first glance sounded like a dispute about numbers too large to apply even to the most grandiose cosmological discussions – could affect the behaviour of a five-gram silicon chip, then there could easily be a billion other systems on the planet at risk of being touched by the very same flaw.

But there was worse to come.

The theory was, we'd located part of the boundary between two incompatible systems of mathematics, both of which were *physically true*, in their respective domains. Any sequence of deductions which stayed entirely on one side of the defect – whether it was the 'near side', where conventional arithmetic applied, or the 'far side', where the alternative took over – would be free from contradictions. But any sequence which crossed the border would give rise to absurdities: hence S could lead to not-S.

So, by examining a large number of chains of inference, some of which turned out to be self-contradictory and some not, it should have been possible to map the area around the defect precisely – to assign every statement to one system or the other.

Alison displayed the first map she'd made. It portrayed an elaborately crenellated fractal border, rather like the boundary between two microscopic ice crystals – as if the two systems had been diffusing out at random from different starting points, and then collided, blocking each other's way. By now, I was almost prepared to believe that I really was staring at a snapshot of the creation of mathematics – a fossil of primordial attempts to define the difference between truth and falsehood.

Then she produced a second map of the same set of statements, and overlaid the two. The defect, the border, had shifted – advancing in some places, retreating in others.

My blood went cold. '*That* has got to be a bug in the software.'

'It's not.'

I inhaled deeply, looking around the square – as if the heedless crowd of tourists and hawkers, shoppers and executives, might offer some simple 'human' truth more resilient than mere arithmetic. But all I could think of was *1984*: Winston

Smith, finally beaten into submission, abandoning every touchstone of reason by conceding that *two and two make five*.

I said, 'OK. Go on.'

'In the early universe, some physical system must have tested out mathematics which was isolated, cut off from all the established results, leaving it free to decide the outcome at random. That's how the defect arose. But by now, *all* the mathematics in this region has been tested, all the gaps have been filled in. When a physical system tests a theorem on the near side, not only has it been tested a billion times before, but all the *logically adjacent* statements around it have been decided, and they imply the correct result in a single step.'

'You mean . . . peer pressure from the neighbours? No inconsistencies allowed, you have to conform? If $x-1 = y-1$, and $x+1 = y+1$, then x is left with no choice but to equal y because there's nothing "near by" to support the alternative?'

'Exactly. Truth is determined locally. And it's the same, deep into the far side. The alternative mathematics has dominated there, and every test takes place surrounded by established theorems which reinforce each other, and the "correct" – nonstandard – result.'

'At the border, though—'

'At the border, every theorem you test is getting contradictory advice. From one neighbour, $x-1 = y-1$ . . . but, from another, $x+1 = y+2$. And the topology of the border is so complex that a near-side theorem can have more far-side neighbours than near-side ones – and vice versa.

'So the truth at the border isn't fixed, even now. Both regions can still advance or retreat. *It all depends on the order in which the theorems are tested.* If a solidly near-side theorem is tested first, and it lends support to a more vulnerable neighbour, that can guarantee that they both stay near-side.' She ran a brief animation which demonstrated the effect. 'But if the order is reversed, the weaker one *will* fall.'

I watched, light-headed. Obscure, but supposedly eternal,

truths were tumbling like chess pieces. 'And . . . you think that physical processes going on *right now* – chance molecular events which keep inadvertently testing and re-testing different theories along the border – cause each side to gain and lose territory?'

'Yes.'

'So there's been a kind of . . . random tide washing back and forth between the two kinds of mathematics, for the past few billion years?' I laughed uneasily, and did some rough calculations in my head. 'The expectation value for a random walk is the square root of N. I don't think we have anything to worry about. The tide isn't going to wash over any useful arithmetic in the lifetime of the universe.'

Alison smiled humourlessly, and held up the notepad again. 'The tide? No. But it's the easiest thing in the world to dig a channel. To bias the random flow.' She ran an animation of a sequence of tests which forced the far-side system to retreat across a small front – exploiting a 'beach-head' formed by chance, and then pushing on to undermine a succession of theorems. 'Industrial Algebra, though, I imagine, would be more interested in the reverse. Establishing a whole network of narrow channels of non-standard mathematics running deep into the realm of conventional arithmetic – which they could then deploy against theorems with practical consequences.'

I fell silent, trying to imagine tendrils of contradictory arithmetic reaching down into the everyday world. No doubt IA would aim for surgical precision, hoping to earn themselves a few billion dollars by corrupting the specific mathematics underlying certain financial transactions. But the ramifications would be impossible to predict – or control. There'd be no way to limit the effect, spatially. They could target certain mathematical truths, but they couldn't confine the change to any one location. *A few billion dollars, a few billion neurons, a few billion stars . . . a few billion people.* Once the basic rules of counting were undermined, the most solid and distinct objects could be rendered as uncertain as swirls of fog. This was not a power I would have entrusted to a cross between Mother Teresa and Carl Friedrich Gauss.

'So what do we do? Erase the map and just hope that IA never find the defect for themselves?'

'No.' Alison seemed remarkably calm – but then, her own long-cherished philosophy had just been confirmed, not razed to the ground, and she'd had time on the flight from Zürich to think through all the *Realmathematik*. 'There's only one way to be sure that they can never use this. We have to strike first. We have to get hold of enough computing power to map the entire defect. And then we either iron the border flat, so it *can't* move: if you amputate all the pincers, there can be no pincer movements. Or – better yet, if we can get the resources – we push the border in, from all directions, and shrink the far-side system down to nothing.'

I hesitated. 'All we've mapped so far is a tiny fragment of the defect. We don't know how large the far side could be. Except that it can't be small, or the random fluctuations would have swallowed it long ago. And it *could* go on for ever; it could be infinite, for all we know.'

Alison gave me a strange look. 'You still don't get it, do you, Bruno? You're still thinking like a Platonist. The universe has only been around for fifteen billion years. It hasn't had time to create infinities. The far side *can't* go on for ever, because somewhere beyond the defect there are theorems which don't belong to *any* system. Theorems which have never been touched, never been tested, never been rendered true or false.

'And if we have to reach beyond the existing mathematics of the universe in order to surround the far side . . . then that's what we'll do. There's no reason why it shouldn't be possible, just so long as we get there first.'

* * *

When Alison took my place, at one in the morning, I was

certain I wouldn't get any sleep. When she shook me awake three hours later, I still felt as though I hadn't.

I used my notepad to send a priming code to the data caches buried in our veins, and then we stood together side by side, left shoulder to right shoulder. The two chips recognised each other's magnetic and electrical signatures, interrogated each other to be sure, and then began radiating lower power microwaves. Alison's notepad picked up the transmission, and merged the two complementary data streams. The result was still heavily encrypted, but, after all the precautions we'd taken so far, shifting the map into a hand-held computer felt about as secure as tattooing it onto our foreheads.

A taxi was waiting for us downstairs. The People's Institute for Advanced Optical Engineering was in Minhang, a sprawling technology park some thirty kilometres south of the city centre. We rode in silence through the grey pre-dawn light, past the giant ugly tower blocks thrown up by the landlords of the new millennium, riding out the fever as the necrotraps and their cargo dissolved into our blood.

As the taxi turned into an avenue lined with biotech and aerospace companies, Alison said, 'If anyone asks, we're PhD students of Yuen's, testing a conjecture in algebraic topology.'

'*Now* you tell me. I don't suppose you have any specific conjecture in mind? What if they ask us to elaborate?'

'On *algebraic topology*? At five o'clock in the morning?'

The Institute building was unimposing – sprawling black ceramic, three storeys high – but there was a five-metre electrified fence, and the entrance was guarded by two armed soldiers. We paid the taxi driver and approached on foot. Yuen had supplied us with visitor's passes, complete with photographs and fingerprints. The names were our own; there was no point indulging in unnecessary deception. If we were caught out, pseudonyms would only make things worse.

The soldiers checked the passes, then led us through an MRI scanner. I forced myself to breathe calmly as we waited for the results; in theory, the scanner could have picked up our symbionts' foreign proteins, lingering breakdown products from the necro-traps, and a dozen other suspicious trace chemicals. But it all came down to a question of what they were looking for; magnetic resonance spectra for billions of molecules had been catalogued, but no machine could hunt for all of them at once.

One of the soldiers took me aside and asked me to remove my jacket. I fought down a wave of panic and then struggled not to overcompensate: if I'd had nothing to hide, I would still have been nervous. He prodded the bandage on my upper arm; the surrounding skin was still red and inflamed. 'What's this?'

'I had a cyst there. My doctor cut it out, this morning.'

He eyed me suspiciously, and peeled back the adhesive bandage with ungloved hands. I couldn't bring myself to look; the repair cream should have sealed the wound completely – at worst there should have been old, dried blood – but I could *feel* a faint liquid warmth along the line of the incision.

The soldier laughed at my gritted teeth, and waved me away with an expression of distaste. I had no idea what he thought I might have been hiding, but I saw fresh red droplets beading the skin before I closed the bandage.

Yuen Ting-fu was waiting for us in the lobby. He was a slender, fit-looking man in his late sixties, casually dressed in denim. I let Alison do all the talking: apologising for our lack of punctuality (although we weren't actually late), and thanking him effusively for granting us this precious opportunity to pursue our unworthy research. I stood back and tried to appear suitably deferential. Four soldiers looked on impassively; they didn't seem to find all this grovelling excessive. And no doubt I would have been giddy with awe if I really had been a student granted time here for some run-of-the-mill thesis.

We followed Yuen as he strode briskly through a second check-point and scanner (this time, no one stopped us), then down a long corridor with a soft grey vinyl floor. We passed a couple of white-coated technicians, but they barely gave us a second glance. I'd had visions of a pair of obvious foreigners attracting as much attention here as we would have done wandering through a military base, but that was absurd. Half the runtime on Luminous was sold to foreign corporations – and because the machine was most definitely *not* linked to any communciations network, commercial users had to come here in person. Just how often Yuen wangled free time for his students – whatever their nationality – was another question, but if he believed it was the best cover for us, I was in no position to argue. I only hoped he'd planted a seamless trail of reassuring lies in the University records and beyond, in case the Institute administration decided to check up on us in any detail.

We stopped in at the operations room, and Yuen chatted with the technicians. Banks of flatscreens covered one wall, displaying status histograms and engineering schematics. It looked like the control centre for a small particle accelerator – which wasn't far from the truth.

Luminous was, literally, a computer made of light. It came into existence when a vacuum chamber, a cube five metres wide, was filled with an elaborate standing wave created by three vast arrays of high-powered lasers. A coherent electron beam was fed into the chamber – and just as a finely machined grating built of solid matter could diffract a beam of light, a sufficiently ordered (and sufficiently intense) configuration of light could diffract a beam of matter.

The electrons were redirected from layer to layer of the light cube, recombining and interfering at each stage, every change in their phase and intensity performing an appropriate computation – and the whole system could be reconfigured, nanosecond by nanosecond, into complex new 'hardware' optimised for the calculations at hand. The auxiliary supercomputers controlling the laser arrays could design, and then instantly build, the perfect machine of light to carry out each particular stage of any program.

83

It was, of course, fiendishly difficult technology, incredibly expensive and temperamental. The chance of ever putting it on the desktops of Tetris-playing accountants was zero, so nobody in the West had bothered to pursue it.

And this cumbersome, unwieldy, impractical machine ran faster than all the pieces of silicon hanging off the Internet, combined.

We continued on to the programming room. At first glance, it might have been the computing centre in a small primary school, with half a dozen perfectly ordinary work stations sitting on white Formica tables. They just happened to be the only six in the world which were hooked up to Luminous.

We were alone with Yuen now. Alison cut the protocol and just glanced briefly in his direction for approval, before hurriedly linking her notepad to one of the work stations and uploading the encrypted map. As she typed in the instructions to decode the file, all the images running through my head of what would have happened if I'd poisoned the soldier at the gate receded into insignificance. We now had half an hour to banish the defect, and we still had no idea how far it extended.

Yuen turned to me; the tension on his face betrayed his own anxieties, but he mused philosophically, 'If our arithmetic seems to fail for these large numbers, does it mean the mathematics, the ideal, is really flawed and mutable, or only that the behaviour of matter always falls short of the ideal?'

I replied, 'If every class of physical objects "falls short" in exactly the same way, whether it's boulders or electrons or abacus beads, what is it that their common behaviour is obeying – or defining – if not the mathematics?'

He smiled, puzzled. 'Alison seemed to think you were a Platonist.'

'Lapsed. Or . . . defeated. I don't see what it can *mean* to talk about standard number theory still being true for these statements – in some vague Platonic sense – if no real objects can ever reflect that truth.'

'We can still imagine it. We can still contemplate the abstraction. It's only the physical act of validation that must fall through. Think of transfinite arithmetic: no one can physically test the properties of Cantor's infinities, can they? We can only reason about them from afar.'

I didn't reply. Since the revelations in Hanoi, I'd pretty much lost faith in my power to 'reason from afar' about anything I couldn't personally describe with Arabic numerals on a single sheet of paper. Maybe Alison's idea of 'local truth' was the most we could hope for; anything more ambitious was beginning to seem like the comic-book 'physics' of swinging a rigid beam ten billion kilometres long around your head, and predicting that the far end would exceed the speed of light.

An image blossomed on the work-station screen: it began as the familiar map of the defect, but Luminous was already extending it at a mind-boggling rate. Billions of inferential loops were being spun around the margins: some confirming their own premises, and thus delineating regions where a single, consistent mathematics held sway; others skewing into self-contradiction, betraying a border crossing. I tried to imagine what it would have been like to follow one of those Möbius-strips of deductive logic in my head; there were no difficult concepts involved, it was only the sheer size of the statements which made that impossible. But would the contradictions have driven me into gibbering insanity, or would I have found every step perfectly reasonable, and the conclusion simply unavoidable? Would I have ended up calmly, happily conceding: *Two and two make five*?

As the map grew – smoothly re-scaled to keep it fitting on the screen, giving the unsettling impression that we were retreating from the alien mathematics as fast as we could, and only just avoiding being swallowed – Alison sat hunched forward, waiting for the big picture to be revealed. The map portrayed the network of statements as an intricate lattice in three dimensions (a crude representational convention, but it was as good as any other). So far, the border between the regions showed no sign of overall curvature, just variously sized random incursions in both directions. For all we knew, it was possible that the far-side mathematics enclosed the near side completely, that the arithmetic we'd once believed stretched out to infinity was really no more than a tiny island in an ocean of contradictory truths.

I glanced at Yuen; he was watching the screen with undisguised pain. He said, 'I read your software, and I thought: Sure, this looks fine, but some glitch on your machines is the real explanation. Luminous will soon put you right.'

Alison broke in jubilantly, 'Look, it's turning!'

She was right. As the scale continued to shrink, the random fractal meanderings of the border were finally being subsumed by an overall convexity – a convexity of the far side. It was as if the viewpoint was backing away from a giant spiked sea-urchin. Within minutes, the map showed a crude hemisphere, decorated with elaborate crystalline extrusions at every scale. The sense of observing some palaeomathematical remnant was stronger than ever now: this bizarre cluster of theorems really did look as if it had exploded out from some central premise into the vacuum of unclaimed truths, perhaps a billionth of a second after the Big Bang, only to be checked by an encounter with our own mathematics.

The hemisphere slowly extended into a three-quarters sphere . . . and then a spiked whole. The far side was bounded, finite. It was the island, not us.

Alison laughed uneasily. 'Was that true before we started, or did we just make it true?' *Had the near side enclosed the far side for billions of years, or had Luminous broken new ground, actively extending the near side into mathematical territory which had never been tested by any physical system before?*

We'd never know. We'd designed the software to advance the mapping along a front in such a way that any unclaimed statements would be instantly recruited into the near side. If we'd reached out blindly, far into the void, we might have tested an isolated statement – and inadvertently spawned a whole new alternative mathematics to deal with.

Alison said, 'OK, now we have to decide. Do we try to seal the border or do we take on the whole structure?'

The software, I knew, was busy assessing the relative difficulty of the tasks.

Yuen replied at once, 'Seal the border, nothing more. You mustn't destroy this.' He turned to me, imploringly. 'Would you smash up a fossil of *Australopithecus*? Would you wipe the cosmic background radiation out of the sky? This may shake the foundations of all my beliefs, but it encodes the truth about our history. We have no right to obliterate it, like vandals.'

Alison eyed me nervously. *What was this, majority rule?* Yuen was the only one with any power here; he could pull the plug in an instant. And yet it was clear from his demeanour that he wanted a consensus; he wanted our moral support for any decision.

I said cautiously, 'If we smooth the border, that'll make it literally impossible for IA to exploit the defect, won't it?'

Alison shook her head. 'We don't know that. There may be a quantum-like component of spontaneous defections, even for statements which appear to be in perfect equilibrium.'

Yuen countered, 'Then there could be spontaneous defections *anywhere*, even far from any border. Erasing the whole structure will guarantee nothing.'

'It will guarantee that IA won't find it! Maybe pinpoint defections *do* occur, all the time, but the next time they're tested they'll always revert. They're surrounded by explicit contradictions; they have no chance of getting a foothold. You can't compare a few transient glitches with this . . . *armoury* of counter-mathematics!'

The defect bristled on the screen like a giant caltrap. Alison and Yuen both turned to me expectantly. As I opened my mouth, the work station chimed. The software had examined the alternatives in detail: destroying the entire far side would take Luminous twenty-three minutes and seventeen seconds – about a minute less than the time we had left. Sealing the border would take more than an hour.

I said, 'That can't be right.'

Alison groaned. 'But it is! There's random interference going on at the border from other systems all the time – and doing anything finicky there means coping with that noise, fighting it. Charging ahead and pushing the border inwards is different: you can exploit the noise to speed the advance. It's not a question of *dealing with a mere surface* versus *dealing with a whole volume*. It's more like . . . trying to carve an island into an absolutely perfect circle while waves are constantly crashing on the beach – versus bulldozing the whole thing into the ocean.'

We had thirty seconds to decide, or we'd be doing neither today. And maybe Yuen had the resources to keep the map safe from IA while we waited a month or more for another session on Luminous, but I wasn't prepared to live with that kind of uncertainty.

'I say we get rid of the whole thing. Anything less is too dangerous. Future mathematicians will still be able to study the map – and if no one believes that the defect itself ever really existed, that's just too bad. IA are too close. We can't risk it.'

Alison had one hand poised above the keyboard. I turned to Yuen; he was staring at the floor with an anguished expression. He'd let us state our views, but in the end it was his decision.

He looked up, and spoke sadly but decisively.

'OK. Do it.'

Alison hit the key, with about three seconds to spare. I sagged into my chair, light-headed with relief.

*   *   *

We watched the far side shrinking. The process didn't look quite as crass as *bulldozing an island* – more like dissolving some quirkily beautiful crystal in acid. Now that the danger was receding before our eyes, though, I was beginning to suffer faint pangs of regret. Our mathematics had coexisted with this strange anomaly for fifteen billion years, and it shamed me to think that, within months of its discovery, we'd backed ourselves into a corner where we'd had no choice but to destroy it.

Yuen seemed transfixed by the process. 'So are we breaking the laws of physics – or enforcing them?'

Alison said, 'Neither. We're merely changing what the laws imply.'

He laughed softly. ' "Merely". For some esoteric set of complex systems, we're rewriting the high-level rules of their behaviour. Not including the human brain, I hope.'

My skin crawled. 'Don't you think that's . . . unlikely?'

'I was joking.' He hesitated, then added soberly, 'Unlikely for humans, but *someone* could be relying on this, somewhere. We might be destroying the whole basis of their existence: certainties as fundamental to them as a child's multiplication tables are to us.'

Alison could barely conceal her scorn. 'This is junk mathematics – a relic of a pointless accident. Any kind of life which evolved from simple to complex forms would have no use for it. Our mathematics works for . . . rocks, seeds, animals in the herd, members of the tribe. *This* only kicks in beyond the number of particles in the universe—'

'Or smaller systems which represent those numbers,' I reminded her.

'And you think life somewhere might have a burning need to do *non-standard trans-astronomical arithmetic*, in order to survive? I doubt that very much.'

We fell silent. Guilt and relief could fight it out later, but no one suggested halting the program. In the end, maybe nothing could outweigh the havoc the defect would have caused if it had ever been harnessed as a weapon, and I was looking forward to composing a long message to Industrial Algebra, informing them of precisely what we'd done to the object of their ambitions.

Alison pointed to a corner of the screen. 'What's that?' A narrow dark spike protruded from the shrinking cluster of statements. For a moment I thought it was merely avoiding the near side's assault, but it wasn't. It was slowly, steadily, growing longer.

'Could be a bug in the mapping algorithm.' I reached for the keyboard and zoomed in on the structure. In close-up, it was several thousand statements wide. At its border, Alison's program could be seen in action, testing statements in an order designed to force tendrils of the near side ever deeper into the interior. This slender extrusion, ringed by contradictory mathematics, should have been corroded out of existence in a fraction of a second. Something was actively countering the assault, though – repairing every trace of damage before it could spread.

'If IA have a bug here—' I turned to Yuen. 'They couldn't take on Luminous directly, so they couldn't stop the whole far side shrinking, but a tiny structure like this . . . What do you think? Could they stabilise it?'

'Perhaps,' he conceded. 'Four or five hundred top-speed work stations could do it.'

Alison was typing frantically on her notepad. She said, 'I'm writing a patch to identify any systematic interference and divert all our resources against it.' She brushed her hair out of her eyes. 'Look over my shoulder, will you, Bruno? Check me as I go.'

'OK.' I read through what she'd written so far. 'You're doing fine. Stay calm.' Her hands were trembling.

The spike continued to grow steadily. By the time the patch was ready, the map was re-scaling constantly to fit it on the screen.

Alison triggered the patch. An overlay of electric blue appeared along the spike, flagging the concentration of computing power, and the spike abruptly froze.

I held my breath, waiting for IA to notice what we'd done – and switch their resources elsewhere? If they did, no second spike would appear – they'd never get that far – but the blue marker on the screen would shift to the site where they'd regrouped and tried to make it happen.

But the blue glow didn't move from the existing spike. And the spike didn't vanish under the weight of Luminous's undivided efforts.

Instead, it began to grow again, slowly.

Yuen looked ill. 'This is *not* Industrial Algebra. There's no computer on the planet—'

Alison laughed derisively. 'What are you saying now? Aliens who need the far side are defending it? Aliens *where*? Nothing we've done has had time to reach even . . . Jupiter.' There was an edge of hysteria in her voice.

'Have you measured how fast the changes propagate? Do you know, for certain, that they can't travel faster than light – with the far-side mathematics undermining the logic of relativity?'

I said, 'Whoever it is, they're not defending all their borders. They're putting everything they've got into the spike.'

'They're aiming at something. A specific target.' Yuen reached over Alison's shoulder for the keyboard. 'We're shutting this down. Right now.'

She turned on him, blocking his way. 'Are you crazy? We're almost holding them off! I'll rewrite the program, fine-tune it, get an edge in efficiency—'

'No! We stop threatening them, then see how they react. We don't know what harm we're doing—'

He reached for the keyboard again.

Alison jabbed him in the throat with her elbow, hard. He staggered backwards, gasping for breath, then crashed to the floor, bringing a chair down on top of him. She hissed at me, 'Quick – shut him up!'

I hesitated, loyalties fracturing; his idea had sounded perfectly sane to me. But if he started yelling for security . . .

I crouched down over him, pushed the chair aside, then clasped my hand over his mouth, forcing his head back with pressure on the lower jaw. We'd have to tie him up and then try brazenly marching out of the building without him. But he'd be found in a matter of minutes. Even if we made it past the gate, we were screwed.

Yuen caught his breath and started struggling; I clumsily pinned his arms with my knees. I could hear Alison typing, a ragged staccato; I tried to get a glimpse of the work-station screen, but I couldn't turn that far without taking my weight off Yuen.

I said, 'Maybe he's right: maybe we should pull back and see what happens.' *If the alterations could propagate faster than light . . . how many distant civilisations might have felt the effects of what we'd done?* Our first contact with extraterrestrial life could turn out to be an attempt to obliterate mathematics which they viewed as . . . what? A precious resource? A sacred relic? An essential component of their entire world view?

The sound of typing stopped abruptly. 'Bruno? Do you feel—'

'What?'

Silence.

'*What?*'

Yuen seemed to have given up the fight. I risked turning around.

Alison was hunched forward, her face in her hands. On the screen, the spike had ceased its relentless linear growth, but now an elaborate dendritic structure had blossomed at its tip. I glanced down at Yuen; he seemed dazed, oblivious to my presence. I took my hand from his mouth, warily. He lay there placidly, smiling faintly, eyes scanning something I couldn't see.

I climbed to my feet. I took Alison by the shoulders and shook her gently; her only response was to press her face harder into her hands. The spike's strange flower was still growing, but it wasn't spreading out into new territory; it was sending narrow shoots back in on itself, criss-crossing the same region again and again with ever finer structures.

Weaving a net? Searching for something?

It hit me with a jolt of clarity more intense than anything I'd felt since childhood. It was like reliving the moment when the whole concept of *numbers* had finally snapped into place – but with an adult's understanding of everything it opened up, everything it implied. It was a lightning-bolt revelation – but there was no taint of mystical confusion: no opiate haze of euphoria, no pseudo-sexual rush. In the clean-lined logic of the simplest concepts, I saw and understood exactly how the world worked—

—Except that it was all wrong, it was all false, it was all impossible.

Quicksand.

Assailed by vertigo, I swept my gaze around the room, counting frantically: *Six work stations. Two people. Six chairs.* I grouped the work stations: three sets of two, two sets of three. One and five, two and four; four and two, five and one.

I weaved a dozen cross-checks for consistency – *for sanity* . . . but everything added up.

They hadn't stolen the old arithmetic; they'd merely blasted the new one into my head, on top of it.

Whoever had resisted our assault with Luminous had reached down with the spike and rewritten our neural meta-mathematics – the arithmetic which underlay our own reasoning *about* arithmetic – enough to let us glimpse what we'd been trying to destroy.

Alison was still uncommunicative, but she was breathing slowly and steadily. Yuen seemed fine, lost in a happy reverie. I relaxed slightly, and began trying to make sense of the flood of far-side arithmetic surging through my brain.

On their own terms, the axioms were . . . trivial, obvious. I could see that they corresponded to elaborate statements about trans-astronomical integers, but performing an exact translation was far beyond me; and thinking about the entities they described in terms of the huge integers they represented was a bit like thinking about *pi* or *the square root of two* in terms of the first ten thousand digits of their decimal expansion: it would be missing the point entirely. These alien 'numbers' – the basic objects of the alternative arithmetic – had found a way to embed themselves in the integers, and to relate to each other in a simple, elegant way, and if the messy corollaries they implied upon translation contradicted the rules integers were supposed to obey . . . well, only a small, remote patch of obscure truths had been subverted.

Someone touched me on the shoulder. I started, but Yuen was beaming amiably, all arguments and violence forgotten.

He said, 'Lightspeed is *not* violated. All the logic which requires that remains intact.' I could only take him at his word; the result would have taken me hours to prove. Maybe the aliens had done a better job on him, or maybe he was just a superior mathematician in either system.

'Then . . . where are they?' At lightspeed, our attack on the far side could not have been felt any further away than Mars, and the strategy used to block the corrosion of the spike would have been impossible with even a few seconds' time lag.

'The atmosphere?'

'You mean *Earth's*?'

'Where else? Or maybe the oceans.'

I sat down heavily. Maybe it was no stranger than any conceivable alternative, but I still baulked at the implications.

Yuen said, 'To us, their structure wouldn't look like "structure" at all. The simplest unit might involve a group of thousands of atoms – representing a trans-astronomical number – not necessarily even *bonded together* in any conventional way, but breaking the normal consequences of the laws of physics, obeying a different set of high-level rules which arise from the alternative mathematics. People have often mused about the chances of intelligence being coded into long-lived vortices on distant gas giants . . . but *these* creatures won't be in hurricanes or tornadoes. They'll be drifting in the most innocuous puffs of air, invisible as neutrinos.'

'Unstable—'

'Only according to our mathematics. Which does not apply.'

Alison broke in suddenly, angrily. 'Even if all of this is true, where does it get us? Whether the defect supports a whole invisible ecosystem or not, IA will still find it, and use it, in exactly the same way.'

For a moment I was dumbstruck. *We were facing the prospect of sharing the planet with an undiscovered civilisation and all she could think about was IA's grubby machinations?*

She was absolutely right, though. Long before any of these extravagant fantasies could be proved or disproved, IA could still do untold harm.

I said, 'Leave the mapping software running, but shut down the shrinker.'

She glanced at the screen. 'No need. They've overpowered it, or undermined its mathematics.' The far side was back to its original size.

'Then there's nothing to lose. Shut it down.'

She did. No longer under attack, the spike began to reverse its growth. I felt a pang of loss as my limited grasp of the far-side mathematics suddenly evaporated; I tried to hold on, but it was like clutching at air.

When the spike had retracted completely, I said, 'Now we try doing an Industrial Algebra. We try bringing the defect closer.'

We were almost out of time, but the task was easy enough. In thirty seconds, we rewrote the shrinking algorithm to function in reverse.

Alison programmed a function key with the commands to revert to the original version, so that if the experiment backfired, one keystroke would throw the full weight of Luminous behind a defence of the near side again.

Yuen and I exchanged nervous glances. I said, 'Maybe this wasn't such a good idea.'

Alison disagreed. 'We need to know how they'll react to this. Better we find out now than leave it to IA.'

She started the program running.

The sea-urchin began to swell, slowly. I broke out in a sweat. The far-siders hadn't harmed us, so far, but this felt like tugging hard at a door which you really, badly, didn't want to see thrown open.

A technician poked her head into the room and announced cheerfully, 'Down for maintenance in two minutes!'

Yuen said, 'I'm sorry, there's nothing—'

The whole far side turned electric blue. Alison's original patch had detected a systematic intervention.

We zoomed in. Luminous was picking off vulnerable statements of the near side, but something else was repairing the damage.

I let out a strangled noise that might have been a cheer.

Alison smiled serenely. She said, 'I'm satisfied. IA don't stand a chance.'

Yuen mused, 'Maybe they have a reason to defend the status quo. Maybe they rely on the border itself, as much as the far side.'

Alison shut down our reversed shrinker. The blue glow vanished; both sides were leaving the defect alone. There were a thousand questions we all wanted answered, but the technicians had thrown the master switch, and Luminous itself had ceased to exist.

*　　*　　*

The sun was breaking through the skyline as we rode back into the city. As we pulled up outside the hotel, Alison started shaking and sobbing. I sat beside her, squeezing her hand. I knew she'd felt the weight of what might have happened, all along, far more than I had.

I paid the driver, and then we stood on the street for a while, silently watching the cyclists go by, trying to imagine how the world would change as it endeavoured to embrace this new contradiction between the exotic and the mundane, the pragmatic and the Platonic, the visible and the invisible.

MISTER VOLITION

'Give me the patch.'

He hesitates, despite the gun, long enough to confirm that the thing must be genuine. He's cheaply dressed but expensively groomed: manicured and depilated, with the baby-smooth skin of rich middle age. Any card in his wallet would be p-cash only, anonymous but encrypted, useless without his own living finger-prints. He's wearing no jewellery, and his watchphone is plastic; the patch is the only thing worth taking. Good fakes cost 15 cents, good real ones 15 K, but he's the wrong age, and the wrong class, to want to wear a fake for the sake of fashion.

He tugs at the patch gently, and it dislodges itself from his skin; the adhesive rim doesn't leave the faintest weal or pluck a single hair from his eyebrow. His newly naked eye doesn't blink or squint, but I know it's not truly sighted yet; the suppressed perceptual pathways take hours to reawaken.

He hands me the patch; I half expect it to stick to my palm, but it doesn't. The outer face is black, like anodised metal, with a silver-grey logo of a dragon in one corner – drawn 'escaping' from a cut-and-folded drawing of itself, to bite its own tail. Recursive Visions, after Escher. I press the gun harder against his stomach to remind him of its presence, while I glance down and turn the thing over. The inner face appears velvet black at first, but as I tilt it I catch the reflection of a street light, rainbow-diffracted by the array of quantum-dot lasers. Some plastic fakes are moulded with pits which give a similar effect, but the sharpness of this image – dissected into colours, but not blurred at all – is like nothing I've ever seen before.

I look up at him, and he meets my gaze warily. I know what he's feeling – that icewater in the bowels – but there's something more than fear in his eyes: a kind of dazed curiosity, as if he's drinking in the strangeness of it all. Standing here at three in the morning with a gun to his intestines. Robbed of his most expensive toy. Wondering what else he's going to lose.

I smile sadly, and I know how that looks through the Balaclava.

'You should have stayed up at the Cross. What did you want to come down here for? Looking for something to fuck? Something to snort? You should have hung around the nightclubs, and it all would have come to you.'

He doesn't reply, but he doesn't avert his eyes. It looks as if he's struggling hard to understand it all: his terror, the gun, this moment. Me. Trying to take it all in and make sense of it, like an oceanographer caught in a tidal wave. I can't decide if that's admirable, or just irritating.

'What were you looking for? *A new experience?* I'll give you a new experience.'

Something skids along the ground behind us in the wind: plastic wrapping, or a cluster of twigs. The street is all terraces converted to office space, barred and silent, wired against intruders but otherwise oblivious.

I pocket the patch, and slide the gun higher. I tell him plainly, 'If I kill you, I'll put a bullet through your heart. Clean and fast, I promise; I won't leave you lying here bleeding your guts out.'

He makes as if to speak, but then changes his mind. He just stares at my masked face, transfixed. The wind rises up again, cool and impossibly gentle. My watch beeps a short sequence of tones which means it's successfully blocking a signal from his personal safety implant. We're alone in a tiny patch of radio silence: phases cancelling, forces finely balanced.

I think: *I can spare him . . . or not* – and the lucidity begins, the tearing of the veil, the parting of the fog. *It's all in my hands now*. I don't look up, but I don't need to: I can feel the stars wheeling around me.

I whisper, 'I can do it, I can kill you.' We're still staring at each other, but I'm staring right through him now; I'm no sadist, I don't need to see him squirm. His fear is outside me, and what matters is within: *My freedom, the courage to embrace it, the strength to face everything I am without flinching*.

My hand has grown numb; I slide my finger across the trigger, waking the nerve ends. I can feel the perspiration cooling on my forearms, the muscles in my jaw aching from my frozen smile. I can feel my whole body, coiled, tensed, impatient but obedient, awaiting my command.

I pull the gun back, then pistol-whip him hard, smashing the handle across his temple. He cries out and collapses to his knees, blood pouring into one eye. I back away, observing him carefully. He puts down his hands to keep himself from falling on his face, but he's too stunned to do anything but kneel there, bleeding and moaning.

I turn and run, tearing off the Balaclava, pocketing the gun, speeding up as I go.

His implant will have made contact with a patrol car in a matter of seconds. I weave through the alleys and deserted side-streets, drunk on the pure visceral chemistry of flight, but still in control, riding instinct smoothly. I hear no sirens, but chances are they wouldn't use them, so I dive for cover at every approaching engine. A map of these streets is burnt into my skull, down to every tree, every wall, every rusting car body. I'm never more than seconds away from shelter of some kind.

Home looms like a mirage, but it's real, and I cross the last lit ground with my heart pounding, trying not to whoop with elation as I unlock the door and slam it behind me.

I'm soaked in sweat. I undress, and pace the house until I'm calm enough to stand beneath the shower, staring up at the ceiling, listening to the music of the exhaust fan. *I could have killed him*. The triumph of it surges through my veins. *It was my choice, alone. There was nothing to stop me.*

I dry myself, and stare into the mirror, watching as the steamed glass slowly clears. Knowing that I could have pulled the trigger is enough. I've faced the possibility; there's nothing left to prove. It's not the act that's important, one way or the other. What matters is overcoming everything that stands in the way of freedom.

But next time?

Next time, I'll do it.

Because I can.

*   *   *

I take the patch to Tran, in his battered Redfern terrace full of posters of deservedly obscure Belgian chainsaw bands. He says, 'Recursive Visions Introscape 3000. Retails at 35 K.'

'I know. I checked.'

'Alex! I'm hurt.' He smiles, showing acid-etched teeth. Too much throwing-up; someone should tell him he's already thin enough.

'So what can you get me?'

'Maybe eighteen or twenty. But it could take months to find a buyer. If you want it off your hands right now, I'll give you twelve.'

'I'll wait.'

'Suit yourself.' I reach out to take it back, but he pulls away. 'Don't be so impatient! He plugs a fibre jack into a tiny socket in the rim, then starts typing on the laptop at the heart of his jury-rigged test bench.

'If you break it, I'll fucking kill you.'

He groans. 'Yeah, my big clumsy photons might smash some delicate little watch-spring in there.'

'You know what I mean. You can still lock it up.'

'If you're going to have it for six months, don't you want to know what software it's running?'

I almost choke. 'You think I'm going to *use* it? It's probably running some executive stress monitor. *Blue Monday*: "Learn to match the colour of the mood display panel with the reference hue beside it, for optimal productivity and total well-being".'

'Don't knock biofeedback till you've tried it. This might even be the premature-ejaculation cure you've been searching for.'

I thump his scrawny neck, then look over his shoulder at the laptop screen, a blur of scrolling hexadecimal gibberish. 'What exactly are you doing?'

'Every manufacturer reserves a block of codes with the ISO, so remotes can't accidentally trigger the wrong devices. But they use the same ones for cabled stuff, too. So we only have to try the codes Recursive Visions—'

An elegant, marbled-grey interface window appears on the screen. The heading says PANDEMONIUM. The only option is a button labelled 'Reset'.

Tran turns to me, mouse in hand. 'Never heard of *Pandemonium*. Sounds like some kind of psychedelic shit. But if it's read his head, and the evidence is in there . . .' He shrugs. 'I'll have to do it before I sell it, so I might as well do it now.'

'OK.'

He fires the button, and a query appears: 'Delete stored map, and prepare for a new wearer?' Tran clicks 'Yes'.

He says, 'Wear and enjoy. No charge.'

'You're a saint.' I take the patch. 'But I'm not going to wear it if I don't know what it does.'

He calls up another database, and types PAN*. 'Ah. No catalogue entry. So it's black market . . . unapproved!' He grins at me, like a school kid daring another to eat a worm. 'But what's the worst it can do?'

'I don't know. Brainwash me?'

'I doubt it. Patches can't show naturalistic images. Nothing strongly representational – and no text. They ran trials with music videos, stock prices, language lessons . . . but the users kept bumping into things. All they can display now is abstract graphics. How do you brainwash someone with that?'

I raise the thing to my left eye experimentally, but I know it won't even light up until it sticks firmly in place.

Tran says, 'Whatever it does . . . if you think of it information-theoretically, it can't show you anything that isn't there in your skull already.'

'Yeah? That much boredom could kill me.'

Still, it does seem crazy to waste the opportunity. Anyone with a machine as expensive as this probably paid a small fortune for the software too, and if it's weird enough to be illegal it might actually be a buzz.

Tran's losing interest. 'It's your decision.'

'Exactly.'

I hold the patch in place over my eye, and let the rim fuse gently with my skin.

*　　*　　*

Mira says, 'Alex? Aren't you going to tell me?'

'Huh?' I peer at her groggily; she's smiling, but she looks faintly hurt.

'I want to know what it showed you!' She leans over and starts tracing the ridge of my cheekbone with her fingertip, as if she'd like to touch the patch itself but can't quite bring herself to do that. 'What did you see? Tunnels of light? Ancient cities bursting into flame? Silver angels fucking in your brain?'

I remove her hand. 'Nothing.'

'I don't believe you.'

But it's true. No cosmic fireworks; if anything, the patterns became more subdued the more I lost myself in the sex. But the details are elusive, as they usually are, unless I've been making a conscious effort to picture the display.

I try to explain. 'Most of the time, I don't see anything. Do you "see" your nose, your eyelashes? The patch is like that.

After the first few hours, the image just . . . vanishes. It doesn't look like anything real, it doesn't move when you move your head, so your brain realises it's got nothing to do with the outside world, and starts filtering it out.'

Mira is scandalised, as if I've cheated her somehow. 'You can't even see what it's showing you? Then . . . what's the point?'

'You don't *see* the image floating in front of you, but you can still know about it. It's like . . . there's a neurological condition called blindsight, where people lose all sense of visual awareness but they can still guess what's in front of them, if they really try, because the information is still coming through—'

'Like clairvoyance. I understand.' She fingers the ankh on her neck chain.

'Yeah, it's uncanny. Shine a blue light in my eye . . . and by some strange magic I'll know that it's blue.'

Mira groans and flops back onto the bed. A car goes by, and the headlights through the curtains illuminate the statue on the bookshelf: a jackal-headed woman in the lotus position, sacred heart exposed beneath one breast. Very hip and syncretic. Mira once told me, deadpan: *This is my soul, passed down from incarnation to incarnation. It used to belong to Mozart – and before that, Cleopatra.* The inscription on the base says Budapest, 2005. But the strangest thing is, they made it like a Russian doll: inside Mira's soul is another soul, and inside that is a third, and a fourth. I said: *This last one's just dead wood. Nothing inside. Doesn't that worry you?*

I concentrate, and try to summon up the image again. The patch constantly measures pupil dilation, and the focal distance of the masked eye's lens – both of which naturally track the unmasked eye – and adjusts the synthetic hologram accordingly. So the image never goes out of focus, or appears too bright or too dim, whatever the unmasked eye is looking at. No real object could ever behave like that; no wonder the brain shunts the data so readily. Even in the first few hours – when I effortlessly saw the patterns superimposed on everything – they seemed more like vivid mental images than any kind of trick with light. Now, the whole idea that I could 'just look' at the hologram and automatically 'see it' is ludicrous; the reality is more like groping an object in the dark, and attempting to picture it.

What I picture is: elaborately branched threads of colour, flashing against the greyness of the room – like pulses of fluorescent dye injected into fine veins. The image seems bright, but not dazzling; I can still see into the shadows around the bed. Hundreds of these branched patterns are flashing simultaneously, but most are faint, and very short-lived. Maybe ten or twelve dominate at any given moment, glowing intensely for about half a second each, before they fade and others take over. Sometimes it seems that one of these 'strong' patterns passes on its strength directly to a neighbouring pattern, summoning it out of the darkness, and sometimes the two can be seen lit up together, tangled edges entwined. At other times, the strength, the brightness, seems to come out of nowhere, though occasionally I catch two or three subtle cascades in the background, each one alone almost too faint and too rapid to follow, converging on a single pattern and triggering a bright, sustained flash.

The wafer of superconducting circuitry buried in the patch is imaging my entire brain. These patterns *could* be individual neurons, but what would be the point of such a microscopic view? More likely, they're much larger systems – networks of tens of thousands of neurons – and the whole thing is some kind of functional map: connections preserved, but distances re-arranged for ease of interpretation. Only a neurosurgeon would care about the actual anatomical locations.

But, exactly which systems am I being shown? And how am I meant to respond to the sight of them?

Most patchware is biofeedback. Measures of stress – or depression, arousal, concentration, whatever – are encoded in the colours and shapes of the graphics. Because the patch image 'vanishes', it's not a distraction, but the information remains accessible. In effect, regions of the brain not naturally wired to 'know about' each other are put in touch, allowing them to modulate each other in new ways. Or that's the hype. But biofeedback patchware should make its target clear: there should be some fixed template held up beside the realtime display showing the result to aim for. All this is showing me is . . . pandemonium.

Mira says, 'I think you'd better go now.'

The patch image almost vanishes, like a cartoon thought-bubble pricked, but I make an effort and manage to hang on to it.

'Alex? I think you should go.'

Hairs rise on the back of my neck. I saw . . . *what?* The same patterns, as she spoke the same words? I struggle to replay the sequence from memory, but the patterns in front of me – the patterns for struggling to remember? – render that impossible. And by the time I let the image fade, it's too late; I don't know what I saw.

Mira puts a hand on my shoulder. 'I want you to leave.'

My skin crawls. Even without the image in front of me, I know the same patterns are firing. '*I think you should go.*' '*I want you to leave.*' I'm not seeing the sounds encoded in my brain. I'm seeing the meaning.

And even now, just thinking about the meaning, I *know* that the sequence is being replayed, faintly.

Mira shakes me angrily, and I finally turn to her. 'What's your problem?' I say. 'You wanted to screw the patch, and I got in the way?'

'Very funny. Just go.'

I dress slowly, to annoy her. Then I stand by the bed, looking at her thin body hunched beneath the sheets. I think: *I could hurt her badly if I wanted to. It would be so simple.*

She watches me uneasily. I feel a surge of shame: the truth is,

106

I don't even want to frighten her. But it's too late; I already have.

She lets me kiss her goodbye, but her whole body is rigid with distrust. My stomach churns. *What's happening to me? What am I becoming?*

Out on the street, though, in the cold night air, the lucidity takes hold. *Love, empathy, compassion* . . . all these obstacles to freedom must be overcome. I need not choose violence, but my choices are meaningless if they're encumbered by social mores and sentimentality, hypocrisy and self-delusion.

Nietzsche understood. Sartre and Camus understood.

I think calmly: *There was nothing to stop me. I could have done anything. I could have broken her neck.* But I chose not to. *I chose.* So how did that happen? How – and where? When I spared the owner of the patch . . . when I chose not to lay a finger on Mira . . . in the end, it was my body that acted one way, not the other, *but where did it all begin?*

If the patch is displaying everything that happens in my brain – or everything that matters: thoughts, meanings, the highest levels of abstraction – then if I'd known how to read those patterns, could I have followed the whole process? *Traced it back to the first cause?*

I halt in mid-step. The idea is vertiginous . . . and exhilarating. Somewhere deep in my brain, there *must* be the 'I': the fount of all action, the self who decides. Untouched by culture, upbringing, genes – the source of human freedom, utterly autonomous, responsible only to itself. I've always known that, but I've been struggling all these years to make it clearer.

If the patch could hold up a mirror to my soul . . . if I could watch *my own will* reaching out from the centre of my being *as I pulled the trigger* . . .

It would be a moment of perfect honesty, perfect understanding.

Perfect freedom.

Home, I lie in the dark, bring back the image, experiment. If I'm going to follow the river upstream, I have to map as much territory as I can. It's not easy: monitoring my thoughts, monitoring the patterns, trying to find the links. Am I seeing the patterns corresponding to the ideas themselves, as I force myself to free-associate? Or am I seeing patterns bound up more with the whole balancing act of attention – between the image itself, and the thoughts which I'm hoping the image reflects?

I turn on the radio, find a talk show, and try to concentrate on the words without letting the patch image slip away. I manage to discern the patterns fired by a few words – or, at least, patterns which are common to every cascade which appears when those words are used – but after the fifth or sixth word I've lost track of the first.

I switch on the light, grab some paper, start trying to sketch a dictionary. But it's hopeless. The cascades happen too fast and everything I do to try to capture one pattern, to freeze the moment, is an intrusion which sweeps the moment away.

It's almost dawn. I give up, and try to sleep. I'll need money for rent soon, I'll have to do something, unless I take up Tran's offer for the patch. I reach under the mattress and check that the gun's still there.

I think back over the last few years. One worthless degree. Three years unemployed. The safe daytime house jobs. Then the nights. Stripping away layer after layer of illusion. Love, hope, morality . . . it all has to be overcome. I can't stop now.

And I know how it has to end.

As light begins to penetrate the room, I feel a sudden shift . . . *in what*? Mood? Perception? I stare up at the narrow strip of sunlight on the crumbling plaster of the ceiling – and nothing looks different, nothing has changed. I scan my body mentally, as if I might be suffering from some kind of pain too unfamiliar to apprehend instantly, but all I get back is the tension of my own uncertainty and confusion.

The strangeness intensifies and I cry out involuntarily. I feel as if my skin is bursting and ten thousand maggots are crawling from the liquid flesh beneath, except that there's nothing to explain this feeling: no vision of wounds, or insects – and absolutely no pain. No itch, no fever, no chilled sweat . . . nothing. It's like some cold-turkey horror story, some nightmare attack of DTs, but stripped of every symptom save the horror itself.

I swing my legs off the bed and sit up, clutching my stomach, but it's an empty gesture: I don't even want to puke. It's not my guts that are heaving.

I sit and wait for the turmoil to pass.

It doesn't.

I almost tear the patch off – *what else can it be?* – but I change my mind. I want to try something first. I switch on the radio.

'. . . cyclone warning for the north-west coast—'

The ten thousand maggots flow and churn; the words hit them like the blast from a firehose. I slam the radio off, stilling the upheaval, and then the words echo in my brain:

. . . cyclone . . .

The cascade runs a loop around the concept, firing off the patterns for the sound itself; a faint vision of the written word; an image abstracted from a hundred satellite weather maps; news footage of wind-blown palms – and more, much more, too much to grasp.

. . . cyclone warning . . .

Most 'warning' patterns were already firing, prepared by the context, anticipating the obvious. The patterns for the height-of-the-storm news footage strengthen, and trigger others for morning-after images of people outside damaged homes.

. . . north-west coast . . .

The pattern for the satellite weather map *tightens*, focusing its energy on one remembered – or constructed – image where the swirl of clouds is correctly placed. Patterns fire for the names of half a dozen north-west towns, and images of tourist spots . . . until the cascade trails away into vague associations with spartan rural simplicity.

And I understand what's happening. (Patterns fire for *understand*, patterns fire for *patterns*, patterns fire for *confused*, *overwhelmed*, *insane* . . .)

The process damps down, slightly (patterns fire for all these concepts). *I can grasp this calmly, I can see it through* (patterns fire). I sit with my head against my knees (patterns fire), trying to focus my thoughts enough to cope with all the resonances, and associations which the patch (patterns fire) keeps showing me through my not-quite-seeing left eye.

There was never any need to do the impossible: to sit down and draw a dictionary on paper. In the last ten days, the patterns have etched their own dictionary into my brain. No need to observe and remember, consciously, which pattern corresponds to which thought; I've spent every waking moment exposed to exactly those associations and they've burned themselves into my synapses from sheer repetition.

And now it's paying off. I don't need the patch to tell me merely what I'd tell myself I'm thinking, but now it's showing me all the rest: all the details too faint and fleeting to capture with mere introspection. Not the single, self-evident stream of consciousness – the sequence defined by the strongest pattern at any moment – but all the currents and eddies churning beneath.

The whole chaotic process of thought.

The pandemonium.

*   *   *

Speaking is a nightmare. I practise alone, talking back to the radio, too unsteady to risk even a phone call until I can learn not to seize up, or veer off track.

I can barely open my mouth without sensing a dozen

110

patterns for words and phrases *rising to the opportunity*, competing for the chance to be spoken – and the cascades which should have zeroed in on one choice in a fraction of a second (they must have, before, or the whole process would never have worked) are kept buzzing inconclusively by the very fact that I've become so aware of all the alternatives. After a while, I learn to suppress this feedback – at least enough to avoid paralysis. But it still feels very strange.

I switch on the radio. A talk-back caller says: 'Wasting taxpayers' money on rehabilitation is just admitting that we didn't keep them in long enough.'

Cascades of patterns flesh out the bare sense of the words with a multitude of associations and connections . . . but they're *already* entwined with cascades building possible replies, invoking their own associations.

I respond as rapidly as I can: 'Rehabilitation is cheaper. And what are you suggesting – locking people up until they're too senile to re-offend?' As I speak, the patterns for the chosen words flash triumphantly, while those for twenty or thirty other words and phrases are only now fading . . . as if hearing what I've actually said is the only way they can be sure that they've lost their chance to be spoken.

I repeat the experiment, dozens of times, until I can 'see' all the alternative reply-patterns clearly. I watch them spinning their elaborate webs of meaning across my mind, in the hope of being chosen.

But . . . *chosen where, chosen how*?

It's still impossible to tell. If I try to slow the process down, my thoughts seize up completely, but if I manage to get a reply out, there's no real hope of following the dynamics. A second or two later, I can still 'see' most of the words and associations which were triggered along the way . . . but trying to trace the decision for what was finally spoken back to its source – *back to my self* – is like trying to allocate blame in a thousand-car pile-up from a single blurred time-exposure of the whole event.

I decide to rest for an hour or two. (Somehow, I decide.) The feeling of decomposing into a squirming heap of larvae has lost its edge, but I can't shut down my awareness of the pandemonium completely. I could try taking off the patch, but it doesn't seem worth the risk of a long slow process of re-acclimatisation when I put it back on.

Standing in the bathroom, shaving, I stop to look myself in the eye. *Do I want to go through with this? Watch my mind in a mirror while I kill a stranger? What would it change? What would it prove?*

It would prove that there's a spark of freedom inside me which no one else can touch, no one else can claim. It would prove that I'm finally responsible for everything I do.

I feel something rising up in the pandemonium. Something emerging from the depths. I close both eyes and steady myself against the sink; then I open them and gaze into both mirrors again.

And I finally see it, superimposed across the image of my face: an intricate, stellated pattern, like some kind of luminous benthic creature, sending delicate threads out to touch ten thousand words and symbols, with all the machinery of thought at its command. It hits me with a jolt of *déjà vu*: I've been 'seeing' this pattern for days. Whenever I thought of myself as a subject, an actor. Whenever I reflected on the power of the will. Whenever I thought back to the moment when I almost pulled the trigger . . .

I have no doubt, this is it. *The self that chooses. The self that's free.*

I catch my eye again, and the pattern streams with light – not at the mere sight of my face, but at the sight of myself watching, and knowing that I'm watching – and knowing that I could turn away, at any time.

I stand and stare at the wondrous thing. *What do I call this?* 'I'? 'Alex'? Neither really fits; their meaning is exhausted. I hunt for the word, the image, which gives the strongest response. My own face in the mirror, from the outside, evokes barely a flicker, but when I *feel* myself sitting nameless in the dark cave of the skull, looking out through the eyes, controlling the body . . . *making the decisions, pulling the strings* . . . the pattern blazes with recognition.

I whisper, 'Mister Volition. That's who I am.'

My head beings to throb. I let the patch image fade from vision.

As I finish shaving, I examine the patch from the outside, for the first time in days. The dragon breaking out of its own insubstantial portrait to attain solidity – or at least, portrayed that way. I think of the man I stole it from, and I wonder if he ever saw into the pandemonium as deeply as I have.

But he can't have, or he never would have let me take the patch. Because now that I've glimpsed the truth, I know I'd defend to the death the power to see it this way.

*　　*　　*

I leave home around midnight, scout the area, take its pulse. Every night there are subtly different flows of activity between the clubs, the bars, the brothels, the gambling houses, the private parties. It's not the crowds I'm after, though. I'm looking for a place where no one has reason to go.

I finally choose a construction site, flanked by deserted offices. There's a patch of ground protected from the two nearest street lights by a large skip near the road, casting a black triangular umbra. I sit on the dew-wet sand and cement dust, gun and Balaclava in my jacket, within easy reach.

I wait calmly. I've learnt to be patient – and there are nights when I've faced the dawn empty-handed. Most nights, though, someone takes a short cut. Most nights, someone gets lost.

I listen for footsteps, but I let my mind wander. I try to follow the pandemonium more closely, seeing if I can absorb the sequence of images passively while I'm thinking of something else – and then replay the memory, the movie of my thoughts.

I make a fist, then open it. I make a fist, then . . . don't. I try to catch Mister Volition in the act, exercising my powers of whim. Reconstructing what I think I 'saw', the thousand-tendrilled pattern certainly flashes brightly, but memory plays strange tricks: I can't get the sequence right. Every time I run the movie in my head, I see most of the other patterns involved in the action flashing *first*, sending cascades converging on Mister Volition, making *it* fire – the very opposite of what I know is true. Mister Volition lights up the instant I feel myself choose . . . so how can anything but mental static precede that pivotal moment?

I practise for more than an hour, but the illusion persists. Some distortion of temporal perception? Some side-effect of the patch?

Footsteps approaching. One person.

I slip on the Balaclava, wait a few seconds. Then I rise slowly to a crouch and sneak a look around the edge of the skip. He's passed it, and he's not looking back.

I follow. He's walking briskly, hands in jacket pocket. When I'm three metres behind him – close enough to discourage most people from making a run – I call out softly: 'Halt.'

He glances back over his shoulder first, then wheels around. He's young, eighteen or nineteen, taller than I am and probably stronger. I'll have to watch out for any dumb bravado. He doesn't quite rub his eyes, but the Balaclava always seems to produce an expression of disbelief. That, and the air of calm: when I fail to wave my arms and scream Hollywood obscenities, some people can't quite bring themselves to accept that it's real.

I move closer. He's wearing a diamond stud in one ear. Tiny, but better than nothing. I point to it, and he hands it over. He looks grim, but I don't think he's going to try anything stupid.

'Take out your wallet, and show me what's in it.'

He does this, fanning the contents for inspection like a hand of cards. I choose the e-cash, 'e' for easily hacked; I can't read the balance, but I slip it into my pocket and let him keep the rest.

'Now take off your shoes.'

He hesitates, and lets a flash of pure resentment show in his eyes. Too afraid to answer back, though. He complies clumsily, standing on one foot at a time. I don't blame him: I'd feel more vulnerable, sitting. Even if it makes no difference at all.

While I tie the shoes by their laces to the back of my belt, one-handed, he looks at me as if he's trying to judge whether I understand that he has nothing else to offer – trying to decide if I'm going to be disappointed, and angry. I gaze back at him, not angry at all, just trying to fix his face in my memory.

For a second, I try to visualise the pandemonium, but there's no need. I'm reading the patterns entirely on their own terms now – taking them in, and understanding them fully, through the new sensory channel which the patch has carved out for itself from the neurobiology of vision.

And I know that Mister Volition is firing.

I raise the gun to the stranger's heart, and click off the safety. His composure melts, his face screws up. He starts shaking, and tears appear, but he doesn't close his eyes. I feel a surge of compassion – *and 'see' it, too* – but it's outside Mister Volition, and only Mister Volition can choose.

The stranger asks simply, pitifully, 'Why?'

'Because I can.'

He closes his eyes, teeth chattering, a thread of mucus dangling from one nostril. I wait for the moment of lucidity, the moment of perfect understanding, the moment I step outside the flow of the world and take responsibility for myself.

Instead, a different veil parts – and the pandemonium shows itself to itself, in every detail:

The patterns for the concepts of *freedom*, *self-knowledge*, *courage*, *honesty* and *responsibility* are all firing brightly.

They're spinning cascades – vast tangled streamers, hundreds of patterns long – but now all the connections, all the causal relationships, are finally crystal clear.

And nothing is flowing out of any fount of action, any irreducible, autonomous self. Mister Volition is firing, but it's just one more pattern among thousands, one more elaborate cog. It taps into the cascades around it with a dozen tentacles and jabbers wildly, 'I I I' – claiming responsibility for everything – but in truth, it's no different from any of the rest.

My throat emits a retching sound, and my knees almost buckle. *This is too much to know, too much to accept.* Still holding the gun firmly in place, I reach up under the Balaclava and tear off the patch.

It makes no difference. The show plays on. The brain has internalised all the associations, all the connections, and the meaning keeps unfolding, relentlessly.

There is no first cause in here, no place where decisions can begin. Just a vast machine of vanes and turbines, driven by the causal flow which passes through it – a machine built out of words made flesh, images made flesh, ideas made flesh.

There is nothing else: only these patterns, and the connections between them. 'Choices' happen everywhere – in every association, every linkage of ideas. The whole structure, the whole machine, 'decides'.

And Mister Volition? Mister Volition is nothing but the idea of itself. The pandemonium can imagine anything: Santa Claus, God . . . the human soul. It can build a symbol for any idea, and wire it up to a thousand others, but that doesn't mean that the thing the symbol represents could ever be real.

I stare in horror and pity and shame at the man trembling in front of me. *Who am I sacrificing him to?* I could have told Mira: *One little soul doll is one too many.* So why couldn't I tell myself? There is no second self inside the self, no inner puppeteer to pull the strings and make the choices. There is only the whole machine.

And under scrutiny, the jumped-up cog is shrivelling. Now that the pandemonium can see itself completely, Mister Volition makes no sense at all.

There is nothing, no one to kill for: no emperor in the mind to defend to the death. And there are no barriers to freedom to be *overcome*. Love, hope, morality . . . tear all that beautiful machinery down, and there'd be nothing left but a few nerve cells twitching at random, not some radiant purified unencumbered *Übermensch*. The only freedom lies in being this machine, and not another.

So this machine lowers the gun, raises a hand in a clumsy gesture of contrition, turns, and flees into the night. Not stopping for breath, and wary as ever of the danger of pursuit, but crying tears of liberation all the way.

Author's note: This story was inspired by the 'pandemonium' cognitive models of Marvin Minsky, Daniel C. Dennett, and others. However, the rough sketch I've presented here is only intended to convey a general sense of how these models work; it doesn't begin to do justice to the fine points. Detailed models are described in *Consciousness Explained* by Dennett, and *The Society of Mind* by Minsky.

COCOON

The explosion shattered windows hundreds of metres away, but started no fire. Later, I discovered that it had shown up on a seismograph at Macquarie University, fixing the time precisely: 3.52 a.m. Residents woken by the blast phoned emergency services within minutes, and our night-shift operator called me just after four, but there was no point rushing to the scene when I'd only be in the way. I sat at the terminal in my study for almost an hour, assembling background data and monitoring the radio traffic on headphones, drinking coffee and trying not to type too loudly.

By the time I arrived, the local fire-service contractors had departed, having certified that there was no risk of further explosions, but our forensic people were still poring over the wreckage, the electric hum of their equipment all but drowned out by birdsong. Lane Cove was a quiet, leafy suburb, mixed residential and high-tech industrial, the lush vegetation of corporate open spaces blending almost seamlessly into the adjacent national park, which straddled the Lane Cove River. The map of the area on my car terminal had identified suppliers of laboratory reagents and pharmaceuticals, manufacturers of precision instruments for scientific and aerospace applications, and no fewer than twenty-seven biotechnology firms – including Life Enhancement International, the erstwhile sprawling concrete building now reduced to a collection of white powdery blocks clustered around twisted reinforcement rods. The exposed steel glinted in the early light, disconcertingly pristine; the building was only three years old. I could understand why the forensic team had ruled out an accident at their first glance; a few drums of organic solvent could not have done anything remotely like *this*. Nothing legally stored in a residential zone could reduce a modern building to rubble in a matter of seconds.

I spotted Janet Lansing as I left my car. She was surveying the ruins with an expression of stoicism, but she was hugging herself. Mild shock, probably. She had no other reason to be chilly; it had been stinking hot all night, and the temperature was already climbing. Lansing was Director of the Lane Cove complex: forty-three years old, with a PhD in molecular biology from Cambridge, and an MBA from an equally reputable Japanese virtual university. I'd had my knowledge miner extract her details, and photo, from assorted databases before I'd left home.

I approached her and said, 'James Glass, Nexus Investigations.'

She frowned at my business card, but accepted it, then glanced at the technicians trawling their gas chromatographs and holography equipment around the perimeter of the ruins. 'They're yours, I suppose?'

'Yes. They've been here since four.'

She smirked slightly. 'What happens if I give the job to someone else? And charge the lot of you with trespass?'

'If you hire another company, we'll be happy to hand over all the samples and data we've collected.'

She nodded distractedly. 'I'll hire you, of course. Since four? I'm impressed. You've even arrived before the insurance people.' As it happened, LEI's 'insurance people' owned 49 per cent of Nexus, and would stay out of the way until we were finished, but I didn't see any reason to mention that. Lansing added sourly, 'Our so-called security firm only worked up the courage to phone me half an hour ago. Evidently a fibre-optic junction box was sabotaged, disconnecting the whole area. They're supposed to send in patrols in the event of equipment failure, but apparently they didn't bother.'

I grimaced sympathetically. 'What exactly were you people making here?'

'Making? Nothing. We did no manufacturing; this was pure R & D.'

In fact, I'd already established that LEI's factories were all in Thailand and Indonesia, with the head office in Monaco, and research facilities scattered around the world. There's a fine line, though, between demonstrating that the facts are at your fingertips, and unnerving the client. A total stranger *ought* to make at least one trivial wrong assumption, ask at least one misguided question. I always do.

'So what were you researching and developing?'

'That's commercially sensitive information.'

I took my notepad from my shirt pocket and displayed a standard contract, complete with the usual secrecy provisions. She glanced at it, then had her own computer scrutinise the document. Conversing in modulated infra-red, the machines rapidly negotiated the fine details. My notepad signed the agreement electronically on my behalf, and Lansing's did the same, then they both chimed happily in unison to let us know that the deal had been concluded.

Lansing said, 'Our main project here was engineering improved syncytiotrophoblastic cells.' I smiled patiently, and she translated for me. 'Strengthening the barrier between the maternal and foetal blood supplies. Mother and foetus don't share blood directly, but they exchange nutrients and hormones across the placental barrier. The trouble is, all kinds of viruses, toxins, pharmaceuticals and illicit drugs can also cross over. The natural barrier cells didn't evolve to cope with HIV, foetal alcohol syndrome, cocaine-addicted babies, or the next thalidomide-like disaster. We're aiming for a single intravenous injection of a gene-tailoring vector, which would trigger the formation of an extra layer of cells in the appropriate structures

120

within the placenta, specifically designed to shield the foetal blood supply from contaminants in the maternal blood.'

'A thicker barrier?'

'Smarter. More selective. More choosy about what it lets through. We know exactly what the developing foetus actually *needs* from the maternal blood. These gene-tailored cells would contain specific channels for transporting each of those substances. Nothing else would be allowed through.'

'Very impressive.' *A cocoon around the unborn child, shielding it from all of the poisons of modern society.* It sounded like exactly the kind of beneficent technology a company called Life Enhancement would be hatching in leafy Lane Cove. True, even a layman could spot a few flaws in the scheme. I'd heard that HIV most often infected children during birth itself, not pregnancy, but presumably there were other viruses which crossed the placental barrier more frequently. And I had no idea whether or not mothers at risk of giving birth to children stunted by alcohol or addicted to cocaine were likely to rush out *en masse* and have gene-tailored foetal barriers installed, but I could picture a strong demand from people terrified of food additives, pesticides, and pollutants. In the long term – if the system actually worked, and wasn't prohibitively expensive – it could even become a part of routine prenatal care.

Beneficent, and lucrative.

In any case, whether or not there were biological, economic and social factors which might keep the technology from being a complete success, it was hard to imagine anyone objecting to *the principle of the thing.*

I said, 'Were you working with animals?'

Lansing scowled. 'Only early calf embryos, and disembodied bovine uteruses on tissue-support machines. If it was an animal-rights group, they would have been better off bombing an abattoir.'

'Mmm.' In the past few years, the Sydney chapter of Animal Equality – the only group known to use such extreme methods

121

– had concentrated on primate research facilities. They might have changed their focus, or been misinformed, but LEI still seemed like an odd target; there were still plenty of laboratories widely known to use whole live rats and rabbits as if they were disposable test tubes – many of them quite close by. 'What about competitors?'

'No one else is pursuing this kind of product line, so far as I know. There's no race being run; we've already obtained individual patents for all of the essential components – the membrane channels, the transporter molecules – so any competitor would have to pay us licence fees, regardless.'

'What if someone simply wanted to damage you financially?'

'Then they should have bombed one of the factories instead. Cutting off our cash flow would have been the best way to hurt us; this laboratory wasn't earning a cent.'

'Your share price will still take a dive, won't it? Nothing makes investors nervous quite so much as terrorism.'

Lansing agreed, reluctantly. 'But then, whoever took advantage of that and launched a takeover bid would suffer the same taint themselves. I don't deny that commercial sabotage takes place in this industry now and then, but not on a level as crude as this. Genetic engineering is a subtle business. Bombs are for fanatics.'

Perhaps. But who would be fanatically opposed to the idea of shielding human embryos from viruses and poisons? Several religious sects flatly rejected any kind of modification to human biology, but the ones who employed violence were far more likely to have bombed a manufacturer of abortifacient drugs than a laboratory dedicated to the task of *safeguarding* the unborn child.

Elaine Chang, head of the forensic team, approached us. I introduced her to Lansing. Elaine said, 'It was a very professional job. If you'd hired demolition experts, they wouldn't have done a single thing differently. But then, they probably would have used identical software to compute the timing and placement of the charges.' She held up her notepad, and displayed a stylised reconstruction of the building, with hypothetical explosive charges marked. She hit a button and the simulation crumbled into something very like the actual mess behind us.

She continued, 'Most reputable manufacturers these days imprint every batch of explosives with a trace element signature, which remains in the residue. We've linked the charges used here to a batch stolen from a warehouse in Singapore five years ago.'

I added, 'Which may not be a great help though, I'm afraid. After five years on the black market, they could have changed hands a dozen times.'

Elaine returned to her equipment. Lansing was beginning to look a little dazed. I said, 'I'd like to talk to you again, later, but I am going to need a list of your employees, past and present, as soon as possible.'

She nodded, and hit a few keys on her notepad, transferring the list to mine. She said, 'Nothing's been lost, really. We had off-site backup for all of our data, administrative and scientific. And we have frozen samples of most of the cell lines we were working on, in a vault in Milson's Point.'

Commercial data backup would be all but untouchable, with the records stored in a dozen or more locations scattered around the world – heavily encrypted, of course. Cell lines sounded more vulnerable. I said, 'You'd better let the vault's operators know what's happened.'

'I've already done that; I phoned them on my way here.' She gazed at the wreckage. 'The insurance company will pay for the rebuilding. In six months' time, we'll be back on our feet. So whoever did this was wasting their time. The work will go on.'

I said, 'Who would want to stop it in the first place?'

Lancing's faint smirk appeared again, and I very nearly asked her what she found so amusing. But people often act incongruously in the face of disasters, large or small; nobody had died, she wasn't remotely hysterical, but it would have been strange if a setback like this hadn't knocked her slightly out of kilter.

She said, 'You tell me. That's your job, isn't it?'

*   *   *

Martin was in the living room when I arrived home that evening. Working on his costume for the Mardi Gras. I couldn't imagine what it would look like when it was completed, but there were definitely feathers involved. Blue feathers. I did my best to appear composed, but I could tell from his expression that he'd caught an involuntary flicker of distaste on my face as he looked up. We kissed anyway, and said nothing about it.

Over dinner, though, he couldn't help himself.

'Fortieth anniversary this year, James. Sure to be the biggest yet. You could at least come and watch.' His eyes glinted; he enjoyed needling me. We'd had this argument five years running, and it was close to becoming a ritual as pointless as the parade itself.

I said flatly, 'Why would I want to watch ten thousand drag queens ride down Oxford Street, blowing kisses to the tourists?'

'Don't exaggerate. There'll only be a thousand men in drag, at most.'

'Yeah, the rest will be in sequined jockstraps.'

'If you actually came and watched, you'd discover that most people's imaginations have progressed far beyond that.'

I shook my head, bemused. 'If people's imaginations had *progressed*, there'd be no Gay and Lesbian Mardi Gras at all. It's a freak show, for people who want to live in a cultural ghetto. Forty years ago, it might have been . . . provocative. Maybe it did some good, back then. But *now*? What's the point? There are no laws left to change, no politics left to address. This kind of thing just recycles the same moronic stereotypes, year after year.'

Martin said smoothly, 'It's a public reassertion of the right to diverse sexuality. Just because it's no longer a *protest march* as well as a celebration doesn't mean it's irrelevant. And complaining about stereotypes is like . . . complaining about the characters in a medieval morality play. The costumes are code, shorthand. Give the great unwashed heterosexual masses credit for some intelligence; they don't watch the parade and conclude that the average gay man spends all his time in a gold lamé tutu. People aren't that literal-minded. They all learnt semiotics in kindergarten, they know how to decode the message.'

'I'm sure they do. But it's still the wrong message: it makes exotic what ought to be mundane. OK, people have the right to dress up any way they like and march down Oxford Street . . . but it means absolutely nothing to me.'

'I'm not asking you to join in—'

'Very wise.'

'—but if one hundred thousand straights can turn up, to show their support for the gay community, why can't you?'

I said wearily, 'Because every time I hear the word *community*, I know I'm being manipulated. If there is such a thing as *the gay community*, I'm certainly not a part of it. As it happens, I don't want to spend my life watching *gay and lesbian* television channels, using *gay and lesbian* news systems . . . or going to *gay and lesbian* street parades. It's all so . . . proprietary. You'd think there was a multinational corporation who had the franchise rights on homosexuality. And if you don't *market the product* their way, you're some kind of second-class, inferior, bootleg, unauthorised queer.'

Martin cracked up. When he finally stopped laughing, he said, 'Go on. I'm waiting for you to get to the part where you say you're no more proud of being gay than you are of having brown eyes, or black hair, or a birthmark behind your left knee.'

I protested, 'That's true. Why should I be "proud" of something I was born with? I'm not proud, or ashamed. I just accept it. And I don't have to join a parade to prove that.'

'So you'd rather we all stayed invisible?'

'*Invisible!* You're the one who told me that the representation rates in movies and TV last year were close to the true demographics. And if you hardly even *notice it* any more when an openly gay or lesbian politician gets elected, that's because it's *no longer an issue.* To most people, now, it's about as significant as . . . being left- or right-handed.'

Martin seemed to find this suggestion surreal. 'Are you trying to tell me that it's now a *non-subject*? That the inhabitants of this planet are now absolutely impartial on the question of sexual preference? Your faith is touching, but . . .' He mimed incredulity.

I said, 'We're equal before the law with any heterosexual couple, aren't we? And when was the last time you told someone you were gay and they so much as blinked? And yes, I know, there are dozens of countries where it's still illegal – along with joining the wrong political parties, or the wrong religions. Parades in Oxford Street aren't going to change *that.*'

'People are still bashed *in this city.* People are still discriminated against.'

'Yeah. And people are also shot dead in peak-hour traffic for playing the wrong music on their car stereos, or denied jobs because they live in the wrong suburbs. I'm not talking about the perfection of human nature. I just want you to acknowledge one tiny victory: leaving out a few psychotics, and a few fundamentalist bigots, most people *just don't care.*'

Martin said ruefully, 'If only that were true.'

The argument went on for more than an hour – ending in a stalemate, as usual. But then, neither of us had seriously expected to change the other's mind.

I did catch myself wondering afterwards, though, if I really believed all of my own optimistic rhetoric. *About as significant as being left- or right-handed?* Certainly, that was the line taken by most Western politicians, academics, essayists, talk-show hosts, soap-opera writers, and mainstream religious leaders, but the same people had been espousing equally high-minded principles of racial equality for decades, and the reality still hadn't entirely caught up on that front. I'd suffered very little discrimination, myself – by the time I reached high school, tolerance was hip, and I'd witnessed a constant stream of improvements since then . . . but how could I ever know precisely how much hidden prejudice remained? By interrogating my own straight friends? By reading the sociologists' latest attitude surveys? People will always tell you what they think you want to hear.

Still, it hardly seemed to matter. Personally, I could get by without the deep and sincere approval of every other member of the human race. Martin and I were lucky enough to have been born into a time and place where, in almost every tangible respect, we were treated as equal.

What more could anyone hope for?

In bed that night, we made love very slowly, at first just kissing and stroking each other's bodies for what seemed like hours. Neither of us spoke, and in the stupefying heat I lost all sense of belonging to any other time, any other reality. Nothing existed but the two of us; the rest of the world, the rest of my life, went spinning away into the darkness.

*   *   *

The investigation moved slowly. I interviewed every current member of LEI's workforce, then started on the long list of past employees. I still believed that commercial sabotage was the most likely explanation for such a professional job, but blowing up the opposition is a desperate measure; a little civilised espionage usually comes first. I was hoping that someone who'd worked for LEI might have been approached in the past and offered money for inside information – and if I could find just one employee who'd turned down a bribe, they might have learnt something useful from their contact with the presumed rival.

Although the Lane Cove facility had been built only three years before, LEI had operated a research division in Sydney for twelve years before that, in North Ryde, not far away. Many of the ex-employees from that period had moved interstate or overseas; quite a few had been transferred to LEI divisions in other countries. Still, almost no one had changed their personal phone numbers, so I had very little trouble tracking them down.

The exception was a biochemist named Catherine Mendelsohn; the number listed for her in the LEI staff records had been cancelled. There were seventeen people with the same surname and initials in the national phone directory; none admitted to being Catherine Alice Mendelsohn, and none looked at all like the staff photo I had.

Mendelsohn's address in the Electoral Roll, an apartment in Newtown, matched the LEI records, but the same address was in the phone directory (and Electoral Roll) for Stanley Goh, a young man who told me that he'd never met Mendelsohn. He'd been leasing the apartment for the past eighteen months.

Credit-rating databases gave the same out-of-date address. I couldn't access tax, banking, or utilities records without a warrant. I had my knowledge miner scan the death notices, but there was no match there.

Mendelsohn had worked for LEI until about a year before the move to Lane Cove. She'd been part of a team working on a gene-tailoring system for ameliorating menstrual side-effects, and although the Sydney division had always specialised in gynaecological research, for some reason the project was about to be moved to Texas. I checked the industry publications; apparently, LEI had been rearranging all of its operations at the time, gathering together projects from around the globe into new multi-disciplinary configurations, in accordance with the latest fashionable theories of research dynamics. Mendelsohn had declined the transfer, and had been retrenched.

I dug deeper. The staff records showed that Mendelsohn had been questioned by security guards after being found on the

North Ryde premises late at night, two days before her dismissal. Workaholic biotechnologists aren't uncommon, but starting the day at two in the morning shows exceptional dedication, especially when the company has just tried to shuffle you off to Amarillo. Having turned down the transfer, she must have known what was in store.

Nothing came of the incident, though. And even if Mendelsohn *had* been planning some minor act of sabotage, that hardly established any connection with a bombing four years later. She might have been angry enough to leak confidential information to one of LEI's rivals, but whoever had bombed the Lane Cove laboratory would have been more interested in someone who'd worked on the foetal barrier project itself – a project which had only come into existence a year after Mendelsohn had been sacked.

I pressed on through the list. Interviewing the ex-employees was frustrating; almost all of them were still working in the biotechnology industry, and they would have been an ideal group to poll on the question of *who would benefit most* from LEI's misfortune, but the confidentiality agreement I'd signed meant that I couldn't disclose anything about the research in question – not even to people working for LEI's other divisions.

The one thing which I *could* discuss drew a blank: if anyone had been offered a bribe, they weren't talking about it – and no magistrate was going to sign a warrant letting me loose on a fishing expedition through a hundred and seventeen people's financial records.

Forensic examination of the ruins, and the sabotaged fibre-optic exchange, had yielded the usual catalogue of minutiae which might eventually turn out to be invaluable, but none of it was going to conjure up a suspect out of thin air.

Four days after the bombing, just as I found myself growing desperate for a fresh angle on the case, I had a call from Janet Lansing.

The backup samples of the project's gene-tailored cell lines had been destroyed.

*　　*　　*

The vault in Milson's Point turned out to be directly underneath a section of the Harbour Bridge – built right into the foundations on the north shore. Lansing hadn't arrived yet, but the head of security for the storage company, an elderly man called David Asher, showed me around. Inside, the traffic was barely audible, but the vibration coming through the floor felt like a constant mild earthquake. The place was cavernous, dry and cool. At least a hundred cryogenic freezers were laid out in rows; heavily clad pipes ran between them, replenishing their liquid nitrogen.

Asher was understandably morose, but co-operative. Celluloid movie film had been archived here, he explained, before everything went digital; the present owners specialised in biological materials. There were no guards physically assigned to the vault, but the surveillance cameras and alarm systems looked impressive, and the structure itself must have been close to impregnable.

Lansing had phoned the storage company, Biofile, on the morning of the bombing. Asher confirmed that he'd sent someone down from their North Sydney office to check the freezer in question. Nothing was missing, but he'd promised to boost security measures immediately. Because the freezers were supposedly tamper-proof, and individually locked, clients were normally allowed access to the vault at their convenience, monitored by the surveillance cameras, but otherwise unsupervised. Asher had promised Lansing that, henceforth, nobody would enter the building without a member of his staff to accompany them – and he claimed that nobody had been inside since the day of the bombing, anyway.

When two LEI technicians had arrived that morning to carry out an inventory, they'd found the expected number of culture flasks, all with the correct bar-code labels, all tightly sealed, but the appearance of their contents was subtly wrong. The translucent frozen colloid was more opalescent than cloudy; an untrained eye might never have noticed the difference, but apparently it spoke volumes to the *cognoscenti*.

The technicians had taken a number of the flasks away for analysis; LEI were working out of temporary premises, a subleased corner of a paint manufacturer's quality-control lab. Lansing had promised me preliminary test results by the time we met.

Lansing arrived, and unlocked the freezer. With gloved hands, she lifted a flask out of the swirling mist and held it up for me to inspect.

She said, 'We've only thawed three samples, but they all look the same. The cells have been torn apart.'

'How?' The flask was covered with such heavy condensation that I couldn't have said if it was empty or full, let alone cloudy or opalescent.

'It looks like radiation damage.'

My skin crawled. I peered into the depths of the freezer; all I could make out were the tops of rows of identical flasks, *but if one of them had been spiked with a radioisotope . . .*

Lansing scowled. 'Relax.' She tapped a small electronic badge pinned to her lab coat, with a dull grey face like a solar cell: a radiation dosimeter. '*This* would be screaming if we were being exposed to anything significant. Whatever the source of the radiation was, it's no longer in here – and it hasn't left the walls glowing. Your future offspring are safe.'

I let that pass. 'You think all the samples will turn out to be ruined? You won't be able to salvage anything?'

Lansing was stoical as ever. 'It looks that way. There are some elaborate techniques we could use to try to repair the DNA, but it will probably be easier to synthesise fresh DNA from scratch, and reintroduce it into unmodified bovine placental cell lines. We still have all the sequence data; that's what matters in the end.'

I pondered the freezer's locking system, the surveillance cameras. 'Are you sure that the source was *inside* the freezer? Or could the damage have been done without actually breaking in – right through the walls?'

She thought it over. 'Maybe. There's not much metal in these things; they're mostly plastic foam. But I'm not a radiation physicist; your forensic people will probably be able to give you a better idea of what happened, once they've checked out the freezer itself. If there's damage to the polymers in the foam, it might be possible to use that to reconstruct the geometry of the radiation field.'

A forensic team was on its way. I said, 'How would they have done it? Walked casually by, and just—?'

'Hardly. A source which could do this in one quick hit would have been unmanageable. It's far more likely to have been a matter of weeks, or months, of low-level exposure.'

'So they must have smuggled some kind of device into *their own freezer*, and aimed it at yours? But then . . . we'll be able to trace the effects right back to the source, won't we? So how could they have hoped to get away with it?'

Lansing said, 'It's even simpler than that. We're talking about a modest amount of a gamma-emitting isotope, not some billion-dollar particle-beam weapon. The effective range would be a couple of metres, at most. If it *was* done from the outside, you've just narrowed down your suspect list to two.' She thumped the freezer's left neighbour in the aisle, then did the same to the one on the right, and said, 'Aha.'

'What?'

She thumped them both again. The second one sounded hollow.

I said, 'No liquid nitrogen? It's not in use?'

Lansing nodded. She reached for the handle.

Asher said, 'I don't think—'

The freezer wasn't locked; the lid swung open easily. Lansing's badge started beeping – and, worse, *there was something in there, with batteries and wires* . . .

I don't know what kept me from knocking her to the floor, but Lansing, untroubled, lifted the lid all the way. She said mildly, 'Don't panic; this dose rate's nothing. Threshold of detectable.'

The thing inside looked superficially like a home-made bomb, but the batteries and timer chip I'd glimpsed were wired to a heavy-duty solenoid, which was part of an elaborate shutter mechanism on one side of a large, metallic grey box.

Lansing said, 'Cannibalised medical source, probably. You know these things have turned up in *garbage dumps*?' She unpinned her badge and waved it near the box; the pitch of the alarm increased, but only slightly. 'Shielding seems to be intact.'

I said, as calmly as possible, 'These people have access to *high explosive*. You don't have any idea what the fuck might be in there, or what it's wired up to do. This is the point where we walk out, quietly, and leave it to the bomb-disposal robots.'

She seemed about to protest, but then she nodded contritely. The three of us went up onto the street, and Asher called the anti-terrorist services contractor. I suddenly realised that they'd have to divert all traffic from the bridge. The Lane Cove bombing had received some perfunctory media coverage, but *this* would lead the evening news.

I took Lansing aside. 'They've destroyed your laboratory. They've wiped out your cell lines. Your data may be almost impossible to locate and corrupt, so the next logical target is you and your employees. Nexus don't provide protective services, but I can recommend a good firm.'

I gave her the phone number; she accepted it with appropriate solemnity. 'So you finally believe me?' she said. 'These people aren't commercial saboteurs. They're dangerous fanatics.'

I was growing impatient with her vague references to 'fanatics'. 'Who exactly do you have in mind?'

She said darkly, 'We're tampering with certain . . . *natural processes*. You can draw your own conclusions, can't you?'

There was no logic to that at all. God's Image would probably want to *force* all pregnant women with HIV infections, or drug habits, to use the cocoon; they wouldn't try to bomb the technology out of existence. Gaia's Soldiers were more concerned with genetically engineered crops and bacteria than trivial modifications to insignificant species like humans – and they wouldn't have used *radioisotopes* if the fate of the planet depended on it. Lansing was beginning to sound thoroughly paranoid; in the circumstances, though, I couldn't really blame her.

I said, 'I'm not drawing any conclusions. I'm just advising you to take some sensible precautions, because we have no way of knowing how far this might escalate. But . . . Biofile must lease freezer space to every one of your competitors. A commercial rival would have found it a thousand times easier than any hypothetical sect member to get into the vault to plant that thing.'

A grey armour-plated van screeched to a halt in front of us; the back door swung up, ramps slid down, and a squat, multi-limbed robot on treads descended. I raised a hand in greeting and the robot did the same; the operator was a friend of mine.

Lansing said, 'You may be right. But then, there's nothing to stop a terrorist from having a day job in biotechnology, is there?'

*　　*　　*

The device turned out not to be booby-trapped at all – just rigged to spray LEI's precious cells with gamma rays for six hours, starting at midnight, every night. Even in the unlikely event that someone had come into the vault in the early hours and wedged themself into the narrow gap between the freezers, the dose they received would not have been much; as Lansing had suggested, it was the cumulative effect over months that had done the damage. The radioisotope in the box was cobalt 60, almost certainly a decomissioned medical source – grown too weak for its original use, but still too hot to be discarded – stolen from a 'cooling off' site. No such theft had been reported, but Elaine Chang's assistants were phoning around the hospitals, trying to persuade them to re-inventory their concrete bunkers.

Cobalt 60 was dangerous stuff, but fifty milligrams in a carefully shielded container wasn't exactly a tactical nuclear weapon. The news systems went berserk, though: ATOMIC TERRORISTS STRIKE HARBOUR BRIDGE! et cetera. If LEI's enemies *were* activists, with some 'moral cause' which they hoped to set before the public, they clearly had the worst PR advisers in the business. Their prospects of gaining the slightest sympathy had vanished the instant the first news reports mentioned the word *radiation*.

My secretarial software issued polite statements of 'No comment' on my behalf, but camera crews began hovering outside my front door, so I relented and mouthed a few newsspeak sentences for them which meant essentially the same thing. Martin looked on, amused – and then I looked on, astonished, as Janet Lansing's own doorstop media conference appeared on TV.

'These people are clearly ruthless. Human life, the environment, radioactive contamination: all mean nothing to them.'

'Do you have any idea who might be responsible for this outrage, Dr Lansing?'

'I can't disclose that yet. All I can reveal right now is that our research is at the very cutting edge of preventative medicine – and I'm not at all surprised that there are powerful vested interests working against us.'

Powerful vested interests? What was *that* meant to be code for, if not the rival biotechnology firm whose involvement she kept denying? No doubt she had her eye on the publicity advantages of being the victim of ATOMIC TERRORISTS, but I thought she was wasting her breath. In two or more years' time, when the product finally hit the market, the story would be long forgotten.

*   *   *

After some tricky jurisdictional negotiations, Asher finally sent me six months' worth of files from the vault's surveillance cameras – all that they kept. The freezer in question had been unused for almost two years; the last authorised tenant was a small IVF clinic which had gone bankrupt. Only about 60 per cent of the freezers were currently leased, so it wasn't particularly surprising that LEI had had a conveniently empty neighbour.

I ran the surveillance files through image-processing software, in the hope that someone might have been caught in the act of opening the unused freezer. The search took almost an hour of supercomputer time and turned up precisely nothing. A few minutes later, Elaine Chang popped her head into my office to say that she'd finished her analysis of the damage to the freezer walls: the nightly irradiation had been going on for between eight and nine months.

Undeterred, I scanned the files again, this time instructing the software to assemble a gallery of every individual sighted inside the vault.

Sixty-two faces emerged. I put company names to all of them, matching the times of each sighting to Biofile's records of the use of each client's electronic key. No obvious inconsistencies showed up; nobody had been seen inside who hadn't used an authorised key to gain access, and the same people had used the same keys, again and again.

I flicked through the gallery, wondering what to do next. Search for anyone glancing slyly in the direction of the radioactive freezer? The software could have done it, but I wasn't quite ready for barrel-scraping efforts like that.

I came to a face which looked familiar: a blonde woman in her mid-thirties, who'd used the key belonging to Federation Centennial Hospital's Oncology Research Unit, three times. I was certain that I knew her, but I couldn't recall where I'd seen her before. It didn't matter; after a few seconds' searching, I found a clear shot of the name badge pinned to her lab coat. All I had to do was zoom in.

The badge read: C. MENDELSOHN.

There was a knock on my open door. I turned from the screen; Elaine was back, looking pleased with herself.

She said, 'We've finally found a place who'll own up to having lost some cobalt 60. What's more, the activity of our source fits their missing item's decay curve exactly.'

'So where was it stolen from?'

'Federation Centennial.'

* * *

I phoned the Oncology Research Unit. Yes, Catherine Mendelsohn worked there – she'd done so for almost four years – but they couldn't put me through to her; she'd been on sick leave all week. They gave me the same cancelled phone number as LEI, but a different address: an apartment in Petersham. The address wasn't listed in the phone directory; I'd have to go there in person.

A cancer-research team would have no reason to want to harm LEI, but a commercial rival – with or without their own key to the vault – could still have paid Mendelsohn to do their work for them. It seemed like a lousy deal to me, whatever they'd offered her – if she was convicted, every last cent would be traced and confiscated – but bitterness over her sacking might have clouded her judgement.

Maybe. Or maybe that was all too glib.

I replayed the shots of Mendelsohn taken by the surveillance cameras. She did nothing unusual, nothing suspicious. She went straight to the ORU's freezer, put in whatever samples she'd brought, and departed. She didn't glance slyly in any direction at all.

The fact that she had been inside the vault – on legitimate business – proved nothing. The fact that the cobalt 60 had been stolen from the hospital where she worked could have been pure coincidence.

And anyone had the right to cancel their phone service.

I pictured the steel reinforcement rods of the Lane Cove laboratory, glinting in the sunlight.

On the way out, reluctantly, I took a detour to the basement. I sat at a console while the armaments safe checked my finger-prints, took breath samples and a retinal blood spectrogram, ran some perception-and-judgement response-time tests, then quizzed me for five minutes about the case. Once it was satisfied with my reflexes, my motives, and my state of mind, it issued me a nine-millimetre pistol and a shoulder holster.

*   *   *

Mendelsohn's apartment block was a 1960s concrete box with front doors opening onto long shared balconies offering no security at all. I arrived just after seven, to the smell of cooking and the sound of game-show applause wafting from a hundred open windows. The concrete still shimmered with the day's heat; three flights of stairs left me coated in sweat. Mendel-sohn's apartment was silent, but the lights were on.

She answered the door. I introduced myself, and showed her my ID. She seemed nervous, but not surprised.

She said, 'I still find it galling to have to deal with people like you.'

'People like—?'

'I was opposed to privatising the police force. I helped organise some of the marches.'

She would have been fourteen years old at the time – a precocious political activist.

She let me in, begrudgingly. The living room was modestly furnished, with a terminal on a desk in one corner.

I said, 'I'm investigating the bombing of Life Enhancement International. You used to work for them, up until about four years ago. Is that correct?'

'Yes.'

'Can you tell me why you left?'

She repeated what I knew about the transfer of her project to the Amarillo division. She answered every question directly, looking me straight in the eye; she still appeared nervous, but she seemed to be trying to read some vital piece of information from my demeanour. *Wondering if I'd traced the cobalt?*

'What were you doing on the North Ryde premises at two in the morning, two days before you were sacked?'

She said, 'I wanted to find out what LEI were planning for the new building. I wanted to know why they didn't want me to stick around.'

'Your job was moved to Texas.'

She laughed drily. 'The work wasn't *that* specialised. I could have swapped jobs with someone who wanted to travel to the States. It would have been the perfect solution, and there would have been plenty of people more than happy to trade places with me. But no, that wasn't allowed.'

'So . . . did you find the answer?'

'Not that night. But later, yes.'

I said carefully, 'So you knew what LEI were doing in Lane Cove?'

'Yes.'

'How did you discover that?'

'I kept an ear to the ground. Nobody who'd stayed on would have told me directly, but word leaked out, eventually. About a year ago.'

'*Three years after you'd left?* Why were you still interested? Did you think there was a market for the information?'

She said, 'Put your notepad in the bathroom sink and run the tap on it.'

I hesitated, then complied. When I returned to the living room, she had her face in her hands. She looked up at me grimly.

'Why was I still interested? Because I wanted to know why *every project* with any lesbian or gay team members was being transferred out of the division. I wanted to know if that was pure coincidence. Or not.'

I felt a sudden chill in the pit of my stomach. I said, 'If you had some problem with discrimination, there are avenues you could have—'

Mendelsohn shook her head impatiently. 'LEI were never *discriminatory*. They didn't sack anyone who was willing to move – and they always transferred the entire team; there was nothing so crude as picking out *individuals* by sexual preference. And they had a rationalisation for everything: projects were being regrouped between divisions to facilitate "synergistic cross-pollination". And if that sounds like pretentious bullshit, it was – but it was plausible pretentious bullshit. Other corporations have adopted far more ridiculous schemes, in perfect sincerity.'

'But if it wasn't a matter of discrimination . . . why should LEI want to force people out of one particular division—?'

I think I'd finally guessed the answer, even as I said those words, but I needed to hear her spell it out, before I could really believe it.

Mendelsohn must have been practising her version for non-biochemists; she had it down pat. 'When people are subject to *stress* – physical or emotional – the levels of certain substances in the bloodstream increase. Cortisol and adrenaline, mainly. Adrenaline has a rapid, short-term effect on the nervous system. Cortisol works on a much longer time frame, modulating all kinds of bodily processes, adapting them for hard times: injury, fatigue, whatever. If the stress is prolonged, someone's cortisol can be elevated for days, or weeks, or months.

'High enough levels of cortisol, in the bloodstream of a pregnant woman, can cross the placental barrier and interact with the hormonal system of the developing foetus. There are parts of the brain where embryonic development is switched into one of two possible pathways, by hormones released by the foetal testes or ovaries. The parts of the brain that control body image and the parts that control sexual preference. Female embryos usually develop a brain wired with a self-image of a female body, and the strongest potential for sexual attraction towards males. Male embryos, vice versa. And it's the sex hormones in the foetal bloodstream which let the growing neurons *know* the gender of the embryo, and which wiring pattern to adopt.

'Cortisol can interfere with this process. The precise inter-actions are complex, but the ultimate effect depends on the timing; different parts of the brain are switched into gender-specific versions at different stages of development. So stress at different times during pregnancy leads to different patterns of sexual preference and body image in the child: homosexual, bisexual, transsexual.

'Obviously, a lot depends on the mother's biochemistry. Pregnancy *itself* is stressful, but everyone responds to that differently. The first sign that cortisol might have an effect came in studies in the 1980s, on the children of German women who'd been pregnant during the most intense bombing raids of World War II, when the stress was so great that the effect showed through despite individual differences. In the nineties, researchers thought they'd found a gene which de-termined male homosexuality, but it was always maternally inherited – and it turned out to be influencing *the mother's stress response*, rather than acting directly on the child.

'If maternal cortisol, and other stress hormones, were kept

from reaching the foetus, then the gender of the brain would always match the gender of the body in every respect. All of the present variation would be wiped out.'

I was shaken, but I don't think I let it show. Everything she said rang true; I didn't doubt a word of it. I'd always known that sexual preference was decided before birth. I'd known that I was gay myself by the age of seven. I'd never sought out the elaborate biological details, though, because I'd never believed that the tedious mechanics of the process could ever matter to me. What turned my blood to ice was not finally learning *the neuroembryology of desire*. The shock was discovering that LEI planned to reach into the womb and take control of it.

I pressed on with the questioning in a kind of trance, putting my own feelings into suspended animation.

I said, 'LEI's barrier is for filtering out *viruses and toxins*. You're talking about a natural substance which has been present for millions of years—'

'LEI's barrier will keep out everything they deem non-essential. The foetus doesn't *need* maternal cortisol in order to survive. If LEI don't explicitly include transporters for it, it won't get through. And I'll give you one guess what their plans are.'

I said, 'You're being paranoid. You think LEI would invest millions of dollars just to take part in a conspiracy to rid the world of homosexuals?'

Mendelsohn looked at me pityingly. 'It's not a *conspiracy*. It's a *marketing opportunity*. LEI don't give a shit about the sexual politics. They could put in cortisol transporters and sell the barrier as an anti-viral, anti-drug, anti-pollution screen. Or they could leave them out and sell it as all of that – plus a means of guaranteeing a heterosexual child. *Which do you think would earn the most money?*'

That question hit a nerve; I said angrily, 'And you had so little faith in people's choice that you *bombed the laboratory* so that no one would ever have the chance to decide?'

Mendelsohn's expression turned stony. 'I did *not* bomb LEI. Or irradiate their freezer.'

'No? We've traced the cobalt 60 to Federation Centennial.'

She looked stunned for a moment, then she said, 'Congratulations. Six thousand other people work there, you know. I'm obviously not the only one of them who's discovered what LEI is up to.'

'You're the only one with access to the Biofile vault. What do you expect me to believe? That having learnt about this project, you were going to do absolutely nothing about it?'

'Of course not! And I still plan to publicise what they're doing. Let people know what it will mean. Try to get the issue debated before the product appears in a blaze of misinformation.'

'You said you've known about the work for a year.'

'Yes – and I've spent most of that time trying to verify all the facts, before opening my big mouth. Nothing would have been stupider than going public with half-baked rumours. I've only told about a dozen people so far, but we were going to launch a big publicity campaign to coincide with this year's Mardi Gras. Although now, with the bombing, everything's a thousand times more complicated.' She spread her hands in a gesture of helplessness. 'But we still have to do what we can, to try to keep the worst from happening.'

'The worst?'

'Separatism. Paranoia. Homosexuality redefined as *pathological*. Lesbians and sympathetic straight women looking for their own technological means to *guarantee* the survival of the culture . . . while the religious far-right try to prosecute them for *poisoning their babies* . . . with a substance God's been happily "poisoning" babies with for the last few thousand years. Sexual tourists travelling from wealthy countries where the technology is in use, to poorer countries where it isn't.'

I was sickened by the vision she was painting, but I pushed on. 'These dozen friends of yours—?'

Mendelsohn said dispassionately, 'Go fuck yourself. I've got nothing more to say to you. I've told you the truth. I'm not a criminal. And I think you'd better leave.'

I went to the bathroom and collected my notepad. In the doorway, I said, 'If you're not a criminal, why are you so hard to track down?'

Wordlessly, contemptuously, she lifted her shirt and showed me the bruises below her rib cage, fading, but still an ugly sight. Whoever it was who'd beaten her – an ex-lover? – I could hardly blame her for doing everything she could to avoid a repeat performance.

On the stairs, I hit the Replay button on my notepad. The software computed the frequency spectrum for the noise of the running water, subtracted it out of the recording, and then amplified and cleaned up what remained. Every word of our conversation came through crystal clear.

From my car, I phoned a surveillance firm and arranged to have Mendelsohn kept under twenty-four-hour observation.

Halfway home, I stopped in a side street, and sat behind the wheel for ten minutes, unable to think, unable to move.

*   *   *

In bed that night, I asked Martin, 'You're left-handed. How would you feel if no one was ever born left-handed again?'

'It wouldn't bother me in the least. Why?'

'You wouldn't think of it as a kind of . . . genocide?'

'Hardly. What's this all about?'

'Nothing. Forget it.'

'You're shaking.'

'I'm cold.'

'You don't feel cold to me.'

As we made love – tenderly, then savagely – I thought: *This is our language, this is our dialect. Wars have been fought over less. And if this language ever dies out, a people will have vanished from the face of the Earth.*

I knew I had to drop the case. If Mendelsohn was guilty, someone else could prove it. To go on working for LEI would destroy me.

Afterwards, though, that seemed like sentimental bullshit. I belonged to no tribe. Every human being possessed his or her own sexuality – and when he or she died, it died with them. If no one was ever born gay again, it made no difference to me.

And if I dropped the case *because I was gay*, I'd be abandoning everything I'd ever believed about my own equality, my own identity . . . not to mention giving LEI the chance to announce: *Yes, of course we hired an investigator without regard to sexual preference, but apparently that was a mistake.*

Staring up into the darkness, I said, 'Every time I hear the word *community*, I reach for my revolver.'

There was no response; Martin was fast asleep. I wanted to wake him, I wanted to argue it all through, there and then, but I'd signed an agreement: I couldn't tell him a thing.

So I watched him sleep, and tried to convince myself that, when the truth came out, he'd understand.

*   *   *

I phoned Janet Lansing, brought her up to date on Mendelsohn – and said coldly, 'Why were you so coy? *"Fanatics"? "Powerful vested interests"?* Are there some words you have trouble pronouncing?'

She'd clearly prepared herself for this moment. 'I didn't want to plant my own ideas in your head. Later on, that might have been seen as prejudicial.'

'Seen as prejudicial *by whom?*' It was a rhetorical question: the media, of course. By keeping silent on the issue, she'd minimised the risk of being seen to have launched a witch-hunt. Telling me to go look for *homosexual terrorists* might have put LEI in a very unsympathetic light, whereas my finding Mendelsohn – for other reasons entirely, despite my ignorance

– would come across as proof that the investigation had been conducted without any preconceptions.

I said, 'You had your suspicions, and you should have disclosed them. At the very least, you should have told me what the barrier was *for*.'

'The barrier,' she said, 'is for protection against viruses and toxins. But anything we do to the body has side-effects. It's not my role to judge whether or not those side-effects are acceptable; the regulatory authorities will insist that we publicise *all* of the consequences of using the product – and then the decision will be up to consumers.'

Very neat: the government would twist their arm, 'forcing them' to disclose their major selling point.

'And what does your market research tell you?'

'That's strictly confidential.'

I very nearly asked her: *When exactly did you find out that I was gay? After you'd hired me – or before?* On the morning of the bombing, while I'd been assembling a dossier on Janet Lansing, had *she* been assembling dossiers on all of the people who might have bid for the investigation? And had she found the ultimate PR advantage, the ultimate seal of impartiality, just too tempting to resist?

I didn't ask. I still wanted to believe that it made no difference: she'd hired me, and I'd solve the crime like any other, and nothing else would matter.

*　　*　　*

I went to the bunker where the cobalt had been stored, at the edge of Federation Centennial's grounds. The trapdoor was solid, but the lock was a joke, and there was no alarm system at all; any smart twelve-year-old could have broken in. Crates full of all kinds of – low-level, short-lived – radioactive waste were stacked up to the ceiling, blocking most of the light from the single bulb; it was no wonder that the theft hadn't been detected sooner. There were even cobwebs – but no mutant spiders, so far as I could see.

After five minutes poking around, listening to my borrowed dosimetry badge adding up the exposure, I was glad to get out, whether or not the average chest X-ray would have done ten times more damage. *Hadn't Mendelsohn realised that: how irrational people were about radiation, how much harm it would do her cause once the cobalt was discovered?* Or had her own – fully informed – knowledge of the minimal risks distorted her perception?

The surveillance teams sent me reports daily. It was an expensive service, but LEI were paying. Mendelsohn met her friends openly, telling them all about the night I'd questioned her, warning them in outraged tones that they were almost certainly being watched. They discussed the foetal barrier, the options for – legitimate – opposition, the problems the bombing had caused them. I couldn't tell if the whole thing was being staged for my benefit, or if Mendelsohn was deliberately contacting only those friends who genuinely believed that she hadn't been involved.

I spent most of my time checking the histories of the people she met. I could find no evidence of past violence or sabotage by any of them, let alone experience with high explosives. But then, I hadn't seriously expected to be led straight to the bomber.

All I had was circumstantial evidence. All I could do was gather detail after detail, and hope that the mountain of facts I was assembling would eventually reach a critical mass, or that Mendelsohn would slip up, cracking under the pressure.

*   *   *

Weeks passed, and Mendelsohn continued to brazen it out. She even had pamphlets printed – ready to distribute at the Mardi Gras – condemning the bombing as loudly as they condemned LEI for its secrecy.

The nights grew hotter. My temper frayed. I don't know what Martin thought was happening to me, but I had no idea how we were going to survive the impending revelations. I couldn't begin to face up to the magnitude of the backlash there'd be once ATOMIC TERRORISTS met GAY BABY-POISONERS in the daily murdochs – and it would make no difference whether it was Mendelsohn's arrest which broke the news to the public, or her media conference blowing the whistle on LEI and proclaiming her own innocence; either way, the investigation would become a circus. I tried not to think about any of it; it was too late to do anything differently, to drop the case, to tell Martin the truth. So I worked on my tunnel vision.

Elaine scoured the radioactive waste bunker for evidence, but weeks of analysis came up blank. I quizzed the Biofile guards, who (supposedly) would have been watching the whole thing on their monitors when the cobalt was planted, but nobody could recall a client with an unusually large and oddly shaped item, wandering casually into the wrong aisle.

I finally obtained the warrants I needed to scrutinise Mendelsohn's entire electronic history since birth. She'd been arrested exactly once, twenty years before, for kicking an – unprivatised – policeman in the shin, during a protest he'd probably, privately, applauded. The charges had been dropped. She'd had a court order in force for the last eighteen months, restraining a former lover from coming within a kilometre of her home. (The woman was a musician with a band called Tetanus Switch-blade; she had two convictions for assault.) There was no evidence of undeclared income, or unusual expenditure. No phone calls to or from known or suspected dealers in arms or explosives, or their known or suspected associates. But every-thing could have been done with pay phones and cash, if she'd organised it carefully.

Mendelsohn wasn't going to put a foot wrong while I was watching. However careful she'd been, though, she could not have carried out the bombing alone. What I needed was someone venal, nervous, or conscience-stricken enough to turn informant. I put out word on the usual channels: I'd be willing to pay, I'd be willing to bargain.

Six weeks after the bombing, I received an anonymous message by e-mail: *Be at the Mardi Gras. No wires, no weapons. I'll find you. 29. 17. 5. 31. 23. 11.*

I played with the numbers for more than an hour, trying to make sense of them, before I finally showed them to Elaine.

She said, 'Be careful, James.'

'Why?'

'These are the ratios of the six trace elements we found in the residue from the explosion.'

*   *   *

Martin spent the day of the Mardi Gras with friends who'd also be in the parade. I sat in my air-conditioned office and tuned in to a TV channel which showed the final preparations, interspersed with talking heads describing the history of the event. In forty years, the Gay and Lesbian Mardi Gras has been transformed from a series of ugly confrontations with police and local authorities, into a money-spinning spectacle advertised in tourist brochures around the world. It was blessed by every level of government, led by politicians and business identities – and the police, like most professions, now had their own float.

Martin was no transvestite (or muscle-bound leather-fetishist, or any other walking cliché); dressing up in a flamboyant costume, one night a year, was as false, as artificial for him as it would have been for most heterosexual men. But I think I understood why he did it. He felt guilty that he could 'pass for straight' in the clothes he usually wore, with the speech and manner and bearing which came naturally to him. He'd never concealed his sexuality from anyone, but it wasn't instantly apparent to total strangers. For him, taking part in the Mardi Gras was a gesture of solidarity with those gay men who were visible, obvious, all year round, and who'd borne the brunt of intolerance because of it.

As dusk fell, spectators began to gather along the route. Helicopters from every news service appeared overhead, turning their cameras on one another to prove to their viewers that this was An Event. Mounted crowd-control personnel – in something very much like the old blue uniform which had vanished when I was a child – parked their horses by the fast-food stands, and stood around fortifying themselves for the long night ahead.

I didn't see how the bomber could seriously expect to find me once I was mingling with a hundred thousand other people, so after leaving the Nexus building I drove my car around the block slowly, three times, just in case.

*　　*　　*

By the time I'd made my way to a vantage point, I'd missed the start of the parade; the first thing I saw was a long line of people wearing giant plastic heads bearing the features of famous and infamous queers. (Apparently the word was back in fashion again, officially declared non-pejorative once more, after several years out of favour.) It was all so Disney I could have gagged – and yes, there was even Bernadette, the world's first lesbian cartoon mouse. I only recognised three of the humans portrayed: Patrick White, looking haggard and suitably bemused, Joe Orton leering sardonically, and J. Edgar Hoover with a Mephistophelian sneer. Everyone wore their names on sashes, though, for what that was worth. A young man beside me asked his girlfriend, 'Who the hell was Walt Whitman?'

She shook her head. 'No idea. Alan Turing?'

'Search me.'

They photographed both of them, anyway.

I wanted to yell at the marchers: *So what? Some queers were famous. Some famous people were queer. What a surprise! Do you think that means you own them?*

150

I kept silent, of course – while everyone around me cheered and clapped. I wondered how close the bomber was, how long he or she would leave me sweating. Panopticon – the surveillance contractors – were still following Mendelsohn and all of her known associates, most of whom were somewhere along the route of the parade, handing out their pamphlets. None of them appeared to have followed me, though. The bomber was almost certainly someone outside the network of friends we'd uncovered.

An anti-viral, anti-drug, anti-pollution barrier, alone – or a means of guaranteeing a heterosexual child. Which do you think would earn the most money? Surrounded by cheering spectators – half of them mixed-sex couples with children in tow – it was almost possible to laugh off Mendelsohn's fears. Who, here, would admit that they'd buy a version of the cocoon which would help wipe out the source of their entertainment? But applauding the freak show didn't mean wanting your own flesh and blood to join it.

An hour after the parade had started, I decided to move out of the densest part of the crowd. If the bomber couldn't reach me through the crush of people, there wasn't much point being here. A hundred or so leather-clad women on – noise-enhanced – electric motorbikes went riding past in a crucifix formation, behind a banner which read DYKES ON BIKES FOR JESUS. I recalled the small group of fundamentalists I'd passed earlier, their backs to the parade route lest they turn into pillars of salt, holding up candles and praying for rain.

I made my way to one of the food stalls, and bought a cold hot dog and a warm orange juice, trying to ignore the smell of horse turds. The place seemed to attract law-enforcement types; J. Edgar Hoover himself came wandering by while I was eating, looking like a malevolent Humpty-Dumpty.

As he passed me, he said, 'Twenty-nine. Seventeen. Five.'
I finished my hot dog and followed him.
He stopped in a deserted side-street, behind a supermarket

parking lot. As I caught up with him, he took out a magnetic scanner.

I said, 'No wires, no weapons.' He waved the device over me. I was telling the truth. 'Can you talk through that thing?'

'Yes.' The giant head bobbed strangely; I couldn't see any eye holes, but he clearly wasn't blind.

'OK. Where did the explosives come from? We know they started off in Singapore, but who was your supplier here?'

Hoover laughed, deep and muffled. 'I'm not going to tell you that. I'd be dead in a week.'

'So what *do* you want to tell me?'

'That I only did the grunt work. Mendelsohn organised everything.'

'No shit. But what have you got that will prove it? Phone calls? Financial transactions?'

He just laughed again. I was beginning to wonder how many people in the parade would know who'd played J. Edgar Hoover; even if he clammed up now, it was possible that I'd be able to track him down later.

That was when I turned and saw six more, identical, Hoovers coming around the corner. They were all carrying baseball bats.

I started to move. Hoover One drew a pistol and aimed it at my face. He said, 'Kneel down slowly, with your hands behind your head.'

I did it. He kept the gun on me, and I kept my eyes on the trigger, but I heard the others arrive, and close into a half-circle behind me.

Hoover One said, 'Don't you know what happens to traitors? Don't you know what's going to happen to you?'

I shook my head slowly. I didn't know what I could say to appease him, so I spoke the truth. 'How can I be a traitor? What is there to betray? Dykes on Bikes for Jesus? The William S. Burroughs Dancers?'

Someone behind me swung their bat into the small of my

back. Not as hard as they might have; I lurched forward, but I kept my balance.

Hoover One said, 'Don't you know any history, Mr Pig? Mr *Polizei*? The Nazis put us in their death camps. The Reaganites tried to have us all die of AIDS. And here you are now, Mr Pig, working for the fuckers who want to wipe us off the face of the planet. That sounds like betrayal to me.'

I knelt there, staring at the gun, unable to speak. I couldn't dredge up the words to justify myself. The truth was too difficult, too grey, too confusing. My teeth started chattering. *Nazis. AIDS. Genocide.* Maybe he was right. Maybe I deserved to die.

I felt tears on my cheeks. Hoover One laughed. 'Boo hoo, Mr Pig.' Someone swung their bat into my shoulders. I fell forward on my face, too afraid to move my hands to break the fall; I tried to get up, but a boot came down on the back of my neck.

Hoover One bent down and put the gun to my skull. He whispered, 'Will you close the case? Lose the evidence on Catherine? You know, your boyfriend frequents some dangerous places; he needs all the friends he can get.'

I lifted my face high enough above the asphalt to reply. 'Yes.'

'Well done, Mr Pig.'

That was when I heard the helicopter.

I blinked the gravel out of my eyes and saw the ground, far brighter than it should have been; there was a spotlight trained on us. I waited for the sound of a bullhorn. Nothing happened. I waited for my assailants to flee. Hoover One took his foot off my neck.

And then they all laid into me with their baseball bats.

I should have curled up and protected my head, but curiosity got the better of me; I turned and stole a glimpse of the chopper. It was a news crew, of course, refusing to do anything unethical like spoil a good story just when it was getting telegenic. That much made perfect sense.

But the goon squad made no sense at all. Why were they

sticking around? Just for the pleasure of beating me for a few seconds longer?

Nobody was that stupid, that oblivious to PR.

I coughed up two teeth and hid my face again. *They wanted it all to be broadcast.* They *wanted* the headlines, the backlash, the outrage. ATOMIC TERRORISTS! BABY-POISONERS! BRUTAL THUGS!

They wanted to demonise the enemy they were pretending to be.

The Hoovers finally dropped their bats and started running. I lay on the ground drooling blood, too weak to lift my head to see what had driven them away.

A while later, I heard hoofbeats. Someone dropped to the ground beside me and checked my pulse.

I said, 'I'm not in pain. I'm happy. I'm delirious.'

Then I passed out.

*   *   *

On his second visit, Martin brought Catherine Mendelsohn to the hospital with him. They showed me a recording of LEI's media conference, the day after the Mardi Gras – two hours before Mendelsohn's was scheduled to take place.

Janet Lansing said, 'In the light of recent events, we have no choice but to go public. We would have preferred to keep this technology under wraps for commercial reasons, but innocent lives are at stake. And when people turn on their own kind . . .'

I burst the stitches in my lips laughing.

LEI had bombed their own laboratory. They'd irradiated their own cells. And they'd hoped that I'd cover up for Mendelsohn, once the evidence led me to her, out of sympathy with her cause. Later, with a tip-off to an investigative reporter or two, the cover-up would have been revealed.

The perfect climate for their product launch.

Since I'd continued with the investigation, though, they'd

154

had to make the best of it: sending in the Hoovers, claiming to be linked to Mendelsohn, to punish me for my diligence.

Mendelsohn said, 'Everything LEI leaked about me – the cobalt, my key to the vault – was already spelt out in the pamphlets I'd printed, but that doesn't seem to cut much ice with the murdochs. I'm the Harbour Bridge Gamma Ray Terrorist now.'

'You'll never be charged.'

'Of course not. So I'll never be found innocent.'

I said, 'When I'm out of here, I'm going after them.' *They wanted impartiality? An investigation untainted by prejudice? They'd get exactly what they paid for, this time. Minus the tunnel vision.*

Martin said softly, 'Who's going to employ you to do that?'

I smiled, painfully. 'LEI's insurance company.'

When they'd left, I dozed off.

I woke suddenly, from a dream of suffocation.

Even if I proved that the whole thing had been a marketing exercise by LEI – even if half their directors were thrown in prison, even if the company itself was liquidated – the technology would still be owned by *someone*.

And one way or another, in the end, it would be *sold*.

That's what I'd missed, in my fanatical neutrality: you can't sell a cure without a disease. So even if I was right to be neutral – even if there was no difference to fight for, no difference to betray, no difference to preserve – the best way to *sell* the cocoon would always be to invent one. And even if it would be no tragedy at all if there was nothing left but heterosexuality in a century's time, the only path which could lead there would be one of lies, and wounding, and vilification.

Would people buy that, or not?

I was suddenly very much afraid that they would.

TRANSITION DREAMS

'We can't tell you what your own transition dreams will be. The only thing that's certain is that you won't remember them.'

Caroline Bausch smiles, reassuringly. Her office, on the sixty-fourth floor of the Gleisner Tower, is so stylish it hurts – her desk is an obsidian ellipse supported by three Perspex circles, and the walls are decorated with the latest in Euclidean Monochrome – but she's not at all the kind of robot the cool, geometric decor seems to demand. I have no doubt that the contrast is intentional, and that her face has been carefully designed to appear more disarmingly natural than even the most cynical person could believe was due to pure guile on the part of her employers.

A few forgettable dreams? That sounds innocuous enough. I very nearly let the matter rest, but I'm puzzled.

'I'll be close to zero degrees when I'm scanned, won't I?'

'Yes. A little below, in fact. Pumped full of antifreeze disaccharides, all your fluids cooled down into a sugary glass.' There's a prickling sensation on my scalp at these words, but the rush I feel is anticipation, not fear; the thought of my body as a kind of ice-confectionary sculpture doesn't seem threatening at all. Several elegant blown-glass figurines decorate the bookshelf behind Bausch's desk. 'Not only does that halt all metabolic processes, it sharpens the NMR spectra. To measure the strength of each synapse accurately, we have to be able to distinguish between subtle variations in neurotransmitter receptor types, among other things. The less thermal noise, the better.'

'I understand. But if my brain has been shut down by hypothermia . . . why will I dream?'

'Your brain won't do the dreaming. The software model we're creating will. But as I said, you won't remember any of it. In the end, the software will be a perfect Copy of your – deeply comatose – organic brain, and it will wake from that coma remembering exactly what the organic brain experienced before the scan. No more, no less. And since the organic brain certainly won't have experienced the transition dreams, the software will have no memory of them.'

The software? I'd expected a simple, biological explanation: a side-effect of the anaesthetic or the antifreeze; neurons firing off a few faint, random signals as they surrendered to the cold.

'Why program the robot's brain to have dreams it won't remember?'

'We don't. Or at least, not explicitly.' Bausch smiles her too-human smile again, not quite masking an appraising glance, a moment spent deciding, perhaps, how much I really need to be told. Or perhaps the whole routine is more calculated reassurance. *Look, even though I'm a robot, you can read me like a book.*

She says, 'Why are Gleisner robots conscious?'

'For the same reason humans are conscious.' I've been waiting for that question since the interview began; Bausch is a counsellor as much as a salesperson, and it's part of her job to ensure that I'm at ease with the new mode of existence I'm buying. 'Don't ask me which neural structures are involved . . . but whatever they are, they must be captured in the scan, and re-created in the model, along with everything else. Gleisner robots are conscious because they process information – about the world, and about themselves – in exactly the same way as humans do.'

'So you're happy with the notion that a computer program which simulates a conscious human brain is, itself, conscious in the very same fashion?'

'Of course. I wouldn't be here if I didn't believe that.' *I wouldn't be talking to you, would I?* I see no need to elaborate – to confess that I've become a thousand times more comfortable with the whole idea ever since the ten-tonne supercomputers in the basements of Dallas and Tokyo began to give way to the ambulatory Gleisner robots, with their compact processors and lifelike bodies. When Copies were finally liberated from their virtual realities – however grand, however detailed they might have been – and given the chance to *inhabit the world* in the manner of flesh-and-blood people, I finally stopped thinking of being scanned as a fate akin to being buried alive.

Bausch says, 'Then you accept that all it takes to *generate experience* is to carry out computations on data structures which encode the same information as the structure of the brain?'

The jargon sounds gratuitous to me, and I don't understand why she's labouring the point, but I say blandly, 'Of course I accept that.'

'Then think about what it implies! Because *the whole process* of creating the finished piece of software which runs a Gleisner robot – the perfect Copy of the unconscious person who was scanned – is one long sequence of computations on data structures which *represent the human brain.*'

I absorb that in silence.

Bausch continues, 'We don't set out to cause the transition dreams, but they're probably unavoidable. Copies have to be *made*, somehow: they can't spring into existence fully formed. The scanner has to probe the organic brain, measure the NMR spectra for billions of different cross-sections, and then process those measurements into a high-resolution anatomical and biochemical map. In other words: carry out several trillion computations on a vast set of data which *represents the brain*. Then, that map has to be used to construct the working computer model, the Copy itself. More computation.'

I think I almost grasp what she's saying, but part of me flatly refuses to accept the notion that merely *imaging the brain* in high enough resolution could cause *the image itself* to dream.

I say, 'None of that computation sets out to mimic the workings of the brain, though, does it? It's all just preparing the way for a program which *will be* conscious, when it's finally up and running.'

'Yes – and once that program *is* up and running, what will it do in order to be conscious? It will generate a sequence of changes in a digital representation of the brain – changes which mimic normal neural activity. But creating that representation in the first place also involves *a sequence of changes*. You can't go from a blank computer memory, to a detailed simulation of a specific human brain, without a few trillion intermediate stages, most of which will represent – in part or in full, in one form or another – possible states of the very same brain.'

'But why should that add up to any kind of mental activity? Rearranging the data, for other reasons entirely?'

Bausch is adamant. 'Reasons don't come into it. The living brain reorganising memories is enough to give rise to ordinary dreams. And just poking an electrode into the temporal lobes is enough to generate *mental activity*. I know: what the brain does is so complex that it's bizarre to think of achieving the same results unintentionally. But all of the brain's complexity is coded into its structure. Once you're dealing with that structure, you're dealing with the stuff of consciousness. Like it or not.'

That does make a certain amount of sense. Almost anything that happens to the brain *feels like something*; it doesn't have to be the orderly process of waking thought. If the random effects of drugs or illness can give rise to distinctive mental events – a fever dream, a schizophrenic episode, an LSD trip – why shouldn't a Copy's elaborate genesis do the same? Each incomplete NMR map, each unfinished version of the simulation software, has no way of 'knowing' that it's not yet *meant* to be self-aware.

159

Still—

'How can you be sure of any of this? If nobody remembers the dreams?'

'The mathematics of consciousness is still in its infancy, but everything we know strongly suggests that the act of constructing a Copy has *subjective content*, even though no trace of the experience remains.'

I'm still not entirely convinced, but I suppose I'll have to take her word for it. The Gleisner Corporation has no reason to invent nonexistent side-effects, and I'm suitably impressed that they bother to warn their customers about *transition dreams* at all. So far as I know, the older companies – the scanning clinics founded in the days when Copies had no physical bodies – never even raised the issue.

We should move on, there are other matters to discuss, but it's hard to drag my thoughts away from this unsettling revelation. I say, 'If you know enough to be certain that there'll always be transition dreams, can't you stretch the mathematics a little further, and tell me what my dreams will be?'

Bausch asks innocently, 'How could we do that?'

'I don't know. Examine my brain, then run some kind of simulation of the Copying process—' I catch myself. 'Ah. But how do you "simulate" a computation without doing it?'

'Exactly. The distinction is meaningless. Any program which could reliably predict the content of the dreams would, itself, *experience them*, as fully as the "you" of the transition process. So what would be the point? If the dreams turned out to be unpleasant, it would be too late to "spare yourself" the trauma.'

Trauma? I'm beginning to wish I'd been satisfied with a reassuring smile and the promise of perfect amnesia. *A few forgettable dreams.*

Now that I – vaguely – understand the reasons for the effect, though, it's a thousand times harder to accept it as inevitable. Neural spasms at the onset of hypothermia might be unavoidable, but anything taking place *inside a computer* is supposed to be subject to limitless control.

'Couldn't you monitor the dreams as they're happening – and intervene, if need be?'

'I'm afraid not.'

'But—'

'Think about it. It would be like prediction, only worse. Monitoring the dreams would mean duplicating the brain-like data structures in still more forms, generating more dreams in the process. So even if we could take charge of the original dreams – deciphering them, and controlling them – all of the software which did that would need *other software watching it*, to see what the side-effects of *its* computations were. And so on. There'd be no end to it.

'As it is, the Copy is constructed by the shortest possible process, the most direct route. The last thing you'd want to do is bring in more computing power, more elaborate algorithms . . . more and more systems mirroring the arithmetic of the experience.'

I shift in my chair, trying to shake off a growing sense of light-headedness. The more I ask, the more surreal the whole subject becomes, but I can't seem to keep my mouth shut.

'If you can't say what the dreams will be about, and you can't control them, can't you at least tell me how long they'll last? Subjectively?'

'Not without running a program which also dreams the dreams.' Bausch is apologetic, but I have a feeling that she finds something elegant, even *proper*, in this state of affairs. 'That's the nature of the mathematics: there are no short-cuts. No answers to hypothetical questions. We can't say for certain what any given conscious system will experience . . . without *creating* that conscious system in the process of answering the question.'

I laugh weakly. *Images of the brain which dream. Predictions of dreams which dream. Dreams which infect any machine which tries to shape them.* I'd thought that all the giddy metaphysics of virtual existence had been banished, now that it was possible to choose to be a Copy living wholly in the physical world. I'd hoped to be able to step from my body into a Gleisner robot without missing a beat . . .

And in retrospect, of course, I will have done just that. Once I've crossed the gulf between human and machine, it will vanish seamlessly behind me.

I say, 'So the dreams are unknowable? And unavoidable? That's close to a mathematical certainty?'

'Yes.'

'But it's equally certain that I won't remember them?'

'Yes.'

'You don't recall anything about your own? Not a single mood? Not a single image?'

Bausch smiles tolerantly. 'Of course not. I woke from a simulated coma. The last thing I remember was being anaesthetised before the scan. There are no buried traces, no hidden memories. No invisible scars. *There can't be.* In a very real sense, *I* never had the transition dreams at all.'

I finally sight a target for my frustration. 'Then, *why warn me*? Why tell me about an experience I'm guaranteed to forget? Guaranteed to end up *not having been through*? Don't you think it would have been kinder to say nothing?'

Bausch hesitates. For the first time, I appear to have discomfited her – and it's a very convincing act. But she must have been asked the same question a thousand times before.

She says, 'When you're dreaming the transition dreams, knowing what you're going through, and why, might make all the difference. Knowing that it's not real. Knowing that it won't last.'

'Perhaps.' It's not that simple, though, and she knows it. 'When my new mind is being pieced together, do you have any idea *when* this knowledge will be part of it? Can you promise me that I'll remember these comforting facts when I need them?

Can you guarantee that anything you've told me will even make sense?'

'No. But—'

'Then what's the point?'

She says, 'Do you think that if we'd kept silent, you would have had *any chance at all* of dreaming the truth?'

*　　*　　*

Out on the street, in the winter sunshine, I try to put my doubts behind me. George Street is still littered with coloured paper from last night's celebrations: after six years of bloodshed – bombings and sieges, plagues and famines – the Chinese civil war finally seems to be over. I feel a surge of elation, just looking down at the tattered remnants of the streamers and reminding myself of the glorious news.

I hug myself and head for Town Hall station. Sydney is going through its coldest June in years, with clear skies bringing sub-zero nights, and frosts lasting long into the mornings. I try to picture myself as a Gleisner robot, striding along the very same route, but choosing not to feel the bite of the wind. It's a cheerful prospect – and I'll be untroubled by anything so tedious as the swelling around my artificial knee and hip joints, once I'm wholly and harmoniously artificial. Unafraid of influenza, pneumonia, or the latest wave of drug-resistant diphtheria sweeping the globe.

I can hardly believe that I've finally signed the contracts and set the machinery in motion, after so many years of making excuses and putting it off. Shaken out of my complacency by a string of near misses: bronchitis, a kidney infection, a mela-noma *on the sole of my right foot*. The cytokine injections don't get my immune system humming the way they did twenty years ago. *One hundred and seven, this August*. The number sounds surreal. But then, so did *twenty-seven*, so did *forty-three*, so did *sixty-one*.

On the train, I examine my qualms one more time, hoping to

lay them to rest. Transition dreams are impossible to avoid, or predict, or control . . . just like ordinary dreams. They'll have a radically different origin, but there's no reason to believe that a different means of invoking the contents of my scrambled brain will give rise to an experience any more disturbing than anything I've already been through. *What horrors do I think are locked up in my skull, waiting to run amok in the data stream from comatose human to comatose machine?* I've suffered occasional nightmares – and a few have been deeply distressing, at the time – but even as a child, I never feared sleep. So why should I fear the transition?

Alice is in the garden, picking string beans, as I come over the hill from Meadowbank station. She straightens up and waves to me. I can never quite believe the size of our vegetable patch, so close to the city. We kiss, and walk inside together.

'Did you book the scan?'

'Yes. Tenth of July.' It should sound matter-of-fact, like that; of all the operations I've had in the last ten years, this will be the safest. I start making coffee; I need something to warm me. The kitchen is luminous with sunlight, but it's colder indoors than out.

'And they answered all your questions? You're happy now?'

'I suppose so.' There's no point keeping it to myself, though; I tell her about the transition dreams.

She says, 'I love the first few seconds after waking from a dream. When the whole thing's still fresh in your mind but you can finally put it in context. When you know exactly what you've been through.'

'You mean the relief of discovering that none of it was real? You didn't actually slaughter a hundred people in a shopping arcade? Stark naked? The police aren't closing in on you after all? It works the other way too, though. Beautiful delusions turning to dust.'

She snorts. 'Anything which turns to dust that easily is no great loss.'

I pour coffee for both of us. Alice muses, 'Transition dreams must have strange endings, though, if you know nothing about them before they start and nothing again by the time they finish.' She stirs her coffee, and I watch the liquid sloshing from rim to rim. 'How would time pass, in a dream like that? It can't run straight through, can it? The closer the computers came to reconstructing every detail of the comatose brain, the less room there'd be for spurious information. At the very beginning, though, there wouldn't be any information at all. Somewhere in the middle, there'd be the most leeway for "memories" of the dream. So maybe time would flow in from the start and the finish, and the dream would seem to end in the middle. What do you think?'

I shake my head. 'I can't even imagine what that would be like.'

'Maybe there are two separate dreams. One running forwards, one running backwards.' She frowns. 'But if they met in the middle, they'd both have to end the same way. How could two different dreams have exactly the same ending, right down to the same memories of everything which happened before? And then, there's the scanner building up its map of the brain . . . and the second stage, transforming that map into the Copy. Two cycles. Two dreams? Or four? Or do you think they'd all be woven together?'

I say irritably, 'I really don't care. I'm going to wake up inside a Gleisner robot, and it will all be academic. I won't have *dreamed any dreams* at all.'

Alice looks dubious. 'You're talking about thoughts and feelings. As real as anything the Copy will feel. How can that be academic?'

'I'm *talking about* a lot of arithmetic. And when you add up everything it does to me, it will all cancel out in the end. Comatose human to comatose machine.'

'Ashes to ashes, dust to dust.'

Words just come out of her mouth sometimes: fragments of

nursery rhymes, lines from old songs – she has no say in it. The hairs stand up on my arms, though. I look down at my withered fingers, my scrawny wrists. *This isn't me.* Ageing feels like a mistake, a detour, a misadventure. When I was twenty years old I was immortal, wasn't I? It's not too late to find my way back.

Alice murmurs, 'I'm sorry.'

I look up at her. 'Let's not make a big deal of this. It's time for me to become a machine. And all I have to do is close my eyes and step across the gap. Then in a few years, it will be your turn. We can do this. There's nothing to stop us. It's the easiest thing in the world.'

I reach across the table and take her hand. When I touch her, I realise I'm shivering with cold.

She says, 'There, there.'

*   *   *

I can't sleep. *Two dreams? Four dreams? Meeting in the middle? Merging into one?* How will I know when they're finally over? The Gleisner robot will emerge from its coma, and blithely carry on; but without a chance to look back on the transition dreams, and recognise them for what they were, how will I ever put them in their place?

I stare up at the ceiling. *This is insane.* I must have had a thousand dreams which I've failed to remember on waking – gone now, for ever, as surely as if my amnesia was computer-controlled and guaranteed. Does it matter if I was terrified of some ludicrous dream-apparition, or believed I'd committed some unspeakable crime, and now I'll never have the chance to laugh off those delusions?

I climb out of bed and, once I'm up, I have no choice but to dress fully to keep from freezing. Since moonlight fills the room, I have no trouble seeing what I'm doing. Alice turns over in her sleep, and sighs. Watching her, a wave of tenderness sweeps through me. *At least I'm going first.* At least I'll be able to reassure her that there's nothing to fear.

In the kitchen, I find I'm not hungry or thirsty at all. I pace to keep warm.

What am I afraid of? It's not as if the dreams were a barrier to be surmounted – a test I might fail, an ordeal I might not survive. The whole transition process will be predetermined, and it *will* carry me safely into my new incarnation. Even if I dream some laborious metaphor for my 'arduous' journey from human to machine – trekking barefoot across an endless plain of burning coals, struggling through a blizzard towards the summit of an unclimbable mountain . . . *and even if I fail to complete that journey* – the computers will grind on, the Gleisner robot will wake, regardless.

I need to get out of the house. I leave quietly, heading for the twenty-four-hour supermarket opposite the railway station.

The stars are mercilessly sharp; the air is still. If I'm colder than I was by day, I'm too numb to tell the difference. There's no traffic at all, no lights in any of the houses. It must be almost three; I haven't been out this late in . . . decades. The grey tones of suburban lawns by moonlight look perfectly familiar, though. When I was seventeen, I seemed to spend half my life talking with friends into the early morning, then trudging home through empty streets exactly like these.

The supermarket's windows glow blue-white around the warmer tones of the advertising signs embedded within them. I enter the building, and explore the deserted aisles. Nothing tempts me, but I feel an absurd pang of guilt about leaving empty-handed, so I grab a carton of milk.

A middle-aged man tinkering with one of the advertising holograms nods at me as I carry my purchase through the exit gate, magnetic fields sensing and recording the transaction.

The man says, 'Good news about the war?'

'Yes! It's wonderful!'

I start to turn away; he seems disappointed. 'You don't remember me, do you?'

I pause and examine him more carefully. He's balding, brown-eyed, kindly-looking. 'I'm sorry.'

'I used to own this shop when you were a boy. I remember you coming in, buying things for your mother. I sold up and left town – eighty-five years ago – but now I'm back, and I've bought the old place again.'

I nod and smile, although I still don't recognise him.

He says, 'I was in a virtual city, for a while. There was a tower which went all the way to the moon. I climbed the stairs to the moon.'

I picture a crystalline spiral staircase, sweeping up through the blackness of space.

'You came out, though. Back into the world.'

'I always wanted to run the old place again.'

I think I remember his face now, but his name still eludes me, if I ever knew it.

I can't help asking: 'Before you were scanned, did they warn you about something called transition dreams?'

He smiles, as if I'd spoken the name of a mutual friend. 'No. Not then. But later, I heard. You know, the Copies used to flow from machine to machine. As the demand for computing power went up and down, and exchange rates shifted, the management software used to take us apart and move us. From Japan, to California, to Texas, to Switzerland. It would break us down into a billion data packets and send us through the network by a thousand different routes, and then put us back together again. Ten times a day, some days.'

My skin crawls. 'And . . . *the same thing happened*? Transition dreams?'

'That's what I heard. We couldn't even tell that we'd been shipped across the planet; it felt to us like no time had passed at all. But I heard rumours that the mathematicians had proved that there were dreams in the data at every stage. In the Copy left behind, as they erased it. In the Copy being pieced together at the new destination. Those Copies had no way of knowing that they were only intermediate steps in the process of moving a frozen snapshot from one place to another – and the changes being made to their digitised brains weren't supposed to *mean* anything at all.'

'So did you stop it happening? Once you found out?'

He chuckles. 'No. There would have been no point. Because even in the one computer, Copies were moved all the time: relocated, shuffled from place to place, to allow memory to be reclaimed and consolidated. Hundreds of times a second.'

My blood turns to ice. *No wonder the old companies never raised the subject of transition dreams.* I was wiser than I ever knew to wait for the Gleisner robots. Merely shifting a Copy around in memory could hardly be comparable to mapping every synapse in a human brain – the dreams it generated would have to be far shorter, far simpler – but just knowing that my life was peppered with tiny mental detours, eddies of consciousness in the wake of every move, would still have been too much to bear.

I head home, clutching the milk carton awkwardly with cold arthritic fingers.

As I come over the hill, I see the light on above our front door, although I'm certain that I left the house in darkness. Alice must have woken and found me missing. I wince at my thoughtlessness; I should have stayed in, or written her a note. I quicken my step.

Fifty metres from home, a tendril of pain flickers across my chest. I look down stupidly to see if I've walked into a protruding branch; there's nothing, but the pain returns – solid as an arrow through the flesh, now – and I sink to my knees.

The bracelet on my left wrist chimes softly, to tell me that it's calling for help. I'm so close to my own front door, though, that I can't resist the urge to rise to my feet and see if I can make the distance.

After two steps, the blood rushes from my head, and I fall again. I crush the milk carton against my chest, spilling the cold liquid, freezing my fingers. I can hear the ambulance in the distance. I know I should relax and keep still, but something compels me to move.

I crawl towards the light.

*   *   *

The orderly pushing me looks like he's just decided that this is the last place on Earth he'd choose to be. I silently concur, and tip my head back to escape his fixed grimace, but then the sight of the ceiling going by above me is even more disconcerting. The corridor's lighting panels are so similar, and their spacing so regular, that it feels as though I'm being wheeled around in a circle.

I say, 'Where's Alice? My wife?'

'No visitors now. There'll be time for that later.'

'I've paid for a scan. With the Gleisner people. If I'm in any danger, they should be told.' All of this is encoded in my bracelet, though; the computers will have read it, there's nothing to fret about. The prospect of having to confront the transition in a matter of hours or minutes fills me with claustrophobic dread, but better that than having left the arrangements too late.

The orderly says, 'I think you're wrong about that.'

'What?' I struggle to get him in sight again. He's grinning nastily, like a nightclub bouncer who's just spotted someone with the wrong kind of shoes.

'I said, I think you're mistaken. Our records don't mention any payment for a scan.'

I break into a sweat of indignation. 'I signed the contracts! Today!'

'Yeah, yeah.' He reaches into a pocket and pulls out a handful of long cotton bandages, then proceeds to stuff them into my mouth. My arms are strapped to my sides; all I can do is grunt in protest, and gag on cotton and saliva.

Someone steps in front of the trolley and keeps pace with us, whispering in Latin.

The orderly says, 'Don't feel bad. The top level's just the tip of the iceberg. The crest of the wave. How many of us can belong to an elite like that?'

I cough and choke, fighting for breath, shuddering with panic; then I calm myself, and force myself to breathe slowly and evenly through my nose.

'The tip of the iceberg! Do you think the organic brain moves by some kind of magic? From place to place? *From moment to moment?* Do you think an empty patch of space-time can be rebuilt into something as complex as a human brain, *without transition dreams*? The physical world has as much trouble shuffling data as any computer. Do you know how much effort it goes to, just to keep *one atom* persisting in the very same spot? Do you think there could *ever* be one coherent, conscious self, enduring through time – without a billion fragmentary minds forming and dying all around it? Transition dreams blossoming, and vanishing into oblivion? The air's thick with them. *Look!*'

I twist my head around and stare down at the floor. The trolley is surrounded by convoluted vortices of light, rainbow sheets like cranial folds, flowing, undulating, spinning off smaller versions of themselves.

'What did you think? You were Mr Big? The one in a billion? The one on top?'

Another spasm of revulsion and panic sweeps through me. I choke on saliva, shivering with fear and cold. Whoever is walking ahead of the trolley lays an icy hand on my forehead; I jerk free.

I struggle to find some solid ground. *So this is my transition dream.* All right. I should be grateful: at least I understand what's happening. Bausch's warning has helped me, after all. And I'm not in any danger; the Gleisner robot is still going to

171

wake. Soon I'll forget this nightmare, and carry on with my life as if nothing had happened. Invulnerable. Immortal.

Carry on with my life. *With Alice, in the house with the giant vegetable garden?* Sweat flows into my eyes; I blink it away. The vegetable garden was at my parents' house. In the back yard, not the front. And that house was torn down long ago.

So was the supermarket opposite the railway station.

Where did I live, then?

What did I do?

Who did I marry?

The orderly says cheerfully, 'So-called Alice taught you in primary school. Ms Something-or-other. A crush on the teacher, who'd have guessed?'

Then, do I have anything straight? The interview with Bausch—?

'Ha ha. Do you think our clever friends at Gleisner would have come right out and *told you* all that? Pull the other one.'

Then how could I know about transition dreams?

'You must have worked it all out for yourself. From the inside. Congratulations.'

The icy hand touches my forehead again; the murmured chant grows louder. I screw my eyes shut, racked with fear.

The orderly says thoughtfully, 'Then again, I could be wrong about that teacher. You could be wrong about that house. There might not even be a Gleisner Corporation. Computerised Copies of human brains? Sounds pretty dodgy to me.'

Strong hands seize me by the shoulders and legs, lift me from the trolley and spin me around. When the blur of motion stops, I'm flat on my back, staring up at a distant rectangle of pale-blue sky.

'Alice' leans into view, and tosses a clod of soil. I ache to comfort her, but I can't move or speak. How can I care so much about her if I didn't love her, if she was never real? Other

172

mourners throw in dirt; none of it seems to touch me, but the sky vanishes in pieces.

Who am I? What do I know for sure about the man who'll wake inside the robot? I struggle to pin down a single certain fact about him, but under scrutiny everything dissolves into confusion and doubt.

Someone chants, 'Ashes to ashes, coma to coma.'

I wait in the darkness, colder than ever.

There's a flickering of light and motion around me. The rainbow vortices, the eddies of transition dreams, weave through the soil like luminous worms – as if even parts of my decomposing brain might be confusing their decay with the chemistry of thought, reinterpreting their disintegration from within, undistracted by the senses, or memory, or truth.

Spinning themselves beautiful delusions, and mistaking death for something else entirely.

SILVER FIRE

I was in my office at home, grading papers for Epidemiology 410, when the call came through from John Brecht in Maryland. Realtime, not a polite message to be dealt with whenever I chose. I'd grown into the habit of thinking of Colonel Brecht as 'my old boss'. Apparently that had been premature.

He said, 'We've found a little Silver Fire anomaly which I think might interest you, Claire. A little blip on the autocorrelation transform which just won't go away. And seeing as you're on vacation—'

'My *students* are on vacation. I still have work to do.'

'Oh, I think Columbia can find someone to take over those menial tasks for a week or two.'

I regarded him in silence for a moment, trying to decide whether or not to tell him to find someone else to take over his own *menial tasks*.

I said, 'What exactly are we talking about?'

Brecht smiled. 'A faint trail. Hovering on the verge of significance. Your specialty.' A map appeared on the screen; his face shrank to an inset. 'It seems to start in North Carolina, around Greensboro, heading west.' The map was peppered with dots marking the locations of recent Silver Fire cases – colour-coded by the time elapsed since a notional 'day of infection', the dots themselves positioned wherever the patient had been at the time. Having been told exactly what to look for, I could just make out a vague spectral progression cutting through the scattered blossoms of localised outbreaks: a kind of smudged rainbow trail from red to violet, dissolving into uncertainty just west of Knoxville, Tennessee. Then again . . . if I squinted, I could discern another structure, about as convincing, sweeping down in an amazingly perfect arc from Kentucky. A few more minutes, and I'd see the hidden face of Groucho Marx. The human brain is far too good at finding patterns; without rigorous statistical tools we're helpless, animists grasping at meaning in every random puff of air.

I said, 'So how do the numbers look?'

'The P value's borderline,' Brecht conceded. 'But I still think it's worth checking out.'

The visible part of this hypothetical trail spanned at least ten days. *Three days* after exposure to the virus, the average person was either dead or in intensive care – not driving blithely across the countryside. Maps tracing the precise routes of infection generally looked like random walks with mean free paths five or ten kilometres long; even air travel, at worst, tended to spawn a multitude of scattered small outbreaks. If we'd stumbled on someone who was infectious but asymptomatic, then that was definitely *worth checking out*.

Brecht said, 'As of now, you have full access to the notifications database. I'd offer you our provisional analysis, but I'm sure you can do better with the raw data yourself.'

'No doubt.'

'Good. Then you can leave tomorrow.'

*   *   *

I woke before dawn and packed in ten minutes, while Alex lay cursing me in his sleep. Then I realised I had three hours to kill, and absolutely nothing left to do, so I crawled back into bed. When I woke for the second time, Alex and Laura were both up, and eating breakfast.

As I sat down opposite Laura, though, I wondered if I was dreaming: one of those insidiously reassuring no-need-to-wake-because-you-already-have dreams. My fourteen-year-old daughter's face and arms were covered in alchemical and zodiacal symbols in iridescent reds, greens and blues. She looked like a character in some dire VR-as-psychedelia movie who'd been mauled by the special-effects software.

She stared back at me defiantly, as if I'd somehow expressed disapproval. In fact, I hadn't yet worked my way around to such a mundane emotion – and by the time I did, I kept my mouth firmly shut. Knowing Laura, these were definitely not fakes which would wash off, but transdermal enzyme patches could still erase them as bloodlessly as the dye-bearing ones which had implanted them. So I was good, I didn't say a word: no cheap reverse-psychology ('Oh, aren't they *sweet*?'), no (honest) complaints about the harassment I'd get from her principal if they weren't gone by the start of term.

Laura said, 'Did you know that Isaac Newton spent more time on alchemy than he did on the theory of gravity?'

'Yes. Did you know he also died a virgin? Role models are great, aren't they?'

Alex gave me a sideways warning look, but didn't buy in. Laura continued, 'There's a whole secret history of science that's been censored from the official accounts. Hidden knowledge that's only coming to light now that everyone has access to the original sources.'

It was hard to know how to respond honestly to this without groaning aloud. I said evenly, 'I think you'll find that most of it has actually "come to light" before. It's just turned out to be of limited interest. But sure, it's fascinating to see some of the blind alleys people have explored.'

Laura smiled at me pityingly. '*Blind alleys!*' She finished picking the toast crumbs off her plate, then she rose and left the room with a spring in her step, as if she'd won some kind of battle.

I said plaintively, 'What did I miss? When did all this start?'

Alex was unfazed. 'I think it's mostly just the music. Or, rather, three seventeen-year-old boys with supernaturally perfect skin and big brown contact lenses, called The Alchemists—'

'Yes, I *know* the band, but New Hermetics is more than the bubblegum music, it's a major cult—'

He laughed. 'Oh, come on! Wasn't your sister deeply in lust with the lead singer of some quasi-Satanic heavy-metal group? I don't recall her ending up nailing black cats to upside-down crucifixes.'

'That was never *lust*. She just wanted to discover his hair-care secrets.'

Alex said firmly, 'Laura is fine. Just . . . relax and sit it out. Unless you want to buy her a copy of *Foucault's Pendulum*?'

'She'd probably miss the irony.'

He prodded me on the arm; mock-violence, but genuine anger. '*That's* unfair. She'll chew up New Hermetics and spit it out in . . . six months, at the most. How long did Scientology last? A week?'

I said, '*Scientology* is crass, transparent gibberish. New Hermetics has five thousand years of cultural adornment to draw on. It's every bit as insidious as Buddhism or Catholicism: there's a tradition, there's a whole aesthetic—'

Alex cut in, 'Yes, and in six months' time she'll understand: the aesthetic can be appreciated without swallowing any of the bullshit. Just because alchemy was a blind alley, that doesn't mean it isn't still elegant and fascinating . . . but *being* elegant and fascinating doesn't render a word of it true.'

I reflected on that for a while, then I leant over and kissed him. 'I hate it when you're right: you always make it sound so obvious. I'm too damn protective, aren't I? She'll work it all out for herself.'

'You know she will.'

I glanced at my watch. '*Shit*. Can you drive me to La Guardia? I'm never going to get a cab now.'

*   *   *

Early in the pandemic, I'd pulled a few strings and arranged for a group of my students to observe a Silver Fire patient close up. It had seemed wrong to bury ourselves in the abstractions of maps and graphs, numerical models and extrapolations – however vital they were to the battle – without witnessing the real physical condition of an individual human being.

We didn't have to don biohazard suits; the young man lay in a glass-walled, hermetically sealed room. Tubes brought him oxygen, water, electrolytes and nutrients – along with antibiotics, antipyritics, immunosuppressants, and pain killers. No bed, no mattress; the patient was embedded in a transparent polymer gel: a kind of buoyant semi-solid which limited pressure sores and drew away the blood and lymphatic fluid weeping out through what used to be his skin.

I surprised myself by crying, silently and briefly, hot tears of anger. Rage dissipating into a vacuum; I knew there was no one to blame. Half the students had medical degrees – but if anything, they seemed more shaken than the green statisticians who'd never set foot in a trauma ward or an operating theatre – probably because they could better imagine what the man would have been feeling without a skull full of opiates.

The official label for the condition was Systemic Fibrotic Viral Scleroderma, but SFVS was unpronounceable, and apparently people's eyes glazed over if news readers spelt out four whole letters. I used the new name like everyone else, but I never stopped loathing it. It was too fucking poetic by far.

When the Silver Fire virus infected fibroblasts in the subcutaneous connective tissue, it caused them to go into overdrive, manufacturing vast quantities of collagen – in a variant form transcribed from the normal gene but imperfectly assembled. This denatured protein formed solid plaques in the extracellular space, disrupting the nutrient flow to the dermis above and eventually becoming so bulky as to shear it off completely. Silver Fire flayed you from within. A good strategy for releasing large amounts of virus, maybe – though when it had stumbled on the trick, no one knew. The presumed animal host in which the parent strain lived, benignly or otherwise, was yet to be found.

If the lymph-glistening sickly white of naked collagen plaques was 'silver', the fever, the autoimmune response, and the sensation of being burned alive was 'fire'. Mercifully, the pain couldn't last long, either way. The standard First World palliative treatment included constant deep anaesthesia – and if you didn't get that level of high-tech intervention, you went into shock, fast, and died.

Two years after the first outbreaks, the origin of the virus remained unknown, a vaccine was still a remote prospect and, though patients could be kept alive almost indefinitely, all attempts to effect a cure by purging the body of the virus and grafting cultured skin had failed.

Four hundred thousand people had been infected, worldwide; nine out of ten were dead. Ironically, rapid onset due to malnutrition had all but eliminated Silver Fire in the poorest nations; most outbreaks in Africa had burned themselves out on the spot. The US not only had more hospitalised victims on life support, per capita, than any other nation; it was heading for the top of the list in the rate of new cases.

A handshake or even a ride in a packed bus could transmit the virus – with a low probability for each contact event, but it added up. The only thing that helped in the medium term was isolating potential carriers, and to date it had seemed that no one could remain infectious and healthy for long. If the 'trail' Brecht's computers had found was more than a statistical mirage, cutting it short might save dozens of lives – and understanding it might save thousands.

*　　*　　*

It was almost noon when the plane touched down at the Triad airport on the outskirts of Greensboro. There was a hire car waiting for me; I waved my notepad at the dashboard to transmit my profile, then waited as the seating and controls rearranged themselves slightly, piezoelectric actuators humming. As I started to reverse out of the parking bay, the stereo began a soothing improvisation, flashing up a deadpan title: *Music for Leaving Airports on 11 June 2008*.

I got a shock driving into town: there were dozens of large plots of tobacco visible from the road. The born-again weed was encroaching everywhere, and not even the suburbs were safe. The irony had become clichéd, but it was still something to witness the reality first-hand: even as nicotine was finally going the way of absinthe, more tobacco was being cultivated than ever before – because tobacco mosaic virus had turned out to be an extremely convenient and efficient vector for introducing new genes. The leaves of these plants would be loaded with pharmaceuticals or vaccine antigens – and worth twenty times as much as their unmodified ancestors at the height of demand.

My first appointment was still almost an hour away, so I drove around town in search of lunch. I'd been so wound up since Brecht's call, I was surprised at just how good I felt to have arrived. Maybe it was no more than travelling south, with the sudden slight shift in the angle of the light – a kind of beneficent latitudinal equivalent of jet lag. Certainly, everything in downtown Greensboro appeared positively luminous after NYC, with modern buildings in pastel shades looking curiously harmonious beside the gleamingly preserved historic ones.

I ended up eating sandwiches in a small diner and going through my notes again, obsessively. It was seven years since I'd done anything like this for real, and I'd had little time to make the mental transition from theoretician back to practitioner.

There'd been four new cases of Silver Fire in Greensboro in the preceding fortnight. Health authorities everywhere had long ago given up trying to establish the path of infection for every last case; given the ease of transmission, and the inability to question the patients themselves, it was a massively labour-intensive process which yielded few tangible benefits. The most useful strategy wasn't backtracking, but rather quarantining the family, workmates and other known contacts of each new case for about a week. Carriers were infectious for two or three days at the most before becoming – very obviously – sick themselves; you didn't need to go looking for them. Brecht's rainbow trail either meant an exception to this rule or a ripple of new cases propagating from town to town without any single carrier.

Greensboro's population was about a quarter of a million, though it depended on exactly where you drew the boundaries. North Carolina had never gone in much for implosive urbanisation; growth in rural areas had actually outstripped growth in the major cities in recent years, and the microvillage movement had taken off here in a big way – at least as much as on the west coast.

I displayed a contoured population density map of the region on my notepad; even Raleigh, Charlotte and Greensboro were only modest elevations against the gently undulating background of the countryside, and only the Appalachians themselves cut a deep trench through this inverted topography. Hundreds of small new communities dotted the map, between the already numerous established towns. The microvillages weren't literally self-sustaining, but they were definitely high-tech Green, with photovoltaics, small-scale local water treatment, and satellite links in lieu of connections to any centralised utilities. Most of their income came from cottage service industries: software, design, music, animation.

I switched on an overlay showing the estimated magnitude of population flows, on the timescale relevant to Silver Fire. The major roads and highways glowed white hot, and the small towns were linked into the skein by their own slender capillaries, but the microvillages all but vanished from the scene: everyone worked from home. So it wasn't all that unlikely for a random Silver Fire outbreak to have spread straight down the interstate, rather than diffusing in a classic drunkard's walk across this relatively populous landscape.

Still . . . the whole point of being here was to find out the one thing that none of the computer models could tell me: whether or not the assumptions they were based on were dangerously flawed.

* * *

I left the diner and set to work. The four cases came from four separate families; I was in for a long day.

All the people I interviewed were out of quarantine, but still suffering various degrees of shock. Silver Fire hit like an express train: there was no time to grasp what was happening before a perfectly healthy child or parent, spouse or lover, all but died in front of your eyes. The last thing you needed was a two-hour interrogation by a total stranger.

It was dusk by the time I reached the last family, and any joy I'd felt at being back in the field had long since worn off. I sat in the car for a minute, staring at the immaculate garden and lace curtains, listening to the crickets, wishing I didn't have to go in and face these people.

Diane Clayton taught high-school mathematics; her husband, Ed, was an engineer, working night shifts for the local power company. They had a thirteen-year-old daughter, Cheryl. Mike, eighteen, was in the hospital.

I sat with the three of them, but it was Ms Clayton who did most of the talking. She was scrupulously patient and courteous with me, but after a while it became clear that she was still in a kind of daze. She answered every question slowly and thoughtfully, but I had no idea if she really knew what she was saying, or whether she was just going through the motions on autopilot.

Mike's father wasn't much help, since the shiftwork had kept him out of synch with the rest of the family. I tried increasing eye contact with Cheryl, encouraging her to speak.

It was absurd, but I felt guilty even as I did it – as if I'd come here to sell the family some junk product, and now I was trying to bypass parental resistance.

'So . . . Tuesday night he definitely stayed home?' I was filling in a chart of Mike Clayton's movements for the week before symptoms appeared – hour-by-hour. It was a fastidious, nit-picking Gestapo routine that made the old days of merely asking for a list of sexual partners and fluids exchanged seem positively idyllic.

'Yes, that's right.' Diane Clayton screwed her eyes shut and ran through her memories of the night again. 'I watched some television with Cheryl, then went to bed around . . . eleven. Mike must have been in his room all the time.' He'd been on vacation from UNC Greensboro, with no reason to spend his evenings studying, but he might have been socialising electronically, or watching a movie.

Cheryl glanced at me uncertainly, then said shyly, 'I think he went out.'

Her mother turned to her, frowning. 'Tuesday night? No!'

I asked Cheryl, 'Do you have any idea where?'

'Some nightclub, I think.'

'He said that?'

She shrugged. 'He was dressed for it.'

'But he didn't say where?'

'No.'

'Could it have been somewhere else? A friend's place? A party?' My information was that no nightclubs in Greensboro were open on Tuesdays.

Cheryl thought it over. 'He said he was going dancing. That's all he said.'

I turned back to Diane Clayton; she was clearly upset at being cut out of the discussion. 'Do you know who he might have gone with?'

If Mike was in a steady relationship he hadn't mentioned the fact, but she gave me the names of three old school friends. She kept apologising to me for her 'negligence'.

I said, 'It's all right. Really. No one can remember every last detail.'

She was still distraught when I left, an hour later. Her son going out without telling her – or the fact that he'd told her, and it had slipped her mind – was now (somehow) the reason for the whole tragedy.

I felt partly to blame for her distress, though I didn't see how I could have handled things any differently. The hospital would have offered her expert counselling – that wasn't my job at all. And there was sure to be more of the same ahead; if I started taking it personally, I'd be a wreck in a matter of days.

I managed to track down all three friends before eleven – about the latest I dared call anyone – but none of them had been with Mike on Tuesday night, or had any idea where he'd been. They helped me cross-check some other details, though. I ended up sitting in the car making calls for almost two hours.

Maybe there'd been a party, maybe there hadn't. Maybe it had been a pretext for something else; the possibilities were endless. Blank spots on the charts were a matter of course; I could have spent a month in Greensboro trying to fill them all in, without success. If the hypothetical carrier *had* been at this hypothetical party (and the other three members of the Greensboro Four definitely hadn't – they were all accounted for on the night), I'd just have to pick up the trail further on.

I checked into a motel and lay awake for a while, listening to the traffic on the interstate; thinking of Alex and Laura – and trying to imagine the unimaginable.

But it couldn't happen to them. They were mine. I'd protect them.

How? By moving to Antarctica?

Silver Fire was rarer than cancer, rarer than heart disease, rarer than death by automobile. Rarer than gunshot wounds, in some cities. But there was no strategy for avoiding it – short of complete physical isolation.

And Diane Clayton was now torturing herself for failing to keep her eighteen-year-old son locked up for the summer vacation. Asking herself, over and over: *What did I do wrong? Why did this happen? What am I being punished for?*

I should have taken her aside, looked her squarely in the eye, and reminded her: 'This is not your fault! There's nothing you could have done to prevent it!'

I should have said: *It just happened. People suffer like this for no reason. There is no sense to be made of your son's ruined life. There is no meaning to be found here. Just a random dance of molecules.*

*   *   *

I woke early and skipped breakfast; I was on the I-40, heading west, by seven-thirty. I drove straight past Winston-Salem; a couple of people had been infected there recently, but not recently enough to be part of the trail.

Sleep had taken the edge off my pessimism. The morning was cool and clear, and the countryside was stunning – or at least, it was where it hadn't been turned over to monotonous biotech crops, or worse: golf courses.

Still, some things had definitely changed for the better. It was on the I-40, more than twenty years before, that I'd first heard a radio evangelist preaching the eighties' gospel of hate: AIDS as God's instrument, HIV as the righteous virus sent down from Heaven to smite adulterers, junkies and faggots. (I'd been young and hot-headed, then; I'd pulled off at the next exit, phoned the radio station, and heaped abuse on some poor receptionist.) But proponents of this subtle theology had fallen curiously silent ever since an immortalised cell line derived from the bone marrow of a Kenyan prostitute had proved more than a match for the omnipotent deity's secret weapon. And if Christian fundamentalism wasn't exactly dead and buried, its power base had certainly gone into decline; the kind of ignorance and insularity it relied upon seemed to be becoming almost impossible to sustain against the tide of information.

Local audio had long since shifted to the net, of course, evangelists and all; the old frequencies had fallen silent. And I was out of range of cellular contact with the beast with 20,000 channels, but the car did have a satellite link. I switched on my notepad, hoping for some light relief.

I'd programmed Ariadne, my knowledge miner, to scan all available media outlets for references to Silver Fire. Maybe it was sheer masochism, but there was something perversely fascinating about the distorted shadow the real pandemic cast in the shallows of media space: rumours and misinformation, hysteria, exploitation.

The tabloid angles, as always, were predictably inane: Silver Fire was a disease from space / the inevitable result of fluoridation / the reason half a dozen celebrities had disappeared from the public gaze. Three false modes of transmission were on offer: today it was tampons, Mexican orange juice, and mosquitoes (again). Several young victims with attractive 'before' shots and family members willing to break down on camera had been duly rounded up. New century, same old foxshit.

The most bizarre item in Ariadne's latest sweep wasn't classic tabloid at all, though. It was an interview on a program called *The Terminal Chat Show* (23.00 GMT, Thursdays, on Britain's Channel 4) with a Canadian academic, James Springer, who was touring the UK (in the flesh) to promote his new hypertext, *The Cyber Sutras*.

Springer was a balding, middle-aged, avuncular man. He was introduced as Associate Professor of Theory at McGill University; apparently only the hopelessly reductionist asked: 'Theory of *what*?' His area of expertise was described as 'computers and spirituality' – but, for reasons I couldn't quite fathom, his opinion was sought on Silver Fire.

'The crucial thing,' he insisted smoothly, 'is that Silver Fire is the very first plague of the Information Age. AIDS was certainly post-industrial and post-modernist, but its onset predated the emergence of true Information Age cultural sensibilities. AIDS, for me, embodied the whole negative *Zeitgeist* of Western materialism confronting its inevitable *fin-de-siècle* crisis of confidence, but with Silver Fire I think we're free to embrace far more positive metaphors for this so-called "disease".'

The interviewer enquired warily, 'So . . . you're hopeful that Silver Fire victims will be spared the stigmatisation and hysteria that accompanied AIDS?'

Springer nodded cheerfully. 'Of course! We've made enormous strides forward in cultural analysis since those days! I mean, if Burroughs' *Cities of the Red Night* had only penetrated the collective subconscious more fully when it appeared, the whole course of the AIDS plague might have been radically different – and that's a hot topic in Uchronic Studies, which one of my doctoral students is currently pursuing. But there's no doubt that Information Age cultural forms have fully prepared us for Silver Fire. When I look at global techno-anarchist raves, trading-card tattoo body comics, and affordable desktop implementations of the Dalai Lama . . . it's clear to me that Silver Fire is a sequence of RNA whose time has come. If it didn't exist, we'd have to synthesise it!'

*   *   *

My next stop was a town called Statesville. A brother and sister in their late teens, Ben and Lisa Walker, and the sister's boyfriend, Paul Scott, were in hospital in Winston-Salem. The families had only just returned home.

Lisa and Ben had been living with their widower father and a nine-year-old brother. Lisa had worked in a local store, alongside the owner, who'd remained symptom-free. Ben had worked in a vaccine-extraction plant, and Paul Scott had been unemployed, living with his mother. Lisa seemed the most likely of the three to have become infected first; in theory, all it took was an accidental brush of skin against skin as a credit card changed hands – albeit with only a 1-in-100 chance of transmission. In the larger cities, some people who dealt with the public in the flesh had taken to wearing gloves, and some (arguably paranoid) subway commuters covered every square centimetre of skin below the neck, even in midsummer, but the absolute risk was so small that few strategies like this had become widespread.

I grilled Mr Walker as gently as I could. His children's movements for most of the week were like clockwork; the only time during the window of infection when they'd been any-where but work or home was Thursday night. Both had been out until the early hours, Lisa visiting Paul, Ben visiting his girlfriend, Martha Amos. Whether the couples had gone any-where, or stayed in, he wasn't certain, but there wasn't much happening locally on a weeknight, and they hadn't mentioned driving out of town.

I phoned Martha Amos; she told me that she and Ben had been at her house, alone, until about two. Since she hadn't been infected, presumably Ben had picked up the virus from his sister sometime later – and Lisa had either been infected by Paul that night, or vice versa.

According to Paul's mother, he'd barely left the house all week, which made him an unlikely entry point. Statesville seemed to be making perfect sense: customer to Lisa in the store (Thursday afternoon), Lisa to Paul (Thursday night), Lisa to Ben (Friday morning). Next stop, I'd ask the store owner what she remembered about their out-of-town customers that day.

But then Ms Scott said, 'Thursday night, Paul was over at the Walkers until late. That's the only time he went out, that I can think of.'

'He went to see Lisa? She didn't come here?'

'No. He left for the Walkers, about half-past eight.'

'And they were just going to hang around the house? They had nothing special planned?'

'Paul doesn't have a lot of money, you know. They can't afford to go out much – it's not easy for them.' She spoke in a relaxed, confiding tone, as if the relationship, with all its minor tribulations, had merely been put on hold. I hoped someone would be around to support her when the truth struck home in a couple of days.

I called at Martha Amos's house. I hadn't paid close enough attention to her when I'd phoned; I could see now that she was not in good shape.

I asked her, 'Did Ben happen to tell you where his sister went with Paul Scott on Thursday night?'

She stared at me expressionlessly.

'I'm sorry, I know this is intrusive, but no one else seems to know. If you can remember anything he said, it could be very helpful.'

Martha said, 'He told me to say he was with me. I always covered for him. His father wouldn't have . . . *approved*.'

'Hang on. Ben wasn't with you on Thursday night?'

'I went with him a couple of times. But it's not my kind of thing. The people are all right. The music's shit, though.'

'Where? Are you talking about some bar?'

'No! *The villages*. Ben and Paul and Lisa went out to the villages, Thursday night.' She suddenly focused on me properly, for the first time since I'd arrived; I think she'd finally realised that she hadn't been making a lot of sense. 'They hold "Events". Which are just dance parties, really. It's no big deal. Only, Ben's father would assume it's all about *drugs*. Which it's not.' She put her face in her hands. 'But that's where they caught Silver Fire, isn't it?'

'I don't know.'

She was shaking; I reached across and touched her arm. She looked up at me and said wearily, 'You know what hurts the most?'

'What?'

'I didn't go with them. I keep thinking: *If I'd gone, it would have been all right*. They wouldn't have caught it then. I would have kept them safe.'

She searched my face, as if for some hint as to what she might have done. *I was hunting down Silver Fire, wasn't I?* I ought to have been able to tell her, precisely, how she could have warded off the curse: what magic she hadn't performed, what sacrifice she hadn't made.

And I'd seen this a thousand times before, but I still didn't know what to say. All it took was the shock of grief to peel away the veneer of understanding: *Life is not a morality play. Disease is just disease; it carries no hidden meaning. There are no gods we failed to appease, no elemental spirits we failed to bargain with*. Every sane adult knew this, but the knowledge was still only skin deep. At some level, we still hadn't swallowed the hardest-won truth of all: *The universe is indifferent*.

Martha hugged herself, rocking gently. 'I know it's crazy, thinking like that. But it still hurts.'

*   *   *

I spent the rest of the day trying to find someone who could tell me more about Thursday night's 'Event' (such as where, exactly, it had taken place; there were at least four possibilities within a twenty-kilometre radius). I had no luck, though; it seemed microvillage culture was very much a minority taste, and Statesville's only three enthusiasts were now *incommunicado*. Drugs weren't the issue with most of the people I talked to; they just seemed to think the villagers were boring tech-heads with appalling taste in music.

Another night, another motel. It was beginning to feel like old times.

Mike Clayton had gone dancing, somewhere, on the Tuesday night. *Out in the villages?* Presumably he hadn't travelled quite this far, but an unknown person – a tourist, maybe –

might easily have been at both Events: Tuesday night near Greensboro, Thursday night near Statesville. If this was true, it would narrow down the possibilities considerably – at least compared with the number of people who'd simply passed through the towns themselves.

I pored over road maps for a while, trying to decide which village would be easiest to add to the next day's itinerary. I'd searched the directories for some kind of 'microvillage nightlife' web site – in vain, but that didn't mean anything. The address had no doubt made its way, by electronic diffusion, to everyone who was genuinely interested; and whichever village I went to, half a dozen people were sure to know all about the Events.

I climbed into bed around midnight, but then reached for my notepad again, to check with Ariadne. Silver Fire had made the big time: video fiction. There was a reference in the latest episode of NBC's 'hit sci-fi drama', *Mutilated Mystic Empaths in N-Space*.

I'd heard of the series, but never watched it before, so I quickly scanned the pilot. 'Don't you know the first law of astronavigation! Ask a *computer* to solve equations in *17-dimensional hyper-geometry* . . . and its rigid, deterministic, linear mind would shatter like a diamond dropped into a black hole! Only *twin telepathic Buddhist nuns*, with seventh-dan black belts in karate, and enough self-discipline to *hack their own legs from their bodies*, could ever hope to master the *intuitive skills* required to navigate the treacherous quantum fluctuations of N-space and rescue that stranded fleet!'

'My God, Captain, you're right – but where will we find . . . ?'

MME was set in the twenty-second century, but the Silver Fire reference was no clumsy anachronism. Our heroines miscalculate a difficult trans-galactic jump (breathing the wrong way during the recitation of a crucial mantra), and end up in present-day San Francisco. There, a small boy and his dog, on the run from Mafia hitmen, help them repair a vital component in their Tantric Energy Source. After humiliating the assassins with a perfectly choreographed display of legless martial arts amid the scaffolding of a high-rise construction site, they track down the boy's mother to a hospital, where she turns out to be infected with Silver Fire.

The camera angles here grow coy. The few glimpses of actual flesh are sanitised fantasies: glowing ivory, smooth and dry.

The boy (whose recently slaughtered accountant-for-the-mob father concealed the truth from him) bursts into tears when he sees her.

But the MMEs are philosophical: 'These well-meaning doctors and nurses will tell you that your Mom has suffered a terrible fate – but in time, the truth will be understood by all. Silver Fire is the closest we can come, in this world, to the Ecstasy of Unbeing. You observe only the frozen shell of her body, but inside, in the realm of *shunyata*, a great and wonderful transformation is at work.'

'Really?'

'Really.'

Boy dries tears, theme music soars, dog jumps up and licks everyone's faces. Cathartic laughter all round.

(Except, of course, from the mother.)

*   *   *

The next day, I had appointments in two small towns further along the highway. The first patient was a divorced forty-five-year-old man, a technician at a textile factory. Neither his brother nor his colleagues could offer me much help; for all they knew, he could have driven to a different town (or village) every single night during the period in question.

In the next town, a couple in their mid-thirties and their eight-year-old daughter had died. The symptoms must have hit all three more or less simultaneously – and escalated more rapidly than usual – because no one had managed to call for help.

The woman's sister told me without hesitation, 'Friday night, they would have gone out to the villages. That's what they usually did.'

'And they would have taken their daughter?'

She opened her mouth to reply, but then froze and just stared at me, mortified, as if I was blaming her sister for recklessly exposing the child to some unspeakable danger. There were photographs of all three on the mantelpiece behind her. This woman had discovered their disintegrating bodies.

I said gently, 'No place is safer than any other. It only looks that way in hindsight. They could have caught Silver Fire anywhere at all – and I'm just trying to trace the path of the infection, after the event.'

She nodded slowly. 'They always took Phoebe. She loved the villages; she had friends in most of them.'

'Do you know which village they went to, that night?'

'I think it was Herodotus.'

Out in the car, I found it on the map. It wasn't much further from the highway than the one I'd chosen purely for convenience; I could probably drive out there and still make it to the next motel by a civilised hour.

I clicked on the tiny dot; the information window told me: *Herodotus, Catawba County. Population 106, established 2004.*

I said, 'More.'

The map said, 'That's all.'

*   *   *

Solar panels, twin satellite dishes, vegetable gardens, water tanks, boxy prefabricated buildings . . . there was no single component of the village which couldn't have been found on almost any large rural property. It was only seeing all of them thrown together in the middle of the countryside that was startling. Herodotus resembled nothing so much as a twentieth-century artist's impression of a pioneering settlement on some Earth-like – but definitely alien – planet.

A major exception was the car park, discreetly hidden behind the huge banks of photovoltaic cells. With only a bus and two other cars, there was room for maybe a hundred more vehicles. Visitors were clearly welcome in Herodotus; there wasn't even a meter to feed.

Despite the prefabs, there was no army-camp feel to the layout; the buildings obeyed some symmetry I couldn't quite parse, clustered around a central square, but they certainly weren't lined up in rows like quonset huts. As I entered the square, I could see a basketball game in progress in a court off to one side; teenagers playing, and younger children watching. It was the only obvious sign of life. I approached, feeling a bit like a trespasser, even if this was as much a public space as the main street of any ordinary town.

I stood by the other spectators and watched the game for a while. None of the children spoke to me, but it didn't feel like I was being actively snubbed. The teams were mixed-sex, and play was intense but good-natured. The kids were Anglo-, African-, Chinese-American. I'd heard rumours that certain villages were 'effectively segregated' – whatever that meant – but it might well have been nothing but propaganda.

The microvillage movement had stirred some controversy when it started, but the lifestyle wasn't exactly radical. A hundred or so people – who would have worked from their homes in towns or cities anyway – pooled their resources and bought some cheap land out in the country, making up for the lack of amenities with a few state-of-the-art technological fixes. Residents were just as likely to be stockbrokers as artists or musicians and, though any characterisation was bound to be unfair, most villages were definitely closer to yuppie sanctuaries than anarchist communes.

I couldn't have faced the physical isolation, myself – and no amount of bandwidth would have compensated – but if the people here were happy, all power to them. I was ready to concede that in fifty years' time, living in Queens would be looked on as infinitely more perverse and inexplicable than living in a place like Herodotus.

A young girl, six or seven years old, tapped my arm.

I smiled down at her. 'Hello.'

She said, 'Are you on the trail of happiness?'

Before I could ask her what she meant, someone called out, 'Hello there!'

I turned; it was a woman – in her mid-twenties, I guessed – shielding her eyes from the sun. She approached, smiling, and offered me her hand.

'I'm Sally Grant.'

'Claire Booth.'

'You're a bit early for the Event. It doesn't start until nine-thirty.'

'I—'

'So if you want a meal at my place, you'd be welcome.'

I hesitated. 'That's very kind of you.'

'Ten dollars sound fair? That's what I'd charge if I opened the cafeteria – only there were no bookings tonight, so I won't be.'

I nodded.

'Well, drop in around seven. I'm number twenty-three.'

'Thank you. Thank you very much.'

I sat on a bench in the village square, shaded from the sunset by the hall in front of me, listening to the cries from the basketball court. I knew I should have told Ms Grant straight away what I was doing here; shown her my ID, asked the questions I was permitted to ask, and left. *But mightn't I learn more by staying to watch the Event? Informally?* Even a few crude first-hand observations of the demographics of this unmodelled contact between the villagers and the other local populations might be useful – and though the carrier was

195

obviously long gone, this was still a chance to get a very rough profile of the kind of person I was looking for.

Uneasily, I came to a decision. There was no reason not to stay for the party and no need to make the villagers anxious and defensive by telling them why I was here.

*　　*　　*

From the inside, the Grants' house looked more like a spacious, modern apartment than a factory-built box which had been delivered on the back of a truck to the middle of nowhere. I'd been unconsciously expecting the clutter of a mobile home, with too many mod cons per cubic metre to leave room to breathe, but I'd misjudged the scale completely.

Sally's husband, Oliver, was an architect. She edited travel guides by day; the cafeteria was a sideline. They were founding residents, originally from Raleigh; there were still only a handful of later arrivals. Herodotus, they explained, was self-sufficient in (vegetarian) staple foods, but there were regular deliveries of all the imports any small town relied on. They both made occasional trips to Greensboro, or interstate, but their routine work was pure telecommuting.

'And when you're not on holidays, Claire?'

'I'm an administrator at Columbia.'

'That must be fascinating.' It certainly turned out to be a good choice; my hosts changed the subject back to themselves immediately.

I asked Sally, 'So what clinched the move for you? Raleigh's not exactly the crime capital of the nation.' I found it hard to believe that the real-estate prices could have driven them out, either.

She replied without hesitation, 'Spiritual criteria, Claire.'

I blinked.

Oliver laughed pleasantly. 'It's all right, you haven't come to the wrong place!' He turned to his wife. 'Did you see her face?

You'd think she'd stumbled onto some enclave of *Mormons* or *Baptists*!'

Sally explained, apologetically, 'I meant the word in its broadest sense, of course: an understanding that we need to *resensitise ourselves* to the *moral dimensions* of the world around us.'

That left me none the wiser, but she was clearly expecting a sympathetic response. I said tentatively, 'And you think . . . living in a small community like this makes your civic responsibilities clearer, more readily apparent?'

Now Sally was bemused. 'Well . . . yes, I suppose it does. But that's just politics, really, isn't it? Not *spirituality*. I meant . . .' She raised her hands, and beamed at me. 'I just *meant* the reason you're here, yourself! We came to Herodotus to find – for a lifetime – what you've come here to find for a few hours, yourself!'

* * *

I heard the other cars begin to arrive while I sat drinking coffee with Sally in the living room. Oliver had excused himself for an urgent meeting with a construction manager in Tokyo. I passed the time with small-talk about Alex and Laura, and my Worst Ever New York Experience horror stories – some of which were true. It wasn't a lack of curiosity that kept me from probing Sally about the Event, I was just afraid of alerting her to the fact that I had no idea what I'd let myself in for. When she left me for a minute, I scanned the room – without rising from my chair – for any sign of what she might have *come here to find for a lifetime*. All I had time to take in were a few CD covers, the half-dozen visible ones on a large rotating rack. Most looked like modern music/video, from bands I'd never heard of. There was one familiar title, though: James Springer's *The Cyber Sutras*.

By the time the three of us crossed the square and approached the village hall – a barn-like structure, resembling a very large cargo container – I was quite tense. There were thirty or forty people in the square, most but not all in their late teens or early twenties, dressed in the kind of diverse mock-casual clothing that might have been seen outside any nightclub in the country. *So what was I afraid was going to happen?* Just because Ben Walker couldn't tell his father about it, and Mike Clayton couldn't tell his mother, didn't mean I'd wandered into some southern remake of *Twin Peaks*. Maybe bored kids just snuck out to the villages to pop hallucinogens at dance parties – my own youth resurrected before my eyes, with safer drugs and better light shows.

As we approached the hall, a small group of people filed in through the self-opening doors, giving me a brief glimpse of bodies silhouetted against swirling lights, and a blast of music. My anxiety began to seem absurd. Sally and Oliver were into psychedelics, that was all, and Herodotus's founders had apparently decided to create a congenial environment in which to use them. I paid the sixty-dollar entry fee, smiling with relief.

Inside, the walls and ceiling were ablaze with convoluted patterns: soft-edged multi-hued fractals pulsing with the music, like vast colour-coded simulations of turbulent fluids cascading down giant fret-boards at Mach 5. The dancers cast no shadows; these were high-power wall-screens, not projections. Stunning resolution – and astronomically expensive.

Sally pressed a fluorescent-pink capsule into my hand. Harmony or Halcyon, maybe; I no longer knew what was fashionable. I tried to thank her and offer some excuse about 'saving it for later', but she didn't hear a word, so we just smiled at each other meaninglessly. The hall's sound insulation was extraordinary (which was lucky for the other villagers); I would never have guessed from outside that my brain was going to be puréed.

Sally and Oliver vanished into the crowd. I decided to hang around for half an hour or so, then slip out and drive on to the motel. I stood and watched the people dancing, trying to keep my head clear despite the stupefying backdrops, though I doubted that I could learn much about the carrier that I didn't already know. *Probably under twenty-five. Probably not towing small children.* Sally had given me all the details I needed to obtain information on Events from here to Memphis – past and future. The search was still going to be difficult, but at least I was making progress.

A sudden loud cheer from the crowd broke through the music – *and the room was transformed before my eyes.* For a moment I was utterly disorientated, and even when the world began to make visual sense again, it took me a while to get the details straight.

The wall-screens now showed dancers in identical rooms to the one I was standing in; only the ceiling continued to play the abstract animation. These identical rooms all had wall-screens themselves, which also showed identical rooms full of dancers . . . much like the infinite regress between a pair of mirrors.

And at first, I thought the 'other rooms' were merely realtime images of the Herodotus dance hall itself. But the swirling vortex pattern on the ceiling joined seamlessly with the animation on the ceilings of 'adjacent' rooms, combining to form a single complex image; there was no repetition, reflected or otherwise. And the crowds of dancers were *not* identical, though they all looked sufficiently alike to make it hard to be sure, from a distance. Belatedly, I turned around and examined the closest wall, just four or five metres away. A young man 'behind' the screen raised a hand in greeting, and I returned the gesture automatically. We couldn't quite make convincing eye contact – and wherever the cameras were placed, that would have been a lot to ask for – but it was, still, almost possible to believe that nothing really separated us but a thin wall of glass.

The man smiled dreamily and walked away.

I had goosebumps. This was nothing new in principle, but the technology here had been pushed to its limits. The sense of being in an infinite dance hall was utterly compelling; I could see no 'furthest hall' in any direction (and when they ran out of real ones, they could have easily recycled them). The flatness of the images, the incorrect scaling as you moved, and the lack of parallax (worst of all when I tried to peer into the 'corner rooms' between the main four, which 'should' have been possible, but wasn't) served more to make the space beyond the walls appear exotically distorted than to puncture the effect. The brain actually struggled to compensate, to cover up the flaws – and if I'd swallowed Sally's capsule, I doubt I would have been nit-picking. As it was, I was grinning like a child on a fairground ride.

I saw people dancing facing the walls, loosely forming couples or groups across the link. I was mesmerised; I forgot all thoughts of leaving. After a while, I bumped into Oliver, who was swaying happily by himself. I screamed into his ear, 'These are all other villages?' He nodded, and shouted back, 'East is east and west is west!' Meaning . . . the virtual layout followed real geography – it just abolished the intervening distances? I recalled something James Springer had said in his *Terminal Chat Show* interview: *We must invent a new cartography, to re-chart the planet in its newborn, protean state. There is no separation, now. There are no borders.*

Yeah . . . and the world was just one giant party. Still, at least they weren't splicing-in live connections to war zones. I'd seen enough we-dance/you-dodge-shells 'solidarity' in the nineties to last a lifetime.

It suddenly occurred to me: *If the carrier really was travelling from Event to Event, then he or she was 'here' with me, right now. My quarry had to be one of the dancers in this giant, imaginary hall.*

And this fact implied no opportunity, let alone any kind of danger. It wasn't as if Silver Fire carriers conveniently fluoresced in the dark. But it still felt like the strangest moment of a long, strange night: to understand that the two of us were finally 'connected', to understand that I'd 'found' the object of my search.

Even if it did me no good at all.

*   *   *

Just after midnight – as the novelty was wearing off, and I was finally making up my mind to leave – some of the dancers began cheering loudly again. This time it took me even longer to see why. People started turning to face the east, and excitedly pointing something out to each other.

Weaving through one of the distant crowds of dancers, in a village three screens removed, were a number of human figures. They might have been naked, some male, some female, but it was hard to be sure: they could only be seen in glimpses, and they were shining so brightly that most details were swamped in their sheer luminosity.

They glowed an intense silver-white. The light transformed their immediate surroundings, though the effect was more like a halo of luminous gas, diffusing through the air, than a spotlight cast on the crowd. The dancers around them seemed oblivious to their presence, as did those in the intervening halls; only the people in Herodotus paid them the kind of attention their spectacular appearance deserved. I couldn't yet tell whether they were pure animation, with plausible paths computed through gaps in the crowd, or unremarkable (but real) actors, enhanced by software.

My mouth was dry. I couldn't believe that the presence of these silver figures could be pure coincidence, but what were they meant to signify? Did the people of Herodotus know about the string of local outbreaks? That wasn't impossible; an independent analysis might have been circulated on the net. Maybe this was meant as some kind of bizarre 'tribute' to the victims.

I found Oliver again. The music had softened, as if in deference to the vision, and he seemed to have come down a little; we managed to have something approaching a conversation.

I pointed to the figures – who were now marching smoothly straight through the image of the image of a wall-screen, proving themselves entirely virtual.

He shouted, 'They're walking the Trail of Happiness!'

I mimed incomprehension.

'Healing the land for us! Making amends! Undoing the Trail of Tears!'

The trail of tears? I was lost for a while, then a memory from high school surfaced abruptly. The 'Trail of Tears' was the brutal forced march of the Cherokee from what was now part of Georgia, all the way to Oklahoma, in the 1830s. Thousands had died along the way; some had escaped, and hidden in the Appalachians. Herodotus, I was fairly sure, was hundreds of kilometres from the historical route of the march, but that didn't seem to be the point. As the silver figures moved across the dance floor twice-removed, I could see them spreading their arms wide, as if performing some kind of benediction.

I shouted, 'But what does *Silver Fire* have to do with—?'

'Their bodies are frozen, so their spirits are free to walk the Trail of Happiness through cyberspace for us! Didn't you know? That's what Silver Fire is *for*! To renew everything! To bring happiness to the land! *To make amends!*' Oliver beamed at me with absolute sincerity, radiating pure goodwill.

I stared at him in disbelief. This man, clearly, hated no one, but what he'd just spewed out was nothing but a New Age remix of the rantings of that radio evangelist, twenty years before, who'd seized upon AIDS as the incontrovertible proof of his own *spiritual beliefs*.

I shouted angrily, 'Silver Fire is a merciless, agonising—'

Oliver tipped his head back and laughed, uproariously, without a trace of malice – as if I was the one telling ghost stories.

I turned and walked away.

The trail-walkers split into two streams as they crossed the hall immediately to the east of us. Half went north, half went south, as they 'detoured around' Herodotus. They couldn't move among us, but this way the illusion remained almost seamless.

And if I'd been drugged out of my skull? If I'd embraced the whole mythology of the Trail of Happiness and come here hoping to see it confirmed? In the morning, would I have half believed that the roaming spirits of Silver Fire patients had marched right past me?

Bestowing their luminous blessing on the crowd.

Near enough to touch.

* * *

I threaded my way towards the camouflaged exit. Outside, the cool air and the silence were surreal; I felt more disembodied and dreamlike than ever. I staggered towards the car park, and waved my notepad to make the hire car flash its lights.

My head cleared as I approached the highway. I decided to drive on through the night; I was so agitated that I didn't think I had much chance of sleeping. I could find a motel in the morning, take a shower, and catch a nap before my next appointment.

I still didn't know what to make of the Event – what solid link there could be between the carrier and the villagers' mad syncretic cyberbabble. If it was nothing but coincidence, the irony was grotesque, but what was the alternative? *Some 'pilgrim' on the Trail of Happiness, deliberately spreading the virus?* The idea was ludicrous – and not just because it was unthinkably obscene. A carrier could only *know* that he or she had been infected if distinctive symptoms had appeared, but *distinctive symptoms* only marked the brutal end stage of the disease; a prolonged mild infection, if such a thing existed, would be indistinguishable from influenza. Once Silver Fire progressed far enough to affect the visible layers of the skin,

203

the only options for cross-country travel all involved flashing lights and sirens.

* * *

At about half-past three in the morning, I switched on my notepad. I wasn't exactly drowsy, but I wanted something to keep me alert.

Ariadne had plenty.

First, a heated debate on *The Reality Studio* – a program on the Intercampus Ideas Network. A freelance zoologist from Seattle named Andrew Feld spoke first, putting the case that Silver Fire 'proved beyond doubt' his 'controversial and paradigm-subverting' S-force theory of life, which 'combined the transgressive genius of Einstein and Sheldrake with the insights of the Maya and the latest developments in superstrings, to create a new, life-affirming biology to take the place of soulless, mechanistic Western science'.

In reply, virologist Margaret Ortega from UCLA explained in detail why Feld's ideas were superfluous, failed to account for – or clashed directly with – numerous observed biological phenomena, and were neither more nor less 'mechanistic' than any other theory which didn't leave everything in the universe to the whim of God. She also ventured the opinion that most people were capable of *affirming life* without casually discarding all of human knowledge in the process.

Feld was a clueless idiot on a wish-fulfilment trip. Ortega wiped the floor with him.

But when the nationwide audience of students voted, he was declared winner by a majority of two to one.

Next item: Protesters were blockading the Medical Research Laboratories of the Max Planck Institute in Hamburg, calling for an end to Silver Fire research. Safety was not the issue. Protest organiser and 'acclaimed cultural agitator' Kid Ransom had held an impromptu press conference:

'We must reclaim Silver Fire from the grey, small-minded

scientists, and learn to tap its wellspring of mythical power for the benefit of all humanity! These technocrats who seek to *explain* everything are like vandals rampaging through a gallery, scrawling equations on all the beautiful works of art!'

'But how will humanity ever find a cure for this disease, without research?'

'There is no such thing as disease! There is only trans-formation!'

There were four more news stories, all concerning (mutually exclusive) proclamations about the 'secret truth' (or secret ineffability) behind Silver Fire, and maybe each one, alone, would have seemed no more than a sad, sick joke. But as the countryside materialised around me – the purple-grey ridge of the Black Mountains to the north starkly beautiful in the dawn – I was slowly beginning to understand. *This was not my world any more.* Not in Herodotus, not in Seattle, not in Hamburg or Montreal or London. Not even in New York.

In my world, there were no nymphs in trees and streams. No gods, no ghosts, no ancestral spirits. *Nothing* – outside our own cultures, our own laws, our own passions – existed in order to punish us or comfort us, to affirm any act of hatred or love.

My own parents had understood this perfectly, but theirs had been the first generation to be so free of the shackles of superstition. And after the briefest flowering of understanding, my own generation had grown complacent. At some level, we must have started taking it for granted that *the way the universe worked* was now obvious to any child, even though it went against everything innate to the species: the wild, undisciplined love of patterns, the craving to extract meaning and comfort from everything in sight.

We thought we were passing on everything that mattered to our children: science, history, literature, art. Vast libraries of information lay at their fingertips. But we hadn't fought hard enough to pass on the hardest-won truth of all: *Morality comes only from within. Meaning comes only from within. Outside our own skulls, the universe is indifferent.*

Maybe, in the West, we'd delivered the death blows to the old doctrinal religions, the old monoliths of delusion, but that victory meant nothing at all.

Because taking their place now, everywhere, was the saccharine poison of *spirituality*.

* * *

I checked into a motel in Asheville. The parking lot was full of campervans, people heading for the national parks; I was lucky, I got the last room.

My notepad chimed while I was in the shower. An analysis of the latest data reported to the Centres for Disease Control showed the 'anomaly' extending almost two hundred kilometres further west along the I-40 – about halfway to Nashville. *Five more people on the Trail of Happiness.* I sat and stared at the map for a while, then I dressed, packed my bag again, and checked out.

I made ten calls as I was driving up into the mountains, cancelling all my appointments with relatives from Asheville to Jefferson City, Tennessee. The time had passed for being cautious and methodical, for gathering every last scrap of data along the way. I *knew* the transmission had to be taking place at the Events; the only question was whether it was accidental or deliberate.

Deliberate how? With a vial full of fibroblasts, teeming with Silver Fire? It had taken researchers at the NIH over a year to learn how to culture the virus – and they'd only succeeded in March. I couldn't believe that their work had been replicated by amateurs in less than three months.

The highway plunged between the lavish wooded slopes of the Great Smoky Mountains, following the Pigeon River most of the way. I programmed a predictive model – by voice – as I drove. I had a calendar for the Events, now, and I had five approximate dates of infection. Case notifications would always be too late; the only way to catch up was to extrapolate. And I could only assume that the carrier would continue moving steadily westwards, never lingering, always travelling on to the next Event.

I reached Knoxville around midday, stopped for lunch, then drove straight on.

The model said: *Pliny, Saturday 14 Jan., 9.30 p.m.* My first chance to search the infinite dance hall for the carrier, without an impassable wall between us.

My first chance to be in the presence of Silver Fire.

* * *

I arrived early, but not so early as to attract the attention of Pliny's equivalents of Sally and Oliver. I stayed in the car for an hour, improvising ways to look busy, recording the licence numbers of arriving vehicles. There were a lot of four-wheel drives and utilities, and a few campervans. Many villagers favoured bicycles, but the carrier would need to have been a real fanatic – and extremely fit – to have cycled all the way from Greensboro.

The Event followed much the same pattern as the one in Herodotus the night before, though Herodotus itself wasn't taking part. The crowd was similar, too: mostly young, but with enough exceptions to keep me from looking completely out of place. I wandered around, trying to commit every face to memory without attracting too much attention. *Had all these people swallowed the Silver Fire myth, as I'd heard it from Oliver?* The possibility was almost too bleak to contemplate. The only thing that gave me any hope was that when I'd compared the number of villages listed on the Event calendar with the number in the region, it was less than one in twenty. The microvillage movement itself had nothing to do with this insanity.

Someone offered me a pink capsule – not for free, this time. I gave her twenty dollars, and pocketed the drug for analysis. There was a slender chance that someone was passing out doctored capsules, although stomach acid tended to make short work of the virus.

A handsome blond kid barely in his twenties hovered around me for a while as the trail-walkers appeared. When they'd vanished into the west, he approached me, took my elbow, and made an offer I couldn't quite hear over the music, though I thought I got the gist of it. I was too distracted to feel amazed or flattered, let alone tempted, and I got rid of him in five seconds flat. He walked away looking wounded, but not long afterwards I saw him leaving with a woman half my age.

I stayed to the very end – and on Saturday nights, that meant five in the morning. I staggered out into the light, discouraged, although I didn't know what I'd seriously hoped to see. *Someone walking around with an aerosol spray, administering doses of Silver Fire?* When I reached the car park I realised that many of the cars had arrived after I'd gone in – and some might have come and gone unseen. I recorded the licence plates I'd missed, trying to be discreet, but almost past caring; I hadn't slept for thirty-six hours.

*   *   *

The nearest Event west of Pliny, on Sunday night, was past the Mississippi and halfway across Arkansas; I made a calculated guess that the carrier would take this as an opportunity for a night off.

Monday evening, I drove into Eudoxus – population 165, established 2002, about an hour from Nashville – ready to spend all night in the car park if I had to. I needed to record every licence plate, or there wasn't much point being here.

I hadn't told Brecht what I was doing; I still had no solid evidence, and I was afraid of sounding paranoid. I'd called Alex before leaving Nashville, but I hadn't told him much, either. Laura had declined to speak to me when he'd called out and told her I was on the line, but that was nothing new. I missed them both already, more than I'd anticipated, but I wasn't sure how I'd manage when I finally made it home, to a daughter who was turning away from reason, and a husband who took it for granted that any bright adolescent would recapitulate five thousand years of intellectual progress in six months.

Thirty-five vehicles arrived between ten and eleven – none I'd seen before – and then the flow tapered off abruptly. I scanned the entertainment channels on my notepad, satisfied by anything with colour and movement; I'd had enough of Ariadne's bad news.

Just before midnight, a blue Ford campervan rolled up and parked in the corner opposite me. A young man and a young woman got out; they seemed excited, but a little wary, as if they couldn't quite believe that their parents weren't watching from the shadows.

As they crossed the car park, I realised that the guy was the blond kid who'd spoken to me in Pliny.

I waited five minutes, then went and checked their licence plate; it was a Massachusetts registration. I hadn't recorded it on Saturday night, so I would have missed the fact that they were following the Trail, if one of them hadn't—

Hadn't *what*?

I stood there frozen behind the van, trying to stay calm, replaying the incident in my mind. I knew I hadn't let him paw me for long, *but how long would it have taken*?

I glanced up at the disinterested stars, trying to savour the irony because it tasted much better than the fear. I'd always known there'd be a risk, and the odds were still heavily in my favour. I could put myself into quarantine in Nashville in the morning; nothing I did right now would make the slightest difference . . .

But I wasn't thinking straight. If they'd *travelled together* all the way from Massachusetts, or even from Greensboro, one should have infected the other long ago. The probability of the two of them sharing the same freakish resistance to the virus was negligible, even if they were brother and sister.

They couldn't both be unwitting, asymptomatic carriers. So either they had nothing to do with the outbreaks—

—or they were transporting the virus outside their bodies, and handling it with great care.

A bumper sticker boasted: STATE-OF-THE-ART SECUR-ITY! I placed a hand against the rear door experimentally; the van didn't emit so much as a warning beep. I tried shaking the handle aggressively; still nothing. If the system was calling a security firm in Nashville for an armed response, I had all the time I needed. If it was trying to call its owners, it wouldn't have much luck getting a signal through the aluminium frame of the village hall.

There was no one in sight. I went back to my car, and fetched the toolkit.

I knew I had no legal right. There were emergency powers I could have invoked, but I had no intention of calling Maryland and spending half the night fighting my way through the correct procedures. And I knew I was putting the prosecution case at risk, by tainting everything with illegal search and seizure.

I didn't care. They weren't going to have the chance to send one more person down the Trail of Happiness, even if I had to burn the van to the ground.

I levered a small, tinted fixed window out of its rubber frame in the door. Still no wailing siren. I reached in, groped around, and unlocked the door.

I'd thought they must have been half-educated biochemists who'd learnt enough cytology to duplicate the published fibroblast-culturing techniques.

I was wrong. They were medical students, and they'd half learnt other skills entirely.

They had their friend cushioned in polymer gel, contained in something like a huge tropical fish tank. They had oxygen set up, a urethral catheter, and half a dozen drips. I played my torch beam over the inverted bottles, checking the various drugs and their concentrations. I went through them all twice, hoping I'd missed one – but I hadn't.

I shone the beam down onto the girl's skinless white face, peering through the delicate streamers of red rising up through the gel. She was in an opiate haze deep enough to keep her motionless and silent, but she was still conscious. Her mouth was frozen in a rictus of pain.

And she'd been like this for sixteen days.

I staggered back out of the van, my heart pounding, my vision going black. I collided with the blond kid; the girl was with him, and they had another couple in tow.

I turned on him and started punching him, screaming incoherently; I don't remember what I said. He put up his hands to shield his face, and the others came to his aid: pinning me gently against the van, holding me still without striking a single blow.

I was crying now. The campervan girl said, 'Sssh. It's all right. No one's going to hurt you.'

I pleaded with her. 'Don't you understand? She's in pain! *All this time, she's been in pain!* What did you think she was doing? *Smiling?*'

'Of course she's smiling. This is what she always wanted. She made us promise that if she ever caught Silver Fire, she'd walk the Trail.'

I rested my head against the cool metal, closed my eyes for a moment, and tried to think of a way to get through to them.

But I didn't know how.

When I opened my eyes, the boy was standing in front of me. He had the most gentle, compassionate face imaginable. He wasn't a torturer, or a bigot, or even a fool. He'd just swallowed some beautiful lies.

He said, 'Don't you understand? All *you* see in there is a woman dying in pain, *but we all have to learn to see more.* The time has come to regain the lost skills of our ancestors: the power to see visions, demons and angels. The power to see the spirits of the wind and the rain. The power to walk the Trail of Happiness.'

REASONS TO BE CHEERFUL

1

In September 2004, not long after my twelfth birthday, I entered a state of almost constant happiness. It never occurred to me to ask why. Though school included the usual quota of tedious lessons, I was doing well enough academically to be able to escape into daydreams whenever it suited me. At home, I was free to read books and web pages about molecular biology and particle physics, quaternions and galactic evolution, and to write my own Byzantine computer games and convoluted abstract animations. And though I was a skinny, uncoordinated child, and every elaborate, pointless organised sport left me comatose with boredom, I was comfortable enough with my body on my own terms. Whenever I ran – and I ran everywhere – it felt good.

I had food, shelter, safety, loving parents, encouragement, stimulation. Why shouldn't I have been happy? And though I can't have entirely forgotten how oppressive and monotonous classwork and schoolyard politics could be, or how easily my usual bouts of enthusiasm were derailed by the most trivial problems, when things were actually going well for me I wasn't in the habit of counting down the days until it all turned sour. Happiness always brought with it the belief that it would last, and though I must have seen this optimistic forecast disproved a thousand times before, I wasn't old and cynical enough to be surprised when it finally showed signs of coming true.

When I started vomiting repeatedly, Dr Ash, our GP, gave

me a course of antibiotics and a week off school. I doubt it was a great shock to my parents when this unscheduled holiday seemed to cheer me up rather more than any mere bacterium could bring me down, and if they were puzzled that I didn't even bother feigning misery it would have been redundant for me to moan constantly about my aching stomach when I was throwing up authentically three or four times a day.

The antibiotics made no difference. I began losing my balance, stumbling when I walked. Back in Dr Ash's surgery, I squinted at the eye chart. She sent me to a neurologist at Westmead Hospital, who ordered an immediate MRI scan. Later the same day, I was admitted as an in-patient. My parents learnt the diagnosis straight away, but it took me three more days to make them spit out the whole truth.

I had a tumour, a medulloblastoma, blocking one of the fluid-filled ventricles in my brain, raising the pressure in my skull. Medulloblastomas were potentially fatal, though with surgery, followed by aggressive radiation treatment and chemotherapy, two out of three patients diagnosed at this stage lived five more years.

I pictured myself on a railway bridge riddled with rotten sleepers, with no choice but to keep moving, trusting my weight to each suspect plank in turn. I understood the danger ahead, very clearly . . . and yet I felt no real panic, no real fear. The closest thing to terror I could summon up was an almost exhilarating rush of vertigo, as if I were facing nothing more than an audaciously harrowing fairground ride.

There was a reason for this.

The pressure in my skull explained most of my symptoms, but tests on my cerebrospinal fluid had also revealed a greatly elevated level of a substance called Leu-enkephalin – an endorphin, a neuropeptide which bound to some of the same receptors as opiates like morphine and heroin. Somewhere along the road to malignancy, the same mutant transcription factor that had switched on the genes enabling the tumour cells to divide unchecked had apparently also switched on the genes needed to produce Leu-enkephalin.

This was a freakish accident, not a routine side-effect. I didn't know much about endorphins then, but my parents repeated what the neurologist had told them, and later I looked it all up. Leu-enkephalin wasn't an analgesic, to be secreted in emergencies when pain threatened survival, and it had no stupefying narcotic effects to immobilise a creature while injuries healed. Rather, it was the primary means of signalling happiness, released whenever behaviour or circumstances warranted pleasure. Countless other brain activities modulated that simple message, creating an almost limitless palette of positive emotions, and the binding of Leu-enkephalin to its target neurons was just the first link in a long chain of events mediated by other neurotransmitters. But for all these subtleties, I could attest to one simple, unambiguous fact: Leu-enkephalin made you feel *good*.

My parents broke down as they told me the news, and I was the one who comforted them, beaming placidly like a beatific little child martyr from some tear-jerking oncological mini-series. It wasn't a matter of hidden reserves of strength or maturity; I was physically incapable of feeling bad about my fate. And because the effects of the Leu-enkephalin were so specific, I could gaze unflinchingly at the truth in a way that would not have been possible if I'd been doped up to the eyeballs with crude pharmaceutical opiates. I was clear-headed but emotionally indomitable, positively radiant with courage.

* * *

I had a ventricular shunt installed, a slender tube inserted deep into my skull to relieve the pressure, pending the more invasive and risky procedure of removing the primary tumour; that operation was scheduled for the end of the week. Dr Maitland, the oncologist, had explained in detail how my treatment would proceed, and warned me of the danger and discomfort I faced in the months ahead. Now I was strapped in for the ride and ready to go.

Once the shock wore off, though, my un-blissed-out parents decided that they had no intention of sitting back and accepting mere two-to-one odds that I'd make it to adulthood. They phoned around Sydney, then further afield, hunting for second opinions.

My mother found a private hospital on the Gold Coast – the only Australian franchise of the Nevada-based 'Health Palace' chain – where the oncology unit was offering a new treatment for medulloblastomas. A genetically engineered herpes virus introduced into the cerebrospinal fluid would infect only the replicating tumour cells, and then a powerful cytotoxic drug, activated only by the virus, would kill the infected cells. The treatment had an 80 per cent five-year survival rate, without the risks of surgery. I looked up the cost myself, in the hospital's web brochure. They were offering a package deal: three months' meals and accommodation, all pathology and radio-logy services, and all pharmaceuticals, for sixty thousand dollars.

My father was an electrician, working on building sites. My mother was a sales assistant in a department store. I was their only child, so we were far from poverty-stricken, but they must have taken out a second mortgage to raise the fee, saddling themselves with a further fifteen or twenty years' debt. The two survival rates were not that different, and I heard Dr Maitland warn them that the figures couldn't really be compared, because the viral treatment was so new. They would have been perfectly justified in taking her advice and sticking to the traditional regime.

Maybe my Leu-enkephalin sainthood spurred them on some-how. Maybe they wouldn't have made such a great sacrifice if I'd been my usual sullen and difficult self, or even if I'd been nakedly terrified rather than preternaturally brave. I'll never know for sure, and, either way, it wouldn't make me think any less of them. But just because the molecule wasn't saturating their skulls, that's no reason to expect them to have been immune to its influence.

On the flight north, I held my father's hand all the way. We'd always been a little distant, a little mutually disappointed in each other. I knew he would have preferred a tougher, more athletic, more extroverted son, while to me he'd always seemed lazily conformist, with a world view built on unexamined platitudes and slogans. But on that trip, with barely a word exchanged, I could feel his disappointment being transmuted into a kind of fierce, protective, defiant love, and I grew ashamed of my own lack of respect for him. I let the Leu-enkephalin convince me that, once this was over, everything between us would change for the better.

* * *

From the street, the Gold Coast Health Palace could have passed for one more high-rise beach-front hotel – and even from the inside, it wasn't much different from the hotels I'd seen on video fiction. I had a room to myself, with a television wider than the bed, complete with network computer and cable modem. If the aim was to distract me, it worked. After a week of tests, they hooked a drip into my ventricular shunt and infused first the virus and then, three days later, the drug.

The tumour began shrinking almost immediately; they showed me the scans. My parents seemed happy but dazed, as if they'd never quite trusted a place where millionaire property developers came for scrotal tucks to do much more than relieve them of their money and offer first-class double-talk while I continued to decline. But the tumour kept on shrinking, and when it hesitated for two days in a row the oncologist swiftly repeated the whole procedure, and then the tendrils and blobs on the MRI screen grew skinnier and fainter even more rapidly than before.

I had every reason to feel unconditional joy now, but when I suffered a growing sense of unease instead I assumed it was just Leu-enkephalin withdrawal. It was even possible that the tumour had been releasing such a high dose of the stuff that literally nothing could have made me *feel better*: if I'd been lofted to the pinnacle of happiness, there'd be nowhere left to go but down. But in that case, any chink of darkness in my sunny disposition could only confirm the good news of the scans.

One morning I woke from a nightmare – my first in months – with visions of the tumour as a clawed parasite thrashing around inside my skull. I could still hear the click of carapace on bone, like the rattle of a scorpion trapped in a jam jar. I was terrified, drenched in sweat . . . *liberated*. My fear soon gave way to a white-hot rage: the thing had drugged me into compliance, but now I was free to stand up to it, to bellow obscenities inside my head, to exorcise the demon with self-righteous anger.

I did feel slightly cheated by the sense of anticlimax that came from chasing my already-fleeing nemesis downhill, and I couldn't entirely ignore the fact that imagining my anger to be driving out the cancer was a complete reversal of true cause and effect – a bit like watching a forklift shift a boulder from my chest, then pretending to have moved it myself by a mighty act of inhalation. But I made what sense I could of my belated emotions, and left it at that.

Six weeks after I was admitted, all my scans were clear, and my blood, CSF and lymphatic fluid were free of the signature proteins of metastasising cells. But there was still a risk that a few resistant tumour cells remained, so they gave me a short, sharp course of entirely different drugs, no longer linked to the herpes infection. I had a testicular biopsy first – under local anaesthetic, more embarrassing than painful – and a sample of bone marrow taken from my hip, so my potential for sperm production and my supply of new blood cells could both be restored if the drugs wiped them out at the source. I lost hair and stomach lining, temporarily, and I vomited more often, and far more wretchedly, than when I'd first been diagnosed. But when I started to emit self-pitying noises, one of the nurses steelily explained that children half my age put up with the same treatment for months.

These conventional drugs alone could never have cured me, but as a mopping-up operation they greatly diminished the chance of a relapse. I discovered a beautiful word: *apoptosis* – cellular suicide, programmed death – and repeated it to myself again and again. I ended up almost relishing the nausea and fatigue; the more miserable I felt, the easier it was to imagine the fate of the tumour cells, membranes popping and shrivelling like balloons as the drugs commanded them to take their own lives. *Die in pain, zombie scum!* Maybe I'd write a game about it, or even a whole series, culminating in the spectacular *Chemotherapy III: Battle for the Brain.* I'd be rich and famous, I could pay back my parents, and life would be as perfect in reality as the tumour had merely made it seem to be.

*   *   *

I was discharged early in December, free of any trace of disease. My parents were wary and jubilant in turn, as if slowly casting off the fear that any premature optimism would be punished. The side-effects of the chemotherapy were gone; my hair was growing back, except for a tiny bald patch where the shunt had been, and I had no trouble keeping down food. There was no point returning to school now, two weeks before the year's end, so my summer holidays began immediately. The whole class sent me a tacky, insincere, teacher-orchestrated get-well e-mail, but my friends visited me at home, only slightly embarrassed and intimidated, to welcome me back from the brink of death.

So why did I feel so bad? Why did the sight of the clear blue sky through the window when I opened my eyes every morning – with the freedom to sleep-in as long as I chose, with my father or mother home all day treating me like royalty, but keeping their distance and letting me sit unnagged at the computer screen for sixteen hours if I wanted – why did that first glimpse of daylight make me want to bury my face in the pillow, clench my teeth and whisper: '*I should have died. I should have died*'?

Nothing gave me the slightest pleasure. Nothing – not my favourite netzines or web sites, not the *njari* music I'd once revelled in, not the richest, the sweetest, the saltiest junk food that was mine now for the asking. I couldn't bring myself to read a whole page of any book, I couldn't write ten lines of code. I couldn't look my real-world friends in the eye, or face the thought of going online.

Everything I did, everything I imagined, was tainted with an overwhelming sense of dread and shame. The only image I could summon up for comparison was from a documentary about Auschwitz that I'd seen at school. It had opened with a long tracking shot, a newsreel camera advancing relentlessly towards the gates of the camp, and I'd watched that scene with my spirits sinking, already knowing full well what had happened inside. I wasn't delusional; I didn't believe for a moment that there was some source of unspeakable evil lurking behind every bright surface around me. But when I woke and saw the sky, I felt the kind of sick foreboding that would only have made sense if I'd been staring at the gates of Auschwitz.

Maybe I was afraid that the tumour would grow back, but not *that* afraid. The swift victory of the virus in the first round should have counted for much more, and on one level I did think of myself as lucky, and suitably grateful. But I could no more rejoice in my escape, now, than I could have felt suicidally bad at the height of my Leu-enkephalin bliss.

My parents began to worry, and dragged me along to a psychologist for 'recovery counselling'. The whole idea seemed as tainted as everything else, but I lacked the energy for resistance. Dr Bright and I 'explored the possibility' that I was subconsciously choosing to feel miserable because I'd learnt to associate happiness with the risk of death, and I secretly feared that re-creating the tumour's main symptom could resurrect the thing itself. Part of me scorned this facile explanation, but part of me seized on it, hoping that if I owned up to such sub-terranean mental gymnastics it would drag the whole process into the light of day, where its flawed logic would become untenable. But the sadness and disgust that everything induced in me – birdsong, the pattern of our bathroom tiles, the smell of toast, the shape of my own hands – only increased.

I wondered if the high levels of Leu-enkephalin from the tumour might have caused my neurons to reduce their popu-lation of the corresponding receptors, or if I'd become 'Leu-enkephalin-tolerant' the way a heroin addict became opiate-tolerant, through the production of a natural regulatory mo-lecule that blocked the receptors. When I mentioned these ideas to my father, he insisted that I discuss them with Dr Bright, who feigned intense interest but did nothing to show that he'd taken me seriously. He kept telling my parents that everything I was feeling was a perfectly normal reaction to the trauma I'd been through, and that all I really needed was time, and patience, and understanding.

*　　*　　*

I was bundled off to high school at the start of the new year, but when I did nothing but sit and stare at my desk for a week, arrangements were made for me to study online. At home, I did manage to work my way slowly through the curriculum, in the stretches of zombie-like numbness that came between the bouts of sheer, paralysing unhappiness. In the same periods of relative clarity, I kept thinking about the possible causes of my afflic-tion. I searched the biomedical literature and found a study of the effects of high doses of Leu-enkephalin in cats, but it seemed to show that any tolerance would be short-lived.

Then, one afternoon in March – staring at an electron micrograph of a tumour cell infected with herpes virus, when I should have been studying dead explorers – I finally came up with a theory that made sense. The virus needed special proteins to let it dock with the cells it infected, enabling it to stick to them long enough to use other tools to penetrate the cell membrane. But if it had acquired a copy of the Leu-enkephalin gene from the tumour's own copious RNA transcripts, it might have gained the ability to cling, not just to replicating tumour cells, but to every neuron in my brain with a Leu-enkephalin receptor.

And then the cytotoxic drug, activated only in infected cells, would have come along and killed them all.

Deprived of any input, the pathways those dead neurons normally stimulated were withering away. Every part of my brain able to feel pleasure was dying. And though at times I could, still, simply feel nothing, mood was a shifting balance of forces. With nothing to counteract it, the slightest flicker of depression could now win every tug-of-war, unopposed.

I didn't say a word to my parents; I couldn't bear to tell them that the battle they'd fought to give me the best possible chance of survival might now be crippling me. I tried to contact the oncologist who'd treated me on the Gold Coast, but my phone calls floundered in a Muzak-filled moat of automated screening, and my e-mail was ignored. I managed to see Dr Ash alone, and she listened politely to my theory, but she declined to refer me to a neurologist when my only symptoms were psychological: blood and urine tests showed none of the standard markers for clinical depression.

The windows of clarity grew shorter. I found myself spending more and more of each day in bed, staring out across the darkened room. My despair was so monotonous, and so utterly disconnected from anything real, that to some degree it was blunted by its own absurdity: no one I loved had just been slaughtered, the cancer had almost certainly been defeated, and I could still grasp the difference between what I was feeling and the unarguable logic of real grief, or real fear.

But I had no way of casting off the gloom and feeling what I wanted to feel. My only freedom came down to a choice between hunting for reasons to justify my sadness – deluding myself that it was my own, perfectly natural response to some contrived litany of misfortunes – or disowning it as something alien, imposed from without, trapping me inside an emotional shell as useless and unresponsive as a paralysed body.

My father never accused me of weakness and ingratitude; he just silently withdrew from my life. My mother kept trying to get through to me, to comfort or provoke me, but it reached the point where I could barely squeeze her hand in reply. I wasn't literally paralysed or blind, speechless or feeble-minded. But all the brightly lit worlds I'd once inhabited – physical and virtual, real and imaginary, intellectual and emotional – had become invisible, and impenetrable. Buried in fog. Buried in shit. Buried in ashes.

By the time I was admitted to a neurological ward, the dead regions of my brain were clearly visible on an MRI scan. But it was unlikely that anything could have halted the process even if it had been diagnosed sooner.

And it was certain that no one had the power to reach into my skull and restore the machinery of happiness.

2

The alarm woke me at ten, but it took me another three hours to summon up the energy to move. I threw off the sheet and sat on the side of the bed, muttering half-hearted obscenities, trying to get past the inescapable conclusion that I shouldn't have bothered. Whatever pinnacles of achievement I scaled today (managing not only to go shopping, but to buy something other than a frozen meal), and whatever monumental good fortune befell me (the insurance company depositing my allowance before the rent was due), I'd wake up tomorrow feeling exactly the same.

Nothing helps, nothing changes. Four words said it all. But

I'd accepted that long ago; there was nothing left to be disappointed about. And I had no reason to sit here lamenting the bleeding obvious for the thousandth time.

Right?

Fuck it. Just keep moving.

I swallowed my 'morning' medication, the six capsules I'd put out on the bedside table the night before, then went into the bathroom and urinated a bright-yellow stream consisting mainly of the last dose's metabolites. No antidepressant in the world could send me to Prozac Heaven, but this shit kept my dopamine and serotonin levels high enough to rescue me from total catatonia – from liquid food, bedpans and sponge baths.

I splashed water onto my face, trying to think of an excuse to leave the flat when the freezer was still half full. Staying in all day, unwashed and unshaven, did make me feel worse: slimy and lethargic, like some pale parasitic leech. But it could still take a week or more for the pressure of disgust to grow strong enough to move me.

I stared into the mirror. Lack of appetite more than made up for lack of exercise – I was as immune to carbohydrate comfort as I was to runner's high – and I could count my ribs beneath the loose skin of my chest. I was thirty years old, and I looked like a wasted old man. I pressed my forehead against the cool glass, obeying some vestigial instinct which suggested that there might be a scrap of pleasure to be extracted from the sensation. There wasn't.

In the kitchen, I saw the light on the phone: there was a message waiting. I walked back into the bathroom and sat on the floor, trying to convince myself that it didn't have to be bad news. No one had to be dead. And my parents couldn't break up twice.

I approached the phone and waved the display on. There was a thumbnail image of a severe-looking middle-aged woman, no one I recognised. The sender's name was Dr Z. Durrani, Department of Biomedical Engineering, University of

Cape Town. The subject line read: 'New Techniques in Prosthetic Reconstructive Neuroplasty'. That made a change; most people skimmed the reports on my clinical condition so carelessly that they assumed I was mildly retarded. I felt a refreshing absence of disgust, the closest I could come to respect, for Dr Durrani. But no amount of diligence on her part could save the cure itself from being a mirage.

Health Palace's no-fault settlement provided me with a living allowance equal to the minimum wage, plus reimbursement of approved medical costs; I had no astronomical lump sum to spend as I saw fit. However, any treatment likely to render me financially self-sufficient could be paid for in full, at the discretion of the insurance company. The value of such a cure to Global Assurance – the total remaining cost of supporting me until death – was constantly falling, but then so was medical research funding, worldwide. Word of my case had got around.

Most of the treatments I'd been offered so far had involved novel pharmaceuticals. Drugs *had* freed me from institutional care, but expecting them to turn me into a happy little wage-earner was like hoping for an ointment that made amputated limbs grow back. From Global Assurance's perspective, though, shelling out for anything more sophisticated meant gambling with a much greater sum – a prospect that no doubt sent my case manager scrambling for his actuarial database. There was no point indulging in rash expenditure decisions when there was still a good chance that I'd suicide in my forties. Cheap fixes were always worth a try, even if they were long shots, but any proposal radical enough to stand a real chance of working was guaranteed to fail the risk/cost analysis.

I knelt by the screen with my head in my hands. I could erase the message unseen, sparing myself the frustration of knowing exactly what I'd be missing out on . . . but then, not knowing would be just as bad. I tapped the Play button and looked away; meeting the gaze of even a recorded face gave me a feeling of intense shame. I understood why: the neural circuitry needed to

225

register positive non-verbal messages was long gone, but the pathways that warned of responses like rejection and hostility had not merely remained intact, they'd grown skewed and hypersensitive enough to fill the void with a strong negative signal, whatever the reality.

I listened as carefully as I could while Dr Durrani explained her work with stroke patients. Tissue-cultured neural grafts were the current standard treatment, but she'd been injecting an elaborately tailored polymer foam into the damaged region instead. The foam released growth factors that attracted axons and dendrites from surrounding neurons, and the polymer itself was designed to function as a network of electrochemical switches. Via microprocessors scattered throughout the foam, the initially amorphous network was programmed first to reproduce generically the actions of the lost neurons, then fine-tuned for compatibility with the individual recipient.

Dr Durrani listed her triumphs: sight restored, speech restored, movement, continence, musical ability. My own deficit – measured in neurons lost, or synapses, or raw cubic centimetres – lay beyond the range of all the chasms she'd bridged to date. But that only made it more of a challenge.

I waited almost stoically for the one small catch, in six or seven figures. The voice from the screen said, 'If you can meet your own travel expenses and the cost of a three-week hospital stay, my research grant will cover the treatment itself.'

I replayed these words a dozen times, trying to find a less favourable interpretation – one task I was usually good at. When I failed, I steeled myself and e-mailed Durrani's assistant in Cape Town, asking for clarification.

There was no misunderstanding. For the cost of a year's supply of the drugs that barely kept me conscious, I was being offered a chance to be whole again for the rest of my life.

* * *

Organising a trip to South Africa was completely beyond me,

but once Global Assurance recognised the opportunity it was facing, machinery on two continents swung into action on my behalf. All I had to do was fight down the urge to call everything off. The thought of being hospitalised, of being powerless again, was disturbing enough, but contemplating the potential of the neural prosthesis itself was like staring down the calendar at a secular Judgement Day. On 7 March 2023, I'd either be admitted into an infinitely larger, infinitely richer, infinitely better world . . . or I'd prove to be damaged beyond repair. And in a way, even the final death of hope was a far less terrifying prospect than the alternative; it was so much closer to where I was already, so much easier to imagine. The only vision of *happiness* I could summon up was myself as a child, running joyfully, dissolving into sunlight – which was all very sweet and evocative, but a little short on practical details. If I'd wanted to be a sunbeam, I could have cut my wrists anytime. I wanted a job, I wanted a family, I wanted ordinary love and modest ambitions, because I knew these were the things I'd been denied. But I could no more imagine what it would be like, finally, to attain them than I could picture daily life in twenty-six dimensional space.

I didn't sleep at all before the dawn flight out of Sydney. I was escorted to the airport by a psychiatric nurse, but spared the indignity of a minder sitting beside me all the way to Cape Town. I spent my waking moments on the flight fighting paranoia, resisting the temptation to invent reasons for all the sadness and anxiety coursing through my skull. *No one on the plane was staring at me disdainfully. The Durrani technique was not going to turn out to be a hoax.* I succeeded in crushing these 'explanatory' delusions . . . but, as ever, it remained beyond my power to alter my feelings, or even to draw a clear line between my purely pathological unhappiness and the perfectly reasonable anxiety that anyone would feel on the verge of radical brain surgery.

Wouldn't it be bliss, not to have to fight to tell the difference all the time? Forget happiness; even a future full of abject misery would be a triumph, so long as I knew that it was always for a reason.

* * *

Luke De Vries, one of Durrani's postdoctoral students, met me at the airport. He looked about twenty-five, and radiated the kind of self-assurance I had to struggle not to misread as contempt. I felt trapped and helpless immediately: he'd arranged everything; it was like stepping on to a conveyor belt. But I knew that if I'd been left to do anything for myself the whole process would have ground to a halt.

It was after midnight when we reached the hospital in the suburbs of Cape Town. Crossing the car park, the insect sounds were wrong, the air smelt indefinably alien, the constellations looked like clever forgeries. I sagged to my knees as we approached the entrance.

'Hey!' De Vries stopped and helped me up. I was shaking with fear, and then shame too, at the spectacle I was making of myself.

'This violates my Avoidance Therapy.'

'Avoidance Therapy?'

'Avoid hospitals at all costs.'

De Vries laughed, though if he wasn't merely humouring me I had no way of telling. Recognising the fact that you'd elicited genuine laughter was a pleasure, so those pathways were all dead.

He said, 'We had to carry the last subject in on a stretcher. She left about as steady on her feet as you are.'

'That's bad?'

'Her artificial hip was playing up. Not our fault.'

We walked up the steps and into the brightly lit foyer.

* * *

The next morning – Monday, 6 March, the day before the

228

operation – I met most of the surgical team who'd perform the first, purely mechanical, part of the procedure: scraping clean the useless cavities left behind by dead neurons, prising open with tiny balloons any voids that had been squeezed shut, and then pumping the whole oddly shaped totality full of Durrani's foam. Apart from the existing hole in my skull from the shunt eighteen years before, they'd probably have to drill two more.

A nurse shaved my head and glued five reference markers to the exposed skin, then I spent the afternoon being scanned. The final, three-dimensional image of all the dead space in my brain looked like a spelunker's map, a sequence of linked caves complete with rockfalls and collapsed tunnels.

Durrani herself came to see me that evening. 'While you're still under anaesthetic,' she explained, 'the foam will harden, and the first connections will be made with the surrounding tissue. Then the microprocessors will instruct the polymer to form the network we've chosen to serve as a starting point.'

I had to force myself to speak; every question I asked – however politely phrased, however lucid and relevant – felt as painful and degrading as if I was standing before her naked asking her to wipe shit out of my hair. 'How did you find a network to use? Did you scan a volunteer?' Was I going to start my new life as a clone of Luke De Vries – inheriting his tastes, his ambitions, his emotions?

'No, no. There's an international database of healthy neural structures – 20,000 cadavers who died without brain injury. More detailed than tomography; they froze the brains in liquid nitrogen, sliced them up with a diamond-tipped microtome, then stained and electron-micrographed the slices.'

My mind baulked at the number of exabytes she was casually invoking; I'd lost touch with computing completely. 'So you'll use some kind of composite from the database? You'll give me a selection of typical structures, taken from different people?'

Durrani seemed about to let that pass as near enough, but

she was clearly a stickler for detail, and she hadn't insulted my intelligence yet. 'Not quite. It will be more like a multiple exposure than a composite. We've used about 4,000 records from the database – all the males in their twenties or thirties – and wherever someone has neuron A wired to neuron B, and someone else has neuron A wired to neuron C, you'll have connections to both B *and* C. So you'll start out with a network that in theory could be pared down to any one of the 4,000 individual versions used to construct it, but in fact you'll pare it down to your own unique version instead.'

That sounded better than being an emotional clone or a Frankenstein collage; I'd be a roughly hewn sculpture, with features yet to be refined. But—

'Pare it down how? How will I go from being potentially anyone to being . . . ?' *What?* My twelve-year-old self, resurrected? Or the thirty-year-old I should have been, conjured into existence as a remix of these 4,000 dead strangers? I trailed off; I'd lost what little faith I'd had that I was talking sense.

Durrani seemed to grow slightly uneasy herself, whatever my judgement was worth on that. She said, 'There should be parts of your brain, still intact, which bear some record of what's been lost. Memories of formative experiences, memories of the things that used to give you pleasure, fragments of innate structures that survived the virus. The prosthesis will be driven automatically towards a state that's compatible with everything else in your brain; it will find itself interacting with all these other systems, and the connections that work best in that context will be reinforced.' She thought for a moment. 'Imagine a kind of artificial limb, imperfectly formed to start with, that adjusts itself as you use it: stretching when it fails to grasp what you reach for, shrinking when it bumps something unexpectedly, until it takes on precisely the size and shape of the phantom limb implied by your movements. Which itself is nothing but an image of the lost flesh and blood.'

That was an appealing metaphor, though it was hard to

believe that my faded memories contained enough information to reconstruct their phantom author in every detail – that the whole jigsaw of who I'd been, and might have become, could be filled in from a few hints along the edges and the jumbled-up pieces of 4,000 other portraits of happiness. But the subject was making at least one of us uncomfortable, so I didn't press the point.

I managed to ask a final question. 'What will it be like, before any of this happens? When I wake up from the anaesthetic and all the connections are still intact?'

Durrani confessed, 'That's one thing I'll have no way of knowing, until you tell me yourself.'

* * *

Someone repeated my name, reassuringly but insistently. I woke a little more. My neck, my legs, my back were all aching, and my stomach was tense with nausea.

But the bed was warm, and the sheets were soft. It was good just to be lying there.

'It's Wednesday afternoon. The operation went well.'

I opened my eyes. Durrani and four of her students were gathered at the foot of the bed. I stared at her, astonished: the face I'd once thought of as 'severe' and 'forbidding' was . . . riveting, magnetic. I could have watched her for hours. But then I glanced at Luke De Vries, who was standing beside her. He was just as extraordinary. I turned one by one to the other three students. Everyone was equally mesmerising; I didn't know where to look.

'How are you feeling?'

I was lost for words. These people's faces were loaded with so much significance, so many sources of fascination, that I had no way of singling out any one factor: they all appeared wise, ecstatic, beautiful, reflective, attentive, compassionate, tranquil, vibrant . . . a white noise of qualities, all positive, but ultimately incoherent.

231

But as I shifted my gaze compulsively from face to face, struggling to make sense of them, their meanings finally began to crystallise, like words coming into focus, though my sight had never been blurred.

I asked Durrani, 'Are you smiling?'

'Slightly.' She hesitated. 'There are standard tests, standard images for this, but, please, describe my expression. Tell me what I'm thinking.'

I answered unselfconsciously, as if she'd asked me to read an eye chart. 'You're . . . curious? You're listening carefully. You're interested, and you're hoping that something good will happen. And you're smiling because you think it will. Or because you can't quite believe that it already has.'

She nodded, smiling more decisively. 'Good.'

I didn't add that I now found her stunningly, almost painfully, beautiful. But it was the same for everyone in the room, male and female: the haze of contradictory moods that I'd read into their faces had cleared, but it had left behind a heart-stopping radiance. I found this slightly alarming – it was too indiscriminate, too intense – though in a way it seemed almost as natural a response as the dazzling of a dark-adapted eye. And after eighteen years of seeing nothing but ugliness in every human face, I wasn't ready to complain about the presence of five people who looked like angels.

Durrani asked, 'Are you hungry?'

I had to think about that. 'Yes.'

One of the students fetched a prepared meal, much the same as the lunch I'd eaten on Monday: salad, a bread roll, cheese. I picked up the roll and took a bite. The texture was perfectly familiar, the flavour unchanged. Two days before, I'd chewed and swallowed the same thing with the usual mild disgust that all food induced in me.

Hot tears rolled down my cheeks. I wasn't in ecstasy; the experience was as strange and painful as drinking from a fountain with lips so parched that the skin had turned to salt and dried blood.

As painful, and as compelling. When I'd emptied the plate, I asked for another. *Eating was good, eating was right, eating was necessary.* After the third plate, Durrani said firmly, 'That's enough'. I was shaking with the need for more; she was still supernaturally beautiful, but I screamed at her, outraged.

She took my arms, held me still. 'This is going to be hard for you. There'll be surges like this, swings in all directions, until the network settles down. You have to try to stay calm, try to stay reflective. The prosthesis makes more things possible than you're used to, but you're still in control.'

I gritted my teeth and looked away. At her touch I'd suffered an immediate, agonising erection.

I said, 'That's right. I'm in control.'

*   *   *

In the days that followed, my experiences with the prosthesis became much less raw, much less violent. I could almost picture the sharpest, most ill-fitting edges of the network being – metaphorically – worn smooth by use. To eat, to sleep, to be with people, remained intensely pleasurable, but it was more like an impossibly rosy-hued dream of childhood than the result of someone poking my brain with a high-voltage wire.

Of course, the prosthesis wasn't sending signals into my brain in order to make my brain feel pleasure. The *prosthesis itself* was the part of me that was feeling all the pleasure – however seamlessly that process was integrated with everything else: perception, language, cognition . . . the rest of me. Dwelling on this was unsettling at first, but on reflection no more so than the thought experiment of staining blue all the corresponding organic regions in a healthy brain, and declaring, '*They* feel all the pleasure, not you!'

I was put through a battery of psychological tests – most of which I'd sat through many times before, as part of my annual insurance assessments – as Durrani's team attempted to quantify their success. Maybe a stroke patient's fine control of a formerly paralysed hand was easier to measure objectively, but I must have leapt from bottom to top of every numerical scale for positive affect. And far from being a source of irritation, these tests gave me my first opportunity to use the prosthesis in new arenas – to be happy in ways I could barely remember experiencing before. As well as being required to interpret mundanely rendered scenes of domestic situations – what has just happened between this child, this woman, and this man; who is feeling good and who is feeling bad? – I was shown breathtaking images of great works of art, from complex allegorical and narrative paintings to elegant minimalist essays in geometry. As well as listening to snatches of everyday speech, and even unadorned cries of joy and pain, I was played samples of music and song from every tradition, every epoch, every style.

That was when I finally realised that something was wrong.

Jacob Tsela was playing the audio files and noting my responses. He'd been deadpan for most of the session, carefully avoiding any risk of corrupting the data by betraying his own opinions. But after he'd played a heavenly fragment of European classical music, and I'd rated it 20 out of 20, I caught a flicker of dismay on his face.

'What? You didn't like it?' I said.

Tsela smiled opaquely. 'It doesn't matter what I like. That's not what we're measuring.'

'I've rated it already; you can't influence my score.' I regarded him imploringly; I was desperate for communication of any kind. 'I've been dead to the world for eighteen years. I don't even know who the composer was.'

He hesitated. 'J. S. Bach. And I agree with you: it's sublime.' He reached for the touchscreen and continued the experiment.

So what had he been dismayed about? I knew the answer

immediately; I'd been an idiot not to notice before, but I'd been too absorbed in the music itself.

I hadn't scored any piece lower than 18. And it had been the same with the visual arts. From my 4,000 virtual donors I'd inherited, not the lowest common denominator, but the widest possible taste – and in ten days, I still hadn't imposed any constraints, any preferences, of my own.

All art was sublime to me, and all music. Every kind of food was delicious. Everyone I laid eyes on was a vision of perfection.

Maybe, after my long drought, I was just soaking up pleasure wherever I could get it, but it was only a matter of time before I grew sated and became as discriminating, as focused, as *particular*, as everyone else.

'Should I still be like this? *Omnivorous?*' I blurted out the question, starting with a tone of mild curiosity, ending with an edge of panic.

Tsela halted the sample he'd been playing – a chant that might have been Albanian, Moroccan, or Mongolian for all I knew, but which made hair rise on the back of my neck, and sent my spirits soaring. Just like everything else had.

He was silent for a while, weighing up competing obligations. Then he sighed and said, 'You'd better talk to Durrani.'

*   *   *

Durrani showed me a bar graph on the wallscreen in her office: the number of artificial synapses that had changed state within the prosthesis – new connections formed, existing ones broken, weakened or strengthened – for each of the past ten days. The embedded microprocessors kept track of such things, and an antenna waved over my skull each morning collected the data.

Day one had been dramatic, as the prosthesis adapted to its environment; the 4,000 contributing networks might all have been perfectly stable in their owners' skulls, but the Everyman version I'd been given had never been wired up to anyone's brain before.

Day two had seen about half as much activity, day three about a tenth.

From day four on, though, there'd been nothing but background noise. My episodic memories, however pleasurable, were apparently being stored elsewhere – since I certainly wasn't suffering from amnesia – but after the initial burst of activity, the circuitry for defining what pleasure *was* had undergone no change, no refinement at all.

'If any trends emerge in the next few days, we should be able to amplify them, push them forward – like toppling an unstable building, once it's showing signs of falling in a certain direction.' Durrani didn't sound hopeful. Too much time had passed already, and the network wasn't even teetering.

I said, 'What about genetic factors? Can't you read my genome, and narrow things down from that?'

She shook her head. 'At least 2,000 genes play a role in neural development. It's not like matching a blood group or a tissue type; everyone in the database would have more or less the same small proportion of those genes in common with you. Of course, some people must have been closer to you in temperament than others, but we have no way of identifying them genetically.'

'I see.'

Durrani said carefully, 'We could shut the prosthesis down completely, if that's what you want. There'd be no need for surgery: we'd just turn it off, and you'd be back where you started.'

I stared at her luminous face. *How could I go back?* Whatever the tests and the bar graphs said, *how could this be failure?* However much useless beauty I was drowning in, I wasn't as screwed-up as I'd been with a head full of Leu-enkephalin. I was still capable of fear, anxiety, sorrow; the tests had revealed universal shadows, common to all the donors. Hating Bach or

Chuck Berry, Chagall or Paul Klee was beyond me, but I'd reacted as sanely as anyone to images of disease, starvation, death.

And I was not oblivious to my own fate, the way I'd been oblivious to the cancer.

But what was my fate if I kept using the prosthesis? Universal happiness, universal shadows . . . half the human race dictating my emotions? In all the years I'd spent in darkness, if I'd held fast to anything, hadn't it been the possibility that I carried a kind of seed within me: a version of myself that might grow into a living person again, given the chance? *And hadn't that hope now proved false?* I'd been offered the stuff of which selves were made – and though I'd tested it all, and admired it all, I'd claimed none of it as my own. All the joy I'd felt in the last ten days had been meaningless. I was just a dead husk, blowing around in other peoples' sunlight.

I said, 'I think you should do that. Switch it off.'

Durrani held up her hand. 'Wait. If you're willing, there is one other thing we could try. I've been discussing it with our ethics committee, and Luke has begun preliminary work on the software, but in the end it will be your decision.'

'To do what?'

'The network can be pushed in any direction. We know how to intervene to do that – to break the symmetry, to make some things a greater source of pleasure than others. Just because it hasn't happened spontaneously, that doesn't mean it can't be achieved by other means.'

I laughed, suddenly light-headed. 'So, if I say the word, *your ethics committee* will choose the music I like, and my favourite foods, and my new vocation? They'll decide who I become?' Would that be so bad? Having died, myself, long ago, to grant life now to a whole new person? To donate, not just a lung or a kidney, but my entire body, irrelevant memories and all, to an arbitrarily constructed, but fully functioning, *de novo* human being?

Durrani was scandalised. 'No! We'd never dream of doing that! But we could program the microprocessors to let *you* control the network's refinement. We could give you the power to choose for yourself, consciously and deliberately, the things that make you happy.'

*   *   *

De Vries said, 'Try to picture the control.' I closed my eyes. He said, 'Bad idea. If you get into the habit, it will limit your access.'

'Right.' I stared into space. Something glorious by Beethoven was playing on the lab's sound system; it was difficult to concentrate. I struggled to visualise the stylised, cherry-red, horizontal slider control that De Vries had constructed, line by line, inside my head five minutes before. Suddenly it was more than a vague memory: it was superimposed over the room again, as clear as any real object, at the bottom of my visual field. 'I've got it.' The button was hovering at around 19.

De Vries glanced at a display, hidden from me. 'Good. Now try to lower the rating.'

I laughed weakly. *Roll over Beethoven.* 'How? How can you try to like something less?'

'You don't. Just try to move the button to the left. Visualise the movement. The software's monitoring your visual cortex, tracking any fleeting imaginary perceptions. Fool yourself into seeing the button moving – and the image will oblige.'

It did. I kept losing control briefly, as if the thing was sticking, but I managed to manoeuvre it down to 10 before stopping to assess the effect. 'Fuck.'

'I take it it's working?'

I nodded stupidly. The music was still . . . *pleasant*, but the spell was broken completely. It was like listening to an electrifying piece of rhetoric, then realising halfway through that the speaker didn't believe a word of it – leaving the original poetry and eloquence untouched, but robbing it of all its real force.

I felt sweat break out on my forehead. When Durrani had explained it, the whole scheme had sounded too bizarre to be real. And since I'd already failed to assert myself over the prosthesis – despite billions of direct neural connections, and countless opportunities for the remnants of my identity to interact with the thing and shape it in my own image – I'd feared that when the time came to make a choice, I'd be paralysed by indecision.

But I knew, beyond doubt, that I should *not* have been in a state of rapture over a piece of classical music that I'd either never heard before, or – since apparently it was famous, and ubiquitous – sat through once or twice by accident, entirely unmoved.

And now, in a matter of seconds, I'd hacked that false response away.

There was still hope. I still had a chance to resurrect myself. I'd just have to do it consciously, every step of the way.

De Vries, tinkering with his keyboard, said cheerfully, 'I'll colour-code virtual gadgets for all the major systems in the prosthesis. With a few days' practice it'll all be second nature. Just remember that some experiences will engage two or three systems at once . . . so if you're making love to music that you'd prefer not to find so distracting, make sure you turn down the red control, not the blue.' He looked up and saw my face. 'Hey, don't worry. You can always turn it up again later if you make a mistake. Or if you change your mind.'

3

It was nine p.m. in Sydney when the plane touched down. Nine o'clock on a Saturday night. I took a train into the city centre, intending to catch the connecting one home, but when I saw the crowds alighting at Town Hall station I put my suitcase in a locker and followed them up to the street.

I'd been in the city a few times since the virus, but never at night. I felt as if I'd come home after half a lifetime in another country, after solitary confinement in a foreign gaol. Everything was disorienting, one way or another. I felt a kind of giddy *déjà vu* at the sight of buildings that seemed to have been faithfully preserved, but still weren't quite as I remembered them, and a sense of hollowness each time I turned a corner to find that some private landmark, some shop or sign I remembered from childhood, had vanished.

I stood outside a pub, close enough to feel my eardrums throb to the beat of the music. I could see people inside, laughing and dancing, sloshing armfuls of drinks around, faces glowing with alcohol and companionship. Some alive with the possibility of violence, others with the promise of sex.

I could step right into this picture myself, now. The ash that had buried the world was gone; I was free to walk wherever I pleased. And I could almost feel the dead cousins of these revellers – reborn now as harmonics of the network, resonating to the music and the sight of their soul-mates – clamouring in my skull, begging me to carry them all the way to the land of the living.

I took a few steps forward, then something in the corner of my vision distracted me. In the alley beside the pub, a boy of ten or twelve sat crouched against the wall, lowering his face into a plastic bag. After a few inhalations he looked up, dead eyes shining, smiling as blissfully as any orchestra conductor.

I backed away.

Someone touched my shoulder. I spun around and saw a man beaming at me. 'Jesus loves you, brother! Your search is over!' He thrust a pamphlet into my hand. I gazed into his face, and his condition was transparent to me: he'd stumbled on a way to produce Leu-enkephalin at will, but he didn't know it, so he'd reasoned that some divine wellspring of happiness was responsible. I felt my chest tighten with horror and pity. At least I'd known about my tumour. And even the fucked-up kid in the alley understood that he was just sniffing glue.

And the people in the pub? Did they know what they were doing? Music, companionship, alcohol, sex . . . where did the border lie? When did justifiable happiness turn into something as empty, as pathological, as it was for this man?

I stumbled away, and headed back towards the station. All around me, people were laughing and shouting, holding hands, kissing, and I watched them as if they were flayed anatomical figures, revealing a thousand interlocking muscles working together with effortless precision. Buried inside me, the machinery of happiness recognised itself, again and again.

I had no doubt, now, that Durrani really had packed every last shred of the human capacity for joy into my skull. But to claim any part of it, I'd have to swallow the fact – more deeply than the tumour had ever forced me to swallow it – that happiness itself meant nothing. Life without it was unbearable, but as an end in itself it was not enough. I was free to choose its causes, and to be happy with my choices, but whatever I felt once I'd bootstrapped my new self into existence, the possibility would remain that all my choices had been wrong.

* * *

Global Assurance had given me until the end of the year to get my act together. If my annual psychological assessment showed that Durrani's treatment had been successful – whether or not I actually had a job – I'd be thrown to the even less tender mercies of the privatised remnants of Social Security. So I stumbled around in the light, trying to find my bearings.

On my first day back I woke at dawn. I sat down at the phone and started digging. My old net workspace had been archived; at current rates it was only costing about ten cents a year in storage fees, and I still had $36.20 credit in my account. The whole bizarre informational fossil had passed intact from company to company through four takeovers and mergers. Working through an assortment of tools to decode the obsolete data formats, I dragged fragments of my past life into the present and examined them, until it became too painful to go on.

The next day I spent twelve hours cleaning the flat, scrubbing every corner – listening to my old *njari* downloads, stopping only to eat, ravenously. And though I could have refined my taste in food back to that of a twelve-year-old salt-junky, I made the choice – thoroughly un-masochistic, and more pragmatic than virtuous – to crave nothing more toxic than fruit.

In the following weeks I put on weight with gratifying speed, though when I stared at myself in the mirror, or used morphing software running on the phone, I realised that I could be happy with almost any kind of body. The database must have included people with a vast range of ideal self-images, or who'd died perfectly content with their actual appearances.

Again, I chose pragmatism. I had a lot of catching up to do, and I didn't want to die at fifty-five from a heart attack if I could avoid it. There was no point fixating on the unattainable or the absurd, though, so after morphing myself to obesity, and rating it zero, I did the same for the Schwarzenegger look. I chose a lean, wiry body – well within the realms of possibility, according to the software – and assigned it 16 out of 20. Then I started running.

I took it slowly at first, and though I clung to the image of myself as a child, darting effortlessly from street to street, I was careful never to crank up the joy of motion high enough to mask injuries. When I limped into a chemist's, looking for liniment, I found something called prostaglandin modulators, anti-inflammatory compounds that allegedly minimise damage without shutting down any vital repair processes. I was sceptical, but the stuff did seem to help; the first month was still painful, but I was neither crippled by natural swelling nor rendered so oblivious to danger signs that I tore a muscle.

And once my heart and lungs and calves were dragged screaming out of their atrophied state, *it was good*. I ran for an hour every morning, weaving around the local back streets, and on Sunday afternoons I circumnavigated the city itself. I didn't push myself to attain ever faster times; I had no athletic ambitions whatsoever. I just wanted to exercise my freedom.

Soon the act of running melted into a kind of seamless whole. I could revel in the thudding of my heart and the feeling of my limbs in motion, or I could let those details recede into a buzz of satisfaction and just watch the scenery, as if from a train. And having reclaimed my body, I began to reclaim the suburbs, one by one. From the slivers of forest clinging to the Lane Cove river to the eternal ugliness of Parramatta Road, I criss-crossed Sydney like a mad surveyor, wrapping the landscape with invisible geodesics then drawing it into my skull. I pounded across the bridges at Gladesville and Iron Cove, Pyrmont, Meadowbank, and the Harbour itself, daring the planks to give way beneath my feet.

I suffered moments of doubt. I wasn't drunk on endorphins – I wasn't pushing myself that hard – but it still felt too good to be true. *Was this glue-sniffing?* Maybe ten thousand generations of my ancestors had been rewarded with the same kind of pleasure for pursuing game, fleeing danger, and mapping their territory for the sake of survival, but to me it was all just a glorious pastime.

Still, I wasn't deceiving myself, and I wasn't hurting anyone. I plucked those two rules from the core of the dead child inside me, and kept on running.

*   *   *

Thirty was an interesting age to go through puberty. The virus hadn't literally castrated me, but having eliminated pleasure from sexual imagery, genital stimulation, and orgasm – and having partly wrecked the hormonal regulatory pathways reaching down from the hypothalamus – it had left me with nothing worth describing as sexual function. My body disposed of semen in sporadic joyless spasms, and without the normal lubricants secreted by the prostate during arousal every unwanted ejaculation tore at the urethral lining.

When all of this changed, it hit hard, even in my state of relative sexual decrepitude. Compared with wet dreams of broken glass, masturbation was wonderful beyond belief, and I found myself unwilling to intervene with the controls to tone it down. But I needn't have worried that it would rob me of interest in the real thing; I kept finding myself staring openly at people on the street, in shops and on trains, until by a combination of willpower, sheer terror, and prosthetic adjustment I managed to kick the habit.

The network had rendered me bisexual, and though I quickly ramped my level of desire down considerably from that of the database's most priapic contributors, when it came to choosing to be straight or gay everything turned to quicksand. The network was not some kind of population-weighted average; if it had been, Durrani's original hope that my own surviving neural architecture could hold sway would have been dashed whenever the vote was stacked against it. So I was not just 10 to 15 per cent gay; the two possibilities were present with equal force, and the thought of eliminating *either* felt as alarming, as disfiguring, as if I'd lived with both for decades.

But was that just the prosthesis defending itself, or was it partly my own response? I had no idea. I'd been a thoroughly asexual twelve-year-old, even before the virus; I'd always assumed that I was straight, and I'd certainly found some girls attractive, but there'd been no moonstruck stares or furtive groping to back up that purely aesthetic opinion. I looked up the latest research, but all the genetic claims I recalled from various headlines had since been discredited, so even if my sexuality had been determined from birth there was no blood test that could tell me, now, what it would have become. I even tracked down my pre-treatment MRI scans, but they lacked the resolution to provide a direct, neuroanatomical answer.

I didn't want to be bisexual. I was too old to experiment like a teenager; I wanted certainty, I wanted solid foundations. I wanted to be monogamous – and even if monogamy was rarely an effortless state for anyone, that was no reason to lumber myself with unnecessary obstacles. *So who should I slaughter?* I knew which choice would make things easier, but if everything came down to a question of which of the 4,000 donors could carry me along the path of least resistance, whose life would I be living?

Maybe it was all a moot point. I was a thirty-year-old virgin with a history of mental illness, no money, no prospects, no social skills – and I could always crank up the satisfaction level of my only current option, and let everything else recede into fantasy. I wasn't deceiving myself, I wasn't hurting anyone. It was within my power to want nothing more.

* * *

I'd noticed the bookshop, tucked away in a back street in Leichhardt, many times before. But one Sunday in June, when I jogged past and saw a copy of *The Man Without Qualities* by Robert Musil in the front window, I had to stop and laugh.

I was drenched in sweat from the winter humidity, so I didn't go in and buy the book. But I peered in through the display towards the counter, and spotted a HELP WANTED sign.

Looking for unskilled work had seemed futile; the total unemployment rate was 15 per cent, the youth rate three times higher, so I'd assumed there'd always be a thousand other applicants for every job: younger, cheaper, stronger, and certifiably sane. But though I'd resumed my on-line education, I was getting not so much nowhere, fast, as everywhere, slowly. All the fields of knowledge that had gripped me as a child had expanded a hundredfold, and while the prosthesis granted me limitless energy and enthusiasm there was still too much ground for anyone to cover in a lifetime. I knew I'd have to sacrifice 90 per cent of my interests if I was ever going to choose a career, but I still hadn't been able to wield the knife.

I returned to the bookshop on Monday, walking up from Petersham Station. I'd fine-tuned my confidence for the occasion, but it rose spontaneously when I heard that there'd been no other applicants. The owner was in his sixties, and he'd just done his back in; he wanted someone to lug boxes around, and take the counter when he was otherwise occupied. I told him the truth: I'd been neurologically damaged by a childhood illness, and I'd only recently recovered.

He hired me on the spot, for a month's trial. The starting wage was exactly what Global Assurance were paying me, but if I was taken on permanently I'd get slightly more.

The work wasn't hard, and the owner didn't mind me reading in the back room when I had nothing to do. In a way, I was in heaven – ten thousand books, and no access fees – but sometimes I felt the terror of dissolution returning. I read voraciously, and on one level I could make clear judgements: I could pick the clumsy writers from the skilled, the honest from the fakers, the platitudinous from the inspired. But the prosthesis still wanted me to enjoy everything, to embrace everything, to diffuse out across the dusty shelves until I was no one at all, a ghost in the Library of Babel.

*   *   *

She walked into the bookshop two minutes after opening time, on the first day of spring. Watching her browse, I tried to think clearly through the consequences of what I was about to do. For weeks I'd been on the counter five hours a day, and with all that human contact I'd been hoping for . . . *something*. Not wild, reciprocated love at first sight, just the tiniest flicker of mutual interest, the slightest piece of evidence that I could actually desire one human being more than all the rest.

246

It hadn't happened. Some customers had flirted mildly, but I could see that it was nothing special, just their own kind of politeness, and I'd felt nothing more in response than if they'd been unusually, formally, courteous. And though I might have agreed with any bystander as to who was conventionally good-looking, who was animated or mysterious, witty or charming, who glowed with youth or radiated worldliness, I just didn't care. The 4,000 had all loved very different people, and the envelope that stretched between their farflung characteristics encompassed the entire species. That was never going to change, until I did something to break the symmetry myself.

So for the past week, I'd dragged all the relevant systems in the prosthesis down to 3 or 4. People had become scarcely more interesting to watch than pieces of wood. Now, alone in the shop with this randomly chosen stranger, I slowly turned the controls up. I had to fight against positive feedback; the higher the settings, the more I wanted to increase them, but I'd set limits in advance, and I stuck to them.

By the time she'd chosen two books and approached the counter, I was feeling half defiantly triumphant, half sick with shame. I'd struck a pure note with the network at last; what I felt at the sight of this woman rang true. And if everything I'd done to achieve it was calculated, artificial, bizarre and abhorrent, I'd had no other way.

I was smiling as she bought the books, and she smiled back warmly. No wedding or engagement ring – but I'd promised myself that I wouldn't try anything, no matter what. This was just the first step: to notice someone, to make someone stand out from the crowd. I could ask out the tenth, the hundredth woman who bore some passing resemblance to her.

I said, 'Would you like to meet for a coffee sometime?'

She looked surprised, but not affronted. Indecisive, but at least slightly pleased to have been asked. And I thought I was prepared for this slip of the tongue to lead nowhere, but then something in the ruins of me sent a shaft of pain through my chest as I watched her make up her mind. If a fraction of that had shown on my face, she probably would have rushed me to the nearest vet to be put down.

She said, 'That would be nice. I'm Julia, by the way.'

'I'm Mark.' We shook hands.

'When do you finish work?'

'Tonight? Nine o'clock.'

'Ah.'

I said, 'How about lunch? When do you have lunch?'

'One.' She hesitated. 'There's that place just down the road . . . next to the hardware store?'

'That would be great.'

Julia smiled. 'Then I'll meet you there. About ten-past. OK?'

I nodded. She turned and walked out. I stared after her, dazed, terrified, elated. I thought: This is simple. Anyone in the world can do it. It's like breathing.

I started hyperventilating. I was an emotionally retarded teenager, and she'd discover that in five minutes flat. Or, worse, discover the 4,000 grown men in my head offering advice.

I went into the toilet to throw up.

* * *

Julia told me that she managed a dress shop a few blocks away. 'You're new at the bookshop, aren't you?'

'Yes.'

'So what were you doing before that?'

'I was unemployed. For a long time.'

'How long?'

'Since I was a student.'

She grimaced. 'It's criminal, isn't it? Well, I'm doing my bit. I'm job-sharing, half-time only.'

'Really? How are you finding it?'

'It's wonderful. I mean, I'm lucky, the position's well enough paid that I can get by on half a salary.' She laughed. 'Most people assume I must be raising a family. As if that's the only possible reason.'

'You just like to have the time?'

'Yes. Time's important. I hate being rushed.'

We had lunch again two days later, and then twice again the next week. She talked about the shop, a trip she'd made to South America, a sister recovering from breast cancer. I almost mentioned my own long-vanquished tumour, but apart from fears about where that might lead, it would have sounded too much like a plea for sympathy. At home, I sat riveted to the phone – not waiting for a call, but watching news broadcasts, to be sure I'd have something to talk about besides myself. *Who's your favourite singer/author/artist/ actor? I have no idea.*

Visions of Julia filled my head. I wanted to know what she was doing every second of the day; I wanted her to be happy, I wanted her to be safe. *Why?* Because I'd chosen her. But . . . why had I felt compelled to choose anyone? Because, in the end, the one thing that most of the donors must have had in common was the fact that they'd desired, and cared about, one person above all others. *Why?* That came down to evolution. You could no more help and protect everyone in sight than you could fuck them, and a judicious combination of the two had obviously proved effective at passing down genes. So my emotions had the same ancestry as everyone else's; what more could I ask?

But how could I pretend that I felt anything real for Julia, when I could shift a few buttons in my head, anytime, and make those feelings vanish? Even if what I felt was strong enough to keep me from wanting to touch that dial . . .

Some days I thought: it must be like this for everyone. People make a decision, half shaped by chance, to get to know someone; everything starts from there. Some nights I sat awake for hours, wondering if I was turning myself into a pathetic slave, or a dangerous obsessive. Could anything I discovered about Julia drive me away, now that I'd chosen her? Or even trigger the slightest disapproval? And if, when, she decided to break things off, how would I take it?

We went out to dinner, then shared a taxi home. I kissed her goodnight on her doorstep. Back in my flat, I flipped through sex manuals on the net, wondering how I could ever hope to conceal my complete lack of experience. Everything looked anatomically impossible; I'd need six years of gymnastics training just to achieve the missionary position. I'd refused to masturbate since I'd met her; to fantasise about her, to *imagine her* without consent, seemed outrageous, unforgivable. After I gave in, I lay awake until dawn trying to comprehend the trap I'd dug for myself, and trying to understand why I didn't want to be free.

*　　*　　*

Julia bent down and kissed me, sweatily. 'That was a nice idea.' She climbed off me and flopped onto the bed.

I'd spent the last ten minutes riding the blue control, trying to keep myself from coming without losing my erection. I'd heard of computer games involving exactly the same thing. Now I turned up the indigo for a stronger glow of intimacy, and when I looked into her eyes I knew that she could see the effect on me. She brushed my cheek with her hand. 'You're a sweet man. Did you know that?'

I said, 'I have to tell you something.' *Sweet? I'm a puppet, I'm a robot, I'm a freak.*

'What?'

I couldn't speak. She seemed amused, then she kissed me. 'I know you're gay. That's all right; I don't mind.'

'I'm not gay.' *Any more?* 'Though I might have been.'

Julia frowned. 'Gay, bisexual . . . I don't care. Honestly.'

I wouldn't have to manipulate my responses much longer; the prosthesis was being shaped by all of this, and in a few weeks I'd be able to leave it to its own devices. Then I'd feel, as naturally as anyone, all the things I was now having to choose.

I said, 'When I was twelve, I had cancer.'

I told her everything. I watched her face, and saw horror, then growing doubt. 'You don't believe me?'

She replied haltingly, 'You sound so matter-of-fact. *Eighteen years?* How can you just say, "I lost eighteen years"?'

'How do you want me to say it? I'm not trying to make you pity me. I just want you to understand.'

When I came to the day I met her my stomach tightened with fear, but I kept on talking. After a few seconds I saw tears in her eyes, and I felt like I'd been knifed.

'I'm sorry. I didn't mean to hurt you.' I didn't know whether to try to hold her, or to leave right then. I kept my eyes fixed on her, but the room swam.

She smiled. 'What are you sorry about? You chose me. I chose you. It could have been different for both of us. But it wasn't.' She reached down under the sheet and took my hand. 'It wasn't.'

*　　*　　*

Julia had Saturdays off, but I had to start work at eight. She kissed me goodbye sleepily when I left at six; I walked all the way home, weightless.

I must have grinned inanely at everyone who came into the shop, but I hardly saw them. I was picturing the future. I hadn't spoken to either of my parents for nine years; they didn't even know about the Durrani treatment. But now it seemed possible to repair anything. I could go to them now and say: *This is your son, back from the dead. You did save my life, all those years ago.*

There was a message on the phone from Julia when I arrived home. I resisted viewing it until I'd started things cooking on the stove; there was something perversely pleasurable about forcing myself to wait, imagining her face and her voice in anticipation.

I hit the Play button. Her face wasn't quite as I'd pictured it.

I kept missing things and stopping to rewind. Isolated phrases stuck in my mind. *Too strange. Too sick. No one's fault.* My explanation hadn't really sunk in the night before. But now she'd had time to think about it, and she wasn't prepared to carry on a relationship with 4,000 dead men.

I sat on the floor, trying to decide what to feel: the wave of pain crashing over me, or something better, by choice. I knew I could summon up the controls of the prosthesis and make myself happy – happy because I was 'free' again, happy because I was better off without her, happy because Julia was better off without me. Or even just happy because happiness meant nothing, and all I had to do to attain it was flood my brain with Leu-enkephalin.

I sat there wiping tears and mucus off my face while the vegetables burned. The smell made me think of cauterisation, sealing off a wound.

I let things run their course, I didn't touch the controls, but just knowing that I could have changed everything. And I realised then that, even if I went to Luke De Vries and said, 'I'm cured now, take the software away, I don't want the power to choose anymore,' I'd never be able to forget where everything I felt had come from.

* * *

My father came to the flat yesterday. We didn't talk much, but he hasn't remarried yet, and he made a joke about us going nightclub-hopping together.

At least I hope it was a joke.

Watching him, I thought: he's there inside my head, and my mother too, and ten million ancestors, human, proto-human, remote beyond imagining. What difference did 4,000 more make? Everyone had to carve a life out of the same legacy: half universal, half particular; half sharpened by relentless natural selection, half softened by the freedom of chance. I'd just had to face the details a little more starkly.

And I could go on doing it, walking the convoluted border between meaningless happiness and meaningless despair. Maybe I was lucky; maybe the best way to cling to that narrow zone was to see clearly what lay on either side.

When my father was leaving, he looked out from the balcony across the crowded suburb, down towards the Parramatta river, where a storm drain was discharging a visible plume of oil, street litter, and garden run-off into the water.

He asked dubiously, 'You happy with this area?'

I said, 'I like it here.'

OUR LADY OF CHERNOBYL

We knew not whether we were in heaven or on earth, for surely there is no such splendour or beauty anywhere upon earth.

>The envoy of Prince Vladimir of Kiev, describing the Church of the Divine Wisdom in Constantinople, 987.

It is the rustiest old barn in heathendom.

>– S. L. Clemens, ditto, 1867.

Luciano Masini had the haunted demeanour and puffy complexion of an insomniac. I'd picked him as a man who'd begun to ask himself, around two a.m. nightly, if his twenty-year-old wife really had found the lover of her dreams in an industrialist three times her age – however witty, however erudite, however wealthy. I hadn't followed his career in any detail, but his most famous move had been to buy the entire superconducting cables division of Pirelli, when the parent company was dismembered in '09. He was impeccably dressed in a grey silk suit, the cut precisely old fashioned enough to be stylish, and he looked as if he'd once been strikingly handsome. A perfect candidate, I decided, for vain self-delusion and belated second thoughts.

I was wrong. What he said was: 'I want you to locate a package for me.'

'A package?' I did my best to sound fascinated – although if adultery was stultifying, lost property was worse. 'Missing *en route* from—?'

'Zürich.'

'To Milan?'

'Of course!' Masini almost flinched, as if the idea that he might have been shipping his precious cargo elsewhere, intentionally, caused him physical pain.

I said carefully, 'Nothing is ever really lost. You might find that a strongly worded letter from your lawyers to the courier is enough to work miracles.'

Masini smiled humourlessly. 'I don't think so. The courier is dead.'

Afternoon light filled the room; the window faced east, away from the sun, but the sky itself was dazzling. I suffered a moment of strange clarity, a compelling sense of having just shaken off a lingering drowsiness, as if I'd begun the conversation half asleep and only now fully woken. Masini let the copper orrery on the wall behind me beat twice, each tick a soft, complicated meshing of a thousand tiny gears. Then he said, 'She was found in a hotel room in Vienna three days ago. She'd been shot in the head at close range. And no, she was not meant to take any such detour.'

'What was in the package?'

'A small icon.' He indicated a height of some thirty centimetres. 'An eighteenth-century depiction of the Madonna. Originally from the Ukraine.'

'The Ukraine? Do you know how it came to be in Zürich?' I'd heard that the Ukrainian government had recently launched a renewed campaign to persuade certain countries to get serious about the return of stolen artwork. Crateloads had been smuggled out during the turmoil and corruption of the eighties and nineties.

'It was part of the estate of a well-known collector, a man with an impeccable reputation. My own art dealer examined all the paperwork, the bills of sale, the export licences, before giving his blessing to the deal.'

'Paperwork can be forged.'

Masini struggled visibly to control his impatience. 'Anything can be *forged*. What do you want me to say? I have no reason to suspect that this was stolen property. I'm not a criminal, Signor Fabrizio.'

'I'm not suggesting that you are. So . . . money and goods changed hands in Zürich? The icon was yours when it was stolen?'

'Yes.'

'May I ask how much you paid for it?'

'Five million Swiss francs.'

I let that pass without comment, although for a moment I wondered if I'd heard correctly. I was no expert, but I did know that Orthodox icons were usually painted by anonymous artists, and were intended to be as far from unique as individual copies of the Bible. There were exceptions, of course – a few treasured, definitive examples of each type – but they were a great deal older than eighteenth-century. However fine the craftsmanship, however well preserved, five million sounded far too high.

I said, 'Surely you insured—?'

'Of course! And in a year or two, I may even get my money back. But I'd much prefer to have the icon. That's why I purchased it in the first place.'

'And your insurers will agree. They'll be doing their best to find it.' If another investigator had a head start on me, I didn't want to waste my time – least of all if I'd be competing against a Swiss insurance firm on their home ground.

Masini fixed his bloodshot eyes on me. 'Their *best* is not good enough! Yes, they'll want to save themselves the money, and they'll treat this potential loss with great seriousness . . . like the accountants they are. And the Austrian police will try very hard to find the murderer, no doubt. Neither are moved by any sense of urgency. Neither would be greatly troubled if nothing were resolved for months. Or years.'

If I'd been wrong about Masini's nocturnal visions of

adultery, I'd been right about one thing: there was a passion, an obsession, driving him which ran as deep as jealousy, as deep as pride, as deep as sex. He leant forward across the desk, restraining himself from seizing my shirtfront, but commanding and imploring me with as much arrogance and pathos as if he had.

'Two weeks! I'll give you two weeks – and you can name your fee! Deliver the icon to me within a fortnight . . . and everything I have is yours for the asking!'

*　　*　　*

I treated Masini's extravagant offer with as much seriousness as it deserved, but I accepted the case. There were worse ways to spend a fortnight, I decided, than consulting with informants on the fringes of the black market over long lunches in restaurants fit for connoisseurs of fine art.

The obvious starting point, though, was the courier. Her name was Gianna De Angelis: twenty-seven years old, five years in the business, with a spotless reputation; according to the regulatory authorities, not a single complaint had ever been lodged against her, by customer or employer. She'd been working for a small Milanese firm with an equally good record: this was their first loss, in twenty years, of either merchandise or personnel.

I spoke to two of her colleagues; they gave me the barest facts, but wouldn't be drawn into speculation. The transaction had taken place in a Zürich bank vault, then De Angelis had taken a taxi straight to the airport. She'd phoned head office to say that all was well, less than five minutes before she was due to board the flight home. The plane had left on time, but she hadn't been on it. She'd bought a ticket from Tyrolean Airlines – using her own credit card – and flown straight to Vienna, carrying the attaché case containing the icon as hand luggage. Six hours later, she was dead.

I tracked down her fiancé, a TV sound technician, to the

apartment they'd shared. He was red-eyed, unshaven, hungover. Still in shock, or I doubt he would have let me through the door. I offered my condolences, helped him finish a bottle of wine, then gently inquired whether Gianna had received any unusual phone calls, made plans to spend extravagant sums of money, or had appeared uncharacteristically nervous or excited in recent weeks. I had to cut the interview short when he began trying to crack my skull open with the empty bottle.

I returned to the office and began trawling the databases, from the official public records right down to the patchwork collections of mailing lists and crudely collated electronic debris purveyed by assorted cyberpimps. One system, operating out of Tokyo, could search the world's digitised newspapers, and key frames from TV news reports, looking for a matching face – whether or not the subject's name was mentioned in the caption or commentary. I found a near-twin walking arm in arm with a gangster outside a Buenos Aires courthouse in 2007, and another weeping in the wreckage of a village in the Philippines, her family killed in a typhoon, in 2010, but there were no genuine sightings. A text-based search of local media yielded exactly two entries; she'd only made it into the papers at birth and at death.

So far as I could discover, her financial position had been perfectly sound. No one had any kind of dirt on her, and there wasn't the faintest whiff of an association with organised crime. The icon would have been far from the most valuable item she'd ever laid her hands on – and I still thought Masini had paid a vastly inflated price for it. Artwork, anonymous or not, wasn't exactly the most liquid of assets. So why had she sold out, on this particular job, when there must have been a hundred opportunities which had been far more tempting?

Maybe she hadn't been trying to sell the icon in Vienna. Maybe she'd been coerced into going there. I couldn't imagine anyone 'kidnapping' her in the middle of the airport, marching her over to the ticket office, through the security scanners and onto the plane. She'd been armed, highly trained, and carrying all the electronics she could possibly need to summon immediate assistance. But even if she hadn't had an X-ray-transparent gun pointed at her heart every step of the way, maybe a more subtle threat had compelled her.

As dusk fell on the first day of my allotted fourteen, I paced the office irritably, already feeling pessimistic. De Angelis's image smiled coolly on the terminal; her grieving lover's wine tasted sour in my throat. This woman was dead, *that was the crime*, and I was being paid to hunt for a faded piece of kitsch. If I found the killers it would be incidental. And the truth was, I was hoping I wouldn't.

I opened the blinds and looked down towards the city centre. Flea-sized specks scurried across the Piazza del Duomo, the cathedral's forest of mad Gothic pinnacles towering above them. I rarely noticed the cathedral: it was just another part of the expensive view (like the Alps, visible from the reception room); and the view was just part of the whole high-class image which enabled me to charge twenty times as much for my services as any back-alley operator. Now I blinked at the sight of it as if it were a hallucination: it seemed so alien, so out of place, beside the gleaming dark ceramic buildings of twenty-first-century Milan. Statues of saints, or angels, or gargoyles – I couldn't remember and, at this distance, I couldn't really tell them apart – stood atop every pinnacle, like a thousand demented stylites. The whole roof was encrusted with pink-tinged marble, dizzyingly, surrealistically ornate, looking in places like lacework, and in places like barbed wire. Good atheist or not, I'd been inside once or twice, though I struggled to remember when and why; some unavoidable ceremonial occasion. In any case, I'd grown up with the sight of it; it should have been a familiar landmark, nothing more. But at that moment, the whole structure seemed utterly foreign, utterly strange; it was as if the mountains to the north had shed their snow and greenery and topsoil and revealed themselves to be giant artefacts, pyramids from Central America, relics of a vanished civilisation.

I closed the blinds, and wiped the dead courier's face from my computer screen.

Then I bought myself a ticket to Zürich.

*   *   *

The databases had had plenty to say about Rolf Hengartner. He'd worked in electronic publishing, making deals on some ethereal plane where Europe's biggest software providers carved up the market to their mutual satisfaction. I imagined him skiing, snow and water, with Ministers of Culture and satellite magnates . . . although probably not in the last few years, in his seventies, with acute lymphoma. He'd started out in film finance, orchestrating the funding of multinational coproductions; one of the photographs of him in the reception room to what was now his assistant's office showed him raising a clenched fist beside a still-young Depardieu at an anti-Hollywood demonstration in Paris twenty years before.

Max Reif, his assistant, had been appointed executor of the estate. I'd downloaded the latest overpriced *Schweitzerdeutsch* software for my notepad, in the hope that it would guide me through the interview without too many blunders, but Reif insisted on speaking Italian, and turned out to be perfectly fluent.

Hengartner's wife had died before him, but he was survived by three children and ten grandchildren. Reif had been instructed to sell all of the art, since none of the family had ever shown much interest in the collection.

'What was his passion? Orthodox icons?'

'Not at all. Herr Hengartner was eclectic, but the icon was a complete surprise to me. Something of an anomaly. He owned some French Gothic and Italian Renaissance works with religious themes, but he certainly didn't specialise in the Madonna, let alone the Eastern tradition.'

Reif showed me a photograph of the icon in the glossy brochure which had been put together for the auction; Masini had mislaid his copy of the catalogue, so this was my first chance to see exactly what I was searching for. I read the Italian section in the pentalingual commentary on the facing page:

A stunning example of the icon known as the Vladimir Mother of God, probably the most ancient variation of the icons of 'loving-kindness' (Greek *eleousa*, Russian *umileniye*). It depicts the Virgin holding the Child, His face pressed tenderly to His mother's cheek, in a powerful symbol of both divine and human compassion for all of creation. According to tradition, this icon derives from a painting by the Evangelist Luke. The surviving exemplar, from which the type takes its name, was brought to Kiev from Constantinople in the 12th century, and is now in the Tretyakov Gallery, Moscow. It has been described as the greatest holy treasure of the Russian nation.

Artist unknown. Ukrainian, early 18th century. Cyprus panel, 293 x 204 mm, egg tempera on linen, exquisitely decorated with beaten silver.

The reserve price was listed as eighty thousand Swiss francs. Less than a fiftieth what Masini had paid for it.

The aesthetic attraction of the piece was lost on me; it wasn't exactly a Caravaggio. The colours were drab, the execution was crude – deliberately two-dimensional – and even the silver was badly tarnished. The paintwork itself appeared to be in reasonable condition; for a moment I thought there was a hairline crack across the full width of the icon, but on closer inspection it looked more like a flaw in the reproduction: a scratch on the printing plate, or some photographic intermediate.

Of course, this wasn't meant to be 'high art' in the Western tradition. No expression of the artist's ego, no indulgent idiosyncrasies of style. It was, presumably, a faithful copy of the Byzantine original, intended to play a specific role in the

261

practice of the Orthodox religion, and I was in no position to judge its value in that context. But I had trouble imagining either Rolf Hengartner or Luciano Masini as secret converts to the Eastern church. So was it purely a matter of a good investment? Was this nothing but an eighteenth-century baseball card, to them? If Masini's only interest was financial, though, why had he paid so much more than the market value? And why was he so desperate to get it back?

I said, 'Can you tell me who bid for the icon, besides Signor Masini?'

'The usual dealers, the usual brokers. I'm afraid I couldn't tell you on whose behalf they were acting.'

'But you did monitor the bidding?' A number of potential buyers, or their agents, had visited Zürich to view the collection in person – Masini among them – but the auction itself had taken place by phone line and computer.

'Of course.'

'Was there a consensus for a price close to Masini's final bid? Or was he forced up to it by just one of those anonymous rivals?'

Reif stiffened, and I suddenly realised what that must have sounded like.

I said, 'I certainly didn't mean to imply—'

'*At least* three other bidders,' he said icily, 'were within a few hundred thousand francs of Signor Masini all the way. I'm sure he'll confirm that, if you take the trouble to ask him.' He hesitated, then added less defensively, 'Obviously the reserve price was set far too low. But Herr Hengartner anticipated that the auction house would undervalue this item.'

That threw me. 'I thought you didn't know about the icon until after his death. If you'd discussed its value with him—'

'I didn't. But Herr Hengartner left a note beside it in the safe.' He hesitated, as if debating with himself whether or not I deserved to be privy to the great man's insights.

I didn't dare plead with him, let alone insist; I just waited in silence for him to continue. It can't have been more than ten or fifteen seconds, but I swear I broke out in a sweat.

Reif smiled, and put me out of my misery. 'The note said: *Prepare to be surprised*.'

*   *   *

In the early evening I left my hotel room and wandered through the city centre. I'd never had reason to visit Zürich before, but, language aside, it was already beginning to feel just like home. The same fast-food chains had colonised the city. The electronic billboards displayed the same advertisements. The glass fronts of the VR parlours glowed with surreal images from the very same games, and the twelve-year-olds inside had all succumbed to the same unfortunate Texan fashions. Even the smell of the place was exactly like Milan on a Saturday night: french fries, popcorn, Reeboks and Coke.

Had Ukrainian secret service agents killed De Angelis to get the icon back? Was this the flip-side of all the diplomatic efforts to recover stolen artwork? That seemed unlikely. If there were the slightest grounds for the return of the icon, then dragging the matter through the courts would have meant far better publicity for the cause. Slaughtering foreign citizens could play havoc with international aid, and the Ukraine was in the middle of negotiating an upgrading of its trade relationship with Europe. I couldn't believe that any government would risk so much for a single work of art, in a country full of more or less interchangeable copies of the very same piece. It wasn't as if Hengartner had got his hands on the twelfth-century original.

Who, then? Another collector, another obsessive hoarder, whom Masini had outbid? Someone, perhaps, unlike Hengartner, who already owned several other baseball cards, and wanted a complete set? Maybe Masini's insurance firm had the connections and clout needed to find out who the true bidders at the auction had been; I certainly didn't. A rival collector wasn't the only possibility; one of the bidders could have been a dealer who was so impressed by the price the icon fetched that he or she decided it was worth acquiring by other means.

The air was growing cold faster than I'd expected; I decided to return to the hotel. I'd been walking along the west bank of the Limmat River, down towards the lake; I started to cross back over at the first bridge I came to, then I paused midway to get my bearings. There were cathedrals either side of me, facing each other across the river; unimposing structures compared with Milan's giant Nosferatu Castle, but I felt a – ridiculous – *frisson* of unease, as if the pair of them had conspired to ambush me.

My *Schweitzerdeutsch* package came with free maps and tour guides; I hit the Where am I? button, and the GPS unit in the notepad passed its co-ordinates to the software, which proceeded to demystify my surroundings. The two buildings in question were the Grossmunster (which looked like a fortress, with two brutal towers side by side, not quite facing the river's east bank) and the Fraumunster (once an abbey, with a single slender spire). Both dated from the thirteenth century, although modifications of one kind or another had continued almost to the present. Stained-glass windows by, respectively, Giacometti and Chagall. And Ulrich Zwingli had launched the Swiss Reformation from the pulpit of the Grossmunster in 1523.

I was staring at one of the birthplaces of a sect which had endured for five hundred years, and it was far stranger than standing in the shadow of the most ancient Roman temple. To say: *Christianity has shaped the physical and cultural landscape of Europe for two thousand years, as relentlessly as any glacier, as mercilessly as any clash of tectonic plates,* is to state the fatuously obvious. But if I'd spent my whole life surrounded by the evidence, it was only now – now that the legacy of those millennia was beginning to seem increasingly bizarre to me – that I had any real sense of what it meant. Arcane theological disputes between people as alien to me as the ancient Egyptians had transformed the entire continent – along with a thousand purely political and economic forces, for sure – but, nevertheless, modulating the development of almost every human activity, from architecture to music, from commerce to warfare, at one level or another.

And there was no reason to believe that the process had halted. Just because the Alps were no longer rising didn't mean geology had come to an end.

'Do you wish to know more?' the tour guide asked me.

'Not unless you can tell me the word for a pathological fear of cathedrals.'

It hesitated, then replied with impeccable fuzzy logic, 'There are cathedrals across the length and breadth of Europe. Which particular cathedrals did you have in mind?'

*   *   *

De Angelis's colleagues had provided me with the name of the taxi company she'd used for her trip from the bank to the airport – the last thing she'd paid for with her business credit card. I'd spoken to the manager of the company by phone from Milan, and there was a message from her when I arrived back at the hotel, with the name of the driver for the journey in question. He was far from the last person who'd seen De Angelis alive – but possibly the last before she'd been persuaded, by whatever means, to take the icon to Vienna. He was due to report for work at the depot that evening at nine. I ate quickly, then set out into the cold again. The only taxis outside the hotel were from a rival company. I went on foot.

I found Phan Anh Tuan drinking coffee in a corner of the garage. After a brief exchange in German, he asked me if I'd prefer to speak French, and I gratefully switched. He told me he'd been an engineering student in East Berlin when the Wall came down. 'I always meant to find a way to finish my degree and go home. I got sidetracked, somehow.' He gazed out at the dark icy street, bemused.

I put a photo of De Angelis on the table in front of him; he looked long and hard. 'No, I'm sorry. I didn't take this woman anywhere.'

I hadn't been optimistic; still, it would have been nice to have gleaned some small clue about her state of mind; had she been humming 'We're in the Money' all the way to the airport, or what?

I said, 'You must have a hundred customers a day. Thanks for trying.' I started to take the photo back; he caught my hand.

'I'm not telling you I must have forgotten her. I'm telling you I'm sure I've never seen her before.'

I said, 'Last Monday. Two twelve p.m. Intercontinental Bank to the airport. The despatcher's records show—'

He was frowning. 'Monday? No. I had engine trouble. I was out of service for almost an hour. Until nearly three.'

'Are you sure?'

He fetched a handwritten log book from his vehicle, and showed me the entry.

I said, 'Why would the despatcher get it wrong?'

He shrugged. 'It must have been a software glitch. A computer takes the calls, allocates them . . . it's all fully automated. We flick a switch on the radio when we're unavailable – and I can't have forgotten to do that, because I kept the radio on all the time I was working on the car, and no fares came through to me.'

'Could someone else have accepted a job from the despatcher, pretending to be you?'

He laughed. 'Intentionally? No. Not without changing the ID number of their radio.'

'And how hard would that be? Would you need a forged chip, with a duplicate serial number?'

'No. But it would mean pulling the radio out, opening it up, and resetting thirty-two DIP switches. Why would anyone bother?' Then I saw it click in his eyes.

I said, 'Do you know of anyone here having a radio stolen recently? The two-way, not the music?'

He nodded sadly. 'Both. Someone had both stolen. About a month ago.'

*   *   *

I returned in the morning and confirmed with some of the other drivers most of what Phan had told me. There was no easy way of proving that he hadn't lied about the engine trouble and driven De Angelis himself, but I couldn't see why he would have invented an 'alibi' when there was no need for one – when he could have said 'Yes, I drove her, she hardly spoke a word,' and no one would have had the slightest reason to doubt him.

So: someone had gone to a lot of trouble to be alone in a fake taxi with De Angelis . . . and then they'd let her walk into the airport and phone home. To delay the moment when head office would realise that something had gone wrong, presumably, but why had she gone along with that? *What had the driver said to her, in those few minutes, to make her so co-operative?* Was it a threat to her family, her lover? Or a bribe, large enough to convince her to make up her mind on the spot? And then she hadn't bothered to cover her trail, because she knew there'd be no way to do so convincingly? She'd accepted the fact that her guilt would be obvious, and that she'd have to become a fugitive?

That sounded like one hell of a bribe. So how could she have been so naïve as to think that anyone would actually pay it?

Outside the Intercontinental Bank, I took her photo from my wallet and held it up towards the armoured-glass revolving doors, trying to imagine the scene. *The taxi arrives, she climbs in, they pull out into the traffic. The driver says: Nice weather we're having. By the way, I know what you've got in the attaché case. Come to Vienna with me and I'll make you rich.*

She stared back at me accusingly. I said, 'All right, De Angelis, I'm sorry. I don't believe you were that stupid.'

I gazed at the laser-printed image. Something nagged at me. *Digital radios with driver IDs?* For some reason, that had surprised me. It shouldn't have. Perhaps movie scenes of taxi drivers and police communicating in incomprehensible squawks still lingered in my subconscious, still shaped my expectations on some level, in spite of the kind of technology I used myself every day. The word 'auction' still conjured up scenes of a man or woman with a hammer, shouting out bids in a crowded room, though I'd never witnessed anything remotely like that, except in the movies. In real life, everything was computerised, everything was digital. This 'photograph' was digital. Chemical film had started disappearing from the shops when I was fourteen or fifteen years old, and even in my childhood it was strictly an amateur medium; most commercial photographers had been using CCD arrays for almost twenty years.

So why did there appear to be a fine scratch across the photograph of the icon? The few hundred copies of the auction catalogue would have been produced without using a single analogue intermediate; everything would have gone from digital camera to computer to laser printer. The glossy end-product was the one anachronism – and a less conservative auction house would have offered an on-line version, or an interactive CD.

Reif had let me keep the catalogue; back in my hotel room, I inspected it again. The 'scratch' definitely wasn't a crack in the paintwork; it cut right across the image, a perfectly straight, white line of uniform thickness, crossing from paint to raised silverwork without the slightest deviation.

A glitch in the camera's electronics? Surely the photographer would have noticed that, and tried again. And even if the flaw had been spotted too late for a retake, one keystroke on any decent image-processing package would have removed it instantly.

I tried to phone Reif; it took almost an hour to get through to him. I said, 'Can you tell me the name of the graphic designers who produced the auction catalogue?'

He stared at me as if I'd called him in the middle of sex to ask who'd murdered Elvis. 'Why do you need to know that?'

'I just want to ask their photographer—'

'Their photographer?'

'Yes. Or whoever it was who photographed the items in the collection.'

'It wasn't necessary to have the collection photographed. Herr Hengartner already had photographs of everything, for insurance purposes. He left a disk with the image files, and detailed instructions for the layout of the catalogue. He knew that he was dying. He had everything organised, everything prepared. Does that answer your question? Does that satisfy your curiosity?'

Not quite. I steeled myself, and grovelled: Could I have a copy of the original image file? I was seeking advice from an art historian in Moscow, and the best colour fax of the catalogue wouldn't do justice to the icon. Reif begrudgingly had an assistant locate the data and transmit it to me.

The line, the 'scratch', was there in the file.

Hengartner – who'd treasured this icon in secret, and who'd somehow known that it would fetch an extraordinary price – had left behind an image of it with a small but unmistakable flaw, and made sure that it was seen by every prospective buyer.

That had to mean something, but I had no idea what.

*   *   *

A list of the dates when Lombardy had fallen in and out of Austrian hands, committed to memory when I was sixteen years old, just about exhausted my knowledge of the Habsburg empire. Which should hardly have mattered in 2013, but I felt disconcertingly ill prepared all the same.

In my hotel room, I unpacked my bags, then looked out warily across the rooftops of Vienna. I could see Saint Stephen's Cathedral in the distance; the southern tower, almost detached from the main hall, was topped with a spire like a filigree radio antenna. The roof of the hall was decorated with richly coloured tiles, forming an eye-catching zigzag pattern of chevrons and diamonds – as if someone had draped a giant Mongolian rug over the building to keep it warm. But then, anything less exotic would have been a disappointment.

De Angelis had died in the same hotel (in the room directly above me, with much the same view). Booked in under her own name. Paying with her own plastic, when she could have used anonymous cash. *Did that prove that she'd had nothing to be ashamed of – that she'd been threatened, not bribed?*

I spent half the morning trying to persuade the hotel manager that the local police wouldn't lock him up for allowing me to speak to his staff about the murder; the whole idea seemed to strike him as akin to treason. 'If a Viennese citizen died in Milan,' I argued patiently, 'wouldn't you expect an accredited Austrian investigator to receive every courtesy there?'

'We would send a delegation of police to liaise with the Milanese authorities, not a private detective acting alone.'

I was getting nowhere, so I backed off. Besides, I had an appointment to keep.

My long-awaited expense-account lunch with a black-marketeer turned out to be in a health-food restaurant. Back in Milan, I'd paid several million lira to a net-based 'introduction agency' to put me in touch with 'Anton'. He was much younger than I'd expected; he looked about twenty, and he radiated the kind of self-assurance I'd only come across before in wealthy adolescent drug dealers. I managed once again to avoid using my atrocious German; Anton spoke CNN English, with an accent that I took to be Hungarian.

I handed him the auction catalogue, open at the relevant page; he glanced at the picture of the icon. 'Oh yeah. The Vladimir. I could get you another one, exactly like this. Ten thousand US dollars.'

'I don't want a forged replica.' Attractive as the idea was, Masini would never have fallen for it. 'Or even a similar contemporary piece. I want to know who asked for *this*. Who spread the word that it was going to change hands in Zürich, and that they'd pay to have it brought east.'

I had to make a conscious effort not to look down to see where he'd placed his feet. Before he'd arrived, I'd discreetly dropped a pinch of silica microspheres onto the floor beneath the table. Each one contained a tiny accelerometer – an array of springy silicon beams a few microns across, fabricated on the same chip as a simple, low-power microprocessor. If just one, out of the fifty thousand I'd scattered, still adhered to his shoes the next time we met, I'd be able to interrogate it in infra-red and learn exactly where he'd been. Or exactly where he kept this pair of shoes when he changed into another.

Anton said, 'Icons move west.' He made it sound like a law of nature. 'Through Prague or Budapest, to Vienna, Salzburg, Munich. That's the way everything's set up.'

'For five million Swiss francs, don't you think someone might have made the effort to switch from their traditional lines of supply?'

He scowled. '*Five million!* I don't believe that. What makes this worth five million?'

'You're the expert. You tell me.'

He glared at me as if he suspected that I was mocking him, then looked down at the catalogue again. This time he even read the commentary. He said cautiously, 'Maybe it's older than the auctioneers thought. If it's really, say, fifteen century, the price could almost make sense. Maybe your client guessed the true age . . . and so did someone else.' He sighed. 'It will be expensive finding out who, though. People will be very reluctant to talk.'

I said, 'You know where I'm staying. Once you find someone who needs persuading, let me know.'

He nodded sullenly, as if he'd seriously hoped I might have handed over a large wad of cash for miscellaneous bribes. I almost asked him about the 'scratch' – *Could it be some kind of coded message to the* cognoscenti *that the icon is older than it seems?* – but I didn't want to make a fool of myself. He'd seen it, and said nothing; perhaps it was just a meaningless computer glitch after all.

When I'd paid the bill, he stood up to depart, then bent down towards me and said quietly, 'If you mention what I'm doing, to anyone, I'll have you killed.'

I kept a straight face, and replied, 'Vice versa.'

When he was gone, I tried to laugh. *Stupid, swaggering child.* I couldn't quite get the right sound out, though. I didn't imagine he'd be very happy if he found out what he'd trodden in. I took out my notepad, consulted the appointments diary, then let my right arm hang beside me for a second, dousing the floor with a fry-your-brains code to the remaining microspheres.

Then I took the pictures of De Angelis from my wallet and held it in front of me on the table.

I said, 'Am I in any danger? What do you think?'

She stared back at me, not quite smiling. The expression in her eyes might have been amusement, or it might have been concern. Not indifference; I was sure of that. But she didn't seem prepared to start dispensing predictions or advice.

*   *   *

Just as I was psyching myself up to tackle the hotel manager again, the relevant bureaucrat in the city government finally agreed to fax the hotel a pro-forma statement acknowledging that my licence was recognised throughout the jurisdiction. That seemed to satisfy the manager, though it said no more than the documents I'd already shown him.

The clerk at the check-in desk barely remembered De Angelis; he couldn't say if she'd been cheerful or nervous, friendly or terse. She'd carried her own luggage; a porter remembered seeing her with the attaché case, and an overnight bag. (She'd spent the night in Zürich before collecting the icon.) She hadn't used room service, or any of the hotel restaurants.

The cleaner who'd found the body had been born in Turin, according to his supervisor. I wasn't sure if that was going to be a help or a hindrance. When I tracked him down in a basement storeroom, he said stubbornly, in German, 'I told the police everything. Why are you bothering me? Go and ask them, if you want to know the facts.'

He turned his back on me. He seemed to be stock-taking carpet shampoo and disinfectant, but he made it look like a matter or urgency.

I said, 'It must have been a shock for you. Someone so young. An eighty-year-old guest dying in her sleep, you'd probably take it in your stride. But Gianna was twenty-seven. A tragedy.'

He tensed up at the sound of her name; I could see his shoulders tighten. *Six days later? A woman he'd never even met?*

I said, 'You didn't see her any time before, did you? You didn't talk to her?'

'No.'

I didn't believe him. The manager was a small-minded cretin; fraternising was probably strictly forbidden. This guy was in his twenties, good-looking, spoke the same language. What had he done? Flirted with her harmlessly in a corridor for thirty seconds? And now he was afraid he'd lose his job if he admitted it?

'No one else will find out, if you tell me what she said. You have my word. It's not like the cops; nothing has to be official. All I want to do is help lock up the fuckers who killed her.'

He put down the bar-code scanner and turned to face me. 'I just asked her where she was from. What she was doing in town.'

Hairs stood up on the back of my neck. It had taken me so

273

long to get even this close to her, I couldn't quite believe it was happening.

'How did she react?'

'She was polite. Friendly. She seemed nervous, though. Distracted.'

'And what did she say?'

'She said she was from Milan.'

'What else?'

'When I asked her why she was in Vienna, she said she was playing chaperone.'

'*What?*'

'She said she wasn't staying long. And she was only here to play chaperone. To an older lady.'

*   *   *

Chaperone? I lay awake half the night, trying to make sense of that. Did it imply that she hadn't given up custodianship of the icon? That she was still guarding it when she died? That she considered it to be Luciano Masini's property, and still fully intended to deliver it to him, right to the end?

What had the 'taxi driver' said to her? Bring the icon to Vienna for a day? No need to let it out of your sight? We don't want to steal it . . . we just want to borrow it? To pray to it one last time before it vanishes into another Western bank vault? But what was so special about *this* copy of the Vladimir Mother of God that made it worth so much trouble? The same thing that made it worth five million Swiss francs to Masini, possibly – but what?

And why had De Angelis blown her job, and risked imprisonment, to go along with the scheme? Even if she'd been blind to the obvious fact that it was all a set-up, what could they have offered her in exchange for flushing her career and reputation down the drain?

I'd only been asleep ten or twenty minutes when I was woken by someone pounding on the door of my room. By the time I'd staggered out of bed and pulled on my trousers, the police had grown impatient and let themselves in with a pass key. It wasn't quite two a.m.

There were four of them, two in uniform. One waved a photograph in front of my face. I squinted at it.

'Did you speak to this man? Yesterday?'

It was Anton. I nodded. If they didn't already know the answer, they wouldn't have asked the question.

'Will you come with us, please?'

'Why?'

'Because your friend is dead.'

They showed me the body, so I could confirm that it really was the same man. He'd been shot in the chest and dumped near the canal. Not in it; maybe the killers had been disturbed. In the morgue, the corpse was definitely shoeless, but it would have been worth sending out the microspheres' code, just in case – the things could end up in the strangest places (nostrils, for a start). But before I could think of a plausible excuse to take the notepad from my pocket, they'd pulled the sheet back over his head and led me away for questioning.

The police had found my name and number in 'Anton's' notepad (if they knew his real name, they were keeping it to themselves . . . along with several other things I would have liked to have known, such as whether or not the ballistics matched the bullet used on De Angelis). I recounted the whole conversation in the restaurant, but left out the (illegal) microspheres; they'd find them soon enough, and I had nothing to gain by volunteering a confession.

I was treated with appropriate disdain, but not even verbally abused, really – a five-star rating; I'd had ribs broken in Seveso, and a testicle crushed in Marseille. At half-past four, I was free to leave.

Crossing from the interview room to the elevator, I passed half a dozen small offices; they were separated by partitions, but not fully enclosed. On one desk was a cardboard box, full of items of clothing in plastic bags.

I walked past, then stopped just out of sight. There was a man and a woman in the office, neither of whom I'd seen before, talking and making notes.

I walked back and poked my head into the office. I said, 'Excuse me . . . could you tell me . . . please—?' I spoke German with the worst accent I could manage; I had a head start, it must have been dire. They stared at me, appalled. Visibly struggling for words, I pulled out my notepad and hit a few keys, fumbling with the phrasebook software, walking deeper into the office. I thought I saw a pair of shoes out of the corner of my eye, but I couldn't be certain. 'Could you tell me please where I could find the nearest public convenience?'

The man said, 'Get out of here before I kick your head in.'

I backed out, smiling uncertainly. '*Grazie*, signore! *Danke schön!*'

There was a surveillance camera in the elevator; I didn't even glance at the notepad. Ditto for the foyer. Out on the street, I finally looked down.

I had the data from two hundred and seven microspheres. The software was already busy reconstructing Anton's trail.

I was on the verge of shouting for joy, when it occurred to me that I might have been better off if I hadn't been able to follow him.

*　　*　　*

The first place he'd gone from the restaurant looked like home; no one answered the door, but I could glimpse posters of several of the continent's most pretentious rock bands through the windows. If not his own, maybe a friend's place, or a girlfriend's. I sat in an open-air café across the street, sketching the visible outline of the apartment, guessing at walls and furniture, playing back the trace for the hours he'd spent there, then modifying my guesses, trying again.

The waiter looked over my shoulder at the multiple exposure of stick figures filling the screen. 'Are you a choreographer?'

'Yes.'

'How exciting! What's the name of the dance?'

' "Making Phone Calls And Waiting Impatiently". It's an *hommage* to my two idols and mentors, Twyla Tharp and Pina Bausch.' The waiter was impressed.

After three hours, and no sign of life, I moved on. Anton had stopped by at another apartment, briefly. This one was occupied by a thin blonde woman in her late teens.

I said, 'I'm a friend of Anton's. Do you know where I could find him?'

She'd been crying. 'I don't know anyone by that name.' She slammed the door. I stood in the hallway for a moment, wondering: *Did I kill him? Did someone detect the spheres, and put a bullet in his heart because of them?* But if they'd found them, they would have destroyed them; there would have been no trail to follow.

He'd only visited one more location before taking a car trip to the canal, lying very still. It turned out to be a detached two-storey house in an upmarket district. I didn't ring the doorbell. There was no convenient observation post, so I did a single walk-by. The curtains were drawn; no vehicles were parked near by.

A few blocks away, I sat on a bench in a small park and started phoning databases. The house had been leased just three days before; I had no trouble finding out about the owner – a corporate lawyer with property all over the city – but I couldn't get hold of the new tenant's name.

Vienna had a centralised utilities map, to keep people from digging into underground power cables and phone lines by accident. Phone lines were useless to me; no one who made the slightest effort could be bugged that way any more. But the houses had natural gas; easier to swim through than water, and much less noisy.

I bought a shovel, boots, gloves, a pair of white overalls, and a safety helmet. I captured an image of the gas company logo from its telephone directory entry, and jet-sprayed it onto the helmet; from a distance, it looked quite authentic. I summoned up all the bravado I had left, and returned to the street – beyond sight of the house, but as close to it as I dared. I shifted a few paving slabs out of the way, then started digging. It was early afternoon; there was light traffic, but very few pedestrians. An old man peeked out at me from a window of the nearest house. I resisted the urge to wave to him; it wouldn't have rung true.

I reached the gas main, climbed down into the hole, and pressed a small package against the PVC; it extruded a hollow needle which melted the plastic chemically, maintaining the seal as it penetrated the walls of the pipe. Someone passed by on the footpath, walking two large slobbering dogs; I didn't look up.

The control box chimed softly, signalling success. I refilled the hole, replaced the paving slabs, and returned to the hotel for some sleep.

* * *

I'd left a narrow fibre-optic cable leading from the buried control box to the unpaved ground around a nearby tree, the end just a few millimetres beneath the soil. The next morning, I collected all the stored data, then went back to the hotel to sift through it.

Several hundred bugs had made it into the house's gas pipes and back to the control box, several times – eavesdropping in hour-long overlapping shifts, then returning to disgorge the results. The individual sound tracks were often abysmal, but by processing all of them together the software could usually come up with intelligible speech.

There were five voices, three male, two female. All used

French, though I wouldn't have sworn it was everyone's native tongue.

I pieced things together slowly. They didn't have the icon; they'd been hired to find it, by someone called Katulski. Apparently they'd paid Anton to keep an ear to the ground, but he'd come back to them asking for more money, in exchange for not switching his loyalty to me. The trouble was, he really had nothing tangible to offer . . . and they'd just had a tip-off from another source. References to his murder were oblique, but maybe he'd tried to blackmail them in some way when they'd told him he was no longer needed. One thing was absolutely clear, though; they were taking turns watching an apartment on the other side of the city, where they believed the man who'd killed De Angelis would eventually show up.

I hired a car and followed two of them when they set out to relieve the watch. They'd rented a room across the street from their target; with my IR binoculars I could see where they were aiming theirs. The place under observation looked empty; all I could make out through the tatty curtains was peeling paint.

I called the police from a public phone; the synthesized voice of my notepad spoke for me. I left an anonymous message for the cop who'd interrogated me, giving the code which would unlock the data in the microspheres. Forensic would have found them almost immediately, but extracting the information by brute-force microscopy would have taken days.

Then I waited.

Five hours later, around three a.m., the two men I'd followed left in a hurry, without replacements. I took out my photo of De Angelis and inspected it in the moonlight. I still don't understand what it was about her that held me in her sway; she was either a thief or a fool. Possibly both. And whatever she was, it had killed her.

I said, 'Don't just stand there smirking like you know all the answers. How about wishing me luck?'

The building was ancient, and in bad repair. I had no trouble picking the lock on the front door, and though the stairs creaked all the way to the top floor I encountered no one.

There was a tell-tale pattern of electric fields detectable through the door of apartment 712; it looked like it was wired-up with ten different kinds of alarm. I picked the lock of the neighbouring apartment. There was an access hatch in the ceiling – fortuitously right above the sofa. Someone below moaned in their sleep as I pulled my legs up and closed the hatch. My heart was pounding from adrenaline and claustrophobia, burglary in a foreign city, fear, anticipation. I played a torch-beam around: mice went scurrying.

The corresponding hatch in 712 was guarded just like the door. I moved to another part of the ceiling, lifted away the thermal insulation, then cut a hole in the plaster and lowered myself into the room.

I don't know what I'd expected to find. A shrine covered with icons and votive candles? Occult paraphernalia and a stack of dusty volumes on the teachings of Slavonic mystics?

There was nothing in the room but a bed, a chair, and a VR rig, plugged into the phone socket. Vienna had kept up with the times; even this dilapidated apartment had the latest high-bandwidth ISDN.

I glanced down at the street; there was no one in sight. I put my ear to the door; if anyone was ascending the stairs, they were far quieter than I'd been.

I slipped the helmet over my head.

The simulation was a building, larger than anything I'd ever seen, stretching out around me like a stadium, like a Colosseum. In the distance – perhaps two hundred metres away – were giant marble columns topped with arches, holding up a balcony with an ornate metal railing, and another set of Columns, supporting another balcony . . . and so on, to six tiers. The floor was tile, or parquetry, with delicate angular braids out-lining a complex hexagonal pattern in red and gold. I looked up – and, dazzled, threw my arms in front of my face (to no effect). The hall of this impossible cathedral was topped with a massive dome, the scale defying calculation. Sunlight poured in through dozens of arched windows around the base. Above, covering the dome, was a figurative mosaic, the colours exquisite beyond belief. My eyes watered from the brightness; as I blinked away the tears, I could begin to make out the scene. A haloed woman stretched out her hand—

Someone pressed a gun barrel to my throat.

I froze, waiting for my captor to speak. After a few seconds, I said in German, 'I wish someone would teach me to move that quietly.'

A young male voice replied, in heavily accented English: ' "He who possesses the truth of the word of Jesus can hear its silence." Saint Ignatius of Antioch.' Then he must have reached over to the rig control box and turned down the volume – I'd planned to do that myself, but it had seemed redundant – because I suddenly realised that I'd been listening to a blanket of white noise.

He said, 'Do you like what we're building? It was inspired by the Hagia Sophia in Constantinople – Justinian's Church of the Divine Wisdom – but it's not a slavish copy. The new archi-tecture has no need to make concessions to gross matter. The original in Istanbul is a museum now, and of course it was used as a mosque for five centuries before that. But there's no prospect of either fate befalling this holy place.'

'No.'

'You're working for Luciano Masini, aren't you?'

I couldn't think of a plausible lie which would make me any more popular. 'That's right.'

'Let me show you something.'

I stood rigid, prepared, hoping he was about to take the helmet off me. I felt him moving as the gun barrel shifted slightly, then I realised that he was slipping on the rig's data glove.

He pointed his hand, and moved my viewpoint; blindly for him, which impressed me. I seemed to slide across the cathedral floor straight towards the sanctuary, which was separated from the nave by a massive, gilded latticework screen, covered in hundreds of icons. From a distance, the screen glinted opulently, the subjects of the paintings impossible to discern, the coloured panels making up a weirdly beautiful abstract mosaic.

As I drew closer, though, the effect was overwhelming.

The images were all executed in the same 'crude' two-dimensional style which I'd derided in Masini's missing baseball card – but here, together *en masse*, they seemed a thousand times more expressive than any overblown Renaissance masterpiece. It was not just the fact that the colours had been 'restored' to a richness no physical pigment had ever possessed: reds and blues like luminous velvet, silver like white-hot steel. The simple, stylised human geometry of the figures – the angle of a head bowed in suffering, the strange dispassionate entreaty of eyes raised to heaven – seemed to constitute a whole language of emotions, with a clarity and precision which cut through every barrier to comprehension. It was like writing before Babel, like telepathy, like music.

Or maybe the gun at my throat was helping to broaden my aesthetic sensibilities. Nothing like a good dose of endogenous opiates to throw open the doors of perception.

My captor pointed my eyes at an empty space between two of the icons.

'This is where Our Lady of Chernobyl belongs.'

'Chernobyl? That's where it was painted?'

'Masini didn't tell you anything, did he?'

'Didn't tell me what? That the icon was really fifteenth-century?'

'Not fifteenth. *Twentieth*. 1986.'

My mind was racing, but I said nothing.

He recounted the whole story in matter-of-fact tones, as if he'd been there in person. 'One of the founders of the True Church was a worker at the number four reactor. When the accident happened, he received a lethal dose within hours. But he didn't die straight away. It was two weeks later, when he truly understood the scale of the tragedy – when he realised that it wasn't just hundreds of volunteers, firemen and soldiers who'd die in agony in the months to follow, but *tens of thousands of people* dying in years to come; land and water contaminated for decades; sickness for generations – that Our Lady came to him in a vision, and She told him what to do.

'He was to paint Her as the Vladimir Mother of God, copying every detail, respecting the tradition. But in truth, he would be the instrument for the creation of a new icon – and She would sanctify it, pouring into it all of Her Son's compassion for the suffering which had taken place, His rejoicing in the courage and self-sacrifice His people had shown, and His will to share the burden of the grief and pain that was yet to come.

'She told him to mix some spilt fuel into the pigments he used, and when it was completed to hide it away until it could take its rightful place on the iconostasis of the One True Church.'

I closed my eyes, and saw a scene from a TV documentary: celluloid movie footage taken just after the accident, the image covered with ghostly flashes and trails. Particle tracks recorded in the emulsion; radiation damage to the film itself. *That was what Hengartner's 'scratch' had meant* – whether it was a real effect which appeared when he photographed the icon with a modern camera, or just a stylised addition created by computer. It was a message to any prospective buyer who knew how to read the code: This is not what the commentary says. This is a rarity, a brand-new icon, an original. *Our Lady of Chernobyl.* Ukrainian, 1986.

I said, 'I'm surprised anyone ever got it onto a plane.'

'The radiation is barely detectable now; most of the hottest fission products decayed years ago. Still, you wouldn't want to kiss it. And maybe it killed that superstitious old man a little sooner than he would have died otherwise.'

Superstitious? 'Hengartner . . . thought it would cure his cancer?'

'Why else would he have bought it? It was stolen in '93, and it disappeared for a long time, but there were always rumours circulating about its *miraculous powers*.' His tone was contemptuous. 'I don't know what religion that old fart believed in. *Homeopathy*, maybe. A dose of what ailed him, to put it right again. The best whole-body scanners can pick up the smallest trace of strontium-90, and date it to the accident; if Chernobyl caused his cancer, he would have known it. But your own boss, I imagine, is just an old-fashioned Mariolater, who thinks he can save his granddaughter's life if he burns all his money at a shrine to the Virgin.'

Maybe he thought he was goading me; I didn't give a shit what Masini believed, but a surge of careless anger ran through me. 'And the courier? *What about her?* Was she just another dumb, superstitious peasant to you?'

He was silent for a while; I felt him change hands on the gun. I knew precisely where he was now; with my eyes closed, I could see him in front of me.

'My brother told her there was a boy from Kiev, dying from leukaemia in Vienna, who wanted a chance to pray to Our Lady of Chernobyl.' All of the contempt had gone out of his voice now. And all of the pompous scriptural certainty. 'Masini had told her about his granddaughter. She knew how obsessed he was; she knew he'd never part with the icon willingly, not even for a couple of hours. So she agreed to take it to Vienna. To deliver it a day late. She didn't believe it would cure anyone. I don't think she believed in God at all. But my brother convinced her that the boy had the right to pray to the icon, to take some comfort from doing that. Even if he didn't have five million Swiss francs.'

I threw a punch, the hardest I'd thrown in my life. It connected with flesh and bone, jarring my whole body like an electric shock. For a moment I was so dazed that I didn't know whether or not he'd squeezed the trigger and blown half my face away. I staggered, and pushed the helmet off, icy sweat dripping from my face. He was lying on the floor, shuddering with pain, still holding the gun. I stepped forward and trod on his wrist, then bent down and took the weapon, easily. He was fourteen or fifteen years old, long-limbed but very emaciated, and bald. I kicked him in the ribs, viciously.

'And you played the pious little cancer victim, did you?'

'Yes.' He was weeping, but whether it was from pain or remorse, I couldn't tell.

I kicked him again. 'And then you killed her? To get your hands on the fucking Virgin of Chernobyl who doesn't even work any fucking miracles?'

'I didn't kill her!' He was bawling like an infant. 'My brother killed her, and now he's dead too.'

His brother was dead? 'Anton?'

'He went to tell Katulski's goons about you.' He got the words out between sobs. 'He thought they'd keep you busy . . . and he thought, maybe if they were fighting it out with you, we might have a chance to get the icon out of the city.'

I should have guessed. What better way to hunt for a stolen icon than to traffic in them yourself? And what better way to keep track of your rivals than to pretend to be their informant?

'So where is it now?'

He didn't reply. I slipped the gun into my back pocket, then bent down and picked him up under the arms. He must have weighed about thirty kilos, at the most. Maybe he really was dying of leukaemia; at the time, I didn't much care. I slammed him against the wall, let him fall, then picked him up and did it again. Blood streamed out of his nose; he started choking and

285

spluttering. I lifted him for a third time, then paused to inspect my handiwork. I realised I'd broken his jaw when I'd hit him, and probably one of my fingers.

He said, 'You're nothing. Nothing. A blip in history. Time will swallow up the secular age – and all the mad, blasphemous cults and superstitions – like a mote in a sandstorm. Only the True Church will endure.' He was smiling bloodily, but he didn't sound smug, or triumphant. He was just stating an opinion.

The gun must have reached body temperature in the pocket of my jeans; when he pressed the barrel to the back of my head, at first I mistook it for his thumb. I stared into his eyes, trying to read his intentions, but all I could see was desperation. In the end, he was just a child alone in a foreign city, overwhelmed by disasters.

He slid the barrel around my head, until it was aimed at my temple. I closed my eyes, clutching at him involuntarily. I said, 'Please—'

He took the gun away. I opened my eyes just in time to see him blow his brains out.

*   *   *

All I wanted to do was curl up on the floor and sleep, and then wake to find that it had all been a dream. Some mechanical instinct kept me moving, though. I washed off as much of the blood as I could. I listened for signs that the neighbours had woken. The gun was an illegal Swedish weapon with an integral silencer; the round itself had made a barely audible hiss, but I wasn't sure how loudly I'd been shouting.

I'd been wearing gloves from the start, of course. The ballistics would confirm suicide. But the hole in the ceiling and the broken jaw and the bruised ribs would have to be explained, and the chances were I'd shed hair and skin all over the room. Eventually, there would have to be a trial. And I would have to go to prison.

I was almost ready to call the police. I was too tired to think of fleeing, too sickened by what I'd done. I hadn't literally killed the boy – just beaten him, and terrorised him. I was still angry with him, even then; he was partly to blame for De Angelis's death. At least as much as I was to blame for his.

And then the mechanical part of me said: *Anton was his brother. They might have met, the day he was killed – at Anton's place, or the apartment with the thin blonde girl. Trodden the same floor for a while. Wiped their feet on the same doormat. And since that time, he might have moved the icon from one hiding place to another.*

I took out my notepad, knelt at the feet of the corpse, and sent out the code.

Three spheres responded.

* * *

I found it just before dawn, buried under rubble in a half-demolished building on the outskirts of the city. It was still in the attaché case, but all the locks and alarms had been disabled. I opened the case, and stared at the thing itself for a while. It looked like the catalogue photograph. Drab and ugly.

I wanted to snap it in two. I wanted to light a bonfire and burn it. Three people were dead because of it.

But it wasn't that simple.

I sat on the rubble with my head in my hands. I couldn't pretend that I didn't know what the icon meant to its rightful owners. I'd seen the church they were building, the place where it belonged. I'd heard the story, however apocryphal, of its creation. And if talk of divine compassion for the dead of Chernobyl being channelled into a radioactive Christmas card was meaningless, ludicrous bullshit to me, that wasn't the point. De Angelis had believed none of it, but she'd still blown her job, she'd still gone to Vienna of her own free will. And I could dream of a perfect, secular, rational world all I liked, but I still had to live, and act, in the real one.

I was sure I could get the icon to Masini before I was arrested. He wasn't likely to hand over all his worldly goods, as promised, but I'd probably be able to extract several billion lira from him – before the kid died, and his gratitude faded. Enough to buy myself some very good lawyers. Good enough, perhaps, to keep me out of prison.

Or I could do what De Angelis should have done when it came to the crunch, instead of defending Masini's fucking property rights to the death.

I returned to the apartment. I'd switched off all the alarms before leaving; I could enter through the door this time. I put on the VR helmet and glove, and wrote an invisible message with my fingertip in the empty space on the iconostasis.

Then I pulled out the phone plug, breaking the connection, and went looking for a place to hide until nightfall.

* * *

We met just before midnight, outside the fairground to the city's north-east, within sight of the Ferris wheel. Another frightened, expendable child, putting on a brave front. I might have been the cops. I might have been anyone.

When I handed over the attaché case, he opened it and glanced inside, then looked up at me as if I were some kind of holy apparition.

I said, 'What will you do with it?'

'Extract the true icon from the physical representation. And then destroy it.'

I almost replied: *You should have stolen Hengartner's image file instead, and saved everyone a lot of trouble*. But I didn't have the heart.

He pressed a multilingual pamphlet into my hands. I read it on my way to the subway. It spelt out the theological differences between the True Church and the various national versions of Orthodoxy. Apparently it all came down to the question of the incarnation; God had been made information, not flesh, and anyone who'd missed that important distinction needed to be set right as soon as possible. It went on to explain how the True Church would unify the Eastern Orthodox – and eventually the entire Christian – world, while eradicating superstitions, apocalyptic cults, virulent nationalism, and atheistic materialism. It didn't say anything, one way or the other, about anti-Semitism, or the bombing of mosques.

The letters decayed on the page, minutes after I'd read them. Triggered by exhaled carbon dioxide? These people had appropriated the methods of some strange gurus indeed.

I took out my photo of De Angelis.

'Is this what you wanted of me? Are you satisfied?'

She didn't reply. I tore up the image and let the pieces flutter to the ground.

I didn't take the subway. I needed the cold air to clear my head. So I walked back into the city, making my way between the ruins of the incomprehensible past, and the heralds of the unimaginable future.

THE PLANCK DIVE

Gisela was contemplating the advantages of being crushed – almost certainly to death, albeit as slowly as possible – when the messenger appeared in her homescape. She noted its presence but instructed it to wait, a sleek golden courier with winged sandals stretching out a hand impatiently, frozen in mid-stride twenty delta away.

The scape was currently an expanse of yellow dunes beneath a pale-blue sky, neither too stark nor too distracting. Gisela, reclining on the cool sand, was intent on a giant, scruffy triangle hovering at an incline over the dunes, each edge resembling a loose bundle of straw. The triangle was a collection of Feynman diagrams, showing just a few of the many ways a particle could move between three events in spacetime. A quantum particle could not be pinned down to any one path, but it could be treated as a sum of localised components, each following a different trajectory and taking part in a different set of interactions along the way.

In 'empty' spacetime, interactions with virtual particles caused each component's phase to rotate constantly, like the hand of a clock. But the time measured by any kind of clock travelling between two events in flat spacetime was greatest when the route taken was a straight line – any detours caused time dilation, shortening the trip – and so a plot of phase shift versus detour size also reached its peak for a straight line. Since this peak was smooth and flat, a group of nearly straight paths clustered around it all had similar phase shifts, and these paths allowed many more components to arrive in phase with each other, reinforcing each other, than any equivalent group on the slopes. Three straight lines, glowing red through the centre of each 'bundle of straw', illustrated the result: the classical paths, the paths of highest probability, were straight lines.

In the presence of matter, all the same processes became slightly skewed. Gisela added a couple of nanograms of lead to the model – a few trillion atoms, their world lines running vertically through the centre of the triangle, sprouting their own thicket of virtual particles. Atoms were neutral in charge and colour, but their individual electrons and quarks still scattered virtual photons and gluons. Every kind of matter interfered with some part of the virtual swarm, and the initial disturbance spread out through spacetime by scattering virtual particles itself, rapidly obliterating any difference between the effect of a tonne of rock or a tonne of neutrinos, growing weaker with distance according to a roughly inverse square law. With the rain of virtual particles – and the phase shifts they created – varying from place to place, the paths of highest probability ceased obeying the geometry of flat spacetime. The luminous red triangle of most-probable trajectories was now visibly curved.

The key idea dated back to Sakharov: gravity was nothing but the residue of the imperfect cancellation of other forces; squeeze the quantum vacuum hard enough and Einstein's equations fell out. But since Einstein, every theory of gravity was also a theory of *time*. Relativity demanded that a free-falling particle's rotating phase agree with every other clock that travelled the same path, and once gravitational time dilation was linked to changes in virtual particle density, every measure of time – from the half-life of a radioisotope's decay (stimulated by vacuum fluctuations) to the vibrational modes of a sliver of quartz (ultimately due to the same phase effects as those giving rise to classical paths) – could be reinterpreted as a count of interactions with virtual particles.

It was this line of reasoning that had led Kumar – a century after Sakharov, building on work by Penrose, Smolin and Rovelli – to devise a model of spacetime as a quantum sum of every possible network of particle world lines, with classical 'time' arising from the number of intersections along a given strand of the net. This model had been an unqualified success, surviving theoretical scrutiny and experimental tests for centuries. But it had never been validated at the smallest length scales, accessible only at absurdly high energies, and it made no attempt to explain the basic structure of the nets, or the rules that governed them. Gisela wanted to know where those details came from. She wanted to understand the universe at its deepest level, to touch the beauty and simplicity that lay beneath it all.

That was why she was taking the Planck Dive.

The messenger caught her eye again. It was radiating tags indicating that it represented Cartan's mayor: non-sentient software that dealt with the maintenance of good relations with other polises, observing formal niceties and smoothing away minor points of conflict in those cases where no real citizen-to-citizen connections existed. Since Cartan had been in orbit around Chandrasekhar, ninety-seven light years from Earth, for almost three centuries – and was currently even further from all the other spacefaring polises – Gisela was at a loss to imagine what urgent diplomatic tasks the mayor could be engaged in, let alone why it would want to consult her.

She sent the messenger an activation tag. Deferring to the scape's aesthetic of continuity, it sprinted across the dunes, coming to a halt in front of her in a cloud of fine dust. 'We're in the process of receiving two visitors from Earth.'

Gisela was astonished. 'Earth? Which polis?'

'Athena. The first one has just arrived; the second will be in transit for another ninety minutes.'

Gisela had never heard of Athena, but ninety minutes per person sounded ominous. Everything meaningful about an individual citizen could be packed into less than an exabyte, and sent as a gamma-ray burst a few milliseconds long. If you wanted to simulate an entire flesher body – cell by cell, redundant viscera and all – that was a harmless enough eccentricity, but lugging the microscopic details of your 'very own' small intestine ninety-seven light years was just being precious.

'What do you know about Athena? In brief.'

'It was founded in 2312, with a charter expressing the goal of "regaining the lost flesher virtues". In public fora, its citizens have shown little interest in exopolitan reality – other than flesher history and artforms – but they do participate in some contemporary interpolis cultural activities.'

'So why have these two come here?' Gisela laughed. 'If they're refugees from boredom, surely they could have sought asylum a little closer to home?'

The mayor took her literally. 'They haven't adopted Cartan citizenship; they've entered the polis with only visitor privileges. In their transmission preamble they stated that their purpose in coming was to witness the Planck Dive.'

'Witness – not take part in?'

'That's what they said.'

They could have witnessed as much from home as any non-participant here in Cartan. The Dive team had been broadcasting everything – studies, schematics, simulations, technical arguments, metaphysical debates – from the moment the idea had coalesced out of little more than jokes and thought experiments, a few years after they'd gone into orbit around the black hole. But at least Gisela now knew why the mayor had picked on her; she'd volunteered to respond to any requests for information about the Dive that couldn't be answered automatically from public sources. No one seemed to have found their reports to be lacking a single worthwhile detail, though, until now.

'So the first one's suspended?'

'No. She woke as soon as she arrived.'

That seemed even stranger than their excess baggage. If you

were travelling with someone, why not delay activation until your companion caught up? Or, better yet, package yourselves as inter-leaved bits?

'But she's still in the arrival lounge?'

'Yes.'

Gisela hesitated. 'Shouldn't I wait until the other one's all here? So I can greet them together?'

'No.' The mayor seemed confident on this point. Gisela wished interpolis protocol allowed non-sentient software to play host; she felt woefully ill prepared for the role. But if she started consulting people, seeking advice, and looking into Athena's culture in depth, the visitors would probably have toured Cartan and gone home before she was ready for them.

She steeled herself, and jumped.

* * *

The last person who'd whimsically redesigned the arrival lounge had made it a wooden pier surrounded by grey, wind-swept ocean. The first of the two visitors was still standing patiently at the end of the pier, which was just as well; it was unbounded in the other direction, and walking a few kilodelta to no avail might have been a bit dispiriting. Her fellow traveller, still in transit, was represented by a motionless placeholder. Both icons were highly anatomical-realist, clothed but clearly male and female, the unfrozen female much younger-looking. Gisela's own icon was more stylised, and her surface, whether 'skin' or 'clothing' – either could gain a tactile sense if she wished – was textured with diffuse reflection rules not quite matching the optical properties of any real substance.

'Welcome to Cartan. I'm Gisela.' She stretched out her hand, and the visitor stepped forward and shook it – though it was possible that she perceived and executed an entirely different act, cross-translated through gestural interlingua.

'I'm Cordelia. This is my father, Prospero. We've come all the way from Earth.' She seemed slightly dazed, a response

Gisela found entirely reasonable. Back in Athena, whatever elaborate metaphoric action they'd used to instruct the communications software to halt them, append suitable explanatory headers and checksums, then turn the whole package bit by bit into a stream of modulated gamma rays, it could never have fully prepared them for the fact that in a subjective instant they'd be stepping ninety-seven years into the future, and ninety-seven light years from home.

'You're here to observe the Planck Dive?' Gisela chose to betray no hint of puzzlement; it would have been pointlessly cruel to drive home the fact that they could have seen everything from Athena. Even if you fetishised realtime data over lightspeed transmissions, it could hardly be worth slipping one-hundred-and-ninety-four years out of synch with your fellow citizens.

Cordelia nodded shyly, and glanced at the statue beside her. 'My father, really . . .'

Meaning what? It was all his idea? Gisela smiled encouragingly, hoping for clarification, but none was forthcoming. She'd been wondering why a Prospero had named his daughter Cordelia, but now it struck her as only prudent – if you had to succumb to a Shakespearean-names fad at all – not to put anyone from the same play together in one family.

'Would you like to look around? While you're waiting for him?'

Cordelia stared at her feet, as if the question was profoundly embarrassing.

'It's up to you.' Gisela laughed. 'I have no idea what constitutes the polite treatment of half-delivered relatives.' It was unlikely that Cordelia did, either; citizens of Athena clearly didn't make a habit of crossing interstellar distances, and the connections on Earth all had so much bandwidth that the issue would never arise. 'But if it was me in transit, I wouldn't mind at all.'

Cordelia hesitated. 'Could I see the black hole, please?'

'Of course.' Chandrasekhar possessed no blazing accretion disk – it was six billion years old, and had long ago swept the region clean of gas and dust – but it certainly left the imprint of its presence on the ordinary starlight around it. 'I'll give you the short tour, and we'll be back long before your father's awake.' Gisela examined the bearded icon; with his gaze fixed on the horizon and his arms at his side, he appeared to be on the verge of bursting into song. 'Assuming he's not running on partial data already. I could have sworn I saw those eyes move.'

Cordelia smiled slightly, then looked up and said solemnly, 'That's not how we were packaged.'

Gisela sent her an address tag. 'Then he'll be none the wiser. Follow me.'

*   *   *

They stood on a circular platform in empty space. Gisela had inflected the scape's address to give the platform 'artificial gravity' – a uniform one gee, regardless of their motion – and a transparent dome full of air at standard temperature and pressure. Presumably all Athena citizens were set up to ignore any scape parameters that might cause them discomfort, but it still seemed like a good idea to err on the side of caution. The platform itself was a compromise, five delta wide – offering some protection from vertigo, but small enough to let its occupants see some forty degrees below 'horizontal'.

Gisela pointed. 'There it is: Chandrasekhar. Twelve solar masses. Seventeen thousand kilometres away. It might take you a moment to spot it; it looks about the same as the new moon from Earth.' She'd chosen their co-ordinates and velocity carefully; as she spoke, a bright star split in two, then flared for a moment into a small, perfect ring as it passed directly behind the hole. 'Apart from gravitational lensing, of course.'

Cordelia smiled, obviously delighted. 'Is this a real view?'

'Partly. It's based on all the images we've received so far from a whole swarm of probes, but there are still viewpoints that have never been covered and need to be interpolated. That includes the fact that we're almost certainly moving with a different velocity than any probe that passed through the same location, so we're seeing things differently, with different Doppler shifts and aberration.'

Cordelia absorbed this with no sign of disappointment. 'Can we go closer?'

'As close as you like.'

Gisela sent control tags to the platform, and they spiralled in. For a while it looked as if there'd be nothing more to see; the featureless black disk ahead of them grew steadily larger, but it clearly wasn't going to blossom with any kind of detail. Gradually, though, a congested halo of lensed images began to form around it, and you didn't need the flash of an Einstein ring to see that light was behaving strangely.

'How far away are we now?'

'About thirty-four M.' Cordelia looked uncertain. Gisela added, 'Six hundred kilometres, but if you convert mass into distance in the natural way, that's thirty-four times Chandrasekhar's mass. It's a useful convention; if a hole has no charge or angular momentum, its mass sets the scale for all the geometry: the event horizon is always at two M, light forms circular orbits at three M, and so on.' She conjured up a spacetime map of the region outside the hole, and instructed the scape to record the platform's world line on it. 'Actual distances travelled depend on the path you take, but if you think of the hole as being surrounded by spherical shells on which the tidal force is constant – something tangible you can measure on the spot – you can give them each a radius of curvature without caring about the details of how you might travel all the way to their centre.' With one spatial dimension omitted to make room for time, the shells became circles, and their histories on the map were shown as concentric translucent cylinders.

As the disk itself grew, the distortion around it spread faster. By ten M, Chandrasekhar was less than sixty degrees wide, but even constellations in the opposite half of the sky were visibly crowded together, as incoming light rays were bent into more radial paths. The gravitational blue shift, uniform across the sky, was strong enough now to give the stars a savage glint – not so much icy, as blue-hot. On the map, the light cones dotted along their world line – structures like stylised conical hourglasses, made up of all the light rays passing through a given point at a given moment – were beginning to tilt towards the hole. Light cones marked the boundaries of physically possible motion; to cross your own light cone would be to outrace light.

Gisela created a pair of binoculars and offered them to Cordelia. 'Try looking at the halo.'

Cordelia obliged her. 'Ah! Where did all those stars come from?'

'Lensing lets you see the stars behind the hole, but it doesn't stop there. Light that grazes the three-M shell orbits part-way around the hole before flying off in a new direction – and there's no limit to how far it can swing around, if it grazes the shell close enough.' On the map, Gisela sketched half a dozen light rays approaching the hole from various angles; after wrapping themselves in barber's-pole helices at slightly different distances from the three-M cylinder, they all headed off in almost the same direction. 'If you look into the light that escapes from those orbits, you see an image of the whole sky, compressed into a narrow ring. And at the inner edge of that ring, there's a smaller ring, and so on – each made up of light that's orbited the hole one more time.'

Cordelia pondered this for a moment. 'But it can't go on forever, can it? Won't diffraction effects blur the pattern, eventually?'

Gisela nodded, hiding her surprise. 'Yeah. But I can't show you that here. This scape doesn't run to that level of detail!'

They paused at the three-M shell itself. The sky here was perfectly bisected: one hemisphere in absolute darkness, the other packed with vivid blue stars. Along the border, the halo arched over the dome like an impossibly geometricised Milky Way. Shortly after Cartan's arrival, Gisela had created a homage to Escher based on this view, tiling the half-sky with interlocking constellations that repeated at the edge in ever smaller copies. With the binoculars on 1000 X, they could see a kind of silhouette of the platform itself 'in the distance': a band of darkness blocking a tiny part of the halo in every direction.

Then they continued towards the event horizon, oblivious to both tidal forces and the thrust they would have needed to maintain such a leisurely pace in reality.

The stars were now all brightest at ultraviolet frequencies, but Gisela had arranged for the dome to filter out everything but light from the flesher visible spectrum, in case Cordelia's simulated skin took descriptions of radiation too literally. As the entire erstwhile celestial sphere shrank to a small disk, Chandrasekhar seemed to wrap itself around them – and this optical illusion had teeth. If they'd fired off a beam of light away from the hole, but failed to aim it at that tiny blue window, it would have bent right around like the path of a tossed rock and dived back into the hole. No material object could do better; the choice of escape routes was growing narrower. Gisela felt a *frisson* of claustrophobia; soon she'd be doing this for real.

They paused again to hover – implausibly – just above the horizon, with the only illumination a pin-prick of heavily blue-shifted radio waves behind them. On the map, their future light cone led almost entirely into the hole, with just the tiniest sliver protruding from the two-M cylinder.

Gisela said, 'Shall we go through?'

Cordelia's face was etched in violet. 'How?'

'Pure simulation. As authentic as possible, but not so authentic that we'll be trapped, I promise.'

Cordelia spread her arms, closed her eyes, and mimed falling backwards into the hole. Gisela instructed the platform to cross the horizon.

The speck of sky blinked out, then began to expand again rapidly. Gisela was slowing down time a millionfold; in reality they would have reached the singularity in a fraction of a millisecond.

Cordelia said, 'Can we stop here?'

'You mean freeze time?'

'No, just hover.'

'We're doing that already. We're not moving.' Gisela suspended the scape's evolution. 'I've halted time; I think that's what you wanted.'

Cordelia seemed about to dispute this, but then she gestured at the now-frozen circle of stars. 'Outside, the blue shift was the same right across the sky, but now the stars at the edge are much bluer. I don't understand.'

Gisela said, 'In a way it's nothing new; if we'd let ourselves free-fall towards the hole, we would have been moving fast enough to see a whole range of Doppler shifts superimposed on the gravitational blue shift, long before we crossed the horizon. You know the starbow effect?'

'Yes.' Cordelia examined the sky again, and Gisela could almost see her testing the explanation, imagining how a blue-shifted starbow should look. 'But that only makes sense if we're moving – and you said we weren't.'

'We're not, by one perfectly good definition. But it's not the definition that applied outside.' Gisela highlighted a vertical section of their world line, where they'd hovered on the three-M shell. 'Outside the event horizon – given a powerful enough engine – you can always stay fixed on a shell of constant tidal force. So it makes sense to choose that as a definition of being "motionless" – making time on this map strictly vertical. But inside the hole, that becomes completely incompatible with experience; your light cone tilts so far that your world line *must* cut through the shells. And the simplest new definition of being "motionless" is to burrow straight through the shells – the complete opposite of trying to cling to them – and to make "map time" strictly horizontal, pointing towards the centre of the hole.' She highlighted a section of their now-horizontal world line.

Cordelia's expression of puzzlement began to give way to astonishment. 'So when the light cones tip over far enough . . . the definitions of "space" and "time" have to tip with them?'

'Yes! The centre of the hole lies in our future, now. We won't hit the singularity face-first, we'll hit it future-first – just like hitting the Big Crunch. And the direction on this platform that used to point towards the singularity is now facing "down" on the map – into what seems from the outside to be the hole's past, but is really a vast stretch of space. There are billions of light years laid out in front of us – the entire history of the hole's interior, converted into space – and it's expanding as we approach the singularity. The only catch is, elbow room and head room are in short supply. Not to mention time.'

Cordelia stared at the map, entranced. 'So the inside of the hole isn't a sphere at all? It's a spherical shell in two directions, with the shell's history converted into space as the third . . . making the whole thing the surface of a hypercylinder? A hypercylinder that's increasing in length, while its radius shrinks.' Suddenly her face lit up. 'And the blue shift is like the blue shift when the universe starts contracting?' She turned to the frozen sky. 'Except this space is only shrinking in two directions – so the more the angle of the starlight favours those directions, the more it's blue-shifted?'

'That's right.' Gisela was no longer surprised by Cordelia's rapid uptake; the mystery was how she could have failed to learn everything there was to know about black holes, long ago. With unfettered access to a half-decent library and rudimentary tutoring software, she would have filled in the gaps in no time. But if her father had dragged her all the way to Cartan just to witness the Planck Dive, how could he have stood by and allowed Athena's culture to impede her education? It made no sense.

Cordelia raised the binoculars and looked sideways, around the hole. 'Why can't I see us?

'Good question.' Gisela drew a light ray on the map, aimed sideways, leaving the platform just after they'd crossed the horizon. 'At the three-M shell, a ray like this would have followed a helix in spacetime, coming back to our world line after one revolution. But here, the helix has been flipped over and squeezed into a spiral – and, at best, it only has time to travel halfway around the hole before it hits the singularity. None of the light we've emitted since crossing the horizon can make it back to us.

'That's assuming a perfectly symmetrical Schwarzschild black hole, which is what we're simulating. And an ancient hole like Chandrasekhar probably has settled down to a fair approximation of the Schwarzschild geometry. But close to the singularity, even infalling starlight would be blue-shifted enough to disrupt it, and anything more massive – like us, if we really were here – would cause chaotic changes even sooner.' She instructed the scape to switch to Belinsky–Khalatnikov–Lifshitz geometry, then restarted time. The stars began to shimmer with distortion, as if seen through a turbulent atmosphere, then the sky itself seemed to boil, red shifts and blue shifts sweeping across it in churning waves. 'If we were embodied, and strong enough to survive the tidal forces, we'd feel them oscillating wildly as we passed through regions collapsing and expanding in different directions.' She modified the spacetime map accordingly, and enlarged it for a better view. Close to the singularity, the once-regular cylinders of constant tidal force now disintegrated into a random froth of ever finer, ever more distorted bubbles.

Cordelia examined the map with an expression of

consternation. 'How are you going to do any kind of computation in an environment like that?'

'We're not. This is chaos, but chaotic systems are highly susceptible to manipulation. You know Tiplerian theology? The doctrine that we should try to reshape the universe to allow infinite computation to take place before the Big Crunch?'

'Yes.'

Gisela spread her arms to take in all of Chandrasekhar. 'Reshaping a black hole is easier. With a closed universe, all you can do is rearrange what's already there; with a black hole, you can pour new matter and radiation in from all directions. By doing that, we're hoping to steer the geometry into a more orderly collapse – not the Schwarzschild version, but one that lets light circumnavigate the space inside the hole many times. Cartan Null will be made of counter-rotating beams of light, modulated with pulses like beads on a string. As they pass through each other, the pulses will interact; they'll be blue-shifted to energies high enough for pair-production, and eventually even high enough for gravitational effects. Those beams will be our memory, and their interactions will drive all our computation – with luck, down almost to the Planck scale: ten-to-the-minus-thirty-five metres.'

Cordelia contemplated this in silence, then asked hesitantly, 'But how much computation will you be able to do?'

'In total?' Gisela shrugged. 'That depends on details of the structure of spacetime at the Planck scale – details we won't know until we're inside. There are some models that would allow us to do the whole Tiplerian thing in miniature: infinite computation. But most give a range of finite answers, some large, some small.'

Cordelia was beginning to look positively gloomy. Surely she'd known about the Divers' fate all along?

Gisela said, 'You do realise we're sending in clones? No one's moving their sole version into Cartan Null!'

'I know.' Cordelia averted her eyes. 'But once you *are* the clone . . . won't you be afraid of dying?'

Gisela was touched. 'Only slightly. And not at all, at the end. While there's still a slender chance of infinite computation, or even some exotic discovery that might allow us to escape, we'll hang on to fear of death. It should help motivate us to examine all the options! But if and when it's clear that dying is inevitable, we'll switch off the old instinctive response, and just accept it.'

Cordelia nodded politely, but she didn't seem at all convinced. If you'd been raised in a polis that celebrated 'the lost flesher virtues', this probably sounded like cheating at best, and self-mutilation at worst.

'Can we go back now, please? My father will be awake soon.'

'Of course.' Gisela wanted to say something to this strange, solemn child to put her mind at ease, but she had no idea where to begin. So they jumped out of the scape together – out of their fictitious light cones – abandoning the simulation before it was forced to admit that it was offering neither the chance of new knowledge, nor the possibility of death.

*   *   *

When Prospero woke, Gisela introduced herself and asked what he wished to see. She suggested a schematic of Cartan Null; it didn't seem tactful to mention that Cordelia had already toured Chandrasekhar, but offering him a scape that neither had seen seemed like a diplomatic way of side-stepping the issue.

Prospero smiled at her indulgently. 'I'm sure your Falling City is ingeniously designed, but that's of no interest to me. I'm here to scrutinise your motives, not your machines.'

'Our motives?' Gisela wondered if there'd been a translation error. 'We're curious about the structure of spacetime. Why else would someone dive into a black hole?'

Prospero's smile broadened. 'That's what I'm here to

304

determine. There's a wide range of choices besides the Pandora myth: Prometheus, Quixote, the Grail of course . . . perhaps even Orpheus. Do you hope to rescue the dead?'

'Rescue the dead?' Gisela was dumbfounded. 'Oh, you mean Tiplerian resurrection? No, we have no plans for that at all. Even if we obtained infinite computing power, which is unlikely, we'd have far too little information to re-create any specific dead fleshers. As for resurrecting everyone by brute force, simulating every possible conscious being, there'd be no sure way to screen out in advance simulations that would experience extreme suffering – and statistically, they're likely to outnumber the rest by about ten thousand to one. So the whole thing would be grossly unethical.'

'We shall see.' Prospero waved her objections away. 'What's important is that I meet all of Charon's passengers as soon as possible.'

'Charon's . . . ? You mean the Dive team?'

Prospero shook his head with an anguished expression, as if he'd been misunderstood, but he said, 'Yes, assemble your "Dive team". Let me speak to them all. I can see how badly I'm needed here!'

Gisela was more bewildered than ever. 'Needed? You're welcome here, of course . . . but in what way are you needed?'

Cordelia reached over and tugged at her father's arm. 'Can we wait in the castle? I'm so tired.' She wouldn't look Gisela in the eye.

'Of course, my darling!' Prospero leant down and kissed her forehead. He pulled a rolled-up parchment out of his robe and tossed it into the air. It unfurled into a doorway, hovering above the ocean beside the pier, leading into a sunlit scape. Gisela could see vast, overgrown gardens, stone buildings, winged horses in the air. It was a good thing they'd compressed their accommodation more efficiently than their bodies, or they would have tied up the gamma-ray link for about a decade.

Cordelia stepped through the doorway, holding Prospero's

hand, trying to pull him through. Trying, Gisela finally realised, to shut him up before he could embarrass her further.

Without success. With one foot still on the pier, Prospero turned to Gisela. 'Why am I needed? I'm here to be your Homer, your Virgil, your Dante, your Dickens! I'm here to extract the mythic essence of this glorious, tragic endeavour! I'm here to grant you a gift infinitely greater than the immortality you seek!'

Gisela didn't bother pointing out, yet again, that she had every expectation of a much shorter life inside the hole than out. 'What's that?'

'I'm here to make you *legendary*!' Prospero stepped off the pier, and the doorway contracted behind him.

Gisela stared out across the ocean, unseeing for a moment, then sat down slowly and let her feet dangle in the icy water.

Certain things were beginning to make sense.

* * *

'Be nice,' Gisela pleaded. 'For Cordelia's sake.'

Timon feigned wounded puzzlement. 'What makes you think I won't be nice? I'm always nice.' He morphed briefly from his usual angular icon – all rib-like frames and jointed rods – into a button-eyed teddy bear.

Gisela groaned softly. 'Listen. If I'm right – if she's thinking of migrating to Cartan – it will be the hardest decision she's ever had to make. If she could just walk away from Athena she would have done it by now, instead of going to all the trouble of making her father believe that it was his idea to come here.'

'What makes you so sure it wasn't?'

'Prospero has no interest in reality; the only way he could have heard of the Dive is by Cordelia bringing it to his attention. She must have chosen Cartan because it's far enough from Earth to make a clean break, and the Dive gave her the excuse she needed, a fit subject for her father's "talents" to dangle in front of him. But until she's ready to tell him that she's not going back, we mustn't alienate him. We mustn't make things harder for her than they already are.'

Timon rolled his eyes into his anodised skull. 'All right! I'll play along! I suppose there is a chance you might be reading her correctly. But if you're mistaken . . .'

Prospero chose that moment to make his entrance, robes billowing, daughter in tow. They were in a scape created for the occasion, to Prospero's specifications: a room shaped like two truncated square pyramids joined at their bases, panelled in white, with a twenty-M view of Chandrasekhar through a trapezoidal window. Gisela had never seen this style before; Timon had christened it 'Athenian Astrokitsch'.

The five members of the Dive team were seated around a semi-circular table. Prospero stood before them while Gisela made the introductions: Sachio, Tiet, Vikram, Timon. She'd spoken to them all, making the case for Cordelia, but Timon's half-hearted concession was the closest thing she'd received to a guarantee. Cordelia shrank into a corner of the room, eyes downcast.

Prospero began soberly. 'For nigh on a thousand years, we, the descendants of the flesh, have lived our lives wrapped in dreams of heroic deeds long past. But we have dreamed in vain of a new Odyssey to inspire us, new heroes to stand beside the old, new ways to re-tell the eternal myths. Three more days, and your journey would have been wasted, lost to us for ever.' He smiled proudly. 'But I have arrived in time to pluck your tale from the very jaws of gravity!'

Tiet said, 'Nothing was at risk of being lost. Information about the Dive is being broadcast to every polis, stored in every library.' Tiet's icon was like a supple jewelled statue carved from ebony.

Prospero waved a hand dismissively. 'A stream of technical jargon. In Athena, it might as well have been the murmuring of the waves.'

Tiet raised an eyebrow. 'If your vocabulary is impoverished, augment it – don't expect us to impoverish our own. Would you give an account of classical Greece without mentioning the name of a single city-state?'

'No. But those are universal terms, part of our common heritage—'

'They're terms that have no meaning outside a tiny region of space, and a brief period of time. Unlike the terms needed to describe the Dive, which are applicable to every quartic femto-metre of spacetime.'

Prospero replied, a little stiffly, 'Be that as it may, in Athena we prefer poetry to equations. And I have come to honour your journey in language that will resonate down the corridors of the imagination for millennia.'

Sachio said, 'So you believe you're better qualified to portray the Dive than the participants?' Sachio appeared as an owl, perched inside the head of a flesher-shaped wrought-iron cage full of starlings.

'I am a narratologist.'

'You have some kind of specialised training?'

Prospero nodded proudly. 'Though in truth, it is a vocation. When ancient fleshers gathered around their campfires, I was the one telling stories long into the night, of how the gods fought among themselves, and even mortal warriors were raised up into the sky to make the constellations.'

Timon replied, deadpan, 'And I was the one sitting opposite, telling you what a load of drivel you were spouting.' Gisela was about to turn on him, to excoriate him for breaking his promise, when she realised that he'd spoken to her alone, routing the data outside the scape. She shot him a poisonous glance.

Sachio's owl blinked with puzzlement. 'But you find the Dive itself incomprehensible. So how are you suited to explain it to others?'

Prospero shook his head. 'I have come to create enigmas, not explanations. I have come to shape the story of your descent into a form that will live on long after your libraries have turned to dust.'

'Shape it how?' Vikram was as anatomically correct as a Da Vinci sketch, when he chose to be, but he lacked the tell-tale signs of a physiological simulation: no sweat, no dead skin, no shed hair. 'You mean change things?'

'To extract the mythic essence, mere detail must become subservient to a deeper truth.'

Timon said, 'I think that was a yes.'

Vikram frowned amiably. 'So what exactly will you change?' He spread his arms, and stretched them to encompass his fellow team members. 'If we're to be improved upon, do tell us how.'

Prospero said cautiously, 'Five is a poor number, for a start. Seven, perhaps, or twelve.'

'Whew.' Vikram grinned. 'Shadowy extras only; no one's for the chop.'

'And the name of your vessel . . .'

'Cartan Null? What's wrong with that? Cartan was a great flesher mathematician, who clarified the meaning and consequences of Einstein's work. "Null" because it's built of null geodesics: the paths followed by light rays.'

'Posterity,' Prospero declared, 'will like it better as "The Falling City" – its essence unencumbered by your infelicitous words.'

Tiet said coolly, 'We named this polis after Elie Cartan. Its clone inside Chandrasekhar will be named after Elie Cartan. If you're unwilling to respect that, you might as well head back to Athena right now, because no one here is going to offer you the slightest co-operation.'

Prospero glanced at the others, possibly looking for some evidence of dissent. Gisela had mixed feelings; Prospero's mythopoeic babble would not outlive the truth in the libraries, whatever he imagined, so in a sense it hardly mattered what it contained. But if they didn't draw the line somewhere, she could imagine his presence rapidly becoming unbearable.

He said, 'Very well. Cartan Null. I am an artisan as well as an artist; I can work with imperfect clay.'

As the meeting broke up, Timon cornered Gisela. Before he could start complaining, she said, 'If you think three more days of *that* is too awful to contemplate, imagine what it's like for Cordelia.'

Timon shook his head. 'I'll keep my word. But now that I've seen what she's up against, I really don't think she's going to make it. If she's been wrapped in propaganda about the golden age of fleshers all her life, how can you expect her to see through it? A polis like Athena forms a closed trapped memetic surface: concentrate enough Prosperos in one place, and there's no escape.'

Gisela eyed him balefully. 'She's here, isn't she? Don't try telling me that she's bound to Athena for ever, just because she was created there. Nothing's as simple as that. Even black holes emit Hawking radiation.'

'Hawking radiation carries no information. It's thermal noise; you can't tunnel out with it.' Timon swept two fingers along a diagonal line, the gesture for 'QED'.

Gisela said, 'It's only a metaphor, you idiot, not an iso-morphism. If you can't tell the difference, maybe you should fuck off to Athena yourself.'

Timon mimed pulling his hand back from something biting it, and vanished.

Gisela looked around the empty scape, angry with herself for losing her temper. Through the window, Chandrasekhar was calmly proceeding to crush spacetime out of existence, as it had for the past six billion years.

She said, 'And you'd better not be right.'

*   *   *

Fifty hours before the Dive, Vikram instructed the probes in the lowest orbits to begin pouring nanomachines through the event horizon. Gisela and Cordelia joined him in the control scape, a

310

vast hall full of maps and gadgets for manipulating the hardware scattered around Chandrasekhar. Prospero was off interrogating Timon, an ordeal Vikram had just been through himself. 'Oedipal urges' and 'womb/vagina symbolism' had figured prominently, though Vikram had cheerfully informed Prospero that, as far as he knew, no one in Cartan had ever shown much interest in either organ. Gisela found herself wondering precisely how Cordelia had been created; slavish simulations of flesher childbirth didn't bear thinking about.

The nanomachines comprised only a trickle of matter, a few tonnes per second. Deep inside the hole, though, they'd measure the curvature around them – observing both starlight and signals from the nanomachines following behind – then modify their own collective mass distribution in such a way as to steer the hole's future geometry closer to the target. Every deviation from free fall meant jettisoning molecular fragments and sacrificing chemical energy, but before they'd entirely ripped themselves apart they'd give birth to photonic machines tailored to do the same thing on a smaller scale.

It was impossible to know whether or not any of this was working as planned, but a map in the scape showed the desired result. Vikram sketched in two counter-rotating bundles of light rays. 'We can't avoid having space collapsing in two directions and expanding in the third – unless we poured in so much matter that it collapsed in all three, which would be even worse. But it's possible to keep changing the direction of expansion, flipping it ninety degrees again and again, evening things out. That allows light to execute a series of complete orbits – each taking about one hundredth the time of the previous one – and it also means there are periods of contraction across the beams, which counteract the defocusing effects of the periods of expansion.'

The two bundles of rays oscillated between circular and elliptical cross-sections as the curvature stretched and squeezed them. Cordelia created a magnifying glass and followed them 'in': forwards in time, towards the singularity. She said, 'If the orbital periods form a geometric series, there's no limit to the number of orbits you could fit in before the singularity. And the wavelength is blue-shifted in proportion to the size of the orbit, so diffraction effects never take over. So what's there to stop you doing infinite computation?'

Vikram replied cautiously, 'For a start, once colliding photons start creating particle-antiparticle pairs, there'll be a range of energies for each species of particle when it will be travelling so much slower than lightspeed that the pulses will begin to smear. We think we've shaped and spaced the pulses in such a way that all the data will survive, but it would take only one unknown massive particle to turn the whole stream into gibberish.'

Cordelia looked up at him with a hopeful expression. 'What if there are no unknown particles?'

Vikram shrugged. 'In Kumar's model, time is quantised, so the frequency of the beams can't keep rising without limit. And most of the alternative theories also imply that the whole setup will fail eventually, for one reason or another. I only hope it fails slowly enough for us to understand *why*, before we're incapable of understanding anything.' He laughed. 'Don't look so mournful! It will be like . . . the death of one branch of a tree. And maybe we'll gain some knowledge for a while that we could never even glimpse, outside the hole.'

'But you won't be able to do anything with it,' Cordelia protested. 'Or tell anyone.'

'Ah, technology and fame.' Vikram blew a raspberry. 'Listen, if my Dive clone dies learning nothing, he'll still die happy, knowing that I continued outside. And if he learns everything I'm hoping he'll learn, he'll be too ecstatic to go on living.' Vikram composed his face into a picture of exaggerated earnestness, deflating his own hyperbole, and Cordelia actually smiled. Gisela had been beginning to wonder if morbid grief over the fate of the Divers would be enough to put her off Cartan altogether.

Cordelia said, 'What would make it worthwhile, then? What's the most you could hope for?'

Vikram sketched a Feynman diagram in the air between them. 'If you take spacetime for granted, rotational symmetry plus quantum mechanics gives you a set of rules for dealing with a particle's spin. Penrose turned this inside out, and showed that the whole concept of "the angle between two directions" can be created from scratch in a network of world lines, so long as they obey those spin rules. Suppose a system of particles with a certain total spin throws an electron to another system, and in the process the first system's spin decreases. If you knew the angle between the two spin vectors, you could calculate the probability that the second spin was increased rather than decreased . . . but if the concept of "angle" doesn't even exist yet, you can work backwards and *define it* from the probability you get by looking at all the networks for which the second spin is increased.

'Kumar and others extended this idea to cover more abstract symmetries. From a list of rules about what constitutes a valid network, and how to assign a phase to each one, we can now derive all known physics. But I want to know if there's a deeper explanation for those rules. Are spin and the other quantum numbers truly elementary, or are they the product of something more fundamental? And when networks reinforce or cancel each other according to the phase difference between them, is that something basic we just have to accept, or is there hidden machinery beneath the mathematics?'

Timon appeared in the scape, and drew Gisela aside. 'I've committed a small infraction – and, knowing you, you'll find out anyway. So this is a confession in the hope of leniency.'

'What have you done?'

Timon regarded her nervously. 'Prospero was rambling on about flesher culture as the route to all knowledge.' He morphed into a perfect imitation, and replayed Prospero's voice: ' "The key to astronomy lies in the study of the great

Egyptian astrologers, and the heart of mathematics is revealed in the rituals of the Pythagorean mystics . . ." '

Gisela put her face in her hands; she would have been hard-pressed not to respond herself. 'And you said—?'

'I told him that if he was ever embodied in a spacesuit, floating among the stars, he ought to try sneezing on the face plate to improve the view.'

Gisela cracked up laughing. Timon asked hopefully, 'Does that mean I'm forgiven?'

'No. How did he take it?'

'Hard to tell.' Timon frowned. 'I'm not sure that he's cap-able of grasping insults. It would require imagining that some-one could believe that he's less than essential to the future of civilisation.'

Gisela said sternly, 'Two more days. Try harder.'

'Try harder yourself. It's your turn now.'

'What?'

'Prospero wants to see you.' Timon grinned with malicious pleasure. 'Time to have your own *mythic essence* extracted.'

Gisela glanced towards Cordelia; she was talking animatedly with Vikram. Athena, and Prospero, had suffocated her; it was only away from both that she came to life. The decision to migrate was hers alone, but Gisela would never forgive herself if she did anything to diminish the opportunity.

Timon said, 'Be nice.'

*　　*　　*

The Dive team had decided against any parting of the clones; their frozen snapshots would be incorporated into the blueprint for Cartan Null without ever being run outside Chandrasekhar. When Gisela had told Prospero this, he'd been appalled, but he'd cheered up almost immediately; it left him all the more room to invent some ritual farewell for the travellers, without being distracted by the truth.

The whole team did gather in the control scape, though,

along with Prospero and Cordelia, and a few dozen friends. Gisela stood apart from the crowd as Vikram counted down to the deadline. On 'ten', she instructed her exoself to clone her. On 'nine', she sent the snapshot to the address being broadcast by an icon for the Cartan Null file – a stylised set of counter-rotating light beams – hovering in the middle of the scape. When the tag came back confirming the transaction, she felt a surge of loss; the Dive was no longer part of her own linear future, even if she thought of the clone as a component of her extended self.

Vikram shouted exuberantly, 'Three! Two! One!' He picked up the Cartan Null icon and tossed it into a map of the spacetime around Chandrasekhar. This triggered a gamma-ray burst from the polis to a probe with an eight-M orbit; there, the data was coded into nanomachines designed to re-create it in active, photonic form – and those nanomachines joined the stream cascading into the hole.

On the map, the falling icon veered into a 'motionless' vertical world line as it approached the two-M shell. Successive slices of constant time in the static frame outside the hole never crossed the horizon, they merely clung to it; by one definition, the nanomachines would take for ever to enter Chandrasekhar.

By another definition, the Dive was over. In their own frame, the nanomachines would have taken less than one-and-a-half milliseconds to fall from the probe to the horizon, and not much longer to reach the point where Cartan Null was launched. And however much subjective time the Divers had experienced, however much computing had been done along the way, the entire region of space containing Cartan Null would have been crushed into the singularity a few micro-seconds later.

'If the Divers tunnelled out of the hole, there'd be a paradox, wouldn't there?' Gisela turned; she hadn't noticed Cordelia behind her. 'Whenever they emerged, they wouldn't have fallen in yet, so they could swoop down and grab the nanomachines, preventing their own births.' The idea seemed to disturb her.

Gisela said, 'Only if they tunnelled out close to the horizon. If they appeared further away – say, here in Cartan, right now – they'd already be too late. The nanomachines have had too much of a head start; the fact that they're almost standing still in our reference frame doesn't make them an easy target if you're actually chasing after them. Even at lightspeed, nothing could catch them from here.'

Cordelia appeared to take heart from this. 'So escape isn't impossible?'

'Well . . .' Gisela thought of listing some of the other hurdles, but then she began to wonder if the question was about something else entirely. 'No. It's not impossible.'

Cordelia gave her a conspiratorial smile. 'Good.'

Prospero cried out, 'Gather round! Gather round now and hear *The Ballad of Cartan Null*!' He created a podium, rising beneath his feet. Timon sidled up to Gisela and whispered, 'If this involves a lute, I'm sending my senses elsewhere.'

It didn't; the blank verse was delivered without musical accompaniment. The content, though, was even worse than Gisela had feared. Prospero had ignored everything she and the others had told him. In his version of events, 'Charon's passengers' entered 'gravity's abyss' for reasons he'd invented out of thin air: to escape, respectively, a failed romance/vengeance for an unspeakable crime/ the ennui of longevity; to resurrect a lost flesher ancestor; to seek contact with 'the gods'. The universal questions the Divers had actually hoped to answer – the structure of spacetime at the Planck scale, the underpinnings of quantum mechanics – didn't rate a mention.

Gisela glanced at Timon, but he seemed to be taking the news that his sole version had just fled into Chandrasekhar to avoid punishment for an unnamed atrocity extremely well; there was disbelief on his face, but no anger. He said softly,

'This man lives in Hell. Mucus on the face plate is all he'll ever see.'

The audience stood in silence as Prospero began to 'describe' the Dive itself. Timon stared at the floor with a bemused smile. Tiet wore an expression of detached boredom. Vikram kept peeking at a display behind him, to see if the faint gravitational radiation emitted by the inflowing nanomachines was still conforming to his predictions.

It was Sachio who finally lost control and interjected angrily, 'Cartan Null is some ghostly image of a scape, full of ghostly icons, floating through the vacuum, down into the hole?'

Prospero seemed more startled than outraged by the interruption. 'It is a city of light. Translucent, ethereal . . .'

The owl in Sachio's skull puffed its feathers out. 'No photon state would look like that. What you describe could never exist, and even if it could it would never be conscious.' Sachio had worked for decades on the problem of giving Cartan Null the freedom to process data without disrupting the geometry around it.

Prospero spread his arms in a conciliatory gesture. 'An archetypal quest narrative must be kept simple. To burden it with *technicalities*—'

Sachio inclined his head briefly, fingertips to forehead, downloading information from the polis library. 'Do you have any idea what archetypal narratives *are*?'

'Messages from the gods, or from the depths of the soul; who can say? But they encode the most profound and mysterious—'

Sachio cut him off impatiently. 'They're the product of a few chance attractors in flesher neurophysiology. Whenever a more complex or subtle story was disseminated through an oral culture, it would eventually degenerate into an archetypal narrative. Once writing was invented, they were only ever created deliberately by fleshers who failed to understand what they were. If all of antiquity's greatest statues had been dropped into a glacier, they would have been reduced to a predictable spectrum of spheroidal pebbles by now; that does not make the spheroidal pebble the pinnacle of the artform. What you've created is not only devoid of truth, it's devoid of aesthetic merit.'

Prospero was stunned. He looked around the room expectantly, as if waiting for someone to speak up in defence of the *Ballad*.

No one made a sound.

This was it: the end of diplomacy. Gisela spoke privately to Cordelia, whispering urgently: 'Stay in Cartan! No one can force you to leave!'

Cordelia turned to her with an expression of open astonishment. 'But I thought . . .' She fell silent, reassessing something, hiding her surprise.

Then she said, 'I can't stay.'

'*Why not?* What is there to stop you? You can't stay buried in Athena—' Gisela caught herself; whatever bizarre hold the place had on her, disparaging it wouldn't help.

Prospero was muttering in disbelief now, 'Ingratitude! Base ingratitude!'

Cordelia regarded him with forlorn affection. 'He's not ready.' She faced Gisela, and spoke plainly. 'Athena won't last for ever. Polises like that form and decay; there are too many real possibilities for people to cling to one arbitrary sanctified culture, century after century. But he's not prepared for the transition; he doesn't even realise it's coming. I can't abandon him to that. He's going to need someone to help him through.' She smiled suddenly, mischievously. 'But I've cut two centuries off the waiting time. If nothing else, the trip did that.'

Gisela was speechless for a moment, shamed by the strength of this child's love. Then she sent Cordelia a stream of tags. 'These are references to the best libraries on Earth. You'll get the real stuff there, not some watered-down version of flesher physics.'

Prospero was shrinking the podium, descending to ground

318

level. 'Cordelia! Come to me now. We're leaving these barbarians to the obscurity they deserve!'

For all that she admired Cordelia's loyalty, Gisela was still saddened by her choice. She said numbly, 'You belong in Cartan. It should have been possible. We should have been able to find a way.'

Cordelia shook her head: no failure, no regrets. 'Don't worry about me. I've survived Athena so far; I think I can see it through to the end. Everything you've shown me, everything I've done here, will help.' She squeezed Gisela's hand. 'Thank you.'

She joined her father. Prospero created a doorway, opening up onto a yellow-brick road through the stars. He stepped through, and Cordelia followed him.

Vikram turned away from the gravitational wave trace and asked mildly, 'All right, you can own up now: who threw in the additional exabyte?'

*   *   *

'*Freeeeee-dom!*' Cordelia bounded across Cartan Null's control scape, a long platform floating in a tunnel of colour-coded Feynman diagrams that were streaming through the darkness like the trails of a billion colliding and disintegrating sparks.

Gisela's first instinct was to corner her and shout in her face: *Kill yourself now! End this now!* A brief side-branch, cut short before there was time for personality divergence, hardly counted as a real life and a real death. It would be a forgotten dream, nothing more.

That analysis didn't hold up, though. From the instant she'd become conscious, this Cordelia had been an entirely separate person: the one who'd left Athena for ever, the one who'd escaped. Her extended self had invested far too much in this clone to treat it as a mistake and cut its losses. Beyond anything it hoped for itself, the clone knew exactly what its existence meant for the original. To betray that, even if it could never be found out, would be unthinkable.

Tiet said sharply, 'You didn't raise her hopes, did you?'

Gisela thought back over their conversations. 'I don't think so. She must know there's almost no chance of survival.'

Vikram looked troubled. 'I might have put our own case too strongly. She might believe the same discoveries will be enough for her, but I'm not sure they will.'

Timon sighed impatiently. 'She's here. That's irreversible; there's no point agonising about it. All we can do is give her the chance to make what she can of the experience.'

A horrifying thought struck Gisela. 'The extra data hasn't over-burdened us, has it? Ruled out access to the full computational domain?' Cordelia had compressed herself down to a far leaner program than the version she'd sent from Earth, but it was still an unexpected load.

Sachio made a sound of indignation. 'How badly do you think I did my job? I knew someone would bring in more than they'd promised; I left a hundredfold safety margin. One stowaway changes nothing.'

Timon touched Gisela's arm. 'Look.' Cordelia had finally slowed down enough to start examining her surroundings. The primary beams, the infrastructure for all their computation, had already been blue-shifted to hard gamma rays, and the colliding photons were creating pairs of relativistic electrons and positrons. In addition, a range of experimental beams with shorter wavelengths probed the physics of length scales ten thousand times smaller – physics that would apply to the primary beams about a subjective hour later. Cordelia found the window with the main results from these beams. She turned and called out, 'Lots of mesons full of top and bottom quarks ahead, but nothing unexpected!'

'Good!' Gisela felt the knot of guilt and anxiety inside her begin to unwind. Cordelia had chosen the Dive freely, just like the rest of them. The fact that it had been a hard decision for her to make was no reason to assume that she'd regret it.

Timon said, 'Well, you were right. I was wrong. She certainly tunnelled out of Athena.'

'Yeah. So much for your theory of closed trapped memetic surfaces.' Gisela laughed. 'Pity it was just a metaphor, though.'

'Why? I thought you'd be overjoyed that she made it.'

'I am. It's just a shame that it says nothing at all about our own chances of escape.'

*   *   *

Each orbit gave them thirty minutes of subjective time, while the true length and time scales of Cartan Null shrank a hundredfold. Sachio and Tiet scrutinised the functioning of the polis, checking and re-checking the integrity of the 'hardware' as new species of particles entered the pulse trains. Timon reviewed various methods for shunting information into new modes if the opportunity arose. Gisela struggled to bring Cordelia up to speed, and Vikram, whose main work had been the nanomachines, helped her.

The shortest-wavelength beams were still recapitulating the results of old particle accelerator experiments; the three of them pored over the data together. Gisela summarised as best she could. 'Charge and the other quantum numbers generate a kind of angle between world lines in the networks, just like spin does, but in this case they act like angles in five-dimensional space. At low energies what you see are three separate subspaces, for electromagnetism and the weak and strong forces.'

'Why?'

'An accident in the early universe with Higgs bosons. Let me draw a picture . . .'

There was no time to go into all the subtleties of particle physics, but many of the issues that were crucial outside Chandrasekhar were becoming academic for Cartan Null anyway. Broken symmetries were being restored as they spoke, with increasing kinetic energy diluting differences in rest mass into insignificance. The polis was rapidly mutating into a hybrid of every possible particle type; what governed their future would not be the theory of any one force, but the nature of quantum mechanics itself.

'What lies behind the frequency and wavelength of a particle?' Vikram sketched a snapshot of a wave packet on a spacetime diagram. 'In its own reference frame, an electron's phase rotates at a constant rate: about once every ten-to-the-minus-twenty seconds. If it's moving, we see that rate slowed down by time dilation, but that's not the whole picture.' He drew a set of components fanning out at different velocities from a single point on the wave, then marked off successive points where the phase came full circle for each one. The locus of these points formed a set of hyperbolic wavefronts in spacetime, like a stack of conical bowls – packed more tightly, in both time and space, where the components' velocity was greater. 'The spacing of the original wave is only reproduced by components with just the right velocity; they trace out identical copies of the wave at later times, all neatly superimposed. Components with the wrong velocity scramble the phase, so their copies all cancel out.' He repeated the entire construction for a hundred points along the wave, and it propagated neatly into the future. 'In curved spacetime the whole process becomes distorted, but, given the right symmetries, the *shape* of the wave can be preserved while the wavelength shrinks and the frequency rises.' Vikram warped the diagram to demonstrate. 'Our own situation.'

Cordelia took this all in, scribbling calculations, cross-checking everything to her own satisfaction. 'OK. So why does that have to break down? Why can't we just keep being blue-shifted?'

Vikram zoomed in on the diagram. 'All phase shifts ultimately come from *interactions* – intersections of one world line with another. In the Kumar model, every network of world

322

lines has a finite weave. At each intersection, there's a tiny phase shift that makes time jump by about ten-to-the-minus-forty-three seconds . . . and it's meaningless to talk about either a smaller phase shift or a shorter time scale. So if you try to blue-shift a wave indefinitely, eventually you reach a point where the whole system no longer has the resolution to keep reproducing it.' As the wave packet spiralled in, it began to take on a blurred, jagged approximation of its former shape. Then it disintegrated into unrecognisable noise.

Cordelia examined the diagram carefully, tracing individual components through the final stages of the process. Finally she said, 'How long before we see evidence of this? Assuming the model's correct?'

Vikram didn't reply; he seemed to be having second thoughts about the wisdom of the whole demonstration. Gisela said, 'In about two hours we should be able to detect quantised phase in the experimental beams. And then we'll have another hour or so before . . .' Vikram glanced meaningfully at her – privately, but Cordelia must have guessed why the sentence trailed off, because she turned on him.

'What do you think I'm going to do?' she demanded indignantly. 'Collapse into hysterics at the first glimmering of mortality?'

Vikram looked stung. Gisela said, 'Be fair. We've only known you three days. We don't know what to expect.'

'No.' Cordelia gazed up at the stylised image of the beam that encoded them, swarming now with everything from photons to the heaviest mesons. 'But I'm not going to ruin the Dive for you. If I'd wanted to brood about death, I would have stayed at home and read bad flesher poetry.' She smiled. 'Baudelaire can screw himself. I'm here for the physics.'

* * *

Everyone gathered round a single window as the moment of truth for the Kumar model approached. The data it displayed came from what was essentially a two-slit interference experiment, complicated by the need to perform it without anything resembling solid matter. A sinusoidal pattern showed the numbers of particles detected across a region where an electron beam recombined with itself after travelling two different paths; since there were only a finite number of detection sites, and each count had to be an integer, the pattern was already 'quantised', but the analysis software took this into account, and the numbers were large enough for the image to appear smooth. At a certain wavelength, any genuine Planck scale effects would rise above these artefacts, and once they appeared they'd only grow stronger.

The software said, 'Found something!' and zoomed in to show a slight staircasing of the curve. At first it was so subtle that Gisela had to take the program's word that it wasn't merely showing them the usual, unavoidable jagging. Then the tiny steps visibly broadened, from two horizontal pixels to three. Sets of three adjacent detection sites, which moments ago had been registering different particle counts, were now returning identical results. The whole apparatus had shrunk to the point where the electrons couldn't tell that the path lengths involved were different.

Gisela felt a rush of pure delight, then an aftertaste of fear. They were reaching down to brush their fingertips across the weave of the vacuum. It was a triumph that they'd survived this far, but their descent was almost certainly unstoppable.

The steps grew wider; the image zoomed out to show more of the curve. Vikram and Tiet cried out simultaneously, a moment before the analysis software satisfied itself with rigorous statistical tests. Vikram repeated softly, 'That's wrong.' Tiet nodded, and spoke to the software. 'Show us a single wave's phase structure.' The display changed to a linear staircase. It was impossible to measure the changing phase of a single wave directly, but assuming that the two versions of the beam were undergoing identical changes this was the progression implied by the interference pattern.

Tiet said, 'This is *not* in agreement with the Kumar model. The phase is quantised, but the steps aren't equal – or even random, like the Santini model. They're structured across the wave, in cycles. Narrower, broader, narrower again . . .'

Silence descended. Gisela gazed at the pattern and struggled to concentrate, elated that they'd found something unexpected, terrified that they might fail to make sense of it. Why wouldn't the phase shift come in equal units? This cyclic pattern was a violation of symmetry, allowing you to pick the phase with the smallest quantum step as a kind of fixed reference point – an idea that quantum mechanics had always declared to be as meaningless as singling out one direction in empty space.

But the rotational symmetry of space wasn't perfect: in small enough networks, the usual guarantee that all directions would look the same no longer held up. *Was that the answer?* The angles the two beams had to take to reach the detector were themselves quantised, and that effect was superimposed on the phase?

No. The scale was all wrong. The experiment was still taking place over too large a region.

Vikram shouted with joy, and did a backwards somersault. 'There are world lines crossing *between the nets*! That's what creates phase!' Without another word, he began furiously sketching diagrams in the air, launching software, running simulations. Within minutes, he was almost hidden behind displays and gadgets.

One window showed a simulation of the interference pattern, a perfect fit to the data. Gisela felt a stab of jealousy: she'd been so close, she should have been first. Then she began to examine more of the results, and the feeling evaporated. This was elegant, this was beautiful, this was right. It didn't matter who'd discovered it.

Cordelia was looking dazed, left behind. Vikram ducked out

from the clutter he'd created, leaving the rest of them to try to make sense of it. He took Cordelia's hands and they waltzed across the scape together. 'The central mystery of quantum mechanics has always been: why can't you just *count* the ways things can happen? Why do you have to assign each alternative a phase, so they can cancel as well as reinforce each other? We knew the rules for doing it, we knew the consequences, but we had no idea what phases were, or where they came from.' He stopped dancing, and conjured up a stack of Feynman diagrams, five alternatives for the same process, layered one on top of the other. 'They're created the same way as every other relationship: common links to a larger network.' He added a few hundred virtual particles, criss-crossing between the once-separate diagrams. 'It's like spin. If the networks have created directions in space that make two particles' spins parallel, when they combine they'll simply add together. If they're anti-parallel, in opposing directions, they'll cancel. Phase is the same, but it acts like an angle in two dimensions, and it works with every quantum number together: spin, charge, colour, everything – if two components are perfectly out-of-phase, they vanish completely.'

Gisela watched as Cordelia reached into the layered diagram, followed the paths of two components, and began to understand. They hadn't discovered any deeper structure to the individual quantum numbers, as they'd hoped they might, but they'd learnt that a single vast network of world lines could account for everything the universe built from those indivisible threads.

Was this enough for her? Her original, struggling for sanity back in Athena, might take comfort from the hope that the Dive clone had witnessed a breakthrough like this – but as death approached, would it all turn to ashes for the witness? Gisela felt a pang of doubt herself, though she'd talked it through with Timon and the others for centuries. Did everything she felt at this moment lose all meaning, just because there was no chance to carry the experience back to the wider world? She couldn't deny that it would have been better to know that she could reconnect with her other selves, tell all her distant family and friends what she'd learnt, follow through the implications for millennia.

But the whole universe faced the same fate. Time *was* quantised; there was no prospect of infinite computation before the Big Crunch, for anyone. If everything that ended was void, the Dive had merely spared them the prolonged false hope of immortality. If every moment stood alone, complete in itself, then nothing could rob them of their happiness.

The truth, of course, lay somewhere in between.

Timon approached her, grinning with delight. 'What are you pondering here by yourself?'

She took his hand. 'Small networks.'

Cordelia said to Vikram, 'Now that you know precisely what phase is, and how it determines probabilities . . . is there any way we could use the experimental beams to manipulate the probabilities for the geometry ahead of us? Twist back the light cones just enough to keep us skirting the Planck region? Spiral back up around the singularity for a few billion years, until the Big Crunch comes, or the hole evaporates from Hawking radiation?'

Vikram looked stunned for a moment, then he began launching software. Sachio and Tiet came and helped him, searching for computational short cuts. Gisela looked on, light-headed, hardly daring to hope. To examine every possibility might take more time than they had, but then Tiet found a way to test whole classes of networks in a single calculation, and the process sped up a thousandfold.

Vikram announced the result sadly. 'No. It's not possible.'

Cordelia smiled. 'That's all right. I was just curious.'

Thanks to Caroline Oakley, Anthony Cheetham, John Douglas, Peter Robinson, Kate Messenger, Philip Patterson, Tony Gardner, Russ Galen, David Pringle, Lee Montgomerie, Gardner Dozois, Sheila Williams and Bill Congreve.

ACKNOWLEDGEMENTS

'Transition Dreams' was first published in *Interzone No. 76*, October 1993.

'Chaff' was first published in *Interzone No. 78*, December 1993.

'Cocoon' was first published in *Asimov's Science Fiction*, May 1994.

'Our Lady of Chernobyl' was first published in *Interzone No. 83*, May 1994.

'Mitochondrial Eve' was first published in *Interzone No. 92*, February 1995.

'Luminous' was first published in *Asimov's Science Fiction*, September 1995.

'Mister Volition' was first published in *Interzone No. 100*, October 1995.

'Silver Fire' was first published in *Interzone No. 102*, December 1995.

'Reasons to be Cheerful' was first published in *Interzone No. 118*, April 1997.

'The Planck Dive' was first published in *Asimov's Science Fiction*, February 1998.